Dear Readers,

Hello, friends, I'm back once more, delighted by Silhouette's decision to publish *Thorne's Way* and *Thorne's Wife* in one volume. Let me tell you why, and let you in on one my personal secrets.

I just love Jonas Thorne. Of all the heroes populating my sixty-odd books, Jonas is one of my favorites. You might ask, "How come?" As, though ruggedly handsome and rather wealthy, he also is tough, hard-edged, demanding and more than a little arrogant. Not your sensitive new millennium man or your everyday guy next door.

True, Jonas is neither of those types. But then, I know the sensitive, new millennium man and the guy next door—fine, upstanding men. Still for my own reading taste, they are not the stuff of fictional heroes, most especially romance fiction heroes.

Perhaps I'm old-fashioned, but give me a fictional hero who can be strong as well as gentle, tough as well as tender, arrogant as well as understanding. It doesn't hurt if he's handsome and rich, too!

As a matter of fact, I like Valerie almost as much as I like Jonas. I'd tell you why, except that would be giving away too much. And I certainly do not want to ruin the two stories for any of you. Hope you enjoy reading them, as much as I enjoyed writing them.

All my best,

Joan Hohl

JOAN HOHL

More Than Anything

Published by Silhouette Books

America's Publisher of Contemporary Romance

SILHOUETTE BOOKS

MORE THAN ANYTHING

Copyright © 2002 by Harlequin Books S.A.

ISBN 0-373-48467-4

The publisher acknowledges the copyright holder of the individual works as follows:

THORNE'S WAY
Copyright © 1982 by Joan M. Hohl

THORNE'S WIFE
Copyright © 1989 by Joan Hohl

Visit Silhouette at www.eHarlequin.com

Printed in U.S.A.

CONTENTS

THORNE'S WAY

Chapter 1

The shrill whine of the engines increased in volume as the executive jet charged down the runway. With an arrogant-looking lift to its pointed nose, the plane soared into the deep blue of the late afternoon sky.

Unfastening the confining seat belt, Valerie shifted into a more comfortable position in the overstuffed chair. Her hand idly smoothing the velour-covered arm of the chair, she let her eyes roam over the plane's fantastic interior.

Except for the fact that she *knew* she was thousands of feet above the ground, she could have been sitting in a small, plush living room. The carpet beneath her feet was deep pile, the color of antique gold. Near the rear of the compartment was a gleaming walnut cabinet that opened into a well-stocked bar. The seven other chairs in the compartment were exactly like the one she sat on, overstuffed loungers in varying shades of brown.

A brief smile tugged the corners of her mouth as her eyes rested on the woman sitting on one of those chairs. At the moment the swivel chair was turned to the side and all Valerie could see was her friend's profile and the curly cap of her light brown hair. Her head was bent over a small stack of papers on her lap and when her full, red lips moved Valerie heard the soft murmur of her voice, although her words did not register. A much deeper, though equally soft voice came in reply and Valerie's eyes sought the source of that voice.

The man sitting opposite the curly-haired woman spoke again in that low, soft voice, but as before, the actual content of his words did not reach Valerie. His head was bent also as he studied a paper held in his long-fingered hand. She could see only his profile, not his complete face. But then, she did not have to see his full face. The look of him had been imprinted on her mind at first sight. Glancing away, Valerie closed her eyes and let her mind wander back to that first meeting less than an hour ago.

They had arrived at the airport, she and Janet, flustered and out of breath and five minutes early. The dark blue Mercedes limo had glided smoothly to a stop exactly on time. Before the car's engine could be shut off, the door to the back seat was flung open and a dark masculine figure became visible. There was a moment's hesitation, as if the man had paused to say something to the other occupant of the back seat, and then he purposefully exited the car.

The first thing that struck Valerie was the fact that the hair at his temples was almost the exact silver-gray color of his suit. That observation fled, replaced by a series of others as the man straightened to his full height of over six feet.

From the distance that separated them, Valerie's immediate impression was that he was in his late forties or early fifties. But that impression was contradicted by his athletic physique. His face was lean and dark. The cheeks were high, the jaw and chin thrustingly firm, the nose long and hawkish. His thin, compressed lips were a slashing, straight line in his face. The overall picture was of harsh lines and smooth planes and—when he got close enough for her to see his cold blue-gray eyes—rock hard determination. Oddly at variance with the dark-skinned, hard image, his head was covered with a thick, silky-looking crop of wavy ash-blond hair, gone silver-gray at the sides.

He had not paused as he'd drawn near the two women, but had merely nodded curtly and continued in his long-legged stride toward the gleaming white jet poised on the tarmac, awaiting his convenience.

Pushing the button that lowered her chair into a reclining position, Valerie adjusted her body to fit the contour of the seat. A hint of sharpness in the low, male tone scattered her wandering thoughts. Lifting her eyelids fractionally she centered her violet eyes on the man before her.

With studied indifference she noted how the material of his pants stretched tautly over the long, hard thigh that crossed his left leg. Through her lashes she examined with detachment the broad, long-fingered hand as it was raised to rake through ash-blond waves.

Valerie knew now that her first impression had been erroneous. There had been no contradiction between age and body. It was obvious from the supple way he moved that the man was in his prime—probably not more than forty or forty-one.

Had Valerie been impressionable, or looking for a man, she might have reached the decision that this particular male was the most exciting and interesting-looking specimen she'd ever encountered. And had she done so, she would have been joining a long line of women who had reached the same conclusion. But as she was neither impressionable nor interested, she could sum up her opinion of him in one word—formidable.

Despite her yawning indifference Valerie could imagine the impact he had on most people. For a fleeting moment even her detachment had been pierced when, just before they boarded the plane, a sleek-looking Porsche came to a tire-screeching stop alongside the Mercedes and an elegantly dressed woman jumped out to run, very inelegantly, toward the plane, calling, "Darling, wait!"

A grimace of extreme annoyance had twisted his mouth and Valerie had, surprisingly, felt a flash of anger when he'd turned his back and entered the plane with a coldly ordered "Get rid of her" to the uniformed steward.

Stunned by his callousness, Valerie had stared at the empty portal in disbelief until her companion had nudged her forward, advising tersely: "Go inside unless you want to witness the histrionics. This one's an actress and I can just imagine the performance she'll put on for Parker in her attempt to get on the plane to him."

Parker, of course, being the luckless steward.

Valerie had entered the plane just as the woman had begun her pleading, and not really wanting to feel *anything,* let alone compassion, she sighed with relief when, after she had stepped into the small plush compartment, the door was closed behind her, shutting off all outside noises.

Her amazement on entering the compartment had wiped all thoughts of the elegant woman from Valerie's mind. Standing transfixed, she had gazed around, bemused. She had been on private planes before. One had even been jet propelled, but never had she seen anything like the luxury displayed before her now. The abrupt movement of the man as he came to stand in front of her broke her rapt concentration on the lavish appointments of the plane's interior. Her eyes focused on the large hand extended to her at the same time his cool, deep voice reached her ears.

"I gather you are Valerie Jordan?"

Stiffening at his clipped, insolent tone, Valerie nodded shortly and answered with a frigid, "Yes."

A tiny, icy shiver went tiptoeing down her spine at the way his eyes narrowed on her face.

"Jonas Thorne," he snapped curtly, barely touching her fingers before dropping his hand. "Your employer."

The emphasis he'd placed on his last statement left little doubt in Valerie's mind that her coldness annoyed him. What, she asked herself, had he expected? A genuflection? A torrent of gushing thanks for being granted the privilege of her new position? Straightening to her full five feet three inches, she stared into his cold, blue-gray eyes unflinchingly.

"You *do* want the job, Miss Jordan?" The iciness

of his tone sent another chilling tingle down her spine.
There was a definite warning woven into that simple
question. Even in her indifference Valerie did not
miss the message within that warning, and she knew,
without a doubt, that he would dump her back onto
the tarmac without hesitation if her answer did not
please him.

"Yes, sir."

Valerie felt no shame in her meekly voiced reply.
She was indifferent, not stupid. And to be rejected by
him now, through her own perverseness, would be
sheer stupidity. She did not like him, but that was
unimportant. She did not have to like him. If she
found herself, now, standing on the tarmac watching
as his plane became a black dot on the horizon, she
would be not only without employment, but without
a place to live or funds to fall back on, in a country
that was not her own. Only a fool was that indifferent.

Apparently her answer suited him, for he turned
away with a curtly ordered, "You had better sit down
and buckle up. We will be taking off shortly."

Now, studying his harsh profile through the inky
screen of her long black lashes, Valerie had the uncomfortable feeling that she'd allowed herself to be
pushed in the wrong direction. Shifting her gaze, she
studied the curly headed ball of energy who had done
the pushing.

As if she could feel Valerie's brooding perusal, Janet Peterson glanced up. The gentle smile that
touched Janet's lips fleetingly told Valerie that her
friend thought she was asleep. Valerie made no move
to correct Janet's impression. She knew Janet was
concerned about her health—both physical and men-

tal—so she allowed the older woman the satisfaction of believing that she was enjoying the sleep of contentment.

"She's obviously sleeping." The conclusion came from Jonas Thorne in an unconcerned, emotionless tone. Then the tone took on a sardonic inflection as he added, bitingly, "You surprise me, Janet. I had no idea you had latent maternal instincts."

Although she remained still, a startlingly strong curl of anger flashed through Valerie's mind. How dare he attack Janet like that? Janet had done nothing the whole previous week but sing his praises, and here *he* sat slinging verbal abuse at her. The soft chuckle with which Janet received his insult added shock to Valerie's anger.

"I suppose the instinct is in every woman. It's just buried deeper in some than in others." Janet replied calmly. "Valerie has inspired protective feelings in me from the first day I met her seven years ago." Janet paused, then her voice took on a pleading quality that touched Valerie's unwilling conscience. "I promise you won't be sorry about this, Jonas."

"We'll see," came the disbelieving retort.

His tone left little doubt in Valerie's mind that he firmly believed he *would* be sorry. It was at that moment that Valerie decided to prove him wrong. The decision made, she lowered her lids entirely and allowed her thoughts to drift back over the events that had led to her present unenviable position.

Etienne.

Just thinking his name caused pain. Swallowing a moan, Valerie let an image of him form in her mind. At five feet nine inches, he had been only six inches taller than she, and yet she had looked up to him as to a god. Etienne, with his Gallic darkness of skin, hair and eyes, and the classic, aesthetically beautiful face.

Was it possible it was only a little over a year since she had glanced up from her typewriter on hearing someone enter the office, to encounter his dark eyes fastened on her? Even now she could feel the thrill that had twisted pleasurably in her midsection. He had literally stolen her breath and heart with that one warm, caressing glance.

Valerie had known, without conceit, that she was very good at her job as private secretary to the manager of the Paris office of J.T. Electronics. Yet, caught by Etienne's warm-eyed glance, she had sounded like an inarticulate, inexperienced fledgling.

"Can I—uh, may I help you, sir?" she'd stuttered, a warm stain flushing her creamy cheeks.

"Yes, you may, *mignon.*"

The smile he had bestowed on her had scattered her senses. His charmingly accented voice melted her spine. "You may help me enormously by saying you'll have dinner with me this evening."

That had been the beginning. She had said "yes," of course. In her awe of him she could not have refused him anything. She had gone out with him every night for a week and by the end of that week she was hopelessly in love.

Etienne was everything she had ever dreamed of and never hoped to find. Intelligent, urbane and charming—he was all these. But what captured Valerie's heart was the deep streak of tenderness he was unafraid of displaying. He proposed to her six weeks after their first meeting. She had accepted at once, unable to believe her good fortune. But the most amazing thing of all was Etienne's fervently confessed adoration of her.

Valerie had been in France for six years, having requested a transfer to the Paris office of J.T. Electronics soon after her twentieth birthday. Young and eager to taste life, she had availed herself of every opportunity to meet new people and see as much as possible of the country.

Small, delicately boned and wafer thin, she realized without vanity that she was not unattractive. What Valerie had never seen in her mirrored image was the elusively haunting beauty of her small, heart-shaped face, a quality that instilled envy in most women, and the urge to protect in all men. She knew, of course, that her pale-skinned face, large violet eyes, and long, wavy black hair were appealing to men. But she innocently had no idea of exactly how appealing she was. And the fact that she was, so obviously, innocent tripled her appeal. And so, in the years she'd spent in Paris before she met Etienne, Valerie had had no lack of male companionship.

Valerie was not a prude. She was, in a word, fastidious, and she had remained innocent for one reason only. She simply could not engage in indiscriminate sex, and, until Etienne, she had not been aroused enough, either physically or emotionally, to take the final step into full womanhood.

For months she was gloriously happy. It had been early February when they met, and as spring came to breathe new life into Paris, Valerie blossomed in the warmth of Etienne's love. Declaring he could not possibly endure a long engagement, he set the wedding day for the end of May.

Breathless and starry-eyed, Valerie had blinked back tears of happiness as Etienne slipped an exquisitely beautiful ruby-stoned engagement ring on her small finger. She had not been able to keep the tears from rolling down her cheeks when he lifted his handsome head and declared reverently that he would love her forever.

For Valerie and Etienne, forever was to be a very short time.

Blissfully unaware of what the future held, Valerie delighted in the spring weeks they spent together. The weekend after he'd proposed Etienne drove her to his parents' home some miles outside of Paris. The French countryside was bursting with new life, as were the parklike grounds that enclosed the very old, very lovely château that was her beloved's birthplace.

Madame and Monsieur DeBron greeted Valerie like a long-lost daughter, and Etienne's older brother Jean-Paul teased her from the beginning as outrageously as he would have teased a much loved younger sister.

In a state of rosy-hued euphoria, Valerie soared on cloud nine as Etienne introduced her to his friends and favorite places. Never had she enjoyed the sights and sounds of Paris more. Never had she thrilled so deeply to its history and antiquities.

Although Etienne had whispered lovingly that he wished to wait until the wedding night to savor the fullness of their love, in a moment of overwhelming passion, he broke his own self-imposed time limit.

They had had a rare evening alone together and

after a leisurely dinner had returned to Valerie's tiny apartment for a good-night drink. For a half hour or so they relaxed on her low sofa with good brandy and quiet conversation. It was the first time in weeks that they had been alone together in the evening, as their many friends had feted them nightly with dinners and prewedding parties.

"Do you know, I have missed you very much?" Etienne had said as he placed his empty glass on her small coffee table.

"Missed me?" Valerie had laughed. "But, darling, we've been together every evening."

"Yes, together, but not alone." A rueful smile curved his perfectly formed lips. "And, on bringing you home I have had to be satisfied with a quick good-night kiss." His lips turned up into an enticing smile and he held his arms out to her. "Come, let me hold you a moment before I must leave."

Valerie didn't need further coaxing. She had been longing for the feel of his arms and the touch of his lips on hers.

Etienne's kiss began as a tender exploration, but, as Valerie parted her lips with a sigh, she heard him groan and then his kiss deepened with hunger.

"Oh, my precious life," he'd groaned in husky English as he dropped tiny kisses over her face. "These last weeks have been torment for me, being so close to you yet unable to hold you, touch you, kiss you properly."

They were the last words he'd said to her in English that night. As each successive kiss became more urgent with desire, he whispered age-old words of love, made excitingly new to Valerie, in his own tongue.

Not once had it even occurred to Valerie to try to stop him. When he had lifted her into his arms and carried her into the bedroom she had curled her arms around his neck and murmured, "Yes, yes," against his heated skin.

Caressing the silkiness of her body with reverent sweetness, Etienne had tenderly prepared her for their lovemaking. Very, very gently he led her into the knowledge of physical pleasures. Inside the safety of his lightly stroking hands and his whispered words of adoration, Valerie had felt not one moment of fear. When it was over, and she lay within the glow of his love, and the circle of his arms, Valerie's heart was filled to overflowing with happiness and contentment.

Six days later, after yet another prewedding party, that happiness was shattered. Her world came crashing about her head as a drunken driver sent his vehicle skidding across a rain-wet road to crash head-on into Etienne's car.

Telling herself there had to be some sort of mistake, Valerie had rushed to the hospital where Etienne was being treated. Some seven hours later Valerie stood staring at the still, pale face of the man on the bed and felt hope trickle out of her life like sands from an hourglass.

Reality seemed to recede as she glanced around in a desperate effort to maintain some point of contact with the real world. But there was no reality for her in the people around her—Etienne's parents, his brother, the doctor in charge of the case—or in the room itself, or even in the knowledge that the room was in a small private hospital several miles outside Paris. Indeed, even the magical word *Paris,* which she had learned to love during the last six years of her life, held no concrete reality.

No, for Valerie, at 6:15 on a stormy May morning, the only reality existed in that still pale man lying on the sterile-looking bed. Recognizing in that man the lover she'd laughed and danced with only ten hours earlier was a task she was finding next to impossible.

In her imagination the form on the bed changed. For fleeting seconds he became again the smilingly gallant man who had toasted her, his fiancée, such a short time before. After the toast he had lifted her fingers to his lips and murmured, "The next two weeks will seem interminable, my love."

In a purely reflex action Valerie now clutched at that same hand, resting limply on the covers. The contrast between the hand she now held and the vitally warm one that had enclosed hers the night before caused bitter gall to rise chokingly in her throat.

Vitally alive! The descriptive phrase repeated itself painfully in her mind, and she sent up a silent, agonizing plea. Dear God, please, please let Etienne live.

With the unvoiced prayer came the realization she'd managed to block out of her consciousness till now. Etienne DeBron, her fiancé, her love, her entire life, was very likely going to die. And with that realization came rage. A rage that filled the void created by dissolving hope. A rage that clouded her vision and made her hands shake. A rage that finally settled on the unscathed man who had caused the unbelievable anguish of the previous hours.

Damn that drunken fool, she thought furiously.

Damn him to hell! The curse brought an image of the small, skinny farmer and an echo of his whining voice.

"Mon Dieu!" He'd invoked the Lord as his witness. "I didn't see his car," he'd sobbed brokenly. "The rain was lashing against the windscreen so heavily, I could hardly see anything through it."

And even less through your drunken haze, Valerie now accused the farmer silently. For although he was reasonably sober by the time they'd reached the hospital, the man had been very intoxicated when the gendarmes arrived at the scene of the accident.

He had been out with friends, the farmer had nervously explained, celebrating the birth of his long-awaited first child. Perhaps he had imbibed a little too freely, he'd admitted grudgingly. But, he'd qualified in a belligerent tone, the weather was more at fault for his car's crashing into Etienne's than he was himself.

The sheer outrageousness of his claim had stunned an already deeply shocked Valerie, and it was not until this moment, hours later, that the farmer's sniveling excuses fully registered. The man was actually blaming Etienne's injuries on God! Without a twinge of guilt, Valerie silently repeated her curse: Damn him to hell.

The faint movement of the fingers in her clasped hand drew Valerie's attention back to the bed—and the face of her love.

"Je t'aime, Valerie."

Whispered through colorless lips that barely moved, the vow, though faint, touched every ear in the hushed room.

"I love *you,* Etienne."

From a throat dry with fear, Valerie repeated the pledge softly, hoarsely.

A mere hint of a smile feathered over the pale lips, and cold fingers pressed hers weakly in an attempted caress.

Valerie's hand tightened convulsively around his fingers as if willing her strength into him.

The very stillness of the air in the room gave her warning; and then it happened. From deep in his throat came the final exhalation of life.

"Etienne?"

Softly, almost timidly, Valerie called to the still form on the bed.

"Etienne!"

Valerie's tone had sharpened into a demand that defied the truth. Violet eyes, wide with growing horror, searched the white, waxy-looking face for a reason to defy that truth. There was only stillness. A stillness that made her blood run cold.

The white-coated figure of the doctor bent over the still form. Short, blunt fingers moved a stethoscope over the exposed chest, then the doctor straightened, head moving side to side.

From the other side of the bed came the harsh sound of weeping from both Etienne's parents. The strong arm of his brother slid over her shoulders, his hand grasping her upper arm firmly.

"Etienne, no—please no!"

The hand on her arm tightened at her anguished cry and the arm turned her in, against his chest, forcing her eyes from the ashen face. Strong fingers pried loose her grip on the lifeless hand.

"Valerie, he can no longer hear you," Jean-Paul coaxed in his enchantingly accented voice. "Come away, *petite,* he is lost to us."

Valerie lifted her tear-streaked face to gaze pleadingly into his dark eyes, so like Etienne's, bright now with his own unshed tears.

"Can't I stay with him, Jean-Paul?" she begged softly. "Please, he'll be all alone."

"He is not alone, *mignon.*" Jean-Paul's lips moved in a faint, sympathetic smile. "Come." Turning her firmly, he walked to the door, giving her no choice but to go with him. "Etienne would not want you to stay."

Moving like a sleepwalker, Valerie had allowed herself to be led to the door. She'd turned to gaze once more on the beautiful features of the man who was to have become her husband in two weeks' time.

The flame of joyous animation that had burned so brightly inside Valerie had been extinguished with Etienne's last breath. From the moment Jean-Paul led her from that hushed hospital room, Valerie had slipped into a numbed shock. In a blessedly frozen state, she had been able to receive the condolences of friends and co-workers and had stood mutely in the small cemetery while the shell that had contained the essence of Etienne was interred in the family vault.

It was after she was alone in her apartment, having declined Jean-Paul's pleas that she stay with his parents for awhile, that the shock wore off and the real pain began. In an agony of remorseless grief, Valerie sank from despondency into a deep depression that even her closest friends could not break through.

The one person who might have been able to reach

her was unaware of her withdrawn state. Jean-Paul, with a gentle understanding so like his brother's, had respected her request for solitude after the funeral. He had called her at least once a week to ask if there was anything he could do for her. But her answer had always been the same: There was nothing she needed.

Then, three months after Etienne's death, Jean-Paul's company had sent him to New York City. He had stopped to see her before leaving Paris, and again she had assured him there was nothing she needed. He had left with obvious reluctance, his dark, compassionate eyes shadowed with concern.

"Don't worry about me, Jean-Paul," Valerie sighed when he hesitated at her door. "Go and enjoy yourself. You'll love New York."

"Petite," Jean-Paul had murmured. "I cannot help but worry about you. You are—" he had paused, his voice cracking with an emotion Valerie was beyond noticing. "You are special to me," he had finished lamely.

"I will be fine, and I will be here when you return," Valerie promised, sending him on his way. She had been neither.

As the weeks slipped into months, she grew more withdrawn from the people around her. Her work suffered and she didn't care. In fact, she was totally unaware that her boss was frantically covering up for her. Nothing touched her, nothing moved her, and she would have shrugged indifferently had someone told her that her superior's sympathetic efforts had failed and management was all too aware of her slipshod work.

The Paris weather was unusually harsh that winter,

and for the first time in her working life, Valerie was constantly absent from the office. *That* also did not go unnoticed at the home office of J.T. Electronics.

Holed up in her tiny apartment, Valerie could not have cared less about anything. Too disinterested to prepare proper meals, yet continually hungry as a result of emotional emptiness, she ate constantly—all the wrong kinds of foods.

By the time winter was on the wane her hair had lost its gleaming sheen, her complexion was no longer translucently glowing, and she was fifteen pounds heavier. She didn't care.

This, then, was the state of Valerie's existence on a blustery day one week before she found herself taking off in a luxurious private plane. She had once again not gone to the office.

To begin with she had overslept. Then, after glancing out the rain-spattered window, she had shrugged and, after calling the office to inform them she would not be in, she had gone back to bed.

She had been sitting on the sofa, her fingers tracing then retracing, the embossed design on the upholstery, when a sharp, imperative knock on her door broke her fixed stare. For a moment she had considered ignoring the caller—whoever it was—then, with a shrug, she walked listlessly to the door and swung it open. She stood staring in disbelief at Janet Peterson.

"My God, Val!" Janet cried in astonishment the moment she was inside. "What have you done to yourself?"

Valerie's unconcerned shrug told Janet more than any defensive explanation would have. Janet had come to Paris for one purpose, and as she studied

Valerie's appearance that purpose hardened. She didn't bother mincing words.

"I've come to get you, Val," she announced flatly. "I'm taking you home."

"Why?" Valerie asked dully.

"Why? Why!" Janet exclaimed. Grabbing Valerie's arm, she pulled her into the bedroom, not stopping until they stood before the dressing table mirror. "You can look at that reflection and ask me why?" Lifting her hand she caught at the limp, dull ponytail Valerie had secured with a rubber band. "Look at this rat's nest. When was the last time it saw the busy end of a brush?" Her hand moving swiftly, she caught Valerie's chin, turning her head so they faced each other. "Your skin is the color of wet cement," Janet declared brusquely. "And you are literally bursting out of your clothes. What have you been living on? A steady diet of gooey pastries?"

"Pretty much so, yes," Valerie admitted tiredly. "What difference does it make, anyway?"

"I'll tell you what difference," Janet snapped. "The difference between vital, glowing health, and this—" her hand moved to indicate Valerie's figure, "*mess* you've become."

Valerie had enough pride—or sense—left to wince. Taking her reaction as a hopeful sign, Janet forged ahead.

"I knew things weren't good with you, but I had no idea they were this bad. Come back into the living room, Val, and prepare yourself for a much needed lecture."

And lecture she did. For over a solid hour Janet expounded on the fruitlessness of Valerie's withdrawal from the human race. With biting logic, she pointed out the futility and utter waste of becoming a recluse at the age of twenty-seven. On and on she talked, driving her truths home relentlessly.

Valerie had not wanted to listen, had, in fact, tried to shut the sound of Janet's voice out completely. It was impossible. Janet had not reached the executive position she held with J.T. Electronics by being ineffectual. She was smart, and she was quick, and, as the saying goes, she could think on her feet. She brought every one of those talents into play in her bid to save Valerie from herself.

"You've been relieved of duties at the office starting now," Janet tacked on at the end of her lecture. "That means we have what's left of the afternoon and six full days to whip you into shape."

"Relieved of duties?" Valerie had repeated in confusion. "Whip me into shape? What for? Janet, I don't know what you're talking about." A twinge of alarm pierced her indifference. Even when one no longer cared about living, the rent had to be paid. "Janet, are you telling me I've been fired?"

"No, I'm telling you you've been relieved of duty in the Paris office." Janet hesitated, then went on with deadly seriousness. "Val, I want you to listen very carefully to what I have to say. We've been friends almost since the first day you started working for the company—right?"

Her attention fully caught by Janet's tone, Valerie nodded her agreement.

"Well, honey, I'm afraid I may have risked my career for you on the way over here. If I've miscalculated in my belief in you, and you let me down, I just might find myself in line at the unemployment office by the end of next week.''

"But why? How?'' Valerie shook her head in an effort to comprehend what Janet was getting at. "Janet, I don't understand.''

"No, there's no way you possibly could.'' Janet sighed. "I'd better start at the very beginning.'' She paused to glance meaningfully at the postage-stamp-sized kitchen. "How about a cup of coffee while I talk?'' she suggested.

"Yes, of course.'' Valerie had the grace to be embarrassed that she hadn't made the suggestion herself. "I'm sorry, Janet.''

Janet waited until Valerie had placed the tray of coffee things on the table in front of the sofa. Cradling a cup in her hands, she launched into her explanation.

"I've been worrying about you ever since—'' she hesitated, then reworded, "for some time now. I could tell from your short, infrequent notes to me—and from various other sources—that you were more than normally despondent. The last two months I've been wracking my brains thinking of how I could help you.''

"But, Janet, I neither asked nor expected—'' That was as far as Valerie got before Janet cut her off.

"I'm more than aware of that,'' Janet scolded gently. "But I was determined to help you whether you asked for it or not. Anyway, the solution came very unexpectedly last week when Jonas's secretary suddenly skipped town with a married man.'' She grimaced. "Needless to say, he was furious.''

"Mr. Thorne?'' Valerie inserted.

"None other.'' Janet smiled grimly. "His behavior

was somewhat like that of a lion with a thorn in his paw." Janet smiled. "A tiny play of words there."

"Very tiny," Valerie agreed.

"Anyway." Janet shrugged. "She couldn't have picked a worse time if she tried. Besides being in the middle of several contract negotiations, Jonas had finalized appointments for a long-planned trip to Paris. He refused to even think about changing his plans and commandeered his assistant's secretary. Then the agencies were requested to come up with a paragon to fill the desk chair in his outer office."

She stopped speaking long enough to swallow the last of her coffee and refill her cup before continuing her story.

"When a replacement had not been found by yesterday, I badgered Jonas into letting me come over here with him. I sang your praises all during the flight. Finally, in a desperate bid to get him to agree to take you back with him as his new secretary, I said I'd give him my resignation if you weren't as good at your job as I claimed you were." Janet drew a deep breath, then added quietly, "He agreed to give you a chance—if you can be ready to quit Paris permanently in a week's time."

Janet neglected to tell Valerie the exact words Jonas had used: "You are walking a very fine line here, Janet. I've had numerous reports on this 'exceptional secretary,' and in my estimation she has turned her back on life. And I have no time for quitters."

Janet's appalled shock upon laying eyes on Valerie was two-fold. She was, as a friend, sincerely concerned about Val. But she was also suddenly concerned about losing her own job.

In the main, it was this possibility that brought about Valerie's decision to go home. That, and the realization that within weeks spring would be coming to France. And suddenly Valerie knew she could not bear to be in Paris in the springtime without Etienne.

Chapter 2

A soft smile curved Valerie's vulnerable lips as she shifted slightly in the upholstered seat. Behind the barrier of her closed lids, she was unaware of the sharp blue-gray gaze that pondered that soft smile.

The smile was for Janet, and it was prompted by a rush of memories. Valerie had been a frightened, lonely nineteen-year-old when she'd entered the offices of J.T. Electronics for the first time. She had been frightened because it was her first job after leaving the security of business school. She had been lonely simply because she had so suddenly found herself alone.

Her father's death, after a lengthy illness, had not been the cause of her loneliness. There had been sadness, of course. A sadness touched by guilt because, near the end, Valerie had found herself praying for his release from pain. No, it was not her father's death, but the shock of her mother's remarriage, less than three months later, that had brought on her feeling of loneliness. The man was an Australian businessman on vacation in the States. He was, Valerie admitted to herself, charming and good-looking. He was also eight years younger than her beautiful mother. Shock followed shock, the final one coming with her mother's announcement that she was leaving for Australia with her new husband just one short week after her wedding.

Stunned, Valerie had stood by mutely while her mother disposed of her home, furniture, and all the collected belongings that she had shared with Valeric's father.

"Please try to understand," Celia Jordan—now Finny—had pleaded to an unresponsive Valerie. "Edwin must be back in Australia by the end of next week, and he wants me with him. Valerie, he's willing to have you with us. Please come." It was not the first time her mother had made this impassioned request. Valerie's answer had been the same every time.

"No."

She had been filled with bitterness and resentment at what she had considered her mother's disloyalty to her father's memory. In her bitterness she had punished her mother by remaining adamant in her refusal to go with her.

Valerie had moved in with her grandparents, and, with an insolence foreign to her nature, refused to accept any financial aid from her mother. Within two weeks after her mother's tearful departure, Valerie had dropped out of business school and had secured a position in the typing pool at J.T. Electronics.

And so it was that a scared, lonely, very young, but unrepentant Valerie walked through the wide doors of the steel and glass edifice that was the home office of J.T. Electronics—and found there a friend. It was Janet Peterson who had, eventually, brought about the reconciliation between Valerie and her mother.

From the day of their first meeting, which happened to be the second day of Valerie's employment, Janet took Valerie under her wing. The friendship that developed between them surprised everyone, for they were complete opposites.

Janet was a walking advertisement for women's lib. She didn't talk about it. She didn't bore or annoy people about it. She lived it. Yet, despite her rapid rise to an executive position in the firm, she had retained her femininity.

On the other hand, Valerie, at nineteen, had no real personal ambitions. She was a good worker. She was an accurate typist who had the potential of becoming an excellent secretary. But, at that point in her young life, her main concern was collecting her paycheck twice a month. Never would she have believed that one day she would be offered the position of personal secretary to the owner of the company. In fact, she had never so much as set eyes on the man who was her employer.

Valerie was soft, inside and out. Her eyes were soft. Her voice was soft. Her skin was soft. And her attitude to life had been to take the path of least resistance. Until her father's illness had dampened her exuberance she had thought of life as a joyous adventure. Why not enjoy it to the full? His death, and the events that followed it, had wrought a change in her personality. Her gaiety had been overshadowed by resentment, her contentment with life had been poisoned by bitterness. Janet had been instrumental in helping her break these emotional chains.

Ten years her senior, Janet had become many things to Valerie. Besides being her best friend she was surrogate mother, mentor, and at times, the insistent echo of her own conscience.

Two months after meeting Janet, Valerie sat down and composed a letter of apology to her mother. Her mother had reciprocated, with great emotion, by return mail. The mending of the rift lifted a weight off Valerie's shoulders. Free of the encumbrance, her laughing, soft-hearted nature surfaced once more.

During the months that followed, Valerie enjoyed herself enormously. She formed many new friendships in the office and was much sought after by her masculine colleagues for dates. Thus, when her grandmother informed her that when her grandfather retired at the end of the year they would like to follow the sun to Florida, she was able to accept the news philosophically. She would miss them, she assured her grandmother, but she could appreciate their desire to spend their retirement years in the sunshine.

Jonas Thorne had had his office complex erected on the outskirts of Philadelphia and for several weeks Valerie scoured the area for a small apartment. Although Janet had offered her her own extra bedroom, Valerie had declined, with thanks, claiming the urge to taste independence.

Meanwhile her grandparents had begun implementing their plans, and were scheduled to depart Pennsylvania in six weeks' time. Beginning to feel a bit desperate, Valerie had put a deposit on a tiny apartment on the third floor of a rather rundown building in an area she had previously avoided.

That was her situation on entering the office a few days later and discovering a new notice to all departments, posted on the bulletin board. The notice informed all employees of the fact that J.T. Electronics would be opening business offices in Paris in the spring, and it contained a list of positions available to employees interested in working out of the country. The one prerequisite was that the applicant had to speak, read and write French.

For Valerie, the notice had seemed like the answer to her prayers. Her French was not only good, it was excellent. She had learned the language from her paternal grandfather, a Parisian whose family had left France just before the Second World War.

Valerie had been the only woman to apply, and after a brief interview with the personnel manager, she had been given the position of front desk receptionist in the new office. She had left the States nine weeks after her grandparents' departure for Florida. During the weeks between her grandparents' move and her own, she had stayed with Janet.

Now, seven years later, another man's death had brought Janet to her rescue again.

Lifting her eyelids, Valerie studied her friend with admiration. Asleep Janet looked anything but the dynamic executive. The riot of curls that framed her face softened its contours, usually set in determination.

The dark lashes that fanned her cheeks were long and full. And her mouth, in repose, had the soft, appealing curves of a young girl's.

But those lips had not been soft a week ago. Her mouth set grimly, her eyes sharply assessing, Janet had circled Valerie while she made a visual examination of her person.

"Good, God, Val, you do look a mess," Janet had scolded gently. "I can see we are going to have a very busy week." Reaching out, she lifted Valerie's loose over-blouse to reveal the unsnapped waistband of her jeans.

"How much weight have you gained?" she'd asked flatly.

"I don't know." Valerie had shrugged. "Does it matter?"

"If all your clothes fit like these jeans—yes," Janet answered sharply. "Do they?"

"Well—everything I've worn lately has felt a little snug," Valerie admitted.

"And what size is everything you've worn lately?" Janet demanded.

"Threes, mostly."

"I think you have graduated to a five," Janet decreed. "We are going shopping first thing tomorrow morning."

The following morning had been the start of a six-day marathon.

In the dressing room of an elegant shop, stripped to newly purchased lacy panties and bra, Valerie submitted to Janet's smiling survey of her figure. "Well, the *jeune-fille* look is gone." Janet's smile had deepened as her eyes met Valerie's in the mirror. "But, *cherie,* the mature woman, as they used to say where I come from—'' her smile stretched into a grin, ''ain't half bad.''

The evidence before Valerie's eyes confirmed Janet's observation. The young girl look was definitely gone. The diet of quick-to-put-together meals, heavy on starch, that she'd been existing on for months, had filled out her formerly sylphlike figure.

''It's a good thing I came when I did,'' Janet had stated, her eyes following Valerie's over the appealing shape reflected in the mirror. ''Another few weeks of French bread sandwiches and pastry, and your figure would have been too voluptuous.''

Perusing her new figure with detachment, Valerie had to agree with Janet's judgment. Her breasts, though not very large, were full, and owed none of their height to the lacy scrap of material covering them. Her waist, though no longer a twenty-inch span, was still narrow. And, although her hips had flared to a mature roundness, her stomach was still flat, while her slim, shapely legs gave a false illusion of length. Yes, she concurred indifferently, her more mature look was not half bad.

The shopping binge that Janet had initiated all but wiped out Valerie's bank balance. Then, added to the total for clothes, there was the cost of several hair treatments, facials and a manicure. When Valerie took a final reckoning, she was astounded. She had the French equivalent of exactly seventy-two dollars and nine cents left.

''Don't worry about it,'' Janet had advised with a careless wave of her slim hand. ''I'll talk to Jonas.

I'm sure he'll be willing to give you an advance until you get squared away.''

Now, having met Jonas Thorne at last, Valerie decided she wanted no advance from him. As a matter of fact, she wanted nothing from the man. Certainly not the position of private secretary that Janet had talked him into giving her.

Moving her head fractionally, she let her narrowed gaze hone in on the object of her unsettling thoughts. He appeared to be asleep, yet even in repose, his face had lost none of its hardness. Valerie shivered with a chill that feathered down her spine. What a frightening specimen he was. And what satisfaction it would give her to be able to tell him exactly what he could do with his job.

But she wouldn't tell him, and she knew it. She was not concerned for herself; she could always find a job elsewhere. She *was* concerned for Janet, though. Valerie felt certain that if she in any way aroused his displeasure, Jonas Thorne would ruthlessly put an end to Janet's career.

Antagonism, hot and strong, surged through Valerie's mind. The intensity of the emotion shocked her, and Valerie closed her eyes completely to shut out his harsh visage. Never before in her life had she reacted to anyone so strongly—or so adversely. But then, she had never encountered anyone quite so coldly unemotional before, either. Jonas Thorne was so, so— inhuman—the unkind appellation jumped into her mind.

The idea of working with him, day after day, five days every week, was an unpalatable one. She would very likely suffer a severe case of frostbite before the first week was over! The mildly humorous thought was almost as shocking to Valerie as her earlier antagonistic feelings had been.

With a sigh of acceptance, she faced the fact that Janet had talked her into a trap. She had no other choice; she had to work for him. At least, she temporized, until Janet's job was secure again. No, she corrected herself grimly, remembering his disbelieving "We'll see." She didn't just have to work for him; she had to *excel* for him.

Even after being in his presence for only a few minutes, it hardly seemed possible to Valerie that this could be the same man Janet had raved about all week. It had seemed that everything Janet said was prefaced by: "Jonas is" or "Jonas does" or "Jonas doesn't"; her friend had gone on and on with Jonas and more Jonas. Valerie had been convinced she was to meet and work for some sort of paragon. What she had met was a statue that just happened to walk, talk and breathe. One had to assume, she supposed, that somewhere inside that marblelike casing a heart beat with regularity and blood flowed.

Valerie moved restlessly, more uncomfortable with her thoughts than with the padded contour of the chair. She had a prickly feeling, as though a limb had gone numb from being in an awkward position. Only with Valerie the sensation was mental. Her mind had been, figuratively, asleep for months, and its sudden arousal was as unpleasant a sensation as the renewed flow of blood to a numbed arm or leg.

Sighing, Valerie wished fervently that Janet had stayed at home and left her alone in her cocoon of misery. *That* thought made her more restless still. Before Janet's arrival the numbness had been so complete she had been unaware of it. Now, as reality took on new meaning for her, Valerie writhed with the prickly sensation of self-awareness.

And now, unsavory as the thought was, she faced the realization that she had been harboring an unconscious death wish. From the moment that dry, dreadful-sounding rattle whispered through Etienne's pale lips, she had ceased living in any normal sense of the word.

It was unhealthy. It was self-destructive. Janet, with her forceful personality and her rational arguments, had dragged her out of the shadows of self-immolation, and into the sunlight of self-interest.

Valerie was restless, and uncomfortable, and prickly in the mind. But, for the first time in a very long time, she was alive. Not fully, not wholly alive; that would come slowly at first, and then with shattering swiftness.

But it was a beginning, and she was every bit as scared as she had been at age nineteen. The only difference was that this time it didn't show. She was feeling again, but more important, she was thinking again. And that thinking led to the conclusion that, unless she protected herself, this man could hurt her. She wasn't quite sure how he could do it—possibly through Janet—but she felt sure that he could. And she had been hurt enough.

Standing on American soil after a seven-year absence, Valerie felt a fluttering in her stomach. She was home! Suddenly she was very glad Janet had forced this move on her. Blinking against the hot sting of tears brought rushing to her eyes by a welter of emotions, the uppermost being plain old-fashioned patriotism, Valerie hurried across the tarmac in the wake of Jonas Thorne's long strides. Their destination was a long, gleaming, silver-gray Cadillac limousine, which was waiting for them off to the side of the single-building airport.

Valerie, already tired from the trip, was experiencing a mild feeling of disorientation. They had left France late in the afternoon and had been served a very early dinner—due, Valerie had learned, to Jonas Thorne's having skipped lunch—and now, at a small airport some miles outside of Philadelphia, it was not yet dinnertime. Valerie knew her disorientation was caused by the flight through time zones. But knowing why she felt strange didn't help much. The fact that Jonas Thorne seemed totally unaffected by the flight added a layer of irritation to her feelings of strangeness.

"Is he always like this?" Valerie asked Janet softly, hoping against hope that she had analyzed him incorrectly.

"Like what?"

Janet's tone, combined with her look of confusion, was all the answer Valerie needed.

"Never mind," she sighed.

"But, Val, what—" Janet began.

"Janet!" Jonas Thorne snapped impatiently. "You have the entire weekend to gossip with Miss Jordan. Whereas I have an appointment in exactly," his arm shot out and he sent a swift glance to the face of the large, round gold watch on his wrist, "thirty-seven minutes. Will you close your mouth and get in the car?'' His lips curved into a sardonic twist before he added, "Please.''

Detestable man! Valerie had to bite her lip to keep her opinion of him silent. Casting a quick, compassionate glance at Janet, her eyes widened in surprise. Not a hint of indignation or hurt was revealed on Janet's face.

"Sorry," Janet murmured, a small apologetic smile touching her lips as she increased her pace toward the big car. "Hello, Lyle," she said softly to the driver, who had jumped out of the front seat to open the back door.

"Miss Peterson," the small, wiry man murmured as Jonas Thorne strode around the car to the front passenger's door. "Good flight?"

"Yes, very smooth." Janet hesitated, then said quickly, "Lyle, this is Valerie Jordan, Jonas's new secretary." On the last word she bent and stepped into the car.

"How do you do, Miss Jordan?" Lyle smiled broadly as he turned his gaze directly at her.

Valerie took an instant liking to the man. Not much taller than she, he had a very ordinary face and an extraordinarily sweet smile. Although she judged him to be about her own age, he had the look of a man who had experienced much of life, and his compact body had a tough, tempered look. Now, spontaneously returning his smile, she replied, "Fine, thank you, Lyle—?" She lifted her eyebrows in question.

"Magesjski." Lyle's smile deepened.

"Pleasantries over?" Jonas Thorne asked, his tone hard.

Valerie felt a flash of hot anger, followed by baffled

surprise. As had Janet a moment before, Lyle smiled apologetically. Yet, strangely, the eyes Lyle turned to his employer held a glint of laughter.

"Yes, sir."

More strange still, and totally incomprehensible to Valerie, the blue-gray gaze that caught and momentarily held Lyle's reflected that laughter. On the point of entering the back seat, Valerie stopped cold.

"My luggage!" she blurted.

"Val, don't worry—" Janet began from the far corner of the seat.

"Parker will bring it with him." Jonas Thorne's impatient tone cut across Janet's soothing voice. "Your cases will be quite safe with him, Miss Jordan." After folding his long frame into the front seat he twisted around and pinned Valerie—positioned half-in, half-out of the car—with a cold stare.

"In or out, Miss Jordan?" he drawled. "My time has now been cut to thirty-two minutes."

Clamping her lips together, Valerie slid onto the back seat. Sitting stiffly erect, she returned his stare until he deliberately turned his head to the front in a dismissive gesture.

The pink tinge of embarrassment heating her cheeks, Valerie sat glaring at the back of Thorne's head. A light pressure on her arm drew her attention, first to Janet's hand, then to her eyes. Her lips pursed, Janet shook her head while tilting it at Jonas Thorne. At Valerie's frown she gave a shrug, as if to say, "Don't let it bother you."

The drive from the airport to the J.T. Electronics building was made in silence and completed in twenty-five minutes, most of it along a new by-pass road constructed during Valerie's sojourn in France.

"Seven minutes to spare, Jonas." Lyle grinned as he brought the limo to a stop at a private side entrance to the building.

"I'm impressed," Jonas Thorne drawled dryly, flinging his door open and stepping out of the car. "Drop Janet and Miss Jordan off and then come back here," he ordered, already moving toward the private entrance.

Janet sighed as Lyle set the car in motion again. Smiling ruefully, she slid slim fingers through her close-cropped curls.

"If he was in such a hurry," she said, "I'm surprised he didn't have the chopper waiting for him."

"The chopper?" Valerie questioned.

"McAndrew flew to Washington in it this morning," Lyle informed Janet, before adding for Valerie's enlightenment, "The chopper is the company helicopter. We use it mostly for short trips."

"I'm impressed." Valerie imitated Thorne's dry drawl.

The following twenty minutes were interesting ones for Valerie. The changes made in the area during the years she'd been away were startling. Many places were totally unfamiliar to her, because of all the building that had taken place, and the alterations gave her an odd feeling. She had come home and she felt like a stranger; a foreigner in the place where she was born.

Lyle turned off the highway onto a road that led to yet another group of unfamiliar high-rise buildings.

He brought the car to a stop at the covered entrance-way to the one in the forefront.

"Here you are, Janet—Miss Jordan," he announced as he swung open the back door for them. "Delivered as ordered."

"Thanks, Lyle," Janet murmured when she and Valerie were standing on the pavement. "Now you had better scoot back to Jonas. See you Monday."

Janet introduced Valerie to the security guard stationed inside the heavy glass doors, told him the younger woman would be staying with her for awhile, then led the way to a row of elevators on the other side of the wide carpeted lobby. The elevator stopped at the fifth floor. After traversing a long hall, Janet unlocked a door marked 5B.

Compared to her tiny flat in Paris, Janet's apartment seemed enormous to Valerie. The living room was large, as were the two bedrooms. The bedrooms each had connecting baths, and there was a small powder room off the living room for use by guests. There was also a small dining area and a kitchen equipped with all the latest conveniences.

"This place is absolutely beautiful," Valerie breathed as the tour ended in the kitchen. "I wouldn't begin to guess how much it costs."

"Plenty." Janet grinned, pausing in the act of pouring water into the coffeemaker. "But it's worth every dollar." She shrugged. "I've worked very hard to get where I am. This place is the reward I've given myself." She glanced around possessively. "Actually, I owe it all to Jonas," she added.

"I don't buy that," Valerie scoffed. "You would

have succeeded in any company. I think Mr. Thorne probably owes you.''

''Not so.'' Janet shook her head sharply. ''Jonas has been very good to me.'' She frowned. ''Did Jonas bruise your sensitivity in some way, honey?''

''Bruise,'' Valerie repeated consideringly. ''You couldn't have chosen a better word, for I find your Jonas Thorne very abrasive.'' Her voice took on a grating edge. ''I don't like him—at all.''

''Oh, Val!''

Janet's worried exclamation made her feelings clear to Valerie.

''Don't worry, Janet,'' she was quick to promise. ''I have no intention of giving him any reason to be dissatisfied. If your job depends on my performance as his personal secretary, you can consider it secure. I promise you I will be a very, very good little girl— no pun intended.'' She accepted the steaming cup of coffee Janet handed her, sipping at it carefully before giving a little laugh. ''I plan to be the best damned secretary he has ever had—bar none.''

Janet stared, openmouthed, at the vehemence of Valerie's tone. ''Honey, I know Jonas was a little testy once or twice on the flight home,'' she said when she'd found her voice again. ''But I think you'll realize before too long that you've been a little hasty in your evaluation of him.''

''And what's your evaluation of him?'' Valerie asked with unaccustomed sarcasm. ''A diamond in the rough?''

''On the contrary.'' Janet's sharp tone was accompanied by a shake of her curly-haired head. ''I think you'll find him very polished. Oh, he's as hard as the

stone you mentioned," she conceded. "He's had to
be to get where he is today. He's tough, yes," she
went on in a tone that bordered on reverence. "But
all the rough edges he started out with are gone. And
he is, at times, ruthless. But, personally, I find the
combination of a brilliant, tough, ruthless mind in a
supremely fit body quite awesome."

Awesome! Now Valerie was the one to stare openmouthed. And the amazing thing was that Janet had
spoken in deadly earnest. Janet's attitude and a flashing memory of the ease with which both Parker and
Lyle responded to Thorne's rasping sarcasm convinced Valerie the man had the three of them completely buffaloed. Did he perhaps, she wondered, have
all his employees believing he was invincible? Not
me, Valerie promised herself.

Apparently she was the only one who saw him as
the brute he was. Perhaps she could see him more
clearly because she had not been involved with him
all along as the others had.

The chime of the doorbell broke the silence that
had settled between Valerie and Janet.

"That's probably Parker." Janet sighed in obvious
relief as she hurried out of the kitchen. Valerie followed at a more leisurely pace, a smile of welcome
curving her lips when Parker glanced at her.

"Good evening, Miss Jordan." Returning her
smile, Parker dipped his head respectfully before
reaching for the doorknob.

"Would you like a cup of coffee?" Janet asked.

"No, thank you." Parker's tone held regret. "I
have to get back to the plane. Jonas is flying to L.A.

tonight with several business associates, and I want to have everything squared away before he boards.''

"I swear—" Janet smiled ruefully at Valerie when the door closed behind Parker, "ever since Jonas bought that Gulfstream, Parker has cared for it like his own child. And he didn't even buy it new!" She paused, then laughed out loud. "Which isn't too surprising, considering what those babies cost."

"An awful lot?" Valerie queried.

"Millions, I'm told," Janet answered with a grimace.

Millions! Janet had said he'd fought his way up, but Valerie had had no idea she'd meant *that* far up! Her first impression came back to her in a rush; he was a formidable man, indeed.

"Well, he's welcome to it," Valerie observed, picking up her two large suitcases. "Especially tonight." Lugging the cumbersome cases as she trailed Janet to the smaller of the bedrooms, she sighed. "Personally, I'm bushed. I'm glad I don't have to face another flight tonight."

"Me too," Janet agreed heartily. "But I doubt it bothers Jonas one way or the other. He does so much dashing back and forth, I'm beginning to think he's immune to the effects."

Although Janet's tone held bemused admiration, Valerie shivered. The more she heard about him, the more inhuman he seemed. And now the reason for the free time he'd given her before reporting for work was clear. He had not acted out of consideration for her as she'd thought. Not in the least. He simply had no need of her in the office if he was in California.

Valerie lay awake a long time in the strange bed

in Janet's guest room, but for the first time in a long time, her sleeplessness was not caused by tormenting memories of Etienne. She was tired, very tired, but her mind was alert forming plans of how to go about becoming the perfect secretary.

Valerie and Janet spent the weekend catching up on each other's experiences of the last six years. In minute detail, Valerie described the orgy of sightseeing she'd indulged in during the years before she met Etienne.

"It all sounds wonderful," Janet sighed at one point. "Especially Greece. I've promised myself that some day I'll take a long vacation in Europe." Her eyes glowed teasingly. "Maybe I'll save it for my honeymoon."

"Are you planning one?" Valerie asked eagerly.

"Isn't everyone?" Janet drawled, then changed the subject.

In between their many conversations, Valerie practiced her typing on Janet's manual machine and took dictation from her obliging friend.

Janet and Valerie left for the office earlier than Janet's usual time on Monday morning and went directly to the personnel office. After filling out the required forms, Valerie was given a small, plastic-coated identification card and a key to the office she would be working in.

"Charlie McAndrew's secretary handed that key in on Friday afternoon," Janet told her when they left the personnel office. "You remember I told you Jonas had commandeered her?" Valerie nodded, following Janet without question as she started down the familiar hallway. Valerie was finding that the layout of the office came back to her easily, but she had never before had occasion to go up to the executive floor where Jonas Thorne worked.

"She'll be in the office with you today, to help you get acquainted with the routine," Janet went on, turning right into another, shorter hallway. "Charlie's office is just down the hall from Jonas's. His secretary's name is Eileen Skopec, by the way." Janet finished her briefing as they approached a curved, counter-high desk inside a door at the end of the hall.

A tall, burly man of about thirty half sat, half leaned on a high stool behind the desk. From his position he had a clear view of the door and both strokes of the L-shaped hallway. As they walked up to the desk a big smile creased the man's face.

"Good morning, Janet." His smile widened. "You're a little early this morning, aren't you?"

"A little, yes." Janet returned his smile. "Steve, this is Jonas's new secretary, Valerie Jordan—Val, Steve Dunn. He'll be checking you in and out of here every day." Janet nodded at the door. "You'll be using that entrance from now on."

"Welcome to the funny farm, Valerie." Steve grinned broadly.

"Thank you—I think." Valerie smiled uncertainly. "Funny farm?" Her eyebrows went up questioningly.

"Just an expression." Steve laughed. "Even though things can get pretty crazy around here. Especially when the coal cracker goes on a rampage."

Frowning in confusion, Valerie glanced at Janet, who smiled wryly and explained, "Steve is referring to our employer. He's been on a rampage ever since his secretary left.''

''Maybe now that you're here,'' Steve nodded at Valerie, ''Jonas will go back to his normal occasional growl.''

Valerie smiled weakly and groaned silently. Good Lord, she thought, walking to the metal door to glance out of the small square of window. It's not enough that I have Janet's job riding on my shoulders, now I find I'm also expected to soothe Thorne's ruffled feathers. She stood staring out the small pane several seconds before she realized this was the entrance where Lyle had dropped Thorne off on Wednesday afternoon. His own private entrance, she mused wryly, and I'm to be allowed the use of it. How lucky can one girl get? A tiny shiver stole along her spine and she turned back to Janet abruptly.

''Where do we go from here?'' she asked brightly, in an effort to dispel the chill of apprehension.

''Up.'' Janet indicated an elevator across the hall. ''See you later, Steve.'' She waved as she walked away.

''Very likely,'' Steve drawled, before adding, ''Nice meeting you, Valerie. Good luck with the cracker.''

''It was nice meeting you, Steve,'' Valerie called back as she followed Janet into the elevator. The box-like car swept up, then came to a smooth stop. The doors swooshed open to reveal a hallway carpeted in dark green plush. Janet ushered Valerie out with a sweeping of one arm.

''There are only two suites of offices on this floor. Jonas has the larger suite. Charlie has the other.'' She walked down the hall to a walnut door that was devoid of all marking. "This door is locked every night. You'll have to use your key."

After opening the door, Valerie stood back for Janet to precede her into the office. Following her, Valerie took three steps into the room and stopped in her tracks, her lips parting in surprise.

Whoever had decorated the room had considered both efficiency and comfort. The latest model in electric typewriters rested on the side of a large desk. Within easy reach were a word processor and a copying machine. The floor was carpeted with the same plush that covered the hall. The room's two large windows were draped with a loosely woven material in a rich cream color. Three chairs—one behind the desk, two in front of it—were upholstered in tawny, glove-soft leather. The overall effect was both businesslike and sumptuous.

"This, of course, is the cell you'll be working in." Janet laughed at Valerie's bemused expression. Striding across the room, she threw open a door on the wall nearest the desk. "And this," she nudged Valerie inside the room, "is where the warden works."

Jonas Thorne's office was the epitome of understated elegance. The carpet in this room was *not* the same as in the hall. A chocolate brown color, it was wonderfully, luxuriously thick.

The desk looked huge, even in the large room, and gleamed like satin in the morning light. The wall behind the desk had one enormous window draped in a roughly woven beige fabric. A long couch, covered in white leather, was placed along the wall facing the desk. Two chairs in a misty orange leather fronted the desk and a smaller one in the same color rested beside the desk. Valerie did not have to be told the small chair was the one she'd sit in to take dictation.

"And this," Janet walked to a door in the far wall, "leads to Jonas's bath and dressing room." She grinned at Valerie's lifted eyebrows. "Yes, it's a full bath. He has been known to work through the night, then catch a few hours' sleep on the couch. He keeps a closet full of clothes here. When he has those—" she hesitated, as if searching for words, then shrugged "—all-night sessions, he simply has a shower, puts on fresh clothes and starts all over again."

"Is he some kind of workaholic?" Valerie asked, peering into the black-and-gold tiled bathroom.

"Full time," Janet stated.

"Good morning."

"Good morning, Eileen," Janet returned warmly, smiling at the small, plump brunette standing in the doorway between the offices.

After introducing Valerie to Eileen, Janet left the office with a wave of her hand and a promise to come for Valerie at lunchtime.

"Well, I must admit I'm glad to see you," Eileen laughed as Janet swept out.

"Has working for Mr. Thorne been that bad?" Valerie frowned.

"Bad? Not really." Eileen shook her head, leading the way back to the other room. "He's very exact, and he expects his secretary to follow his example—but he's no ogre."

Not very reassuring, Valerie thought, remembering her easygoing boss in Paris. Then she was forced to concentrate as Eileen launched into a detailed explanation of what Thorne expected from his secretary. Time flew by, and, concentrating with every brain cell she possessed, Valerie was unaware of someone's entering the office until, glancing up with a bright smile, Eileen said, ''Good morning, Jonas.''

Digesting the fact that apparently everyone called him by his given name, Valerie turned from the copying machine as Thorne replied:

''Good morning, Eileen—Miss Jordan.''

''Good morning, Mr. Thorne.''

As she returned his greeting, Valerie marveled at the steadiness of her own voice. Her tone had conveyed a cool composure she was far from feeling, for on making eye contact with her employer, an uncomfortably familiar chill ran down the length of her spine.

Within the few seconds he paused before striding to his office, Valerie's eyes took a complete inventory of him. He was, again, suited in gray, a darker shade this time, and his eyes seemed to reflect the color, showing not a hint of blue. His sharply defined features gave his face a coldly forbidding cast that the straight line of his mouth did nothing to dispel. Valerie's estimation of him was exactly as it had been at first sight: he was cold, emotionless, formidable.

Valeric was fully aware that while she assessed him his eyes were flicking coolly over her. As they did, his expression seemed to tighten into implacable hardness. A tiny shiver followed the chill as she felt herself dismissed. At the doorway to his office he paused again to issue a terse order.

''I want one of you in here at once to take dictation.''

For several seconds pure, blind panic gripped Valerie, and then she squashed it as Eileen offered softly, "I'll do it. You stay with the machine."

Reaching for the pad and pencil on the desk, Valerie shook her head determinedly, and even managed a brief smile.

"I've got to start sometime; it may as well be now."

Having issued the brave statement she straightened her spine and walked unhesitatingly into Thorne's office.

"Close the door—please."

The harshness of Thorne's order was not relieved in the least by his sardonically tacked-on "please."

Controlling the sudden urge to slam the door shut, Valerie closed it carefully before walking to the chair beside his huge desk. Seating herself on the edge of the chair, back straight, legs seemingly glued together, she poised the pencil over the pad and glanced up at him with what she hoped was a professionally expectant expression.

Though his own expression was bland, his eyes mocked her little show of secretarial efficiency.

"Are you quite ready?"

"Yes—sir."

The brief flicker in Thorne's eyes at her tiny, but deliberate pause before adding the term of respect sent a small thrill of pleasure coiling through Valerie's midsection. The equally brief flash of amusement that replaced the flicker of annoyance transformed her thrill of pleasure into a disquieting sensation that felt very uncomfortably like *real* respect.

Now Valerie was annoyed—although she succeeded in hiding it. She did not want to feel even a glimmer of respect for this man. This was the monster, Valerie reminded herself harshly, who was prepared to accept Janet's resignation in the event she could not meet his high standards in the execution of her duties.

At this point all other considerations were cut off as Thorne launched into dictation.

By the time his quietly clipped voice came to a halt, Valerie felt like all her nerves had been tied into tight, throbbing knots. Her sole consolation was the somewhat surprising realization that she had kept up with him. As she concentrated on getting out of his office while maintaining at least the frayed remnants of her earlier composure, Valerie sent up a silent prayer of thanks for the urge that had set her to practicing her shorthand with Janet over the weekend.

"How did it go?" Eileen's query came with the closing of the door that connected the two offices.

"The man's a machine," Valerie declared in a tone that held both weariness and hard conviction. "How long was I in there?"

"Exactly two hours and thirty-seven minutes," Eileen laughed, glancing at her watch. "Not too long, really," she murmured. "He's been known to go on a lot longer than that." Her grin turned into a soft, compassionate smile. "The first time is always the hardest. You'll get used to his ways."

"If I survive long enough," Valerie opined softly. "Honestly, Eileen, I feel like I was in there for days." She sighed, then went on, "I'm afraid I'm going to

have to evict you from that chair. He wants these,"
she lifted her steno pad, "typed as soon as possible."

"He always does," Eileen returned quietly, rising
and moving away from the desk. Plucking another
pad from the desk top she added, "I'll give him his
phone messages while you start that."

Valerie had no sooner rolled the first sheet of paper
into the typewriter than Eileen came out of Thorne's
office again, a small, apologetic smile on her lips.

"I've been ordered back to my own desk," she
said in a near whisper. "Apparently Charlie's about
ready to tear his hair out." At Valerie's confused,
questioning look she explained, "Jonas's assistant,
my boss, Charles McAndrew, remember?" Valerie
nodded impatiently, which drew a soft laugh from
Eileen. "Well, it appears the girl from the typing pool
has not handled things to Charlie's satisfaction." She
shook her head sadly. "Charlie is—ah—shall I say—
almost as exacting as Jonas. Poor kid, she is very
young. She's an excellent typist, but not qualified to
keep up with Charlie."

"I see." Valerie hesitated a moment, then asked
flatly, "Is everyone on a first-name basis around
here?"

"Just about," Eileen confirmed, heading for the
door. "I suppose it's a little—well—unorthodox, but,
it is by request." Valerie's frown indicated that she
didn't fully comprehend Eileen's meaning and Eileen
explained. "Everyone you've heard refer to Jonas or
Charlie by their given names has done so because
they have been asked to. Charlie, being in absolute
awe of Jonas, is the next thing to his reflection—in
action and attitude—if not in looks." She paused in

the doorway to smile encouragingly. "Within a week you'll very probably be using their first names as unselfconsciously as all the rest of us."

Valerie seriously doubted Eileen's assertion, but she kept her doubts to herself. She was typing away at an incredible pace when Janet called to her from the doorway.

"Are you ready to go for lunch, Val?"

Startled, Valerie looked at Janet blankly a second before her question registered fully. "Why, I don't know," she answered vaguely, darting a glance at her watch. "I'll check with Mr. Thorne."

With fingers that were suddenly, inexplicably shaky, Valerie lifted the receiver and pressed the button that buzzed the phone on Thorne's desk.

"What is it?" he barked impatiently into his receiver.

Valerie fleetingly considered snapping back at him but then reconsidered and said, very coolly, "I'm going to lunch now, sir."

"All right, Miss Jordan," Jonas replied with much less impatience. Then he rendered Valerie speechless by adding, with an almost human understanding of the morning she'd put in, "Take your time."

Chapter 3

During that first week in the office, Thorne's attitude toward his new secretary was characterized by a bewildering combination of impatience and sensitivity. By late Friday afternoon Valerie couldn't decide if Jonas Thorne was the worst or absolutely the best man she'd ever worked for.

He was, above all, thorough, and he expected the same degree of thoroughness from his secretary. Valerie had never worked so hard in her life. Although she fell into bed early every night silently cursing the man, each successive day of working with him added another layer to the unwanted respect she felt for him.

Even when he was most impatient with her, he was unfailingly polite—tacking on sardonically drawled "thank you"'s and "please"'s—until Valerie found herself swinging between simple dislike and total loathing of him.

Charlie McAndrew, on the other hand, was thoroughly likable. Of medium height, with pale blue eyes, sandy hair, and an abundance of freckles, Charlie looked anything but the ambitious young executive. At their first meeting, late on the afternoon of her first day in the office, Charlie had insisted she call him by his given name. Until she saw him in action the following day, Valerie had some difficulty seeing Charlie in the role of Jonas's live-wire assistant. Blushingly shy and easygoing, Charlie appeared more the type found at a small corner desk, pouring over bookkeeping ledgers.

Which only proved, Valerie decided wryly near the end of the week, exactly how deceptive appearances could be. In action Charlie was almost, but not quite, as dynamic as his idol.

By quitting time Friday, positive she'd failed both Janet and herself miserably, Valerie prepared to slink out of the office in defeat.

"I'm afraid I owe Janet an apology." Jonas's quiet voice drew Valerie's startled eyes to his. She had not heard him open the connecting office door, and seeing him leaning indolently against the doorframe unnerved her. In fact, seeing him in an indolent position *anywhere* would have unnerved her.

"An apology?" Valerie repeated blankly. "What for?"

"You don't know?" The tilt of Jonas's right eyebrow, combined with his dry tone, mocked her show of ignorance. Of course she knew what he was referring to. Hadn't she been deriding herself about it when he'd made his sudden appearance? But how did she go about explaining to him that the sound and sight of him had scattered her thoughts? She had been listening to him, seeing him all day. He'd think she was an idiot, and rightly so, she berated herself. His exasperated sigh told her she'd been quiet too long.

"The—bargain—Janet made with me to secure this position for you," Jonas prompted. "You *were* aware of it?" The words were more a statement than a question.

Valerie was convinced she'd let Janet down, and after a week of exposure to both his cold-eyed observation and the confusing nuances that laced his tone, she was oversensitive to just about everything about him. His chiding remark put an end to the polite facade she had assumed in his presence. Lifting her head, she met his cold stare with equal coldness.

"Yes, sir, I was aware of it," Valerie returned frostily. "You were to have Janet's resignation on demand if I was unable to fulfill your requirements." Valerie's tone went from frosty to icy. "Isn't that correct?"

"Not quite," Jonas clipped acerbically. "*I* made no demands. Janet made the terms of the bargain."

"But you didn't hesitate to accept them," Valerie accused frigidly, even though she had no real proof of her charge.

"Why should I have hesitated?" Jonas's tone betrayed his growing anger. "Janet's been with me a long time; I like and respect her. I simply agreed to her proposition."

"You were prepared to accept her resignation if I fell on my face," Valerie asserted.

"But you did not," Jonas shot back. "So it's a moot point." His glittering steel gray eyes narrowed on her indignant expression. "Unless you persist in rousing my anger more than you already have. I'd advise you to speak carefully, Miss Jordan, or instead of offering Janet my apology I'll be showing her the way out of this firm. Needless to say, should I do so, she will be following *you*." He paused to let his warning sink in, then went on, very softly, "Have I made myself clear?"

"Perfectly," Valcrie whispered through stiff lips. She was not concerned about her own job, she assured herself unconvincingly. But she could not take any chances with Janet's. Nevertheless she grew weak with relief when the object of her thoughts sailed blithely into the office.

"Are you ready to leave, Val?" Before Valerie could respond, Janet spied Jonas in the doorway. "Oh, hi, Jonas, am I interrupting something?"

"Not at all," Jonas replied smoothly. "As a matter of fact, we were discussing you."

"Me?" Although Janet managed to keep her smile intact, her eyes darted from Jonas to Valerie then back to Jonas.

"Yes, you." Jonas's teasing tone drew Valerie's startled eyes to his face. She had heard at least a half-dozen shadings in his voice during that long week, but never one of affectionate teasing. "I was just telling Miss Jordan that I owe you an apology."

"An apology?" Janet echoed Valerie's earlier words. "What for?"

"For doubting your judgment. You were right. I'm not sorry I let you badger me into bringing Miss Jordan back from Paris."

The smile he bestowed on Janet stole Valerie's

breath. It was not until Steve called good-night to her and Janet as they left the building that she pulled herself together. What, she wondered, had Janet and Jonas said to each other? Snatches of their conversation skipped in and out of her mind.

"You mean you're really satisfied with her work?" Janet had asked—thereby revealing exactly how concerned she'd been.

"Very satisfied." Jonas's surprising answer had left Valerie so stunned that the content of his subsequent words was lost to her.

Whatever had come over her? The question tormented Valerie as she walked across the parking lot beside Janet. Clearheaded now, Valerie wondered at her odd reaction to the flashing smile that had transformed his face. Good grief, it was the first time she'd ever seen it!

"Val, are you listening?" Janet's exasperated tone put an end to Valerie's bemused thoughts.

"No, I'm sorry, I wasn't." Valerie smiled ruefully. "What did you say?"

"I *said* I'm proud of you." The frown creasing Janet's face smoothed out as she smiled. "Of course, *I* knew *you* could do it. The thing that worried me was whether *you* knew you could do it."

"I really didn't," Valerie admitted, sliding onto the passenger seat of Janet's car. She fastened her seat belt before adding, "As a matter of fact, I was positive I'd failed. His apology was as much a surprise to me as it was to you."

"He gave no indication that he was satisfied with your work?" Janet asked, placing a cigarette between her lips.

"None."

"Strange." Janet finished lighting her cigarette then turned the key in the ignition. "Usually Jonas is quick to show his approval when he's satisfied."

Thinking wryly that a number of meanings could be put on Janet's statement, Valerie shrugged. "I don't like your Jonas very much, Janet."

"My Jonas!" Janet exclaimed loudly. "He's not *my* Jonas." Bringing the car to a stop in the line of cars waiting to exit the parking lot, she turned a wicked grin on Valerie. "Would that I could call him mine, but I don't think there's a woman alive who can." She gave a mock shiver, and her smile turned dreamy. "God, I've wondered for years what he's like in bed."

Cold, Valerie thought disparagingly. Cold and unemotional and mechanical. Aloud she said, "I doubt he's anything to get excited about—in bed I mean."

"Really?" They moved forward four car lengths, then stopped again, and Janet gave her an arch look. "I don't doubt it for a minute. There have been one hell of a lot of females chasing him for as long as I've known him. He's got something."

"Money." Valerie sneered. "There are one hell of a lot of females anxious to marry it."

"Won't wash." Janet shook her head emphatically. "The way I hear it, the women were after him long before he had the money."

"Before?" Valerie's eyes widened with surprise. "You mean he wasn't born with the proverbial silver spoon?"

"Jonas? Hell no!" Janet's burst of laughter was cut off by the blast of a horn, alerting Janet to the space growing between her car and the now moving line in front.

Janet was quiet as she concentrated on maneuvering the car off the lot and onto the highway. When they had finally merged into the thick throng of traffic, Janet said abruptly, "I think we should celebrate. There's a bar near here where a lot of people from J.T.'s stop most Fridays for an end-of-the-week drink. Let's stop and join them."

"Oh, I don't know," Valerie hedged. "I'm very tired, Janet." Tired hardly described the way she felt—half dead on her feet came a little closer to the mark.

"But that's exactly why we should stop," Janet argued. "Val, honey, you're tighter than an overwound watch. You need to relax, be with other people. Lord, girl, how long has it been since you've had a night out?"

Valerie went stiff with the memory, and she had to force herself to answer. "There—there was a prewedding party—" she moistened her lips "—the night before Etienne—" She couldn't say the words, and, turning her head sharply, she stared out the side window.

"Oh, Val." Janet sighed. "I'm sorry, really sorry about Etienne, but, honey, you have got to pull yourself together. The longer you put off being with others, the harder it will be. I really think we should stop. Okay?"

"I suppose you're right." Valerie didn't suppose anything of the sort. She didn't want to be with other people. What she wanted was to go home and sleep the clock around. But Janet had been more than kind, and so she gave in, grudgingly. "Okay, Janet."

"You don't have to sound like it's a punishment." Janet's laughter fell flat. "You just might enjoy it. They're a good group."

Good group or not, Valerie discounted the possibility of enjoyment. Feeling irritable and tense with the effort to hide it, a sudden thought chilled her and she asked stiffly, "Will Mr. Thorne be there?"

"Jonas! You have got to be kidding." Janet shot her a quick grin before returning her attention to the traffic. "And here it is," she informed her a few minutes later.

Valerie studied the unimpressive two-story frame building as Janet drove the car onto the macadam parking lot that was over half-full of cars. All from J.T's? she wondered, eyeing the sign above the bar entrance.

"The Drop Inn Lounge." She read the words aloud. "Cute. Are you sure Mr. Thorne never drops in?"

"Not that I know of." Stepping out of the car Janet tossed her a questioning glance. "Val, are you afraid of Jonas?"

"Seven days a week." The fervent admission surprised Valerie as much as it did Janet. Falling into step beside her friend she went on harshly, "I think he's as tough as a cheap cut of beef."

"Oh, he's tough all right." Janet frowned at her. "Was he—well—unpleasant to you this week?"

"Unpleasant?" Valerie repeated consideringly. "Not exactly unpleasant. He was more..." She searched for words. At least a half-dozen unkind ones sprang to mind but she settled for "impatient."

"Oh, well." Janet paused, hand on the knob of the bar door. "That's nothing to get worked up over. Jonas is impatient with everyone. Come on." She pulled the door open. "I'll prove it to you."

The inside of the bar was a surprise after the unimpressive exterior. It was dimly lit, but the hand of an excellent decorator was evident. The stools in front of the long bar were covered in a vibrant red fabric, as were the captain's chairs around the dozen or so tables in the room. The indoor-outdoor carpeting was in a black and red tile pattern that was repeated in the material of the café curtains that hung at the four windows. Pewter hurricane lamps burning scented oil were placed in the center of every table. The crowded room buzzed with laughter and conversation and vibrated with music from a flashing jukebox sitting just inside the door.

From the moment she stepped inside, Janet was hailed from every section of the room. Smiling and waving back, Janet headed toward a large round table in the corner, around which sat five women.

Trailing behind Janet, Valerie returned the greetings of several people she'd met at various times during the week, and ignored the suggestive glances of several men she had not yet met. As they approached the table Valerie identified three of the five women. Searching her mind, she named and placed them. The small, chunky, dark-haired woman of about thirty was Doris Mercer, secretary to one of Thorne's executives—Valerie couldn't remember his department. Next to her was Sharon Templin, a tall, slim young woman who worked in the mail room. The third was Judy Blume, a dark-haired woman of about Valerie's own age who was assistant to the manager of the typing pool.

Janet waited until they were seated at the table before introducing Valerie to the other two women.

"Valerie Jordan." Janet waved a slim hand at her, then at the lovely platinum blonde directly across the table. "Annette Liemiester—she keeps the file room from falling apart."

Valerie smiled and returned Annette's "hi," and then her eyes moved to the tall black woman with the very pretty, but somewhat stern, face.

"Loretta Harris." Janet grinned at the solemn-faced woman. "She's the top-kick in personnel."

The lazy smile that Loretta turned on Valerie completely changed her visage from stern to devilish. "Hi, Valerie." Her voice was husky, her tone teasing. "Sorry I missed you Monday morning. How are things going in the high-rent district?"

"I beg—" bemused by the chameleon-swift change in Loretta, Valerie was uncertain of her meaning, then the light clicked on in her head. "Oh!" She laughed softly. "You mean the executive suite. All right I guess. At least I haven't been given notice to vacate as yet."

"And won't be," Janet inserted firmly. "Jonas himself told me he is satisfied with her work."

"That's encouraging," Loretta drawled. Fixing her beautiful brown eyes on Valerie, she pleaded. "Please, try to *keep* him satisfied. For as long as you do, Legree's whip won't fall on *my* back."

Her plea was met by total confusion from Valerie and derisive comments from her four companions.

"Poor Loretta," Doris cooed.

"Summer's coming and she won't be able to bare her scarred back," Sharon chided.

"Work , work, work." Judy lifted a hand languidly to smother a yawn.

"Tote that barge, lift that bale." Annette fluttered incredibly long lashes.

Lifting her glass, Loretta sat back in her chair, her huge grin revealing white teeth. "Oh, the price one pays for being indispensable," she said pleasantly.

"Loretta's been feeling the lash of Jonas's tongue ever since your predecessor took off," Janet explained, taking pity on Valerie's obvious confusion.

"I just don't understand why it was so hard to find a replacement." Annette's long eyelashes swooped down and she swept the faces around her with eyes that glittered from behind narrowed lids. "I'd jump at the chance to work closely with Jonas—really closely, I mean."

"Mmm," Judy agreed, taking a quick gulp of her drink. "Don't say any more. Just *thinking* about it is enough to give me shivers."

"Personally," Loretta murmured huskily, "I enjoy imagining what those late nights in the office might be like."

Valerie felt her skin grow warm. Impossible though it was for her to believe, these women were actually drooling over Jonas Thorne! They're putting me on, she decided. Expecting a burst of laughter at any moment, Valerie glanced around the table, a hollow feeling growing inside as she noted the gleam in several pairs of eyes. They're not putting me on! Even Janet wore an expression of flirtatious interest!

The arrival of a waitress at the table broke the spell, and to Valerie's relief, the subject was dropped. Valerie and Janet ordered drinks and another round was requested for the others.

"On me," Janet declared. "Val and I are celebrating the successful conclusion of her week on the hot seat," she went on to explain. "No pun intended."

The tension slowly eased out of Valerie as easy laughter, followed by teasing banter, flowed around her. The conversation revolved around the doings at J.T.'s. Some of the talk concerned serious matters, but most of it was harmless gossip. Valerie, content to simply sit back and listen, was halfway through her second drink when Doris interrupted a rather juicy anecdote that Sharon was relating. Doris was sitting facing the door, and as she glanced in that direction, her eyes widened in shock.

"I don't believe it!" she exclaimed softly.

"Well, Jean insists it's true," Sharon said defensively, casting Doris a look of annoyance.

"Not that," Doris snapped, not even bothering to look at Sharon. She nodded her head toward the bar's entrance. "That."

Valerie's eyes moved along with five other pairs, and then she froze in her seat.

"Is he real or did we conjure him up?" Loretta asked dryly.

"I agree with Doris," Janet murmured. "I don't believe it."

Valerie, however, was uncomfortably aware of how

real Jonas Thorne was as he made his way through the room. His progress was slow, as he was stopped every few steps by someone either at the bar or at a table. Before he was even a quarter of the way into the room a drink was handed to him by a young man from the accounting department whom Valerie had met the previous afternoon. Thorne accepted the glass with a sardonically raised eyebrow and a brief shrug.

When it became apparent that his destination was their table, Valerie very deliberately withdrew into a state of mental detachment. Secure inside the shelter of self-induced indifference, she awaited his arrival.

"Ladies."

For the second time in less than two hours, Valerie was witness to Jonas Thorne's smile. Only this time, safe in her fortress of indifference, she coolly observed its effect on her companions. Right before her eyes they seemed to melt before the dazzling warmth of that smile.

"Washing away the bad taste of J.T.'s?" The slight dip of his head indicated the glasses on the table.

Valerie remained silent as the others laughingly denied his words. She wanted very badly to label his tone condescending or patronizing. She wanted to, but she could not. He displayed nothing but warmth and friendliness. His eyes circled the table, resting briefly on each face. Was it her imagination or had his eyes sharpened momentarily when they took in her closed expression?

How had they answered him? What had they said? Although Valerie had heard the breathless, fluttery sound of their voices, she had not absorbed their actual words. Her attention focused intently on Thorne and the manner in which he received his near adulation. Expecting arrogance, Valerie grudgingly admitted that though he obviously enjoyed their overtly sexual reaction to him, he did not bask in it.

"I stopped here in the hope of catching you before you went home, Loretta." The abrupt change in his tone announced business as usual. Though his cool, blue-gray eyes were focused now on Loretta's, no one but a fool would think he had singled her out for any personal reason. Loretta was anything but a fool. Straightening in her chair as if snapping to attention, she became once again the efficient personnel manager.

"There's a problem?" The somewhat stern expression was back in place—her tone matched it exactly.

"No, no problem," Thorne replied easily. "I had a phone call from Maria Cinelli a short time ago."

This seemingly innocuous statement had an electrifying effect on every woman at the table, bar one— Valerie frowned her confusion.

"And?" Loretta prompted respectfully.

"She wants her job back." His answer came without inflection of any kind.

Valerie had the sensation of being pinned to her chair by the sympathetic glances turned to her by her tablemates. Seeking an answer, she lifted her eyes to Thorne. His face revealed none of the concern written clearly across the faces of his employees. The silence seemed to stretch interminably, yet in truth it lasted no longer than a few rapid heartbeats. "Find her something to do."

A soft sigh, issued collectively from six throats,

followed the terse order. Shifting her eyes to Loretta, Valerie watched as the woman mentally reviewed available job openings.

"Jonas." Loretta's eyes narrowed in defeat, her tone held an odd pleading note. "I have nothing open for someone of her capabilities."

"I didn't ask you to crown her queen, Loretta." A taunting smile curved his lips. "Only to allow her back at court."

A devilish grin was Loretta's immediate response. "Will do, sir."

"Glad to hear it." His soft drawl banished the taut atmosphere. Doris giggled, and as if it were a signal, Thorne turned to leave, then paused.

"The tab's on me." A wave of his hand indicated their drinks.

"Oh!" Annette fluttered her long lashes at him. "We were planning to have dinner here." She waited prettily.

"Then you've lucked out, haven't you?" Once more they were favored with that dazzling smile. "Enjoy your dinner, and the weekend, ladies." His pause was very, very brief. "You too, Miss Jordan."

Chapter 4

Arrogant swine!

Valerie silently repeated the epithet for at least the fiftieth time since Thorne had delivered his parting shot.

Damned arrogant swine. Valerie threw her leather shoulder bag onto her bed with the force of suppressed anger.

"Pig, pig, pig." Seeking an outlet for the fury that seethed in her mind, she muttered the words aloud, slowly, vehemently. She had no idea exactly what he'd meant by his taunting, "You too, Miss Jordan." She didn't even know exactly why the taunt had enraged her so. All she knew was that he'd pierced her armor of detachment with one carelessly tossed barb. And having to hide her dislike of him from Janet and the others hadn't helped much.

What a gaggle of simpering idiots! Jerking around,

Valerie kicked her shoes in the direction of her closet. What motivates these career women? she asked herself despairingly. All of the women at that table were around Valerie's age or older. Yet none were married. Why? Why hadn't they married, or—in the case of Annette and Judy, who were divorced—remarried? What were their goals? The questions had hammered away at Valerie for hours while she sat, shocked, listening to their comments about Thorne.

Dropping tiredly onto the edge of her bed, she replayed the scene in her mind in an effort to glean something, any small understanding, from it. Loretta had been the first to break the tiny silence that had followed in the wake of Thorne's departure.

"That is one big, sexy man."

"I'll say," Sharon breathed softly. "God, when he smiles like that I have to fight the urge to tear my clothes off."

"Yes, but everyone knows that you're oversexed." Doris laughed. "I know what you mean though. With me the urge is to tear *his* clothes off."

"I get shivery all over just thinking about what he'd look like without his clothes," Judy sighed.

"I live in hope." Annette smiled smugly, her long lashes seeming to tremble as her eyes caressed Thorne's retreating back.

"And you'll very probably die in disappointment," Janet inserted dryly. "I have worked for him for almost fifteen years and in all that time he has singled out only one female employee for personal attention."

"And now the witch is back." Doris moaned.

"Unfortunately," Sharon added.

"We haven't heard from Miss Cinelli's replacement." Annette's lovely face was turned in question to Valerie. "What do you say, Valerie?"

She had plenty she dearly longed to say, but the fleeting expression of alarm that passed over Janet's face cautioned her to mind her tongue.

"Nothing." Valerie gazed calmly into Annette's disbelieving eyes. "I'm not interested. Not in him—or any other man."

"Why?" Annette probed. "Are you a man hater?"

Now that Thorne had made it through the room and out the door all their attention focused on her. Valerie, already angry, was not about to subject herself to an inquisition. Getting to her feet, she smiled sweetly at Annette.

"No, I don't hate men. Now, if you'll excuse me, I'd like to freshen up a little."

She had spent ten minutes in the ladies' room making believe she was touching up her makeup and brushing her hair; but all the while she had chided herself for the disgust their comments about Thorne provoked in her. You are twenty-seven years old, she silently lectured her reflection. You have seen quite a bit of the world. You are not an innocent; you have experienced a man's body.

She lowered her eyelids, blocking out the pain reflected in the violet eyes in the mirror. When she looked again most of the pain was gone, replaced by a shadowed, haunted look. For all your traveling around, you *are* an innocent, she silently informed that lost little face in the mirror. And the reason their blatantly sexual talk offends you is that it has nothing to do with the beauty you shared with Etienne.

Thinking his name hurt. Jumping to her feet, she scooped up her purse and hurried out the door. The atmosphere at the table had undergone a complete change. The subject under discussion was food and the varying degrees of starvation each woman was suffering from. Not once during the rest of the evening was Thorne's name mentioned. Nor did Valerie's avowed disinterest in men come up again.

Now, hours later, still fighting the last remnants of her anger, Valerie paused in the act of unbuttoning her tailored shirt, a sudden thought belatedly striking home. Rebuttoning her shirt as she went, she left her room and walked into the living room where Janet sat watching the late news on TV.

"You told them about Etienne, didn't you?" Valerie accused the back of Janet's head. The head jerked around to reveal eyes soft with understanding.

"Yes," Janet admitted calmly. "While you were in the ladies' room." A small smile touched her lips.

"Janet—why?" Valerie had to bite her lip against crying aloud.

"Because I didn't want you badgered by a lot of questions," Janet explained in the same calm tone. "Val, they are nice people, really. At one time or another they've all experienced loss or rejection. They won't pry."

"Maybe not," Valerie groaned. "But by noon Monday every employee at J.T.'s will know about Etienne."

"Very likely." Janet lifted her shoulders in resignation. "But, if nothing else, it will keep the wolves at bay—at least for a while." The smile tugged more forcibly at her lips. "With your looks it won't be for long, but it will give you some breathing space." Her eyebrows arched. "Have any of the self-proclaimed great lovers made an approach yet?"

Valerie sighed wearily. "Yes, several. And their reasons for coming into my office were suspect, now that you mention it."

"Well, there you are." Janet's shoulders lifted again. "Either you put up with their advances, or they know about Etienne and leave you alone for a respectable period."

Valerie sighed again, this time in defeat. "I suppose so," she muttered, turning to go back to her room. She took two steps then swung back to cry, "Dammit, Janet, why did you have to come after me? I was perfectly all right where I was," she lied.

"You were perfectly miserable and you know it," Janet returned gently. "Give it time, honey; it will pass." Her voice gentled even more. "And, meanwhile, Val, I suggest you rub the stardust out of your eyes."

Janet's advice kept Valerie awake long after she slid between the sheets of her bed. It didn't take an Einstein to figure out that Janet had been well aware of Valerie's adverse reaction to the sexual remarks made by their table companions. Turning and twisting uncomfortably, Valerie tried to conjure up the purity of Etienne's face, and for the first time, the image was shadowy and unclear. Blind panic filled her mind, and lying still, barely breathing, she pleaded: Don't go, please don't leave me.

During the weekend, Valerie repeatedly asked herself two seemingly unrelated questions: Did she really have stardust in her eyes? And, what difference would it make if she suddenly found herself dispossessed by her predecessor?

It would make a lot of difference, she realized on Monday morning as she dressed for work. All during the drive in, and as she unlocked the office that she now thought of as her own domain, Valerie felt a mixture of anger and despair. Damn this faceless Maria, she thought angrily. Damn this ex-secretary, ex-mistress, ex-whatever, for coming back now.

Standing in front of her desk, Valerie was shocked into immobility by the intensity of her feelings. Staring at her neat desk top, she slowly curled her fingers into tight fists. True, Thorne had ordered Loretta to find another job for his ex-secretary, but, if what they said was true, and Maria was also his ex-bed partner—how long would it be before Maria was back at this desk and she found herself out hunting for a job?

"Are you posing for my benefit, Miss Jordan? Or are you simply hung-over?"

Valerie's body jerked violently—as if his taunting tongue had been placed against an exposed nerve. Swinging around, she faced him squarely, lost her cool and blurted, "Do you want me to clean out my desk?"

Nails digging into her palms, she watched the transformation in his face. Amused mockery disappeared to be replaced by a stern, hard look.

"You've decided to leave us?" The very softness of his tone, so at odds with his expression, sent a chill of fear down her spine. "You're going to dash back to Paris—and the past?"

Back to Paris? The past? Valerie shook her head dumbly. What did Paris or the past have to do with

Maria Cinelli? Misinterpreting her vague head movement as a negative response, Thorne snapped. "You've found another, better position perhaps?"

"No!" Valerie denied softly. "I didn't mean—"

"If you haven't got another job, and you're not going to leave the country," Thorne interrupted harshly, "would you care to explain just what the hell you do mean?"

The very hardness of his tone added to Valerie's confusion. Why was he so angry? She'd have thought he'd be delighted at having the way so smoothly paved for his girlfriend's return. Why was he attacking her? That thought stiffened her spine with anger. Who did he think he was talking to?

"I *mean* just what I said." Valerie fairly spat the words at him. "Do you want me to clear out?"

"Miss Jordan," he barked exasperatedly, "as I'm never very good at reading minds on Monday morning, would you kindly explain exactly what the hell you are talking about?"

"About Miss Cinelli," Valerie barked back.

"Miss Cinelli," Thorne repeated slowly as he crossed the room to her. "What about Miss Cinelli?" He stopped less than a foot in front of her and Valerie had to tilt her head back to look up at him.

She didn't particularly like what she saw. Up close he gave the appearance of a man very near the end of his patience. Valerie held her ground, hanging on to her composure by sheer willpower. In truth, he scared the breath out of her.

"I thought you'd want her back," she gulped. The narrowing of his eyelids made her add hastily, "As your secretary."

"You heard what I told Loretta, didn't you?" His tone, though very soft, was threatening. Valerie suddenly found it very difficult to swallow.

"Y-Yes."

"Then why are we wasting time on this discussion?"

"I-I," Valerie paused to wet hot, dry lips. "I just thought—"

"Wrong," he interrupted. "You thought wrong. Now, do you *think* we could get on with the electronics business?"

Valerie wanted very badly to back away from him, but even had her pride allowed her to do so, the solid form of her desk mere inches behind her prevented retreat. To make matters still worse, her legs had begun to tremble with nervous weakness and she wanted very badly to sit down. Feeling trapped, she stared up at him mutely. He was the most fierce-looking male she'd ever encountered. After only one week of listening to the chatter in the cafeteria Valerie was well aware of what the female employees on his staff thought of him. There was evidence of respect in abundance, but, first and foremost, the general consensus was that he was handsome, terrifically put together, exciting, and sexy as the very devil—not necessarily in that order.

Gazing up into his face now, Valerie made her own evaluation. Handsome? Hardly. Etienne had been handsome. Thorne's face was too thin, the bones underneath the tautly drawn skin too prominent. There was not a hint of softness or tenderness in his cold eyes or in the long, slightly arched nose that jutted below. The lines that formed grooves from either side of his nose to the corners of his thin-lipped mouth spoke of harshness, and his sharply defined, not quite square jaw thrust forward in determination. That he was built well, she'd concede. And she had to admit he was exciting—at least as an aggressive business-man. Sexy as the devil?

"Have you reached a verdict?"

Valerie's thoughts splintered like shattered glass at the sardonically drawled question. What in the world was she doing? What must he think?

"I'm sorry." Valerie raked her mind for an expla-nation of her odd behavior. Nothing presented itself. "Mr. Thorne, I—"

"You didn't particularly like what you saw, did you?"

Startled, she blinked at him, then lowered her eyes. How did one answer a question like that tactfully?

"You have a very strong, determined face," she finally managed. The laughter that erupted from him startled her and her eyes flew again to his face. Look-ing at him was a mistake. Friday, his smile had stunned her, now his soft laughter had a paralyzing effect. Fleetingly she wondered why, when he could produce such a delightful sound, he laughed so rarely. Abruptly, he turned and walked to the door of his office. Before entering the room he shot her an amused, meaningful look.

"Strong and determined, huh?" The grin that spread across his face could only be described as wicked. "You don't know the half of it, sweetheart."

Groping behind her, Valerie clutched at the desk for support. The doorway was empty now but she could still hear his low chuckle, which unnerved her even more. Making her way around the desk she dropped into her chair, staring blankly at her shaking hands. She hadn't the vaguest idea how long she'd been sitting just staring at nothing, when the phone rang, bringing her to her senses.

With the first call of the day Valerie eased back into her normal routine. By the time she entered Thorne's office to take dictation she'd pulled herself together enough to speak to him in her usual cool tone of voice. His first, distant "Miss Jordan" assured her that he had also reverted to form.

Before drifting off to sleep that night, Valerie replayed the morning's scene over again in her mind in an attempt to make some sense of it. Why, she wondered sleepily, had Thorne's closeness to her, and his taunting jibe, shaken her so ridiculously? It wasn't as if she cared what he thought of her; she didn't. And she was positive he didn't give a damn what she thought about him. So then why had his face seemed to become taut with tension when he'd asked, "Have you reached a verdict?"

Unable to find any plausible answer for his attitude Valerie sought sleep. She was tired but, for the first time in the last year, she had good reason for her weariness. She had been exceptionally busy all day. The phone had rung incessantly and Thorne had required her presence at several meetings to take notes. Yawning widely she curled up on her side, dismissing all thoughts of the baffling Jonas Thorne.

Midmorning Tuesday, refreshed from a deep, dreamless eight hours of sleep, Valerie shifted her gaze from the keys of her typewriter to the woman who entered her office and felt her breath catch in her throat. The woman was not really beautiful, but she certainly was arresting. Tall in comparison to Valerie, she stood before the desk with the poise instilled by an exclusive finishing school—or a good modeling school—her head tilted slightly as she coolly studied the smaller woman. Her makeup had been applied with an artist's touch to enhance her high cheekbones and full-lipped mouth. Every dark hair on her regally held head was in perfect place, and her brown eyes were filled with disdainful amusement as they finished their perusal of Valerie.

Feeling herself weighed, measured and found decidingly wanting, Valerie felt annoyance prick her mind. Who was this haughty woman? Careful not to let her annoyance show, Valerie responded with her most professional smile.

"May I help you, Miss—?"

"Cinelli," the woman supplied, not bothering to return the smile. "Maria Cinelli, and I want to see Jonas."

Who cares what you want? Valerie had to bite back the retort. So this was the ex-everything, she sneered to herself. Very impressive, I suppose, except I'm not impressed.

"Of course you do," Valerie purred silkily, and felt rewarded by the tiny frown that fleetingly marred Maria's smooth brow. Allowing a glimmer of her own disdain to sneak into her eyes, Valerie swept the tall, elegant form with a dismissive glance as she pressed the button on the intercom.

"What is it, Miss Jordan?"

Valerie stiffened at the smug, catlike smirk of satisfaction that curved Maria Cinelli's lips at the impatience in Thorne's tone.

"Miss Cinelli is in the office, sir," Valerie answered in a neutral tone. "She would like to see you."

"Well, then, send her in."

"Yes, sir." Wondering what the maximum was for murder in Pennsylvania, Valerie forced herself to face the Cheshire smile on Maria's red lips. "You may go right in, Miss Cinelli."

"Of course I may," Maria taunted. "There was never any doubt of that."

Valerie decided then and there that she hated Maria Cinelli. She may as well wear a sign on her back that reads "for sale—expensive," she thought waspishly, as she watched that slender back glide into Thorne's office.

The door clicked shut with what sounded to Valerie like sharp finality. Turning back to her typewriter, she tried to relieve her frustration by attacking the innocent keys.

One white sheet of paper followed another around the roller, and still the connecting door remained firmly closed. Pounding away, making mistakes at a rate she had not equalled since leaving the Paris office, Valerie tried in vain to keep the questions at bay. Is Maria pleading with him to be taken back, into his life as well as the office? Is she succeeding? What *is* going on in there? Valerie shook her head suddenly, fiercely. The questions were bad enough. But with the last one came a mental picture of the long white couch in Jonas's office. The figures on the couch were tangled in an intimate embrace, and on the face of one, red lips curved in a smile of triumph.

"Oh, blast," Valerie muttered aloud as several keys, all positioned to strike the paper at the same time, stuck tightly together. What was the matter with her? Hadn't he as much as told her her job was secure? As to the other part of the picture, what did she care who he fooled around with? Valerie assured herself she did not care—all the while swallowing against the sick feeling that climbed from her stomach to her throat.

Thirty-odd minutes later, Valerie cast the still closed door a sour look as she left the office to go to lunch. When she returned, the door stood wide open and Thorne's office was empty. As she circled her desk to sit down, a dark scrawl across her dictation pad caught her eye.

I'm leaving for the day. Have Charlie keep my 2:30 appointment.

J.T.

Well, that about says it all, Valerie thought tiredly. Suppressing a sigh, she lifted the receiver to call Charlie McAndrew.

By quitting time Valerie was in a mood so foul that even Janet could not tease her out of it. That mood had not changed when she reentered the office Wednesday morning. A call from Charlie McAndrew informing her that Jonas had flown to Chicago for the rest of the week did nothing to relieve her irritability. Nor did the news, imparted by Loretta at lunchtime, that Maria had also left town.

Damn Thorne *and* his paramour, Valerie cursed silently through most of Thursday and Friday. The weekend brought thoughts of escape. Perhaps I'll just chuck the whole thing and hunt for another job, she decided late Sunday night, preferably in another city, or another state. Would Thorne give her a decent reference?

"Good morning, Valerie," Thorne greeted her pleasantly as he strolled into her office five minutes after her arrival on Monday morning.

For some obscure reason his casual use of her given name set the spark to her fuse, which had become very short over the weekend.

"Good morning, *sir,*" she returned with icy brittleness.

The change in his demeanor was both instant and somewhat frightening.

"Something on your mind?" he asked smoothly. Then added, even more smoothly, "Val?"

"Yes," Valerie snapped, unreasonably angered by his deliberate shortening of her name. "I want to tender my resignation."

"Fine," he snapped back, pivoting around and striding to the connecting door. "Tender it in writing."

His mockery of her terminology affecting her like a slap in the face, Valerie flounced around the desk. Without bothering to sit down, she snatched the cover off her typewriter, rolled a sheet of paper into it, and with trembling fingers tapped out her resignation.

Still not pausing to consider the rashness of her actions, she stormed into Thorne's office and presented the sheet of paper to him wordlessly. Moving slowly, lazily, Thorne accepted the paper. Then, after barely glancing at the contents, he tore it in half and dropped it into his waste paper basket.

"Now," he said softly. "Suppose you sit down and tell me what in hell this is all about?"

His soft tone didn't fool her for a second. Suddenly all the annoyance drained out of Valerie, and she felt utterly tired, and unbelievably stupid. What had he done to earn her disdain, really? The words, "Get rid of her," slithered into her mind, and Valerie realized with a shock that she had, in a way, been trying to punish him for them ever since. But what did they have to do with her, for heaven's sake? Had she designated herself the champion of her entire sex? A swift image of Maria's smirking face brought an equally swift answer to her question—not very likely.

"I'm waiting, Valerie." Jonas's sharp tone nudged her into alertness. But what could she say?

"I—I think it would be best if I left your employ," she told him weakly.

"Best for you—or me?"

"For me."

"Why?"

Why? Why? Because the idea of you and Maria together sickens me, that's why. Maria or any other woman. Valerie stiffened visibly as the truth hammered its way through the mental defenses she'd erected. God! She had to get out of here. But first she had to tell him *something*.

"Advancement," Valerie clutched at the first thought that came to mind.

"Strange." His tone, softly musing this time, was belied by his coldly calculating expression. "You didn't strike me as being a career woman." He paused, his eyes measuring her. "What sort of advancement?"

"W-What do you mean?" Valerie was beginning to feel uncomfortable under his penetrating gaze.

"I mean, what are your goals? Your long-range goals? What do you want out of life?"

"Want?" Valerie repeated confusedly.

"Yes, want," Thorne probed relentlessly. "From life, eventually?"

Where, she wondered, had she lost the thread of this conversation? It was obvious Thorne was no longer talking about her job. Unable to figure out his purpose, Valerie answered truthfully.

"The same as most women want, I guess. A home, some contentment. Children."

"Children!" Thorne repeated in feigned astonishment. "That will be difficult to manage, won't it?"

"Why should it be?" Valerie bristled.

Leaning back in his chair, Thorne ran a lazily assessing glance over her. "Well, a mate is required to produce children. Not a husband, necessarily, but a man." His thin lips curved mockingly. "And the word's around that you're off men."

Hot anger seared through Valerie, the power of it making her shake. Clenching her hands into tight fists she stood up just so she could look down on him.

"There will be a husband." She pushed the words through her teeth. "I intend *my* children to have legitimacy as well as a father."

"I'm glad to hear it," Thorne applauded. Goaded beyond caring what she said, Valerie went on the attack.

"And what do *you* want from life?"

Thorne didn't bat an eye. "A son," he replied instantly. "An heir to all this." He waved his hand to encompass the building.

"But I thought you already had an heir!" Valerie exclaimed. Janet had told her that though Thorne was now single, he had been married once. Although the union had been short-lived, it had produced a child.

"That's correct, I have." Thorne nodded. "A daughter."

Valerie blinked in surprise. Why had she thought he was different? Because of Janet and a number of other women who had advanced according to their talent and ability? But then, conferring advancement on employees was not quite the same as conferring an entire company on a daughter.

"And a daughter isn't good enough?"

"Don't be stupid," Thorne retorted. "I'd have been proud to have her take over in time, *if* she had been interested. The sad truth is, Valerie, my daughter's interest in this firm is totally centered on her monthly allowance check, nothing more."

"I'm sorry," Valerie murmured, blushing.

"So am I," Thorne returned. He shrugged. "That's the way it goes." He ran his eyes over her again as he slowly stood up. Then, as if coming to a sudden decision, he shocked her speechless by quietly asking, "Would you consider being my son's mother?"

Valerie felt her mouth drop open slightly. She was powerless to close it. Had she heard him correctly?

Apparently she had, for he repeated his question. Beginning to shake her head, she opened her mouth to answer him. He didn't give her the chance.

"I'm not suggesting anything clandestine, Val." His smile twisted strangely. "I also want legitimacy for my child. I'm asking you to marry me."

"But why me?" she blurted out.

"Why not?" Thorne countered.

"We barely know each other, that's why not," Val cried.

"Does anyone ever know anyone else?" Thorne questioned. "You just told me what you want. You know me well enough to be assured I can give it to you. And I assume you are physically capable of giving me what I want." His eyebrows, arched, "Right?"

Valerie nodded in automatic response.

"Well, then." He forged ahead before she could voice a protest. "Why not join forces and each supply the other's wants?"

"Because I don't—" She got no further.

"I know you are still hanging on to the memory of a dead love," Thorne stated coldly. "But if you are ever going to achieve your goal you're going to have to let go sometime. For your own sake, I think the sooner you let go, the better."

Valerie was trembling from the cruelty of his advice. Gritting her teeth she began, "Mr. Thorne—"

"Jonas." Again he would not let her speak. Striding around the desk he grasped her arms with his big hands. "You're going to have to face cold, hard reality sometime, Val. I'm giving you the opportunity to face it comfortably, from behind a protective cushioning of wealth." He smiled at her widened eyes. "Yes, Val, I'm a wealthy man, and I'm willing to make you a full partner. All you have to do for it is produce one son."

"You can fill a field with daughters, while hoping for a son." Valerie repeated one of her father's sayings, feeling like an idiot even while she spoke.

"I won't ask you to go that far," Thorne drawled. "If you are wise, Valerie, you'll consider your answer very carefully. You said your plans include a husband. Well, as far as husband material goes, I'm probably the best thing going."

Chapter 5

Y ou damned arrogant fool! he silently berated himself.

She was going to say no. And it was his own fault. The best thing going, indeed! Jonas watched the play of emotions on Valerie's face for several long seconds then, when she still did not speak, he released her arms and strode to the window to stare out, his jaw clenched so hard the bones hurt.

God, he wanted her! The sun glaring off the hoods and roofs of the rows of cars parked in the building's rear lot was an assault on the eyes and he narrowed his lids against it. He couldn't remember the last time he'd wanted a woman quite this badly. And she was going to say no. He knew it and the frustration of that knowing clawed at his guts.

He'd never taken time to regret his decisions. He'd never had time for regrets of any kind. But right now, this minute, he was sorry as hell that he'd indulged Janet by bringing Val back with him. I should have left her in Paris, he thought savagely. Left her to wallow in her grief and self-pity.

Sliding his hands into his pants pockets, Jonas massaged his knotted upper thighs with the tips of his fingers. What the hell kind of man had he been, this Etienne, this dead lover of Val's?

Fingertips dug painfully into taut muscles as a picture formed before his eyes, obscuring the sight of lot, cars and even the brilliant sunlight. In the picture Val lay with her glorious black hair spread out around her head. Her breathtaking violet eyes were softened by love and her white arms and whiter legs encircled the shadowy form of a faceless man. Dead or not, Jonas hated the thought of that faceless man.

"Mr. Thorne?"

The soft, hesitant sound of Val's voice dissolved the mirage. Releasing his breath slowly, silently, Jonas turned to face her. "Yes?" At that moment he was sure he knew exactly what a man facing a firing squad feels.

"Could I have some time?" His fingers dug yet deeper as he watched her wet her lips. Had she done that on purpose?

"How much time?" Jonas cursed himself for his cold tone when he saw her wince.

"Until—tomorrow morning?"

A reprieve, and he hadn't even heard the phone ring when the governor called. Reprieve hell! He felt like he was hanging on a very sharp hook. Why don't you tell her to get out of your life and get it over with? he advised himself mockingly. Because I still want her, that's why.

"Of course," he answered coolly. "Would you like the rest of the day to yourself?" Say yes, please, he pleaded silently, and get out of my sight so I can think straight.

"No." The sun struck glinting blue lights off her hair as she shook her head. "That won't be necessary."

That's easy for you to say. Jonas watched the smooth movement of Val's body as she walked to the door. Your mind's been numbed by grief and your body's immune to arousal. The door closed with a final-sounding click. I wish I could say the same for my body.

With a grim smile of self-mockery pulling at his lips, Jonas walked to his desk and lowered his long frame into the padded chair. Resting his head against the back of the chair, he lifted one hand to massage his temple. Lord, he was tired, and he didn't like that. He was hardly ever tired, at least not at this time of the morning. And he could never remember being *this* kind of tired.

It seemed there really was a first time for everything. But who needed all these firsts within less than a month? Never before had he had to fight to suppress an almost relentless physical desire for almost three weeks. Yet the opportunity for satisfaction had presented itself in the very lovely form of Maria Cinelli and he had simply not been interested.

Moving his head restlessly, Jonas closed his eyes, fully aware that he was experiencing another first by ignoring the work on his desk. The physical need for that one particular woman has rattled your brain as well as your libido, he told himself dryly.

Why? Why the urgency to possess this particular woman? Eyes still closed, Jonas examined the question clinically. True, she is a very beautiful woman, in a wistful, elusive way. But thousands of women are beautiful, in as many different ways. So why this one? She'd certainly never given him any encouragement. The only side of her he'd seen thus far had been the prickly side.

The grim smile disappeared. Now you're getting close, Thorne. Close hell, he was on top of it, and knew where his convoluted train of thought was heading right along. He knew exactly why and when.

The ride from Edouard Barres's Paris office to the airport had seemed surprisingly short, and not only because Barres's Mercedes ate up the distance so smoothly. He and Edouard had been involved in business meetings and discussions that whole week and still the ideas and plans flowed like a never-ending river between them. Jonas respected Edouard's knowledge and expertise and he was well aware the respect was reciprocated. Even after the car had pulled to a stop he had paused in the act of alighting to give consideration to Edouard's last remark.

Still pondering the feasibility of Edouard's idea, Jonas had taken very little notice of the two women waiting for him, merely nodding in Janet's direction as he walked to the plane. He had just reached the decision that Barres's ideas was very probably worth the time, energy and money that would be required to develop it when the screech of tires broke through his concentration.

About to enter the plane, he had turned to find the source of the racket, and groaned silently. What's-her-name, the rising young whatever of the French film industry, was running toward the plane screaming, "Darling, wait."

Darling? Sudden irritation quickly bloomed into full anger. Damning Edouard for his stupid dinner party, and himself for going in the first place, he stepped by Parker with a tersely ordered, "Get rid of her," knowing full well that Parker would.

Inside the plane, he headed straight for the bourbon. Glass in hand, he started toward his seat, stopping midstride when Janet's fledgling entered the compartment. In the few seconds the door was open, the pleading, somewhat rehearsed, and definitely hysterical sound of the actress's voice reached him and his anger changed to disgust with the female sex in general. They were all leeches! The only difference being that they sucked a man's money as well as his blood.

The blanket condemnation was unfair, and he knew it. Jonas had been around long enough to realize there were every bit as many male leeches in the world as female; maybe more. At that moment, though, he wasn't too concerned with being fair.

Lifting his glass to sip at the bourbon, he studied the young woman who stood, seemingly mesmerized, just inside the doorway.

Beautiful package, he mused. Lovely face. Good figure. Perfect breasts. Big deal. If what Janet had told him about her was true, and he had no reason to doubt Janet's word, she had turned her back on life. Had he come all this way to end up playing nursemaid to a stupid little fool with a death wish? That thought in no way sweetened his disposition.

Why had Maria picked this particular time to do her disappearing act? Jonas fumed. He knew the answer, of course. She was pushing him, turning the rack. At least, *she* thought she was. Jonas suppressed a sigh. He would have thought, after all this time, that she'd know better than to actually put the screws to him.

All the while he was ruminating on Maria's unwise actions, his eyes remained fixed on Valerie Jordan. Now he moved impatiently to her. Was she in a stupor, for God's sake? Biting down on his anger, he extended his hand.

"I gather you are Valerie Jordan?"

"Yes."

Jonas felt his lids narrow in automatic response to the iciness of her tone. For the first time in his life he had to fight the urge to strike a woman. Sure that if he gripped her hand he'd crush it, he briefly brushed her fingers before withdrawing.

"Jonas Thorne." Jonas made his tone insultingly curt. "Your employer." The last was a deliberate nudge. Watching her closely, he felt a tiny flicker of respect at the fearless way she returned his stare. *Was* she fearless, he wondered, or was she past caring about anything? Jonas decided to find out.

"You *do* want the job, Miss Jordan?"

"Yes, sir."

Ahh, better, much better. At least she cared about something. Pivoting away from her, he advised her to sit down and buckle up, and then he dismissed her from his mind; or he tried to.

Her spark of defiance had drawn an answering spark of interest from him. After the plane was airborne, he got down to work with Janet in an attempt to ignore Valerie's presence. Doing so proved not only difficult, but almost impossible. Janet's concern for her friend was obvious, and she repeatedly shot worried glances across the aisle. That was another thing in Valerie's favor. Jonas knew Janet. She was not a woman to expend time and energy on a total washout.

His inability to give his complete concentration to his work stirred fresh anger in Jonas. Not one to evade any issue, he faced the fact that he was much too aware of Valerie's slightest movement. Although Janet thought she was asleep, Jonas knew better. Valerie Jordan was playing possum, studying them through slitted eyelids. This deepened his anger to the point that when Janet assured him he would not be sorry for taking Valerie back to the States, he deliberately drawled a disbelieving, "We'll see."

When he'd finished briefing Janet on the Paris transactions, he tilted his seat back and played his own game of possum while returning her careful regard.

How had he known? What had been the tip off? She certainly had not betrayed herself. To anyone else watching her she would have appeared soundly asleep. Yet, somehow, Jonas knew the moment she decided to prove him wrong about her. And, at that moment, everything alive inside his body responded to that decision. The feeling of sexual excitement that had gone through his body at that moment was one he had not experienced in a very long time—if ever.

A very sobering thought. Not curative, but sobering. Sitting in his chair, behind the enormous desk, eyes closed, a small smile tugged at Jonas's harshly etched lips. I want that woman. After nearly three weeks of continual want, there's no doubt at all. I want that woman more than I've ever wanted anything. And I'm going to have her. With or without her consent.

Lifting his lids lazily, his gleaming eyes focused on the long white couch. You had better come up with the right answer tomorrow morning, my sweet, he advised Valerie silently. Or you just may find yourself on that couch, giving me what I want without benefit of the legal sanctions.

He was still tormenting himself with picturing the scene when his private phone rang.

His lips twisting in self-mockery, he snatched up the receiver and growled, "Thorne."

"Jonas, it's Marge," his ex-mother-in-law said hesitantly. "Am I disturbing you?"

Not nearly as much as my own thoughts, he answered silently. Aloud, he soothed, "Not at all. What's up, Marge?"

That something unusual had happened he was sure. Marge never called him at the office on a mere whim.

"I got a letter from Mary Beth." Marge's voice hummed with excitement.

"And?" Jonas prompted.

"Jonas, she's coming home." Marge sounded ready to explode. "Our baby's coming home."

"When?" Jonas's tone revealed none of the emotions leaping in his body. Their baby. His baby. His Mary Beth.

"She's booked a flight for May fifteenth, the day after school's over. Oh, Jonas, I can hardly wait. She's been away so long."

"Yes, I know," Jonas murmured. Although he knew the date, his eyes shifted to his desk calendar. April sixth. Six weeks. Six weeks and he'd have her home again. How would she react to Valerie? The thought was a revealing one. Pushing it aside temporarily, Jonas addressed the more immediate question. "I'm afraid you have no choice but to wait, Marge. But I have a suggestion on how you could fill the time."

"Do you? What is it?" Marge's eagerness was endearing.

"Why don't you fix up her bedroom? As a matter of fact, go the whole route, redecorate completely."

"May I, Jonas? Really?"

Jonas could practically see the wheels turning in Marge's head. The image amused him and he laughed softly. "Yes, Marge, you really may." Suddenly the laughter was gone and his voice held a hint of rebuke.

"I would have thought, by now, that you wouldn't have to ask."

"Oh, Jonas—"

"Never mind, Marge." Jonas sighed. How many times had they had this same kind of conversation? "Make as many changes as you like. Don't—I repeat—don't consider cost. Remember, it's all for Mary Beth. Send the bills to me here at the office."

"Thank you, Jonas, I—"

"Marge." Jonas cut in on her teary-sounding voice. "Enough, okay? Oh, yes, don't plan on me for dinner tonight."

"All right." Marge paused, then murmured timidly, "And—Jonas? I love you, you know."

"Yes, Marge, I do know," Jonas replied huskily.

Jonas sat staring at the phone long minutes after he'd replaced the receiver. What a woman, he mused. Too bad the daughter was so unlike the mother.

That thought was the catapult that flung him into the past.

He was seventeen the first time he saw her. Seventeen and hungry for life, starved for affection, filled with unnamed desires.

It was midsummer and it was hot. It was lunchtime, and he was starving, but, as he was also broke, he faced the empty feeling in his stomach stoically. It was nothing new. He was nearly always hungry and always broke.

A sound—half sigh, half groan of relief—hissed through his lips as he entered the small air-conditioned appliance shop. For an ecstatic moment he closed his eyes, savoring the cool air against his sweaty skin. For another moment he gave in to the weariness pulling at him. He'd been up at four and by four-thirty he'd just about finished squeezing the carton of juice oranges for the breakfast trade. The small diner where he'd worked for over a year now as short order cook was not air-conditioned.

Jonas's moment of delight in the sweet coolness came to an abrupt end when someone entered the shop behind him, and a young female voice called, "Daddy, where are you? You've got a customer out here."

Swiveling around, Jonas felt the breath hiss out of him again, only this time not from the cold.

She was young, somewhere around his own age, Jonas guessed, and the most beautiful thing he'd ever laid eyes on. She had sun-kissed gold hair and skin tanned to a golden brown. Bright blue eyes sparkled in a face that belonged on a goddess, and her red mouth pouted prettily at him. As if her face alone were not enough of an assault on his senses, she had a figure that wouldn't quit, with high, pointed breasts that seemed to quiver under his gaze. Suddenly, painfully, all of his vague, unnamed desires were centered on that one female body.

"Hi, can I help you?" She asked sweetly. "I don't know where Daddy is."

"Uh, yeah, that is, I don't know." Feeling like a jerk, Jonas felt his face redden. "I saw the sign in the window." At her blank, frowning expression, he stuttered on, "The—the Help Wanted sign? I—I came in to apply."

"Oh, that." Her red lips parted to reveal small, white teeth. "Sure, you can apply, that is, if I ever find Daddy." She paused to draw a deep breath—an exercise that had Jonas staring in reaction to the thrusting lift of her breasts—then she yelled again, "Daddy?"

"For crying in a bucket, Lynn, I heard you the first time."

Jonas spun to face the rear of the shop and the gruff-voiced man entering it from a back room. Lynn! Her name was Lynn. Beautiful.

"I brought your lunch." Lynn walked to the counter and deposited a brown paper bag Jonas had not even noticed she'd been holding. "And this guy," she tipped her gold head at Jonas, "wants to apply for the job you have open."

"Okay, thanks, honey." Although his tone had altered, the voice was still rough.

Jonas had been aware that he was being scrutinized by sharp blue eyes ever since the medium-size, stocky man had entered the shop. Dragging his gaze from Lynn, he coolly returned her father's appraisal. The man had closely cropped, curly blond hair, a shade darker than his daughter's, and his face had a ruddy hue that spoke of high blood pressure or too much alcohol, or both. He was overweight, but his shoulders and arms were muscular and hard-looking. The bright blue eyes that returned Jonas's stare were shrewd.

"Okay, honey, I'll take care of him." He shot a quick smile at the girl. "Run along."

"Can I have a dollar, Daddy?" she coaxed. "It's so hot. I want to stop for a coke."

The sweetness of her voice charmed Jonas and had he possessed a buck himself he'd have whipped it out and offered it to her. She obviously had a similar effect on her father, for he dug in his pants pocket and withdrew a bill, handing it to her with a rueful grin.

"A coke costs a dollar now?" he teased.

"No, silly," she teased back. "But I want to treat a friend." As she turned to leave she shot Jonas a mischievous smile.

"Stosh Kowalski."

The rough voice penetrated Jonas's bemusement and he shifted his eyes back to Lynn's father.

"Jonas Thorne, sir," he replied respectfully, stepping closer to grip Stosh's outstretched hand. "I came in to inquire about the Help Wanted sign in your window." Not a hint of the stuttering boy remained in Jonas's demeanor. Without Lynn's tongue-tying presence he was all business—and all premature man.

"You know anything about electrical appliances or television repair?" Stosh asked, not unkindly.

"No, sir," Jonas answered truthfully. "But I learn fast, and I work hard." Jonas watched as Stosh ran his gaze over his tall, too skinny frame, and felt his hopes sink. He was unaware that though his lanky body appeared weak, his face had strength of purpose and determination indelibly stamped on it.

"You out of school, son?"

"No, sir," Jonas admitted. "I have one more year to go. But," he went on quickly, "I can work full time for the rest of the summer, and after school during the winter. As many hours as you'd want."

"Wouldn't your parents object?"

"I have no parents, sir," Jonas said steadily. "I live in a foster home."

"And your foster parents would have no objections?" Stosh probed gently, his eyes observing the wisp of a cynical smile that fleetingly touched Jonas's lips.

"No, sir," Jonas answered flatly. Jonas forced himself to breathe normally as Stosh Kowalski's eyes measured his worth. A sigh of released tension whispered through his lips when the older man grinned.

"Okay, Jonas." Stosh nodded his head once, decisively. "I'll give you a try. I usually come in around eight so I can get some uninterrupted work done in back before opening the store at nine-thirty. What time could you start?''

Jonas considered a moment, taking his own measure of Stosh Kowalski, then he decided to lay all his cards on the table. ''I've been working for over a year at the Sunrise Diner on the other side of town. I work the grill for breakfast and finish at eight-thirty when the lunch and suppertime cook comes in. I could be here by ten minutes to nine, if that would be all right?''

''You want to work both jobs?'' Stosh frowned.

''Yes, sir,'' Jonas said firmly.

''I'd want you to stay until six most nights. What time do you start at the Sunrise?''

''Four-thirty.''

''Four-thirty!'' Stosh exclaimed. ''You're talking one hell of a long day, kid. Can you handle it?''

''Yes, sir.''

Something in his tone convinced Stosh, for, after giving Jonas a long, hard stare, he shrugged, then grinned. ''Okay, Jonas, I'll give you a try. You can start tomorrow morning at nine o'clock.''

''Thank you, sir.''

''I appreciate the 'sir', kid, but it's not necessary. We're going to be working together all day. Call me Stosh.''

When he left the shop some ten minutes later, Jonas was so buoyed by the idea of earning more money for his college fund that he almost missed seeing Lynn standing under the tattered awning of a tiny dress shop two buildings away. As he drew alongside her she said, pertly, ''Did you get the job?''

Yanked out of his own thoughts, Jonas turned to

face her and felt the blood begin to pound through his body again. Gosh, she was pretty!

"Yes." He grinned idiotically.

"Good." Lynn grinned back, starting to walk up the street. After only several steps she stopped and jerked her head in a beckoning motion. "How about a coke to celebrate?"

Jonas felt his heart sink. "I don't have any money," he said tightly.

"That's okay." Lynn grinned. "I have a whole dollar. It'll be my treat." When Jonas hesitated, she teased, "Come on, dopey, I've been waiting for you to come out for what seems forever. I'm hot and thirsty. Let's go."

Completely enchanted, Jonas went, feeling as though he'd been blessed by heaven. Even the teasing "dopey" sounded enchanting.

Jonas was hardly aware of his none too clean surroundings as he sat across the table from her in a booth in the corner of a small luncheonette. And afterward he never could remember what they talked about. All he knew was that she was the prettiest thing he'd ever seen and he wanted to touch her gold hair and kiss her red mouth. He didn't, of course. At least, not that afternoon.

"Are your parents dead, Jonas?" Stosh asked quietly five minutes after he'd reported for work the following morning.

"My mother is. She died while I was being born," Jonas answered stiffly. "I don't know about my father. She was alone when she had me. I'm a bastard," he finished starkly.

The bright blue eyes resting on his suddenly harsh-looking face flickered with compassion. "Were there no grandparents or relatives willing to take you in?" Stosh asked in astonishment.

"No." Jonas shook his head slowly. "She wasn't from Tamaqua. In fact, no one could find out where she was from. She just showed up at a rooming house across town one day and rented a room. She worked as a waitress somewhere up until a couple of days before I was born. Apparently she never saw a doctor and if it hadn't been for the owner of the rooming house who heard her muffled screams and sent for his own doctor, she probably wouldn't have lived long enough to deliver me." Jonas paused, amazed at himself for offering the information so freely. He'd never told anyone about his history before, and yet, there was something about Stosh's shrewd blue eyes that instilled the urge to confide. With a fatalistic shrug, Jonas ended his story. "She lived long enough to name me, but I don't know if Thorne was her name or the name of the man who fathered me. When they couldn't find out anything about her I was made a ward of the court and placed in a foster home." As had happened the afternoon before, Jonas's lips twisted cynically over the word "foster." "I've been in five different homes in seventeen years."

"Bad, huh?" Stosh probed.

"A couple of them were okay." Jonas lifted his shoulders in an unconvincingly careless shrug. "Mostly the people just wanted the money they were paid for my keep."

"And the people you're with now?" Stosh probed deeper.

Jonas hesitated, then, looking him straight in the eyes, said bluntly, "He's a brutal slob and she's a shrew."

Stosh was not altogether successful in masking his surprised shock at the open disgust in Jonas's tone.

"That's a strong condemnation, son," he said quietly.

This time Jonas's shrug *was* careless. "Not saying the truth out loud doesn't change it. The day I turn eighteen, I'm getting out." His mouth curled in a sneer. "They'd probably throw me out anyway—that's when the money stops."

"Have they treated you very badly, Jonas?" The slow, measured tempo of Stosh's question revealed the outrage he was feeling.

Jonas shook his head slowly. He was done talking. There was no point in complaining about the physical abuse he'd taken from the heavy-fisted man, or the shrill, vocal abuse he'd been subjected to from the strident-voiced woman. Or even the long hours he'd had to work on the small farm his foster parents owned. Jonas had always been too thin for his long frame and the authorities had genuinely believed that the fresh country air would be beneficial to his health when they'd placed him at the farm. And, in truth, it had been. At least, physically. For, even though he still appeared undernourished, the seven years of hard physical labor he'd put in on the farm had toughened his muscles to tempered steel. The last time his foster-father had struck him—just two months previously—Jonas had curled his large hand into a fist and knocked him flat. Jonas hadn't been abused since. The memory brought a satisfied smile to his face.

Stosh frowned, wondering at the meaning behind the young man's unpleasant smile, but, prudently, he did not probe any further. Leading Jonas into the workroom behind the shop, he said, "Okay, kid, let's get started."

For Jonas, that day was the beginning of a lifelong love affair between his mind and everything electrical. While he was on the job he lost himself completely in his work. During the other hours of the day and night, he was consumed with thoughts of the golden-haired Lynn.

Unwittingly, Stosh himself arranged their second meeting a little over a week after Jonas began working for him.

Although it was not yet nine o'clock that Saturday morning in late July, it was steamy hot. The unusual length and intensity of the heat wave had left even the most hardy residents of Tamaqua wilted and gasping. A humid haze hung like a pall over the city and in every dip and hollow of the heavily mined mountains surrounding it. Even the ugliness of the slag banks was softened by the shimmering heat waves.

Jonas entered the shop as Stosh was putting the telephone receiver in its cradle.

"You remember what I showed you about replacing the timer in a refrigerator on Wednesday?" he asked.

"Yes."

"Do you have a driver's license?"

"Yes," Jonas repeated.

"That was the wife I was talking to when you came in." Stosh indicated the phone. "She called to tell me the fridge is acting up." Stosh grimaced. "And in this weather, too. From the way she described it, I think the timer went. Do you want to take a shot at fixing it?''

"Yes, *sir*.'' Jonas grinned.

"You're on.'' Stosh grinned back. Digging into his pocket he withdrew a ring of keys and tossed them to Jonas. "Take my car. There's a replacement timer in the parts case in the trunk.'' He gave Jonas directions to his small ranch house on the outskirts of town, then waved him off with a warned, "Take your time. I want it done right.''

Jonas had no trouble at all finding Stosh's home. He did have trouble with his breathing when Lynn opened the door seconds after he rang the bell. She was dressed in tight shorts and a halter top that barely covered her small breasts, and it was obvious she'd been sunbathing—her body was covered by a mixture of glistening suntan oil and perspiration.

"Hi, dopey,'' she said dispiritedly. "What do you want?''

"Your dad sent me over to fix the refrigerator,'' Jonas managed to articulate without stuttering. To an older, more experienced man, Lynn's moody eyes and pouting lips would have been a clear indication of her sulkiness. To Jonas, however, her eyes looked sexy and her lips wet and inviting.

"I didn't even know the dumb thing was broken.'' She shrugged, pulling the door wide as she stepped back. "I was lying in the sun. Come in.'' As Jonas walked past her she said, "I hope you know what's wrong with it, 'cause Mom's not here to tell you; she went shopping.''

"I know what's wrong with it,'' Jonas assured her,

his eyes following her every movement as he trailed her to the kitchen.

Plopping herself onto a kitchen chair, Lynn chattered at him the whole time he worked, her petulant tone changing to one of interest as she observed the play of previously unnoticed muscles in his broad shoulders and long arms. She left the kitchen while he was washing his hands at the kitchen sink after the fridge was again running smoothly.

"Jonas, can you come in here and help me, please?"

Lynn's voice floated to him as he dried his hands.

"Sure," he answered, wandering out of the kitchen and into a short hallway. "Where are you?"

"In here," she called from a room about halfway along the hall. Jonas walked to the open doorway and stopped dead when he saw it was her bedroom. "I can't get this knot open. Will you see if you can untie it?" Lynn was standing beside her unmade bed, her back to him, her fingers tugging at the knot closing of her halter top.

His pulses hammering, Jonas crossed the carpeted floor and with trembling fingers brushed her hands away and went to work on the knot. The second the cotton ends fluttered apart, he dropped his hands to his sides.

Before he could move, Lynn swung around to face him, curling her arms up and around her golden head as she turned. Jonas sucked air into his suddenly tight chest as the swathe of white cotton dropped to the floor.

Chapter 6

A part of Jonas's mind knew he should get out of that room, that house, but a bigger part wanted to feast his eyes on the perfection of her small, round, upturned breasts. The bigger part won.

"Do you want to touch me?" Lynn asked softly, teasingly.

"Yes," Jonas answered in a croaking whisper.

"Well, do it then, dopey," she laughed.

Raising an arm that felt weighted by lead, Jonas reached out and touched the tips of his trembling fingers to the smooth skin at the outside curve of one breast.

"Oh, you dopey," Lynn chided. "You call that touching?" Lowering one arm she caught his wrist with her hand. Following the pull of her fingers, he cupped the silky mound with his hand. The hard little nipple seemed to poke at his palm, sending a sweet stab of pain shooting into his loins.

His fingers clutching convulsively, Jonas bent his head to hers, his mouth opening as it made contact.

The feel of her small tongue sent a shudder along the length of his spine. Lynn's hand still grasped his wrist and when she sank onto the rumpled bed she pulled him down on top of her. His lips were dislodged from hers when they hit the mattress and Jonas heard the breath go out of her body.

Concerned that the force of his body striking hers might have hurt her, he rolled over, then pulled her tightly against him. His hips thrust against Lynn's body in automatic urgency.

"Ohh, dopey," Lynn whispered thickly, wriggling her own hips slowly. "Aren't you going to kiss my breasts?" she half demanded, half pleaded.

"God, yes," Jonas groaned, the very idea of placing his lips against her skin exciting him further. The feel of her oiled skin on his lips set his body on fire, and taking the hard little nipple inside his mouth, stroking it with his tongue, was exquisite torture.

Without even being aware of the motions, his hands moved down her slippery body to tug and yank at her shorts. Lynn's hands brushed his away impatiently.

"I'll do it," she whispered. "You worry about your own."

Fumbling in his haste, Jonas got to his feet. After yanking open the snap on the waistband of his worn jeans, he undid the zipper. His shorts followed his jeans to the floor and he stepped out of them.

Jonas was a virgin. Lynn was not. And so, it was Lynn who guided him at first, teaching him the art of lovemaking until instinct took over. And it was in her soft embrace that Jonas gained a knowledge of full manhood.

Summer limped along, and Jonas's life seemed suddenly comprised of highs and lows. The highs were reached simply by stepping into the workroom behind the appliance shop. The lows were caused by the fact that seeing Lynn proved not only difficult, but nearly impossible. He knew she was dating another guy, because he had seen them together. And that knowledge only increased his frustration.

As the weeks of unusually hot humid weather melted one into the other, Jonas burned in two ways: on the outside from the heat of the sun, and on the inside from the constant rage of desire.

That rage was appeased briefly at the very beginning of September. An organization Stosh belonged to was having a Labor Day clambake and when Stosh asked Jonas if he'd like to go as a family guest, Jonas accepted eagerly.

Jonas had never been to a clambake, and although he enjoyed the early part of the day, and the food, he did not enjoy the party's deterioration as the sun trekked westward. Laughter grew shrill and voices grew raucously louder as more and more beer was consumed. At seventeen, Jonas did not like the taste of beer. At eighteen, thinking it adult and sophisticated, Lynn did.

Jonas was not the only one to frown in Lynn's direction when she asked for her third glass of beer. In fact, Marge Kowalski did more than frown. Although she spoke softly, Jonas heard Lynn's mother's words of rebuke.

Jonas had spoken to Marge several times when she'd stopped by the shop, and he liked her. She was friendly in a soft-spoken, quiet way that appealed to him. If one were allowed to *choose* a mother, Jonas would have chosen Marge without hesitation.

Lynn did not share his opinion. Spoiled by Stosh, who indulged her slightest whim, she resented every attempt Marge made to control her.

At Marge's cautionary words about the beer, Lynn drained her glass, slammed it onto the wooden picnic table and flounced off fuming. Jonas trailed behind her like a devoted puppy.

Ignoring everyone who called out to her, Lynn stormed away from the picnic grounds into the wooded area of the foothills. Up until that point Jonas had followed her quietly, but it was growing dark, and he was afraid he'd lose sight of her.

"Lynn, where are you going?" he called out.

"None of your business," Lynn snapped peevishly. Then, as his lengthened stride brought him alongside her, she whined, "Go away. You're as bad as she is. I saw your face when I took that last glass of beer."

"I don't know how you can drink that stuff," Jonas observed mildly.

"I *like* drinking that stuff." Lynn pouted. "It makes me feel good." Coming to an abrupt stop she turned on him angrily. "So what?"

"Oh, Lynn, let's not fight." Jonas sighed longingly.

His tone was not lost on her. With a lightning change in mood, she pouted prettily, suggestively, "Can you think of something better to do?"

Desire, never far away, licked through Jonas's

body. Slowly he leaned toward her. With the touch of his lips on hers, Lynn took the initiative from his far less experienced hands.

Clasping her arms around his waist, she arched her body up against the hardness of him. Jonas stopped thinking entirely. Allowing himself to be led, he obeyed her dictates with hands that shook in his eagerness to learn. Even in his inexperience Jonas realized, jealously, that someone with a certain degree of expertise had been tutoring Lynn.

Jonas started back to school the day after the clambake. Soon his time was completely taken up with his studies and work in the appliance shop and he saw even less of Lynn.

One day near the end of November he found her waiting for him in her father's car when he left the shop.

"I have to talk to you," she said tersely the minute he'd folded his long frame into the passenger seat. Not a hint of premonition gave warning of the bald statement that followed.

"I'm pregnant, Jonas."

Everything froze inside him—his muscles, his blood, his mind.

"Did you hear me?" Lynn cried, breaking into the numbness that gripped his mind. "I said I'm going to have a baby. What are you going to do about it?"

What was he going to do? What could he do? His dreams of college and a career in electronics dissolving in his mind, Jonas answered steadily, "I'm going to marry you."

They drove directly to her home, Lynn's nervousness apparent in the restless movement of her hands on the steering wheel. Jonas was every bit as nervous, though he succeeded in hiding it. He hated the thought of facing Stosh and Marge with his betrayal of their kindness.

The telling was every bit as bad as Jonas had feared it would be. Stosh was at first shocked speechless; then he was very vocally furious. Marge, ever quiet, sat motionless in stunned disbelief. The expression on her face hurt Jonas far more than Stosh's angry tirade. When, finally, Marge did speak, her quiet words surprised them all.

"Stosh, that's enough." Marge's tone held soft command. "What's done is done. At least *Jonas* is willing to marry Lynn." It would be months before Jonas would understand the emphasis she placed on his name and the knowing look she ran over her daughter. "But I think it would be a mistake for him to quit school in his senior year."

Jonas had declared that he'd leave school at once to work full time at the shop. Listening to Marge, hope for his future was reignited.

"As a matter of fact," Marge continued, totally ignoring Jonas's attempted protests, "I see no reason why he should not go on to college as planned."

"Now, Marge, be practical," Stosh began heatedly.

"That is exactly what I am being." Marge cut him off with unaccustomed sharpness. "One of Jonas's teachers is an acquaintance of mine. When she found I know Jonas she told me that, in her opinion, Jonas has a brilliant mind and if he did not continue his education after high school it would be a sinful waste."

Jonas learned two things about Marge that night. First, that when she took a stand she could not be budged. And second, that she could not be intimidated. Nothing moved her, not Stosh's anger, not Lynn's tears, and not Jonas's own persuasive tactics. Marge set down the rules, and the rest of the family meekly carried them out. Lynn and Jonas would be married at once. They would make their home with Marge and Stosh. Jonas would stay in school.

Jonas and Lynn were married in a private ceremony conducted in the rectory of the church the Kowalski family attended. After the wedding Jonas went back to school and back to work. The only difference in his life was that now when he left the shop at night he went to a *real* home and to the accommodating body of his wife.

For the first three months of their marriage, Jonas delighted in their lovemaking, firmly ignoring the realization that his bride was well versed in the art— too well versed. With satisfaction came doubt. And with doubt came the cooling of his ardor.

In late February an ugly suggestion made to Jonas by one of his classmates sent him home in a rage. Slamming into the house, he ordered a startled Lynn into the privacy of their bedroom where he demanded, hotly, "How do you know that kid's mine?"

"W-what do you mean?" Lynn stuttered, obviously frightened.

"I was just informed that the only reason you married me was because the guy you tried to trap into marriage wouldn't have you." Jonas yelled. "Is it true?"

"No, no—I," Lynn's denial dissolved into tears,

but Jonas could read the guilt in her pretty face. Sick at heart, he cried, "Who is he?"

"His name is unimportant, Jonas." The answer came from Marge, who had entered the room unnoticed. "He has looks, and money, and a very bad reputation. Lynn fell for his line and became infatuated with him."

"I love him," Lynn screamed at her mother.

"Although it breaks my heart to admit it, Lynn," Marge said sadly, "I truly think you are incapable of loving anyone but yourself."

"What do you know about anything?" Lynn screamed.

"I know you've treated Jonas unfairly," Marge retorted. "Whether this is his baby or not."

"Unfair!" Lynn exclaimed shrilly. "He's getting what he wants!"

Jonas had heard enough. Brushing past Marge, he left the house. He did not go to work that day. Hands jammed into his jacket pockets, shoulders hunched against the bitter cold wind, he walked the streets for hours. By the time he returned to the house whatever it was he'd felt for Lynn—love, physical attraction, fascination with her lovely face—it was all gone. He did not hate her. He just didn't feel anything for her at all. Entering the house through the back door, Jonas found Marge waiting for him.

"Jonas, about the baby," Marge began timidly.

"I'll raise it," Jonas interrupted. "Whether it's mine or not." The smile that curved his mouth brought tears to Marge's eyes. "I know what it's like to be a bastard."

Though he slept beside her every night, Jonas never

again touched his wife in a personal way. Made cautious by the new, unyielding set to his features, Lynn did not question him.

Jonas turned eighteen three days before his graduation from high school. Two weeks later Lynn was delivered of a baby girl. With his first look at her, Jonas knew the child was his. Marge knew it also.

"Oh, Jonas," she whispered in awe. "I'm so happy for you."

"Poor thing looks just like me," Jonas murmured, emotion clogging his throat. Gazing in mute adoration at the tiny life he'd created, Jonas vowed that never would she want for anything. Not as long as he lived, and even after, if he could arrange it.

Seven weeks after Mary Beth's birth, and one week after her christening, Lynn ran away with the man she claimed to love.

Jonas came home from work to find Stosh and Marge waiting for him in the living room. The baby clasped protectively in her arms, Marge sat rocking back and forth, tears chasing each other down her cheeks.

In silence, Jonas read the note Lynn had left for him.

Jonas,
    Please try to understand. I'm too young to be tied to a man who hates me and a baby I don't want. I want to see something of the world. I want to have some fun. And I want to be with Leon.

                                                    Lynn

"This Leon," Jonas said when he'd finished reading. "Is he the one with the looks and money and reputation?"

"Yes," Marge sobbed.

"Okay," he sighed then, straightening his shoulders. "I'll leave as soon as I can find a place to stay and someone to keep Mary Beth."

"Leave?" Marge and Stosh repeated blankly. "Keep Mary Beth?"

"Yes, I don't expect—" Jonas began, only to be silenced by his in-laws, both speaking at once.

"Where would you go?"

"What about college?"

"I'll have to forget college," Jonas said flatly.

"You'll do nothing of the kind." Marge snorted. "And you will not take my granddaughter out of this house." Clutching the baby even closer to her body, Marge jumped to her feet. "Now you listen to me, Jonas Thorne. You are going to stay right here. Both of you. And you are going to Lehigh as planned. You've worked too hard to have your future snatched away now. Do you understand me?"

Jonas glanced at Stosh as if seeking guidance. Stosh, holding up his hands, avowed, "I'm not going to argue with her. You better do as she says, son."

In September Jonas went to Bethlehem and Lehigh University. In mid-December Stosh suffered a series of massive strokes. Two days after Christmas, Stosh died in his sleep.

Once again Jonas declared his intention of leaving school. And once again Marge refused to let him.

"When you go back to school in January, I want you to look around for an apartment for the three of us," she told him calmly. Before Jonas could protest, she went on, "I'm going to put the house and business up for sale. With Stosh gone there is nothing to keep me in Tamaqua."

Even though Lynn's name was not mentioned, Jonas knew Marge was thinking of her. They had heard nothing at all from his wife. It was not even possible to inform her of her father's death.

Settling Stosh's estate took longer than expected and it was June before the move to Bethlehem was made. The apartment Jonas had rented was far from elegant, but it was large and located in a quiet neighborhood. And the rental was within the budget Jonas had worked out.

With the college grant he'd obtained and the money he earned from his new job at Bethlehem Steel, Jonas figured they could squeak through his school years. Ignoring every one of Marge's pleas, Jonas remained adamant in his refusal to take the money she offered him, claiming she was doing more than her share by taking care of Mary Beth.

For Jonas, life consisted of study and work. He saw very little of his daughter, and was, at intervals, amazed at the rate of her growth. After his fiasco with Lynn, he stayed away from women altogether, remaining celibate by choice.

They heard from Lynn for the first time shortly after Mary Beth's third birthday. Luckily, Jonas was at work when she called. As though history was repeating itself, Jonas came home from work to find

Marge in tears. Understandably, he jumped to the wrong conclusion.

"Is something the matter with Mary Beth?" he asked at once.

"No, she's fine," Marge sniffed.

"Then what's wrong?" Weak with relief, Jonas drew Marge into his arms. "Why are you crying?"

"Lynn called from California today, Jonas." Feeling him stiffen, she rushed on. "She wants you to divorce her so she can get married again."

"She can go to hell," Jonas snapped. "If she wants a divorce, let her get it."

"On what grounds?"

"That's her worry, not mine."

"Do you still love her, Jonas?"

"I never did *love* her." Suddenly realizing that he was speaking to Lynn's mother, Jonas sighed. "I'm sorry, Marge, but—"

"Don't apologize, Jonas, I understand." Brushing at her tears, Marge moved out of his encircling arms. "I told her what time you'd be home. She'll be calling back soon."

"How did she know where we were?"

"She called my lawyer." Eyeing him nervously, Marge said, carefully, "I think you should tell her you'll get the divorce."

"What!" Jonas couldn't believe his ears. "Why should I?"

"For Mary Beth."

Jonas shook his head in bewilderment. "I don't understand, Marge. What has Mary Beth got to do with it?"

"Jonas, think," Marge urged. "If *you* file for divorce you can charge Lynn with desertion and claim sole custody of Mary Beth. If the divorce is granted on those grounds, Lynn would probably have a fight on her hands if she ever tried to take Mary Beth away from you."

"She'd have a fight on her hands in any case," Jonas vowed.

"Do it, Jonas," Marge advised earnestly. "Let her marry this producer or director, or whatever he is."

"Producer or director?" Jonas sneered. "What happened to Leon?"

"I don't know—" she shrugged tiredly "—and I don't care. All I'm concerned about is Mary Beth's future. Do it, Jonas."

Marge's pleading tone set off warning signals in Jonas's head. Studying her carefully, he asked, "Did she threaten to take Mary Beth away if I don't jump through the hoop?"

Marge didn't have to answer, her stricken eyes gave her away.

"Damn," Jonas snarled. "If she were here I'd break her neck."

"Jonas, please," Marge cried. "When she calls back tell her you'll do it. I couldn't stand it if she came and took the baby away."

"She'd have to go through me to reach her," Jonas said grimly, then, his tone gentling, he soothed, "Calm down, Marge. No one's going to take our baby, I promise."

Blinking back fresh tears, Marge looked up at him hopefully. "You'll do it?"

"Marge," Jonas groaned. "I don't have the money, you know that."

"I do," she replied quickly.

"No."

"Jonas, you can think of it as a loan. I don't need it. I do need Mary Beth." Marge's voice had dropped to a pleading whisper. "Please, Jonas."

And so, the divorce paid for with borrowed money, Jonas became a free man again at the advanced age of twenty-one.

After graduation the following year, Jonas did not have to go out and walk the streets looking for work. Finishing very near the top of his class, he found himself much sought after by prospective employers.

He considered each and every offer very carefully and then, to the confused surprise of Marge and the few friends he'd made, he accepted an offer from a relatively small company. But there was a very definite method to Jonas's seeming madness. After a careful evaluation, he had reached the conclusion that though the firm was solvent, it was stagnating. All it needed, he decided, was someone with innovative ideas and enough energy and guts to make them work. Jonas had ideas, energy and guts in abundance.

The owner of the company was a fifty-six-year-old childless widower with an ulcer eating away at his insides. He was smart enough to realize his company needed to gear up if it was not to sink slowly into oblivion. He was also smart enough to be aware of his own limitations. The field of electronics was booming, and he no longer had the strength to keep up. When he interviewed Jonas, he had known this was the man he wanted. But not for even one euphoric second had he thought he had a chance of getting him.

By the end of Jonas's first year with the company it was well on the road to expansion and recovery, and Jonas was treated like a much-loved son. By the end of his second year, the owner made him a full partner. And when the owner retired five years later, he was a millionaire with a completely cured ulcer. At the time of his retirement, the company's name was changed to J.T. Electronics. Its former owner didn't mind—Thorne was his sole heir anyway.

By the time Jonas went striding by his thirty-second birthday—which he would not have remembered had not Marge and Mary Beth insisted on celebrating—he was well on his way to being a very successful, very rich man. Yet his on-going love affair with electronics continued.

His self-imposed celibacy had naturally ended long since. There had been a succession of several different women in his life. From the first, though, he was extremely selective. While still in college he had vowed that he would never again be trapped by a scheming female.

Not long after he took control of the company, Lynn reappeared on the scene, fresh from Mexico and her third divorce.

She was even more lovely than she'd been at eighteen. And it very quickly became apparent to anyone who observed her that she was looking for another husband and hoped to make it Jonas.

Lynn made all the right moves. She thoroughly fascinated her very impressionable teenage daughter. She reestablished a tenuous relationship with her mother. She completely charmed Jonas's small circle of friends. And she flirted with her former husband in a way that had other men aching to be in his shoes.

Jonas had not reached the position he was in by being stupid. He was very well aware of her game plan. He just couldn't decide if he wanted simply to ignore her or to throttle her. In the end he decided to pay her off and ship her out. She finally left, still pouting, for a small villa in the south of France—for which Jonas had paid a very healthy sum of money.

The money didn't bother him. What did was having to agree to allow their daughter to visit her periodically. Seeing Mary Beth off the first time she visited Lynn was one of the hardest things Jonas had ever done in his life. But at least he had his work. For Marge, there was nothing but an empty house until her granddaughter came home again.

The last time Mary Beth had gone away it was not to visit her mother but to attend a finishing school in Switzerland for a year.

And now the year was six weeks' shy of being up. She was coming home! What had happened, Jonas wondered, to her plans to spend a few weeks with Lynn sailing around the Aegean?

A buzz from the intercom prevented further speculation. Still lost in his thoughts, Jonas flipped the switch and growled, "What is it?"

Valerie's brief, but telling, hesitation brought him fully alert.

"There's a long distance call for you from Paris. A Mr. Barres," Valerie said stiffly.

"Put it through."

As he reached for the receiver, Jonas asked himself how he expected to evoke a positive response in her if he snarled and snapped at her all the time.

You were right the first time, he thought wryly. You are an arrogant fool!

Chapter 7

After putting the Paris call through, Valerie sat glaring at the intercom. She would have to be insane to even consider Jonas Thorne's preposterous proposal. She could count on one hand the times she'd witnessed any sort of softening in him. Of course, there was that heart-wrenching smile of his.

The mere memory of that smile shortened Valerie's breath. Disgusted by her involuntary response to him, she swiveled around to face her typewriter. He probably practices that damned smile in front of his mirror, she thought nastily.

She resumed typing where she'd left off when the Paris call came, working furiously for a few minutes before coming to an abrupt stop.

Paris. Etienne.

She couldn't marry Jonas Thorne! She couldn't marry anyone. Until those back-to-back thoughts hit her, Valerie had not wanted to admit to herself that she *was* seriously considering his preposterous proposal!

But how could she! How could she give *any* kind of consideration to it? Jonas Thorne was hard, and he was cold. He was almost impossible to work with. What would he be like to live with? Oh, no, she couldn't, could she?

Trying to view the situation objectively, she imagined herself in the role of his wife. What would it be like, being Mrs. Jonas Thorne? A derisive smile curled her lip. I'd probably see less of him than I do now. Now, there's a thought!

"Valerie."

Valerie jumped at the sound of her name coming from the intercom.

"Yes, sir?" For some obscure reason she jumped again when Jonas chuckled softly.

"You sound a little—uh—nervous," Jonas soothed. "Why don't you go home—Val?"

The pause he'd made before whispering her shortened name had been deliberate, Valerie knew.

"Can I leave my problems here if I do—" she paused in retaliation, "sir?"

"You think you have problems?" His tone went a notch lower. "Come into my office, I'll give you problems."

Was he serious? Did he want her in there to work—or...? Valerie shook her head; no not that, not in the office.

"Should I bring my pad?" she asked coolly.

"Is it big enough for two?"

Her cool melted. Damn him. He was being deliberately provocative. Teasing her the way he had teased Loretta and the others that night at the Drop Inn. Well, not in exactly the same way. Biting her lip, Valerie stared at the intercom suspiciously. Nothing. He was letting the silent seconds work on her composure.

"Valerie."

Valerie blinked in confusion. Never could she have imagined him capable of achieving that—that almost caressing tone.

"Are you going to come in here?" he asked very, very softly.

"Mr. Thorne—I—I—"

"Either you come in here, or I'll come out there," he warned. "What's it going to be?"

"All right," Valerie sighed. "I'll come in."

"I thought you might," Jonas drawled.

Fighting the urge to run out of the office and into the elevator, Valerie slowly stood up, straightening her waistband and smoothing down her skirt automatically. Eyeing the closed door to his office warily, she drew a deep breath, walked over to it and stepped inside.

"Tell me you're afraid of me," Jonas chided disbelievingly as she approached his desk with obvious reluctance.

"I'm afraid of you," Valerie obliged.

His smile, *that* smile, flashed like sunlight through a passing storm cloud. "Like hell you are," he grinned.

She couldn't help it. She grinned back.

"I like that." His glance indicated her grin. "Oh,

yes, I do like that. I was beginning to wonder if you knew how to smile.''

In marked contrast to his manner earlier that morning, he now appeared completely relaxed. Hardly able to believe her eyes or ears, Valerie decided to find out if his mood was real or assumed.

Lowering her eyes, she perched on the chair beside his desk. Then, raising her lids slowly she gazed directly into his eyes and laughed softly. "Oh, yes. I know how to smile. When there is someone to smile at.''

"Watch it, Jonas," he warned himself aloud. "The woman's out to trap you." A slow smile, surprisingly sensuous, curved his lips, changing their usual harsh line into an exciting invitation.

Good heavens! Valerie thought wonderingly. They were all right. All those women who had said he was very, very sexy; they were right! In an effort to hide her reaction from him, Valerie again lowered her eyes.

"I think—" her lashes swept up. "I think it would be unwise for a woman to try to trap you, Mr. Thorne.''

"Mr. Thorne," Jonas repeated musingly without denying her assertion. "A few hours ago I managed to articulate a proposal of marriage." His tone, though easy, held a definite warning. "Do you think you could possibly say the name Jonas?''

"I—" Valerie hesitated, unsure of herself now. "You are my employer," she protested lamely.

"Under the circumstances *that* argument could hardly be described as valid." He paused briefly, his eyes alert for her reactions. "I no longer wish to be your employer. I want to be your husband."

Valerie felt as though a wide band was being drawn tightly around her chest, slowly squeezing all the air from her body. She had to reply to him, say something. But what? Jonas broke the silence.

"I don't quite understand why you hesitate," he observed quietly. "Not only in accepting the use of my first name, but in the acquisition of my surname, as well." He paused long enough to light a cigarette, and to let his words sink in. "You've told me what you want out of life. I'm prepared to fulfill those wants. Much more than adequately, as regards a home and financial security."

"Financial security!" Valerie gasped. "I've placed no price tag on myself. I'm not up for grabs, or for sale."

"There's a saying that everyone has a price," Jonas retorted.

"It became a saying because it's probably true," Valerie retaliated. "But the price does not necessarily have to be paid in money."

"You don't like money?" Jonas ridiculed. "You'd be the first woman I've ever encountered who didn't."

"Yes, I like money," Valerie snapped, goaded to anger by his tone. "And I like all the lovely things I can purchase with it. I'd have no objections to having scads and scads of money. But not if I have to sell myself to get it."

"I'm not suggesting you do that, Valerie," Jonas said tightly.

"Aren't you?" she mocked. "It certainly sounded

like you were. And offering yourself as the highest bidder.''

"If it were that simple, we wouldn't be having this discussion," he assured her coolly. "I *would* be the highest bidder—you can be sure of that."

"Your conceit is exceeded only by your arrogance," Valerie snapped, jumping to her feet. She was shaking with anger, humiliation and a jumble of other emotions she couldn't begin to identify.

"Sit down, Val," Jonas sighed. Then, his lips twitching suspiciously, he teased, "Feisty when you're riled, aren't you?"

Feeling suddenly foolish, Valerie sat down again.

"Aren't *you?*" she returned defensively.

"Yes," he admitted, laughing easily again. "I really think you should accept my offer, Valerie, for your own good."

"My own good?" Valerie frowned. "I don't understand. Why—for my own good?"

"I've drawn more emotion, more animation from you in the last few hours, than you've been reputed to have shown in the last year." Jonas's eyes were steady on hers. Ignoring her soft gasp, he drove the nail home. "At least, with me, you'd know you're alive."

"Jonas, please," Valerie whispered pleadingly.

A wry smile curled his mouth. "Amazing." He shook his head slowly. "I had to hurt you to get you to say my name." The wry smile settled in place. "It's true, you know. We may lock horns, often. You may get hurt, but even feeling pain is part of being alive. Say yes, Val. Not only to me, but to being alive."

Everything he'd said was true. She *did* feel more alive than she had in over a year. She no longer clung to a subconscious death wish. She wanted to live again! Without giving herself time to think, to consider the enormity of the step she'd be taking, Valerie gave in.

"All right, Jonas. I accept your proposal."

The stillness that seemed to grip him puzzled her. Had he been playing some sort of game? she wondered, confused. Or testing her in some way? Had she answered incorrectly? Made a dreadful error?

He studied her face for a moment longer, then came around the desk to take her hand into his.

"You agree to the child as well?" he asked softly.

"Yes." Her answer was equally soft, if strained. "That was part of the proposal, wasn't it? You give me what I want in return for what you want."

"Yes," his eyes bored into hers. "I just wanted that point understood." Swinging away from her, he decreed, "I'm sending you home."

"But—" Realizing protest would be useless, Valerie closed her mouth. He was already holding the telephone receiver to his ear and punching out the numbers of a familiar extension.

"I want Lyle to have my car at the exit in five minutes for Miss Jordan." As he replaced the receiver he turned to study her again. Apparently her pale cheeks and her trembling hands told him how nervous she felt, for he asked, "Are you all right?"

"Yes," she answered. "At least I will be when I get used to the idea—I think."

Once again she was treated to the radiance of his smile. "Go on," he urged. "Get out of here. I have several long distance calls to make and something I want to discuss with Charlie. Do you think you'll be up to seeing me this evening?''

"Yes, of course."

"Of course," he mocked, glancing pointedly at her trembling hands. "Go on, beat it. I'll stop by the apartment tonight. That is, if you get out of here and let me get some work done. We'll talk then."

"Oh, but—"

"Go," he ordered, striding to the door to open it for her. "Lyle will be waiting."

Valerie went; not quite at a run. At the soft click of the door closing behind her she came to an indecisive stop. She breathed deeply a few times to calm her racing pulses, then walked to her desk. She was removing a sheet of paper from her typewriter when the phone rang. Lifting the receiver on the second ring, she gave her automatic response.

"Mr. Thorne's office."

"What time do you think you'll be ready to go to lunch today, Val?" Janet sounded alert and efficient—the complete opposite of how Valerie felt.

"I'm not going to lunch today. I'm being sent home."

"Being sent home!" Janet exclaimed. "Why, are you sick?"

Valerie sighed. She'd have to tell Janet, of course, but not here, not over the phone. "No, Janet, I'm fine. But I can't explain now, Lyle's waiting for me."

"Lyle?" Janet repeated sharply. "Val, honey, why is Lyle—"

"Janet, I can't talk now," Valerie interrupted anxiously. "I'll explain when you get home to—" Valerie saved her breath; Janet had hung up.

After replacing the receiver, Valerie filed the work she'd been transcribing, covered her typewriter, and, draping her new spring raincoat over her shoulders, left the office. The elevator doors hissed apart to reveal a frowning Janet.

"You must be sick," she decided aloud as Valerie stepped into the elevator.

"No," Valerie denied. "I'm not sick, Janet. I— he—" she stuttered, not quite sure how to begin.

"Valerie, you didn't quit?" Janet cried. When Valerie shook her head, she gasped, "Jonas didn't fire you?"

"No, he asked me to marry him."

"He— What?!"

"He—" Valerie broke off as the elevator came to a stop and the doors slid open. "We can't talk here, Janet," she concluded, stepping out.

After a stunned hesitation, Janet hurriedly followed her.

"Lyle's waiting, Miss Jor—" Steve began as Valerie walked toward the exit. Janet cut him off with a tersely ordered, "Call Jonas, Steve. Tell him I'm going home with Miss Jordan."

"Will do, Janet." Steve's reply was punctuated by the door's closing behind them.

Lyle was waiting beside the open door of the silver-gray limo. "Morning, Miss Jordan—Janet."

"Good morning, Lyle," Valerie and Janet answered in unison, Janet adding, "We're going to my apartment, Lyle."

With a short nod of his head, and a smiling, "Okay, Janet," Lyle swung the door closed.

As soon as she was seated, Janet touched the button that operated the glass partition and the minute the window was in place between the front and back seats, she turned and demanded, "Now what's going on?" Not even pausing to give Valerie time to respond, she rapped out, "Were you serious about Jonas asking you to marry him?"

"Yes, I—" Valerie was interrupted by an unfamiliar sound that was not quite a ring, yet not quite a buzz either. In confusion, she glanced around trying to locate the sound.

"I should have expected it," Janet sighed, sliding back the top of the center armrest to reveal a phone nestled inside. Casting Valerie a knowing smile, she lifted the receiver and said, "Yes, Jonas?"

Valerie's eyebrows went up in questioning surprise as Janet's eyes studied her face.

"Yes, she's all right," she said quietly. "A little pale, but all right. I haven't been able to make much sense out of what she's told me, Jonas." Janet's tone invited clarification. She was quiet a moment, then she answered, "Yes." Again she listened, longer this time. "She did!" Her eyes flew to Valerie. "Well, you have my overwhelmed congratulations." Her pause was very short this time. "Well, of course I mean it, Jonas. I've been very worried about her." Pause. "Yes, I will, all right, Jonas."

"What was that all about?" Valerie asked suspiciously. "And why have you been 'very worried' about me?"

"*That* was Jonas." Janet grinned.

"Surprise, surprise," Valerie drawled. "And?"

"And," Janet sobered, "you must have looked a little green around the gills to Steve. Jonas was concerned—" she shrugged— "hence the call." Her voice elaborately casual, she went on. "Jonas said you've agreed to marry him."

"Yes," Valerie concurred. "I have."

"Uh-huh—" Janet wasn't quite successful in masking her injured feelings. "We share the same apartment," she muttered, "and I don't even know you've got a thing going with the boss." Shooting Valerie a hurt look, she complained, "You said you didn't even like him."

"I don't," Valerie protested. "I didn't. Oh, hell, Janet, we don't have, haven't had, a 'thing' going. It's—it's—" Valerie's voice faded. How could she explain? She wasn't sure she fully understood the situation herself.

"Well, I certainly am glad you cleared that up," Janet said dryly. "But don't think for a minute that bunch of gibberish got you off the hook. Prepare yourself for the third degree after we get home."

An hour later Valerie decided Janet would have made a fantastic interrogation officer. Janet probed gently, but persistently, until Valerie gave in and told her about Jonas's unorthodox proposal.

"How like Jonas." Janet smiled wryly. "He does love a challenge. Women of all shapes, sizes and colors willing to do anything, and I do mean *anything,* to get their well-manicured hands on him—and his money—and *he* decides to produce an heir through a gal who is emotionally asleep."

"Janet!"

"You're going to tell me you're not?" Janet's eyebrows shot up. "Honey, do you have the vaguest idea what you are letting yourself in for? Jonas could devour you."

Valerie shook her head. "Janet, I don't know what you're talking about."

"That's what I was afraid of," Janet sighed. "Val, the man you're going to marry is not your everyday ordinary guy next door."

"I know that," Valerie cried indignantly. "The guy next door doesn't have loads of money."

"It's not the money," Janet retorted. "It's the man. In the first place, he's a bastard."

"Janet!" Valerie protested.

"I mean," Janet explained soothingly, "his mother and father were not married. He was also an orphan from day one and I've always had the feeling that he never had much of a childhood. His background made him tough and it made him hard. But that isn't what makes him different." Janet lifted her shoulders in a helpless shrug. "He isn't just ambitious. It's more than that. Jonas has a light in his head, a neon sign that spells out electronics. It consumes him. Everything and everyone else comes second."

Valerie shivered. She had always thought of him as machinelike, but Janet's confirmation of her opinion was unsettling. "You make him sound inhuman," she murmured, uncomfortably aware that she had also considered him so.

"Oh, no," Janet denied. "At least I don't mean to. Jonas is very human. When he's hungry, he eats. When he's tired, he sleeps. And when he feels desire, he takes a woman to his bed. He adores his daughter.

All very natural, normal things—but he *is* different. That difference draws the females like a magnet. That's where my concern for you comes in.'' Janet shrugged again. ''I've seen your reaction to the effect he has on women. Having a wife will not lessen that effect. Can you handle it?''

''Why not?'' Valerie asked. ''It's not as if I had any feelings for him.''

Not fooled for a minute by Valerie's brave words, Janet sighed. ''Val, no woman with any pride is going to sit by calmly while other women fall all over her husband, whether or not she has any feelings for him. It would more than annoy anyone, and you more than most. I've been a witness to it countless times. Quite often the play is none too subtle.''

Janet thought of the dinner party she'd attended with Jonas at Edouard Barres's elegant home outside of Paris. The young actress had been embarrassingly obvious in her pursuit of Jonas. Janet sighed again at the memory of the actress running to the plane—and Jonas. She grimaced. ''A few years ago, even his ex-wife got into the act.''

Valerie felt an odd thrill of apprehension jump in her stomach. Something about Janet's tone unnerved her. Why? Why should the mention of Jonas's first wife make her feel shaky and even more uncertain?

''For a while there it looked like Jonas had finally been corralled.'' Janet's musing voice cut across Valerie's thoughts. ''What a production.'' She grinned. ''A novice to the game could have gained an education by taking notes.''

''What happened?'' Valerie asked unwillingly.

''Who knows?'' Janet laughed. ''He's an elusive

devil. All I know is that one day she was here, living
in his house, and the next day she was gone."

"Living in his house!" Valerie exclaimed softly.

"Yes." Janet nodded. "And she gave everyone the
impression she was there to stay. I don't know." Janet's shoulders went up, then down. "She was fresh
from a divorce, her third. Maybe she decided it would
be more interesting to play the field for a while."

"She's been married three times?" Valerie's eyes
widened with astonishment.

"Yep." Janet nodded. "Each one richer than the
last. Of course—" she grinned "—that wouldn't have
taken much for number two. Jonas didn't have a dime
back then. But, as I understand it, her second had lots
and lots of dimes, all of which he was eager to spend
on his beautiful new bride."

Valerie's spirit nose-dived. "She was beautiful?"

"She *is* beautiful," Janet corrected. "Blond, blue-
eyed, and golden-skinned."

Suddenly very tired, Valerie didn't want to hear
any more. But how to shut Janet up? Food! Of course,
how much talking could Janet do if she was busy
eating? Rising quickly, Valerie started toward the
kitchen.

"I don't know about you," she tossed over her
shoulder, "but I'm ready for lunch."

Janet followed, chiding, "In other words, you want
me to button up, right?"

"I'd appreciate it," Valerie drawled.

"I'll go you one better," Janet laughed. "I'll clear
out tonight so you and Jonas can have your discussion
in private."

"But where will you go?"

Janet's smile was teasing. "Dining, dancing, romancing. All the same old dull stuff." Laughing at Valerie's surprised expression, she added, "Actually, I have a date. So don't worry about me, okay?"

Since Janet didn't volunteer a name, Valerie bit back the questions on her lips. That didn't stop them from tumbling through her mind. Was there a man in Janet's life? Who was he? And why hadn't Janet mentioned him before?

"What time do you expect Jonas?"

Janet's question wiped all idle speculation out of her mind. Jonas! Biting her lip, Valerie tried to shrug unconcernedly. "He didn't give a time, just said he'd stop by tonight."

Janet's laughter filled the kitchen. "I swear, there is no one in the world like that man."

That, Valerie thought uneasily, is what I'm afraid of.

A secret smile curving her mouth, Janet left the apartment shortly after seven, dressed to demoralize most men and all women. Feeling somewhat dowdy in comparison, Valerie changed her clothes three times, finally settling on a dress Janet had insisted she buy in Paris. The soft, almost weightless material clung to her full breasts and caressed her hips and thighs at her slightest movement. Although its dusky pink color lent a glow to her pale cheeks, Valerie, not at all satisfied with her appearance, frowned at her reflection in the dresser mirror. Her eyes, purpled by anxiety, stared back at her, and she sighed, then jumped at the sound of the doorbell. Trembling hands smoothing the material over her hips, she walked with forced steadiness to the door.

Jonas, looking cool and relaxed, and supremely sure of himself, stood at ease in the hall, a bottle of champagne in his hand. His eyes ran over her, coming to rest on her face. "May I come in?" he drawled when she made no move to open the door further.

"Oh! Yes...of course," Valerie blurted out, stepping back hastily.

The moment he was inside, he held the bottle aloft, chiding, "Do you think you could find some glasses? This is chilled and ready to drink."

Biting back a retort, Valerie turned and walked into the kitchen. Breathing deeply in an effort to calm her jangled nerves, she retrieved two fragile-looking wine glasses from the cabinet above the sink, then nearly dropped them when she turned to find Jonas standing behind her.

"Where's Janet?" he asked dryly, peeling the gold foil off the top of the bottle.

"She had a date," Valerie replied shortly. "Why, did you want to see her?"

"Hardly," Jonas drawled, easing the cork from the bottle. "Shall we adjourn to the living room? Or would you prefer to drink to our future here in the kitchen?"

Sarcastic brute! Spinning on her heel, Valerie marched into the living room. Depositing the glasses on the coffee table, she sat down on the sofa and watched as Jonas poured the wine before seating himself beside her.

"To the gratification of all wants." Jonas lifted his glass and touched it lightly to hers before raising it to his lips.

Valerie's entire body was suffused with heat at his

sardonic tone. Well, one could hardly accuse Jonas Thorne of being trite or predictable! Valerie lowered her eyes in embarrassment as she lifted her own glass. One sip and she was transported back to Paris and the last time she'd had champagne—the night before Etienne's accident.

Etienne. Etienne.

Valerie was unaware that her trembling hand had placed the glass safely back on the table, or of the man who sat next to her watching her every move through narrowed lids. His tightly controlled voice jerked her into the present.

"Wake up, Valerie," he advised warningly. "You are here now—with me—Jonas," he gritted, leaving her in no doubt that he knew her mind had flown back in time, to Paris and Etienne. "Pick up your wine and drink to your future, with me, beginning in a few weeks' time."

A few weeks' time? Valerie's head jerked up and she froze as the full meaning of his words registered. Her eyes took in his tall frame and her skin crawled at the idea of that body touching hers. A memory of the night she'd spent in Etienne's arms filled her mind and she had to bite her lip to keep from crying aloud: I can't. I cannot bear the thought of another man replacing Etienne in that way.

"Damn it, Valerie, come back," Jonas commanded harshly.

"What?" Valerie blinked, suddenly aware that she had superimposed Etienne's image onto Jonas's sprawling form.

"*I said come back,*" he muttered darkly. "You cannot live in the past. You cannot exist on memories.

You can starve to death on dreams and wishes.'' Standing abruptly, he pulled her up in front of him. ''We will be married in two weeks. *That* is a reality you can rely on.''

''No!'' Valerie hated the puny weakness of her protest even as she admitted her own meager store of strength was no match for his. Wetting fear-dried lips, she tried again. ''Jonas, please, I—I can't—I—''

''You can and you will.'' His assurance sliced through her stuttering. ''You cannot go back. You cannot stand still. That leaves only one direction— forward. I will make it as easy for you as I can—but I will not let you out of it.'' His hand opened to slide around the back of her neck, holding her still. ''Face it, Val. I will allow no kind of retreat.''

His promise held a distinctly ominous undertone and Valerie sighed with relief when he released her. As he turned away she drew a quick breath. Without thinking, she condemned herself with her opening words. ''Mr. Thorne, please…I…''

''Damn you!'' Jonas turned on her, his eyes blazing. ''If you call me *Mr. Thorne* in that tone one more time I swear I'll hit you. Two weeks, Valerie. You have two weeks to come to terms with yourself and the facts of life.''

The facts of life. Why, Valerie wondered distractedly, was it so important that she face life? She didn't want to face the facts of life; they hurt. She didn't want to face the reality of this hard man glaring at her. She wanted to be left alone. Her thoughts fragmented at the insistent prodding of Jonas's harsh voice.

''Do you understand?''

"I loved him."

Valerie bit down on her lip. She hadn't wanted to say that. She hadn't wanted to say anything. A chill feathered her body at the way Jonas's face settled into harshly defined lines.

"I know," he said tightly, through rigid lips that barely moved. "But he's dead, and you're alive—at least partly so." Ignoring her wince of pain, he went on, roughly, "Life is too precious to waste, Valerie, and I'm not going to let you waste any more of yours."

Escape! It was not a conscious thought but an urge that consumed Valerie's entire being. Jerking away from him, she took off at a run. She didn't know where she was going; all she knew was that she had to get away from this man who used his cold voice and his cruel words to inflict torture.

She didn't get very far. With two long strides he caught up to her, his big hand reaching out to tighten painfully around her upper arm.

"There's only one place left to run to, Val," Jonas grated as he pulled her around to face him. "And that is to me." Grasping her other arm, he held her still. "I don't want to hurt you Val." His voice softened. "And I won't unless you force me to. You accepted me this morning. I'm going to hold you to that acceptance."

Valerie stared at him, violet eyes bright with moisture, confused by his swift change from monster to human. She was behaving like a hysterical teenager, and she knew it. What he'd said was true. She *had* accepted him, and he had every right to hold her to it. Defeat settled heavily on her shoulders.

"Jonas, please." Valerie could not manage more than a whisper. "I'm so tired."

"I know that, too." Although his hands loosened their hurtful pressure, he did not release her. "This weariness dragging at you is unnatural, don't you see that?"

The sense of defeat deepening, Valerie nodded dully. "Yes, I guess so."

Jonas's fingers gripped, then eased again. "Don't guess—know," he urged softly. "Will you keep to our bargain?"

The tension in his body was transmitted to her through his fingertips. Valerie could actually feel it, and it unnerved her.

"Jonas—"

"Will you keep to it?"

Valerie wet her lips and wondered at the brief but sharp pain caused by the convulsive dig of his fingers. "Yes."

He was very still for a moment, and now Valerie imagined she could feel the tension flow out of his body. Shaking her head to dispel the fanciful thought, she murmured, "Jonas, please—"

"I know," he interrupted. "I'm going now." He hesitated, leaning toward her slightly. Then, as if catching himself, he released her arms and stepped back. He hesitated again at the door. "Are you coming into the office tomorrow?"

"Yes, of course." Valerie frowned. "Why shouldn't I?"

A sardonic smile played around the edge of his mouth. "There are going to be a lot of questions."

He shrugged fatalistically. "And a lot of speculation."

Valerie grimaced. "The first of the facts of life I'm going to have to face?"

Jonas nodded once, sharply. "The first of many, I'm afraid."

"So am I," Valerie admitted. "Afraid, I mean."

Chapter 8

Two weeks later, en route between the East and West coasts, Valerie was no longer merely afraid: she was scared to death.

A narrow gold band gleamed on one of the hands gripping the arm of her seat. The entrapping circle of gold had been slipped onto her finger less than four hours earlier, along with a diamond solitaire so large she felt a jolt of shock every time she looked at it.

Valerie shivered and forced her fingernails out of the plush upholstery. Jonas was not in the compartment. Just before takeoff he had stood over her until she'd fastened her seat belt. Then he'd left her with a terse: "I'm going forward for a little while. Try to get some sleep, you look exhausted."

The way I look doesn't tell the half of it, Valerie thought now. Sleep—how she longed for it! It had evaded her since that night in Janet's apartment. Remembering that night, Valerie shivered again. She had felt the trap closing then, yet she hadn't had the strength to break free of it. Maybe, if she'd had another month or so before Jonas commenced his onslaught she would have been strong enough to refuse him—but she hadn't had that month.

God, he scared her! That was one fact she'd faced without any prodding from anyone. She had wanted—no, ached—to tell him to go to hell, but, she simply did not have the nerve. She was filled with self-loathing. What a sniveling little coward she was! A pitiful creature without a backbone, bending in whatever direction Jonas Thorne dictated. She had been defenseless and he'd known it. He'd taken advantage of her weakness ruthlessly.

What did a man like Jonas Thorne want with her, anyway? She had asked herself that question over and over during the last two weeks. And she knew she was not the only one asking it.

Valerie was not disliked at J.T. Electronics. She knew that. But speculation had run rampant through the staff, just as Jonas had predicted it would. Valerie would have had to be deaf, blind, and unconscious not to hear the whispered remarks, see the calculating glances, or be aware of the hum of avid interest that permeated the entire office complex.

How it had affected Jonas, if at all, was just another question Valerie did not have an answer for. Jonas could, and did, don a mask at will. A mask in which his cool eyes observed everything, while revealing nothing.

Luckily, for Valerie's peace of mind, the pace of business in the office the last two weeks had increased considerably. There had been a number of transatlantic telephone calls between Jonas and Edouard Barres in Paris. The results of those calls seemed to electrify Jonas, who, in turn, galvanized the entire staff into action.

Except for Charlie McAndrew, no one, including Valerie, knew as yet exactly what it was all about. All that *was* known was that an office was being readied on the executive floor for someone, presumably from France, who was to work closely with Jonas on something. Valerie was grateful for this new source of gossip—it shifted the spotlight off her precipitous engagement to Jonas. But for all the speculation, the details of whatever was brewing remained securely locked away inside Jonas Thorne's head. He certainly hadn't confided in her!

Giving up all pretense of trying to sleep, Valerie sat up and gazed out the window. The incredible expanse of blue sky went unseen as she reviewed the events of the preceding two weeks.

The morning following Jonas's first visit to Janet's apartment, he had made known his intention to marry simply by leaking the information to the company grapevine via Charlie's secretary, Eileen. Before lunchtime Valerie had had at least a dozen interoffice calls, all with the same query: Was it true?

In the office Jonas was all business. When they were alone he was terse, edgy and impatient with her lack of enthusiasm for any suggestions he made about their wedding. And the more impatience he revealed, the more tense she became until, finally, near the end of that first week, feeling boxed in and panicky, she shouted, "I don't care what you do. Make any plans you wish.'' She had shocked herself with the outburst, yet, once started, she had not been able to stop. Shaking all over, she had released her nameless fears by lashing out at him. ''You're the one that insisted on this farce, do as you please.''

''I always do.''

If he had raised his voice, or even sounded angry, Valerie might have made a bid for freedom. Jonas did neither. Instead, he seemed to close up before her eyes. He stared at her so frigidly she felt her blood run cold.

''I must be out of my mind,'' he said quietly, as if to himself. ''All right, Valerie, I'll allow you to play the role of Sleeping Beauty a little longer. I was considering *your* feelings by asking your preference in the proceedings.'' He was quiet for several minutes, his eyes steady on her pale face. He continued dispassionately. ''Friday morning we'll apply for the license and get the medical requirements out of the way. I have a friend on the bench who, I'm sure, will be delighted to marry us in his chambers—I'll let you know what day.'' This last was drawled sardonically. ''And by the way, we're having dinner with my mother-in-law on Sunday.''

''My mother?''

''I said my mother-in-law,'' Jonas replied tiredly. ''*Your* mother is my *future* mother-in-law, Val. I'm referring to my daughter's grandmother. She wants to meet you.''

Valerie hadn't appreciated his tone of weary boredom. She hadn't particularly enjoyed having her stupidity pointed out either. Nonetheless, she tried to use a reasonable tone when she inquired, softly, ''Why

should your former wife's mother want to meet me?''
She knew she'd failed the moment the question was
voiced, for irritation, not reason, colored her tone.

"Why indeed?" After his previous self-control, Jonas's sudden flare of anger startled her. "I suppose
she thought it might be nice if you two became acquainted before the marriage takes place—seeing as
how you are going to be living in the same house."

"You live with your mother-in-law!" Valerie exclaimed.

"No, she lives with me," Jonas corrected.

"But why?"

"Because I choose to have her do so."

Valerie had been rendered speechless by the blatantly cool arrogance of his statement. She had also
been made uncomfortably aware of the fact that Jonas
did not welcome questions about his motives.

Valerie had followed his directives unquestioningly
as they applied for their marriage license on Friday.
At the end of that very long, tiring day, one bit of
information remained sharply defined in her mind.
Jonas Thorne was only thirty-eight years old!

He had not missed her expression of surprise when
he'd marked that bit of information into the date-of-
birth blank on the license application.

"You thought I was older?" he'd mocked her
softly. "Well, console yourself with the thought that
I will be before too long. I'll be thirty-nine in two
months."

There were times, many times, during that two-
week period when Valerie questioned her own sanity.
How else could she explain her rash, ill-considered
acceptance of Jonas as a life partner? He was cold,

he was mocking, he was derisive—except, she was to find, when he was in the presence of his first wife's mother. To Marge Kowalski, Jonas was charming, and considerate, and very gentle. Somehow, his attitude toward her hurt Valerie, even while she asked herself why it should.

Valerie had looked forward to the dinner with rigidly concealed distaste—well, there *was* something very odd about a thirty-eight-year-old bachelor living with his ex-mother-in-law, wasn't there? But it proved to be a relaxing, enjoyable affair.

In fact, the evening turned out to be surprisingly enlightening. What had she expected? Moving her head restlessly, Valerie examined the plush interior of the expensive aircraft. A mansion. What she had been expecting the previous Sunday was a mansion—and possibly a matriarch in residence.

What she had found once they had left behind the two huge iron gates that guarded the entrance drive was a large, rambling natural stone and glass house. It had drawn a gasp of appreciation from her.

"Does that strangled sound denote approval or dismay?" Jonas asked as he pulled on the hand brake.

"It's absolutely beautiful," Valerie breathed softly.

The late afternoon sun bathed the house in gold, its massive windows reflecting the rays back to the ball of near red hovering on the horizon. She could feel Jonas's eyes studying her rapt expression, but at that moment she didn't care, for what she was experiencing was close to love at first sight. Jonas's amused tone broke into her enthrallment.

"I'm relieved," he drawled. "I'd have hated to give it up."

Marge Kowalski was almost as dramatic a surprise as the house itself.

Having only Janet's carelessly delivered, "You'll like Marge," to go on, Valerie had drawn her own conclusions about what her future husband's mother-in-law would be like. After only a few minutes, she knew that the conclusions she'd reached were wrong.

At sixty-one Marge was, if Valerie but knew it, exactly as she had been when Jonas first met her, at least as far as her personality was concerned. Her expertly arranged hair was completely white and she wore the age lines on her face as proudly as any soldier ever wore a medal of honor. Having, she claimed, earned every white hair and wrinkle, she was comfortable with them.

"Mary Beth, being her father's daughter, kept me running while she was growing up," Marge said easily as she gave Valerie the grand tour of the house before dinner. "I think credit for more than a few silver threads goes to the cracker as well." An expression of pure love lit her face as she indicated Jonas, sauntering along, drink in hand, behind them.

"You worked in the mines?" Valerie asked him, vaguely remembering someone else referring to him as a coal cracker.

"No." Jonas gazed indulgently at Marge. "But it amuses Marge on occasion to call me a coal cracker simply because I come from the coal regions." His smile turned into a soft laugh. "But, she forgets that she came from the same place as I do, so she must be a cracker too."

"Lady residents of Tamaqua are not crackers,"

Marge teased him. "Only male residents hold that honor."

"You made that up," Jonas bantered back. "Admit it."

Marge laughed up at him. "Okay, I admit it. So sue me!"

For some unfathomable reason, their affectionate exchange caused a strange, almost painful sensation in Valerie, possibly, she theorized, because it had been so long since she'd been exposed to the warmth of this kind of affectionate wordplay. Turning away, she concentrated on following Marge up the short, curving stairs that led to the third level of the house.

The lowest level had consisted of a small enclosed area that housed the heater and central air-conditioning units, a good-size laundry room, and a huge family room—in which the largest TV Valerie had ever seen held pride of place.

The second level was comprised of a beautiful, compact kitchen, a large dining room with one wall made of glass, a living room of a size equal to the dining room, four good-size bedrooms, two large, full bathrooms and a powder room.

As she mounted the stairs Valerie hesitated to even guess what would be on the final level. What she found was her future home—with evidence that Jonas had been in residence for some time.

The apartment was self-contained and could be made completely private by the simple act of closing the door directly across the carpeted landing at the top of the curving staircase. Except for the master bedroom, the rooms here were smaller than on the floor below, and sliding glass doors led off the bedroom onto a wide redwood deck, at the end of which was a flight of steps that descended to the three-car garage. The furnishings were contemporary and expensive; warm and welcoming. Had she been viewing it with the idea of renting the apartment, Valerie would have jumped at the chance to live in it. But the prospect of sharing it with Jonas was daunting, and took the edge off her pleasure.

The evening was an unqualified success. By the time Jonas drove her back to Janet's apartment Valerie felt sure she was going to like Marge Kowalski very much. The woman was warm, friendly and obviously willing to do anything to ensure Jonas's happiness.

Numbering her days like a condemned prisoner, Valerie had grown steadily more tense as her wedding day approached. With each passing day she grew more quiet and withdrawn, leaving Jonas obviously irritated and Janet very worried. And even though she knew her behavior was far from mature, Valerie could not shake the feeling of dread.

And last night! Valerie grimaced. Last night had seemed a never ending torture. Not wanting to disturb Janet, Valerie had remained in her room, in her bed, caught up in a wide-awake nightmare. She had a wild desire to jump up, fling some clothes into a suitcase and run for her life.

She couldn't and she didn't, of course, but now, her eyes shifting to the vivid expanse of blue just beyond the small window, she wished that she had.

Everything had gone off like clockwork. With Janet as her attendant, Valerie had met Jonas, Marge and Charlie McAndrew at the exact time Jonas had stipulated. They were in the judge's chambers for exactly sixteen and a half minutes. From there they went directly to the Kona Kai, where a table, complete with hovering waiters, had been prepared for an elegant luncheon. Toasts were given and accepted. Valerie ate, drank, talked and smiled, all the time acting on reflex alone.

Jonas had not lingered over his food. As soon as the meal was eaten and the contents of two bottles of Dom Perignon consumed, he announced: "Time to go."

With the assurances of Janet and Charlie that they'd see Marge back to the house, Jonas led Valerie out of the hotel and into the silver-gray limo. The drive to the airport had been made in total silence.

"I'm going forward for a little while. Try to get some sleep, you look exhausted." Those had been Jonas's first words to her since they had left the hotel. Glancing at her watch, Valerie smiled wryly; Jonas's little while had stretched to two hours and ten minutes.

Though she knew they were going to California, she had no idea of their specific destination—nor did she care. At the moment she didn't care if the plane's wheels never again touched down on a landing strip.

A chill touched her spine as Valerie heard again the echo of the judge's low, melodic voice reciting the traditional marriage ceremony. Her nails dug into the armrest as she again felt the warm touch of the entrapping circle of gold that Jonas had slipped onto her icy finger. And her entire body jerked with a shudder of remembrance at the cold, thin-lipped kiss Jonas had brushed across her mouth.

That...that insult of the lips had brought her previous feelings of dread to the point of smothering panic. After Etienne's gentle tenderness, how had she allowed herself even to consider this union with a man so totally devoid of emotion?

The sound of Jonas's voice preceded him into the compartment, giving Valerie the precious seconds needed to lower the seat back and close her eyes in pretended sleep.

Her feigned sleep soon became real and Valerie knew no more until she was awakened by the touch of his hand.

"It's all right," Jonas murmured when she stiffened. "I'm sorry I disturbed you, but your seat belt had to be buckled. We're coming in to land." The buckling completed, Jonas moved back to his own seat. Minutes after he'd latched his seat belt the plane banked and made its approach to the landing strip.

San Francisco! Valerie had often longed to see this city, considered by some to be the most beautiful city in the world. She had longed to see it, but not with Jonas Thorne! Nevertheless, her eyes were glued to the window of the plane as they made their descent.

Had she been in a frame of mind to be impressed, the elegant hotel would certainly have impressed her. But Valerie viewed the elegant spaciousness of the lobby, the exquisite merchandise displayed by the many shops and the expensively clad patrons through eyes dulled by fatigue.

Mutely, she walked beside Jonas, first to the registration desk, then, following the bellhop, to the elevator, and finally along a carpeted hall. As she was ushered, with something of a flourish, over the threshold to their suite her ennui was dispatched by the blatant luxury of the rooms.

A wry smile curving her lips, Valerie silently surveyed the small sitting room. Bemused by the opulence surrounding her, she was unaware of the door's closing or of Jonas's eyes watching her.

I don't know why I should be surprised, she told herself cynically. After his house, the private jet, the cars—her eyes rested on the open doorway to the bedroom, which was also sumptuously elegant—what in the world did I expect, a tiny, rustic motel room in some backwater town?''

"Well?" Jonas prompted dryly. "What do you think?"

"Lotusland," Valerie replied coolly, disparagingly.

"A suitable setting for the princess of never-never land?" he retorted.

Stung, Valerie spun to face him, her eyes showing life for the first time in weeks. "It's positively immoral," she retaliated. "I can't imagine what it must cost just for one night."

"As I have no intention of telling you," Jonas drawled, "there's no need for you to tax your imagination."

The amusement gleaming in his eyes sparked flashing anger in her own and gave her tongue a sharp edge. "The French kings never knew this kind of indulgence," she snapped, indicating the suite with a condemning wave of her hand.

"Ah, but then," he literally purred, "the French kings never earned an honest dime—or heard of capitalism."

"That—that's exactly what *you* are—a capitalist."

Valerie flung the words at him, fully expecting a quick denial. Wasn't everyone ashamed of the title today? Apparently not. At least, not Jonas Thorne.

"To my back teeth," he admitted easily. "Capitalism has made me a rich man." Now he glanced around the room, waved his hand encompassingly. "I'm not ashamed of my money," he informed her seriously. "I didn't inherit it. I didn't steal it. I *earned* it." Hard arrogance underlined every word. "I'll spend it any damned way I please, without anyone's permission—including yours."

"I never—" Valerie began in protest.

"Stop," he interrupted sharply. "Your prim, shocked expression has made your disapproval of my self-indulgence as clear as any tirade would have done."

Bewildered by his harsh accusation, Valerie cried, "I told you once, I have no objection to money."

"Only mine," he sighed striding away from her into the bedroom.

Feeling unfairly accused, Valerie retreated into hurt silence. Moving listlessly, she walked to the wide window to stare out at the city she had yearned to see with sightless eyes. Oh, God, she thought despondently, what have I let myself in for? This—pretense can't possibly work. I can't even talk to him. How could I have thought I could bear to have him touch me? I can't, I can't, she thought wildly. She spun around, and her eyes fastened on the door to the hall. I have got to get away. Her legs moved to put her thought into action. Where she would go, what she would do were unimportant at that moment, for now, her only objective was getting through the door. She was brought to an abrupt stop by a clipped order issued from the bedroom.

"Come in here, Valerie."

Valerie had heard and responded to that same command so many times over the last month that she did so now without conscious thought. It was not until she was inside the room that she paused to wonder why she had obeyed him. Annoyed with herself, she attacked him.

"Who do you think you're ordering around?" she demanded imperiously. "I'm no longer your secretary, remember? I'm your wife."

"Oh, I remember," Jonas said softly. "It was *your* memory I was concerned about."

Valerie didn't have the vaguest idea of what to say to him. That he had seen her move toward the door was pretty obvious. What *could* she say? I'm sorry, Mr. Thorne, but the very idea of your hands on me makes me sick to my stomach? Hardly. His reaction to a statement of that sort would very probably be swift—not to mention painful.

"I—I haven't forgotten," she whispered.

"No? Then where were you going?"

"I don't know," she admitted.

Jonas's lips twisted wryly. "You were just going to run, huh?" He shook his head. "To what? To where? Val, you are twenty-seven years old—when are you planning to grow up?"

Stung, Valerie lashed out at him wildly, thoughtlessly. "I'm getting pretty tired of hearing from you how immature I am. I *am* grown up. Just because the idea of being married to you doesn't appeal to me, that doesn't mean—"

"That's enough," Jonas barked. "No one twisted your arm or kidnapped you. And, whether I appeal to you or not, you're stuck with me, and I'm stuck with you." He grimaced. "So I guess you'll have to bite the bullet and bear it."

"As you will," Valerie taunted.

"Yes," Jonas sighed. "As I will." He stood rigidly a moment, just staring at her, then he shrugged. "This is getting us nowhere, Val. What's done is done. I'm not about to back out and I'm not going to let you renege, either." The tautness went out of his face and his tone softened. "So, what do you want to do?"

"Do?" Valerie repeated nervously.

"Yes, do." The wry smile was back. "It is now—" he shot a quick glance at his watch "—four-twenty. Would you like to do a little sightseeing? Or would you rather start fresh in the morning?"

"I—" Valerie hesitated, thrown off-balance by his offer. "You're willing to take me sightseeing?" she asked disbelievingly.

"Well, of course I'm willing," Jonas snapped in exasperation. "We *are* on our honeymoon," he added dryly. "Were you afraid I'd planned to confine you to the bedroom?"

His chiding shot hit home and Valerie blushed, her color deepening when he laughed softly.

"You're really a winner," he jibed, still laughing.

"What, exactly, is that supposed to mean?" she demanded.

"You're so transparent." He shook his head wonderingly. "You ought to win a prize for surviving so long with your eyes firmly closed to reality."

Reality—again? Valerie's flush of embarrassment

changed to a flash of irritation. "Watching the man you love die is very real, Mr. Thorne, I assure you." For a few sweet moments she had the satisfaction of watching his face fall, but only for a *very* few short moments. His expression grim, he took one step toward her, then stopped.

"Mr. Thorne?" Jonas gritted. "I'm warning you, *Mrs. Thorne,* don't *Mr. Thorne* me again in that tone of voice. Do you understand?"

"Yes," Valerie gritted back. "If you understand I will not be talked down to. I am sick to death of being treated like a child."

"I was not talking down to you, Valerie. Nor was I implying you are a child," Jonas said patiently. "What I *was* implying is that you are a coward."

Biting her lip, Valerie turned to move away; Jonas moved faster. Crossing the room in a few long strides, he grasped her arm with one hand and her chin with the other, forcing her to look at him.

"I know it took courage for you to watch him die," he said softly. "But I'd be willing to bet you have displayed precious little since. You can't run away from the truth, Val. Sooner or later it will catch up to you." Then all the patience and softness left his tone. "He's dead," he went on brutally, ignoring her gasp of protest. "Nothing is going to change that—*ever.* You are here, and so am I. Accept that fact—and me—and you'll know what is real again.

"I—I can't accept it," Valerie cried.

"You will," he promised grimly. "You have my word on that."

Chapter 9

For one terrifying second Valerie thought he was going to draw her into an embrace, but then he released her and stepped back.

"I think we'll leave the sightseeing till tomorrow," he said decisively. "Even though it's early here, it's past dinnertime in Philly and I'm hungry." His eyes flicked over her. "You barely touched your lunch. I suggest we have dinner here in the hotel and call it a day."

Valerie dawdled over her dinner, convinced Jonas's blandly stated "call it a day" meant one thing—bed. That he was fully aware of the growing tension inside her was made perfectly clear when, after she asked for yet another glass of wine, he chided sardonically:

"If you are deliberately trying to drink yourself insensible in the hope I'll postpone the inevitable, forget it."

His words sent a chill of certainty through Valerie. There was no way she could avoid what was ahead of her, and she knew it. Still she tried.

"Jonas, I—I can't," she whispered pleadingly.

"You can," he stated flatly. "And you will. You were fully cognizant of what was expected of you." He lifted one eyebrow mockingly. "Unless, of course, you know of another, less physical, way of producing an heir?"

Controlling all but a tiny tremor in her fingers, Valerie carefully placed her glass on the table, and with equal care, moved her chair back. Jonas was at her side by the time she stood up and no amount of willpower could prevent the shiver that rippled through her when his fingers curled around her elbow. Holding herself stiffly erect, she allowed him to lead her out of the large, nearly empty dining room and across the lobby to the elevators. On entering the suite, Jonas went directly to the fully stocked drinks cabinet provided by the management.

"I'll have a brandy while you shower," he said tonelessly. "I'll be in when my glass is empty—whether you're out of the shower or not."

Valerie walked into the bedroom with cool dignity, but all pretense ended with the closing of the door. With frantic haste she tugged and yanked her way out of the pale lilac dress Janet had insisted she buy before leaving France. As her fingers fumbled with the hooks at the back of her bra her eyes settled on her still closed and locked suitcase.

"Oh, no," she muttered, digging through her handbag for the key to her case.

Finally, divested of her clothes and with nightgown

in hand, she dashed into the bathroom and under the shower. She was hastily rubbing herself dry when she heard Jonas enter the bedroom.

Grimacing at the outrageously expensive white chiffon gown Janet had given her that morning, Valerie slipped it over her head and reached for the doorknob. It was suddenly yanked away from her fingertips.

"Perfect timing," Jonas drawled as she scurried past him.

Panic rising in her throat, Valerie searched out her hairbrush and tried to calm herself by the age-old method of slow, repetitive brushing. She had no success.

I can't. I can't. The chant repeated itself over and over in her mind as she stood, still as stone, staring through the window at the fog-shrouded twilight.

"Etienne."

Whispering his name aloud called forth a plan. Jonas had repeatedly accused her of not facing reality. Well, now she would deliberately suspend reality. By the simple process of superimposing Etienne's image over Jonas's, she would not only enable herself to get through the coming ordeal, she might even enjoy it.

And so, when she heard the bathroom door open, Valerie turned calmly to face her husband with a warm smile of welcome.

Her smile faltered as her glance encountered his naked body. Concentrating fiercely, she dredged up her recollection of Etienne's form. The image wobbled and refused to stay together.

Etienne. Etienne. Etienne. Valerie repeated his name in time with Jonas's steps in a desperate effort to reassemble the fading image and hang on to her crumbling plan.

It was impossible, for in no way did this tall, lithe, powerful-looking man resemble the fiancé her memory was having such a hard time picturing.

Why couldn't she remember him more clearly? Why now, when she needed...

"It won't work, Valerie." Jonas's softly taunting voice scattered her thoughts.

"Wha—what won't work?" she stuttered.

"Your little game," he grated. "Your smile was the tip-off." His voice dropped to a threatening growl. "I *will not* play stand in for a dead man, Valerie."

Intimidated by his tone and his overwhelming presence, Valerie moistened her suddenly hot, parched lips. Before she could form words of denial, he confused the issue by lifting his hand to finger the gossamer material of her gown, asking softly, "Are you trying to make a statement with this frothy bit of virginal white?"

"No!" The disclaimer was out before she could even consider her chances of getting a reprieve by avowing purity. "The—the gown was a bridal gift from Janet," she finished softly.

Gathering great folds of the chiffon into his hands, he drew it up her body. "In that case I'll remove it very carefully." The material caressed her skin as he lifted it over her head, and it fell to the floor soundlessly when he tossed it aside.

"Jonas, I—Oh!" Her breath caught with a gasp in her throat at the feel of his palm against her breast.

"Your heart's pounding away like mad," he murmured. "Don't be afraid, Val."

Valerie's eyes closed when his mouth brushed her forehead.

"I'm not a brute, you know. I do know how to be gentle."

As if to prove his claim, he dropped feather-light kisses across her forehead to her temple. When, in trembling reaction to his touch, she attempted to move away from him, he grasped her around the waist with a softly cautioning, "No."

Holding her still, Jonas proceeded to cover every inch of her face with light, teasing kisses; every inch, that is, except her quivering lips. He kissed his way with excruciating slowness down her neck, across both shoulders and then, even more slowly, to her breasts. Valerie's trembling increased while her breathing grew slow and labored.

Feeling her senses beginning to swim, Valerie strove to recall her plan. Etie—, Oh, Lord, what is he doing! Eyes flying open in disbelief, she watched Jonas drop to his knees and lower his head to her breast. Raising strangely heavy arms, she gripped his shoulders to push him away, then dug her nails into his flesh at the riot of sensations his nibbling teeth exploded inside her body.

Oh, God!

All thought was swept away in the tide of sensual pleasure that flowed through her being. Jonas's tongue, flicking like the tip of a whip, teased first one then the other of her nipples into hard, aching arousal before his lips continued on their downward trek.

Following the dictates of her clamoring senses,

Valerie let her head fall back, and she moaned softly when Jonas's hands arched her body to his mouth. Driven by a need she was beyond questioning, she moved her hands over his shoulders to the back of his head, the tips of her fingers pressing him closer.

When the hard tip of his tongue stabbed into the small hollow of her navel a shudder of surrender went rippling through her body. As if her shudder was the sign he was waiting for, Jonas tightened his hands, and, using her body as leverage, rose lithely to his feet. Sliding one hand to the center of her back and the other to the base of her spine, he drew her body to the hardness of his own.

Valerie was now aware that Jonas had deliberately by-passed her mouth in anticipation of this moment, but she no longer cared. As he lowered his head her arms curled around his neck, and with lips parted she lifted her head to meet him halfway.

The shock of his mouth swept her over the edge of reason and into the hot, swirling depths of desire. Never would she have believed those thin, hard lips capable of creating such total devastation. Hungrily they devoured her lips while his tongue explored the recesses of her mouth.

Plastered against him, she moved when he did, sinking onto the mattress without protest. With hot, openmouthed, plunging kisses and gently caressing, teasing hands, Jonas brought Valerie to quivering readiness. When his searching fingers found the moist core of her desire, she gasped and cried aloud with pleasure as she parted her thighs in invitation.

Curving his hands around her hips, Jonas moved into position between her soft thighs. Lifting her hips slightly, he entered her carefully, then paused as if savoring the moment of possession. His movements slow, exquisitely sensuous, he drew her with him into the heady realm of passionate expression. Trembling, moaning softly, she clasped his hard body to her until, consumed in the flame of desire, they moved as one. The flame flared higher and higher until Valerie, feeling as though the tension would never end—and not even sure she wanted it to— shuddered with release and cried:

"Oh, God, Jonas!"

"Yes." Jonas drew the word out in a hard tone, deep with satisfaction. "Jonas."

Adrift in an ocean of contentment, she was hardly aware he'd spoken. For an hour, or mere minutes, buoyant with fulfillment, she floated carefree in the netherworld midway between sleep and wakefulness.

As her feeling of euphoria faded, reality returned and she was once again conscious of the not unpleasant weight of Jonas's relaxed body. Her left shoulder, where his head rested, and her side from the waist down, were numb—oddly, that too was not unpleasant.

How was it, she mused sleepily, that this man who held the exclusive power to annoy, frustrate, frighten, dismay and enrage her, all within the short span of a few hours, also held the power to unleash—from deep within her—a powerful, passionate nature she had been ignorant of possessing?

In mute acceptance she faced the realization that Etienne had lacked that power. He had never caused in her a bubbling cauldron of seething emotions. She had believed she loved him passionately. But now, after experiencing Jonas Thorne's passion, she knew better. Comparing the two was like trying to make a comparison between a gentle rain and a deluge. The only similarity was the fact that they were both wet— as Jonas and Etienne were both men—end of comparison.

The introspection created confusion, and was much too much like work. Lazily replete, Valerie simply was not up to the task.

Later, she promised herself drowsily. I'll work it all out later. For now, the temptation to smooth the disheveled strands of Jonas's hair, gleaming silver in the eerie half-light, was too great to resist.

Sliding her fingers through his hair proved very exciting. The silky strands caressed her palm sensuously, triggering a curiosity about how the rest of him might feel. She slid her hand very slowly down the side of his face, testing the feel of his sharply defined cheekbones, the shallow hollow beneath and the hard line that comprised his jaws.

Very nice—but inconclusive. Further investigation was definitely called for. Tinglingly alive to every nuance of sensation, her hand slipped over the edge of his beard-roughened jawbone and down the corded column of his neck.

The skin covering his shoulder was moist and surprisingly satiny, beckoning her hand to further study of the subject matter. Engrossed in her exploration, Valerie was unaware of the subtle change in Jonas's breathing, or the very stillness of his supine frame.

His back was an education in muscular development, his hips and flanks a doctoral degree in bone and sinew. Her fingers traced the line of his leg to the knee, hesitated, then trekked up the inside of his thigh; there *was* still the texture of his stomach and chest to measure.

Her hand moved around to his hip and paused again. Dare she continue? She wondered shyly.

"Oh, God, Valerie," Jonas growled softly into her ear. "Don't stop now."

Made brave by his hoarse plea, Valerie slid her palm over his protruding hipbone and across his taut, flat abdomen, enjoying the feel of his muscles contracting under her hand. Her hand moved up, over his navel and onto the slightly concave area between his ribs, and at that moment his ribs expanded as he drew a deep, ragged breath.

Her own breathing becoming quick and uneven, Valerie allowed her hand to caress the breadth of his chest. The hair her fingers slid through was more coarse than that on his head and it tickled her palm. Valerie decided she liked the sensation.

"Oh, sweet heaven." Jonas's groan was echoed by a gasp from Valerie as his tongue slid down her neck and his hand began stroking the inside of her thigh. As his lips slowly kissed a path to her breasts, Jonas shifted his weight, easing his body between her thighs.

"Mmm." His warm breath caressed her lips. Valerie's arm coiled around his neck as his mouth crushed hers. The downward search of his mouth began again, and Valerie lost her hold on reality as his body slid lower on hers. Moaning aloud, she arched her back when his teeth nipped playfully at her hard nipples, but he ignored her silent invitation. Not one spot on her torso was left unkissed.

Whimpering, mindless with desire, her fingers raking through his hair while her body writhed and arched against his lips, Valerie felt on the point of bursting into flames when he finally edged himself up the length of her body. He kissed her mouth, hard. Then, lifting his head, he ordered, "Look at me, Val."

Valerie's tightly closed lids, heavy with passion, opened slowly to reveal desire-clouded eyes.

"In our bed there will be no barriers, no shame, no holding back. I will know you and you will know me. Now bring me to you, Val."

"Jonas, I—" Her breath was pushed back into her throat by his thrusting tongue.

His mouth still on hers, he groaned, "Guide me in, Val."

She obeyed him simply because she *wanted* to obey him; she wanted to touch him, and, most of all, she wanted to feel the life of him inside, filling her again to completion.

"Who?" he demanded as that completion was attained.

"Jonas," Valerie gasped.

"Yes,—Jonas, and don't ever forget it."

The insistent ringing of the phone roused Valerie. Jonas's low curse as he left the bed brought full wakefulness. Rubbing her eyes sleepily, she watched him snatch up the receiver.

"What is it?" Jonas lifted his hand to rake spread fingers through his ruffled hair and Valerie's mouth went dry at the sight of his naked form. In the dark-

ness his body had felt hard and sinewy against hers.
In the midmorning light he looked magnificent.

"Okay, I'll take the call." Jonas's hard tone drew
her eyes to his equally hard, set features. A chill slid
down her spine as her gaze came to a halt on his lips.
A shiver followed the chill when his lips twisted into
an unpleasant smile.

"This better be good, Charlie." Jonas's tone held
a definite threat and Valerie was feeling sorry for
Charlie McAndrew when she saw Jonas's eyes
sharpen an instant before his lids narrowed. Apparently Charlie's reason for disturbing his employer was
very good.

"For God's sake!" Jonas exploded. "Why did you
even agree to see him?" He paused, listening, then
growled, "I don't give a damn about Trans Electric,
they dug themselves into the hole with inefficient
management, and they can climb out by themselves."
Again he paused to listen, longer this time. "I don't
give a damn about them either," he snarled.

Valerie could hear the excited tones of Charlie's
voice all the way over on her side of the bed. Something had definitely gone wrong in the last twenty-
four hours. Jonas's expression had become positively
grim when he turned to run his eyes over her. For a
fleeting instant conflicting emotions were evident in
his gaze, then his expression locked and he looked
away.

"All right, Charlie," he snapped. "Call Caradin in
Washington and tell him to get up to Philadelphia. I'll
be there in—what the hell time is it, anyway?" He
drew a deep breath. "Okay, I'll be there as soon as I
can." He practically threw the receiver onto its base.

Before it even stopped rattling he snatched it up again.

"Desk, please." There was a pause. "This is Jonas Thorne. I'm checking out. Will you get my bill ready and send the bellhop up in a half hour? Thank you."

This time he replaced the receiver carefully before turning to look at her fully for the first time.

"I'm sorry, Val, but I have to go."

"All right." Valerie heard the disappointment in her tone and cursed herself for it. But—she had so wanted to see San Francisco.

Dropping onto the bed beside her, he caught her face in his hands. "I'll bring you back, I promise." His kiss began as a gentle seal on his promise and quickly changed to a rough, hungry demand. By the time he lifted his mouth from hers her pulses were pounding and she was gasping for breath. His left hand caressed the right side of her body restlessly before honing in on the dark triangle between her legs.

"Jonas!" Valerie protested, even as she arched her body to his hand. "Charlie—Caradin, they'll be waiting for you! And the bellhop will be here...."

"First things first," Jonas whispered. "I'm the boss, remember? Let them wait."

Less than two hours later Valerie was once again strapped into the velour-covered chair, and the Gulfstream was airborne—heading east.

"Come over here."

Jonas's soft command drew her eyes from the small pane of glass to his reclining form.

"What?"

Wedging his body tightly against the arm rest, he patted the small area of exposed seat. "Come here."

His eyes looked heavy-lidded and smoky and Valerie felt her heart thump; oh, yes, they had all been right—he was very, very sexy.

"Come."

She went. After she was settled beside him—very tightly beside him—she found the nerve to risk a question.

"What's going on, Jonas?"

Jonas made no pretense of misunderstanding. "You knew an office was being prepared for someone, didn't you?" Valerie nodded. "That office is for a representative from Edouard Barres. He's coming to work with me on a project Edouard and I are beginning."

This was the first Valerie had heard about any new project, and as Jonas's former personal secretary she felt slightly miffed at being excluded.

"Is this project a secret?" she asked suspiciously. Jonas slanted her a wry glance.

"Not anymore," he replied disgustedly. "The thing started when I was in Paris," he explained. "Edouard was speculating on the feasibility of a smaller, less expensive communications system for space exploration. The idea intrigued me, as I'm sure Edouard had intended it would. I began playing around with it—and came up with a practical solution."

"But—" Valerie frowned. "What does that have to do with Charlie's call?"

"I'm getting to that." Jonas grimaced. "You are

also aware, I assume, that Trans Electric has been having some serious financial trouble?''

"Yes.'' Valerie nodded again. "Everyone in the industry is aware of it.''

"Yes,'' Jonas repeated. "But so far the general public is not, and Trans Electric is scrambling to find a way to improve the situation before it becomes common knowledge.'' He smiled, the same unpleasant smile that had twisted his lips earlier. "Somehow—I don't know how, but I'll find out—'' he inserted grimly, "The president of Trans got wind of the project. Trans wants a piece of my action and they sent their chief negotiator, a fool by the name of Parsons, to tell us so.''

"While you were out of the office,'' Valerie murmured.

"Hell, yes!'' Jonas snorted. "They knew damned well I'd throw him out.''

"But,'' Valerie shook her head, "I don't understand. It's your project. Why would they even dream you'd consider letting them in?''

"Why? Because the president of Trans has friends in high places, of course,'' Jonas enlightened her. "And not an hour after Charlie showed Parsons to the door, he had a call from Washington. The lyrics had changed, but the tune was the same. It went something like this: Trans could be of great assistance to us while we put this show together. Besides we couldn't possibly let a reputable firm like Trans go under—bad for the economy, you know. And, really, all they're asking for is a tiny slice of what could turn out to be an enormous pie. And—here is the zinger,'' Jonas sneered. "It has been brought to *someone's* at-

tention that there are several government regulations
J.T. Electronics is guilty of having ignored. If pressure were to be applied in certain quarters, a number
of our projects could be tied up for an extended period, thereby dealing us a very costly, crippling
blow.''

Noting her somewhat awed expression, Jonas
added, ''They really talk like that. Names or specifics
are never mentioned, but you know the screws are
being applied just the same.''

''And that's why you're bringing George Caradin
up from Washington,'' Valerie surmised.

''That's what I pay him for,'' Jonas concurred.

Valerie was quiet a long time, appalled at the very
idea of someone's trying to undercut Jonas in that
way.

''Jonas,'' she said softly. ''If nothing you or Charlie, or George, or anyone else can do works, you'll
have to go along with Trans, won't you?''

''No.'' Jonas's tone held hard finality. ''It's my pie,
and I won't share even a thin slice of it with them.
No one picks *my* brain, Valerie.''

''But how would you stop them?''

Jonas smiled, crookedly. ''I've only been working
on this a few weeks. Even though *I* know it's feasible,
what I've committed to paper wouldn't mean a thing
to anyone else. The majority of the details are still in
my head.'' His smile became strangely benign. ''If
we can't beat them at their game—I'll set a match to
the plans.''

''You wouldn't!'' Valerie leaned back to stare at
him in astonishment. His arm hauled her close to him
again and he laughed.

''Watch me.''

Chapter 10

Placing her hairbrush on top of the dresser, Valerie turned away from the mirror, then turned back again.

Was it too much? The dress—the makeup? Valerie had lost count of the times she'd run sharply critical eyes over the young woman the mirror reflected back to her. The dress, purchased especially for this day, was very simple, and very chic, the blending of colors from palest pink to deep amethyst complimentary to her white skin and violet eyes. The makeup had been painstakingly, if lightly, applied with all the skill she'd picked up in Paris. Her hair held the sheen of sun striking a raven's wing. Yet she was dissatisfied.

It was so very, very important that she look, if not perfect, then as close to it as possible.

Smoothing her hands nervously over the silky material covering her hips, Valerie let her eyes fasten on the flashing reflection of the diamond on her left hand.

He'd be back soon. They would all be here soon. Jonas and Marge, and—Valerie spun away from the mirror—God, what would she be like, this daughter Jonas was bringing home? Would Mary Beth accept her?

Standing perfectly still, hands clenched at her sides, Valerie slowly closed her eyes. She felt actually sick with nerves, and it was all his fault. Why, why, why had Jonas chosen to do it this way?

He had to have realized that his remarriage would be a shock to his daughter. Yet he hadn't told her a thing about it!

Valerie flinched, experiencing again the shock she'd received the night before. Naturally apprehensive, she'd been seeking reassurance when she'd asked him what Mary Beth's reaction had been to their marriage. Now, the memory of his reply still had the power to horrify her.

"I haven't told her."

Beginning to shake, Valerie dug her beautifully manicured nails into her palms. Somewhat hysterically, she pictured the scene at the airport. Marge would, of course, be teary-eyed. Probably Mary Beth would weep a little also. Then she heard Jonas' emotionless, confident voice saying, "Welcome back, Mary Beth. When we get home I'll introduce you to your new stepmother."

Valerie swallowed convulsively against the nausea that suddenly overcame her. Not again, she moaned silently. Clutching her stomach, Valerie ran into the bathroom. There was nothing, of course. Nothing but the dry, wracking heaves. Her stomach had relieved itself of its contents five minutes after she'd opened her eyes that morning. It was morning sickness, Valerie was certain. She didn't know quite how she knew, but know she did. She *was* pregnant. And so, added to the surprise of having a stepmother would be the news that Mary Beth was also to have a sibling.

Oh, why didn't they come so they could get it over with? The waiting was the hardest part. Moving jerkily, Valerie walked to the sliding door, blinking against the glaring brightness of the early afternoon sun. She didn't see the smooth expanse of green lawn or the delicate, new leaves on the surrounding trees, for her attention was directed inward, reviewing the past four weeks of her marriage to Jonas Thorne.

Perhaps, after the wedding night they'd had, if they'd been allowed a few short days—Valerie sighed. What use to think of that now? They had not had a few days, and the beginnings of closeness she'd felt while sharing his seat on the plane had been lost the moment they'd stepped off the craft.

Not one, but two cars had been waiting for them. Valerie had been installed in the one driven by Lyle and dispatched without a backward glance from Jonas. She had, in all ways but one, remained dispatched.

Valerie shivered in the warm May air. Nothing, nothing that had occurred from the day she met him, had prepared her for the living dynamo Jonas became when he was embroiled in a fight. And his language! Talk about turning the air blue! If she had learned nothing else about him Valerie had learned one thing— Jonas Thorne swore like a seasoned trooper when he was mad. And Jonas had been mad for over three weeks!

Geared for battle, Jonas went almost nonstop. He was always gone in the morning when she woke, no matter how early that was, and it was always late before he retired. And even then he did not rest right away for, whether she was asleep or not, he always drew her to him. Lord, the man's appetite was insatiable!

Had she really ever had doubts? Had she really had moments when she'd wondered if he might lose? In retrospect, it seemed inconceivable that she had, for Jonas was a born winner. Even had he been forced to put a match to his plans, he would have won.

Valerie had known it was over when he'd come home early two days ago. And before he'd said another word she'd known that he'd won. The lines of strain were gone from his face and he'd favored Marge—who claimed falsely that she'd never had any doubts—with a devastating smile.

That night, relaxed for the first time in weeks, and victorious, Jonas had made love to her until she was nearly insensible with her need for him. Valerie shuddered now with remembered ecstasy, her whole body growing warm at the images that flashed through her mind. Turning away from the brightness of the light, Valerie let her gaze rest on the bed. Oh, yes, Jonas had won—more than he was as yet aware of. He'd won her admiration, and her respect, and whether he wanted it or not, her love.

Sighing softly, she walked out of the room. Exactly how little regard Jonas had for her, or her feelings, had been brought forcefully home to her with his cool statement last night.

At Marge's insistence they had been making a last

minute inspection of Mary Beth's newly refurbished room, and Marge had stared at Jonas in shocked disbelief.

"You haven't told her?" Marge had finally blurted. "But I naturally assumed—Jonas, why didn't you tell her? It's unfair, not only to Mary Beth, but to Valerie as well."

Unperturbed, Jonas had shrugged. "I was busy here, and she was busy with winding everything up over there." Turning to the door he gave another, dismissive, shrug. "Anyway, I didn't want to tell her over the phone or in a letter."

"But Valerie told her mother over the phone," Marge persisted, following him.

"That's different," Jonas had replied smoothly. "Valerie's mother isn't coming back to the States. Mary Beth is."

Valerie paused halfway down the curving stairway, the conversation of the night before fading as she thought of that phone call to her mother. Why was it, she asked herself, that trouble always seemed to come all at once? It was over three weeks since she'd made that call and shock waves from it were still reverberating through her mind.

Her mother had taken the news of her marriage quite calmly, then had stunned Valerie with news of her own. She was pregnant! Her mother, at forty-six years of age, was pregnant, and happy about it, as well! And she was due sometime around the end of July!

Valerie grimaced and continued down the last few steps and along the hall to the kitchen.

Dorothy Fister, Jonas's housekeeper for over ten years, was at the stove preparing lunch.

"Everything under control, Dot?" Valerie asked from the doorway.

"Of course," the competent woman replied turning to run her glance over Valerie. "You look lovely, Valerie," she added quietly. Like so many of Jonas's other employees, Dot was on a first-name basis with the family. "Don't be nervous," she advised shrewdly. "Mary Beth is a nice girl. Things will work out."

"I hope so," Valerie murmured fervently, turning to leave.

"Oh, I've made up the guest room, just as you asked," Dot added.

Valerie's only reply was a sigh. Another problem, she thought tiredly as she wandered into the living room. With the tenuous relationship between her and Jonas, and Mary Beth's homecoming, the last thing they needed was a houseguest. Yet, they were getting one, at least temporarily. Jonas had calmly informed them only yesterday that Barres's man would be arriving today, and as a suitable place had not as yet been found for him, he would be staying with them. Stifling a groan, Valerie stared out the front window.

It was some fifteen minutes later that she saw the gleam of the silver limo as it purred up the driveway. She reached the front door as the Cadillac glided to a smooth stop. Opening it, she felt a thrill of apprehension scurry down her spine at the set expression on Jonas's face as he alighted from the front passenger seat. Something was very definitely wrong, for although his face revealed nothing, Valerie somehow knew that he was very angry. What in the world now? she wondered silently. Not another problem? Then she felt shock stiffen her spine as not two, but three women got out of the car.

Marge was the first one out, and Valerie did not miss the anxious glance she shot at her. Behind Marge came a tall, slim, young blonde who anyone at a glance would know was Jonas's daughter. And after her came an older, equally slim blonde, who anyone would recognize as Mary Beth's mother!

Lynn! Disbelief froze Valerie in place.

Mary Beth's smiling face, and Lynn's smug expression, sent a pang of pure panic through Valerie. He hadn't told them! The truth of her deduction was proved by the curious glances both mother and daughter turned on her as they entered the house. The urge to run, anywhere, was squashed by Jonas's arm sliding around her waist.

"Val, I'd like you to meet my daughter, Mary Beth, and her mother, Lynn." Jonas's smooth tone revealed none of the anger being transmitted to her by his fingers digging into her waist. "Mary Beth, Lynn," his pause was infinitesimal, "my wife, Valerie."

For one instant there was total silence, and then Mary Beth and Lynn spoke as one.

"Your wife!"

Mary Beth was the first to articulate her reaction.

"Dad," she cried, looking directly at Valerie. "When did this happen? And why didn't you tell me?"

"I just did," Jonas answered sardonically. "And *this* happened almost a month ago."

"Really, Jonas—" Lynn began angrily, only to be silenced by her mother.

"Lynn, I don't think the foyer is the place for this discussion," Marge cautioned sharply. "I suggest we go into the living room."

Held in place by Jonas's restraining hand, Valerie stood mutely as they entered. After taking a few steps, Mary Beth turned to glance at them over her shoulder.

"Coming, Dad?"

"*Val* and I will be with you in a moment," Jonas assured her.

Feeling like an intruder, Valerie watched Mary Beth frown as she turned to follow her mother and grandmother.

"She's a lovely girl." Valerie wasn't even aware she'd murmured the observation aloud until Jonas agreed softly, "Yes, she is."

Glancing up at him quickly, Valerie caught the softening in his eyes, the gentle smile that touched his lips. If he would only look at me that way, just once—Valerie shrugged the wish away, and the hollowness that had followed it.

"Yes?" Jonas's prompting made it clear he had not missed her scrutiny of him.

"Nothing," she said. Then, at the arching of one disbelieving brow, she temporized, "It sounds strange, hearing Mary Beth call you Dad." It wasn't a complete fabrication. It had sounded strange to her and had caused a strange, aching feeling as well.

"It sounds a little strange to me, too," came his surprising reply. "It's been so long since I've heard it." Releasing her, he turned as Lyle entered the house loaded down with suitcases. "Put the red cases in Mary Beth's room," Jonas instructed. "And drop the white ones here in the foyer for the time being."

Valerie eyed the white cases for several seconds after Lyle had retreated before lifting her eyes to Jonas. "Is she staying…here?"

"She has before," Jonas said dryly.

"But that was before…"

"Dad?" Mary Beth's soft, but impatient call ended Valerie's protest.

"Coming," Jonas called back. Lowering his voice, he argued, "Her daughter and mother are here, where else would she stay?"

A hotel? A motel? Home? Valerie didn't voice her suggestions. Instead, she reminded him, "You have another guest coming today."

"I haven't forgotten, Val," Jonas assured her smoothly. "Now, shall we join the others?"

Her resentment flared at the note of command in his tone. Seething with impotent fury, Valerie allowed him to usher her into the room. The sight of Lynn's elegant body ensconced in Valerie's favorite chair set her teeth on edge. Damn him, if he'd wanted Lynn in his home why hadn't he married *her?* Valerie thought furiously.

Valerie was excluded from much of the ensuing conversation; whether the exclusion was deliberate or not she didn't know, and, at the moment, didn't much care. With cool detachment, she studied Lynn and Mary Beth in turn.

Janet had not been exaggerating when she had said that Lynn was beautiful. She had to be close to forty, Valerie knew, yet she showed none of the usual signs of aging. Valerie decided she hated her.

Mary Beth, on the other hand, was a lovely composite of her mother and father. Tall and slim, with the same high cheekbones and determined jaw as Jonas, she had the blue eyes, pert nose and golden skin of her mother. Her hair color was strictly her own, being a shade between Lynn's gold and Jonas's ash-blond.

Her hand sliding over her still flat belly, Valerie wondered how her coloring would combine with Jonas's in their offspring. Her eyes grew misty as she contemplated a tall, slim youth with a shock of black hair and cool gray eyes. Suddenly she longed to hold the infant version of that youth in her arms.

"Valerie?"

The rough edge to Jonas's tone jerked her out of her pleasant daydreams of the future. "I—I'm sorry." Valerie blinked at him. "I didn't hear what you said."

"I asked if our guest room was in order?" Jonas frowned.

"Yes, of course." A sickening thought sent heat flashing through her. He wouldn't install Lynn in the room next to theirs, would he? She had to ask. "Why?"

"That should be obvious," he rapped. "Our guest room is the only one available for Barres's man."

"If you don't mind, I'd like to go to my room and rest awhile." Lynn, one slim hand hiding a yawn, fluttered long lashes at Jonas.

"Of course," Valerie said crisply, gritting her teeth. "I'll show you to your room."

"Don't bother," Lynn purred oversweetly. "I know the way."

To a lot of bedrooms, I'll bet, Valerie thought nastily.

Rising, Marge reached for Mary Beth's hand. "Come along, young lady, I have a surprise for you."

During the ensuing confusion and chatter, Valerie escaped up the stairs, feeling unloved, unwanted and totally unnoticed.

Although the third floor contained a kitchen and dining area, Jonas and Valerie had always eaten dinner with Marge in the larger dining room downstairs. That evening dinner was, for Valerie, an ordeal. Lynn kept up a constant stream of chatter, much of which was designed to make Valerie uncomfortable.

"You replaced Maria Cinelli, didn't you?" the older woman began. "Tell me, is he as much of a bear at the office as he is at home? He's always had an awful temper, you know—" casting a sugar smile at Jonas "—swears like a dock worker, too."

Tell me about it, Valerie longed to purr cattily. Actually, by the time they left the table she longed to hiss and claw like a cat. Lynn was, she decided, an absolute witch.

Jonas, seemingly unaware of the battle raging between his past and present wives, was sublimely going about the business of getting reacquainted with his daughter.

Seating herself in an easy chair as far away from Lynn as possible, Valerie concentrated on the conversation between her husband and his daughter.

"By the way," Jonas quizzed Mary Beth, "what happened to your plans to cruise the Aegean this summer?"

"Well—" Mary Beth began, only to be interrupted by the tinkling sound of Lynn's laughter.

"I'm afraid I squashed those plans, Jonas," Lynn cooed. "We were supposed to go on a yacht that belongs to a friend of mine, but when this friend began talking about a match between his penniless nephew and Mary Beth, I decided I'd better bring her home to Daddy."

"Indeed?" Jonas drawled before arching a brow at his daughter. "Do you want to marry this young man?"

"Heavens no!" Mary Beth choked, roaring with laughter. "I'd probably have to share my allowance with him."

"No, you wouldn't," Jonas corrected dryly. "If you married a fortune hunter you'd have no allowance to share."

That shot sobered Mary Beth. "You mean," she gasped incredulously, "if I marry a man you don't approve of, you'll stop my allowance?"

"That is exactly what I mean, honey-girl," Jonas drawled.

"But—" Mary Beth began.

"But, Jonas, that's ridiculous!" Lynn's shrill voice cut in.

Jonas's eyebrows shot up. "Why ridiculous? Strange, I was under the impression a husband was supposed to support his wife—not her father." His lids narrowed. "I intend to keep what's mine up till the last minute," he warned softly.

"Don't be silly, Jonas," Lynn snapped, obviously upset. "Mary Beth will get the majority of it eventually, anyway."

"Not the majority of it," Jonas corrected even more softly. "At least, not if there's another heir."

"Another heir?" Lynn and Mary Beth cried in unison.

"I see." Lynn's blue eyes glittered. "Is that the *real* reason you married a woman only a few years older than your daughter?"

Valerie steeled herself for Jonas's answer, but just as he opened his mouth to speak, the doorbell rang.

"Ah," he grinned. "Literally saved by the bell. That will be Barres's rep. I'll answer it." His grin widening, he got to his feet and sauntered out of the room.

With his departure three pairs of blue eyes were turned on Valerie. Lynn's in condemnation, Mary Beth's in confusion, and Marge's in commiseration. Unwilling to answer questions, or to withstand their stares, Valerie lowered her eyes. When she lifted them again Jonas stood framed in the archway, a man several years younger than he at his side. Hardly daring to believe her eyes, Valerie whispered:

"Jean-Paul."

Then, with a near shout, she jumped out of her chair.

"Jean-Paul!"

"Valerie?"

Jean-Paul was no less surprised than Valerie and as he cried her name he opened his arms.

Unmindful of the tears that blurred her vision, Valerie ran across the room and into his embrace.

For several minutes the air was filled with babbling French.

"Oh, Jean-Paul, it's so good to see you."

"Little one, I've been out of my mind with worry about you."

"Never would I have dreamed you'd be the rep from Barres."

"My sweet girl, why did you leave without a word?"

"But I wrote to your parents!"

"They were visiting me in New York, then they went on to visit with *maman*'s sister in Quebec."

"You look fantastic, but you've lost a little weight."

"You are beautiful as ever, but you've gained a little weight."

"I see you've met my wife, DeBron." Jonas's cold English sliced through the noise of their happy reunion.

"Your wife," Jean-Paul answered, his eyes darting from Jonas to Valerie then back to Jonas.

"*My* wife," Jonas emphasized.

Jean-Paul shifted his eyes to gaze questioningly at Valerie.

"I'll explain everything later, darling," Valerie promised, not seeing the way Jonas stiffened at the endearment. "Please, come in."

Inside the living room, his voice tight, Jonas made the introductions.

"Jean-Paul DeBron—my daughter, Mary Beth."

"*Mademoiselle.*"

"And her grandmother, Mrs. Kowalski."

"*Madame.*"

"And her mother, Lynn Varga."

"*Enchan*—her mother?" Jean-Paul shot a puzzled look from Lynn to Valerie.

"Yes, Mary Beth's mother." Lynn's honeyed tone drew Jean-Paul's eyes back to her. "I'm Jonas's *first* wife," she purred.

"I assume," Jonas spoke with deceptive softness, "you met my wife while she was living in France?"

"But of course," Jean-Paul replied, still looking puzzled.

"Jonas," Valerie said quietly, "Jean-Paul is Etienne's brother."

Valerie stood under the shower spray as long as she dared. Jonas was angry. Wrong. He was furious. In fact, he had seemed to be in a black fury for most of the last month, ever since Jean-Paul had arrived, come to think of it. Wasn't Jean-Paul's work up to Jonas's expectations? Was that why he had been constantly on the edge of anger all these weeks? And tonight she had pushed him over the edge.

Valerie sighed. Why, why had she risen to Lynn's taunting and allowed herself to ruin Jonas's birthday dinner by lashing out the way she had? He had seemed so genuinely pleased, too. You're a fool, she chided herself. But, even a fool can take only so much torment. And Lynn had made sure Valerie got more than her fair share.

Four weeks of snide remarks and veiled innuendos had proved to be Valerie's limit. It was Lynn who had so carelessly told her that Maria Cinelli was back in Jonas's good graces *and* in his office. It was Lynn who inferred that Jonas was paying the rent on Maria's apartment. It was Lynn who hinted that Jonas had dropped several obscure remarks to the effect that he was now sorry he'd married so hastily. But the real topper came when Lynn slyly suggested that, should Valerie waken one night to find herself alone, she should check Lynn's room first. It was because of Lynn that Valerie had not yet told Jonas that she thought she was pregnant.

And then, tonight, something had just snapped inside of Valerie. Again she sighed. I could have taken it for myself, Valerie thought angrily, but why did she have to start on Jean-Paul? God! The memory of Mary Beth's stricken face made her want to weep. Hadn't Lynn seen the love growing between Mary Beth and Jean-Paul? How could she have missed it? But then, Valerie knew Jonas had not seen it either. But, of course, that was different. Jonas was much too busy to see anything as unelectronic as love. He hadn't even seen his own wife's love for him!

Which still doesn't answer that question of why I had to ruin Jonas's dinner by flying to Jean-Paul's defense when Lynn made that disgusting remark about how she'd heard somewhere that French brothers shared their women. Even though Lynn had laughed as if teasing when she said it, she had hurt two people who were close to Valerie: Jean-Paul and Mary Beth—who was now dear to Valerie *because* of Jean-Paul. So I told her to shut her filthy mouth! It was long past time *someone* did. The problem was, now she had to face Jonas.

With sudden determination she turned the shower off. What could he do, stand her against the wall and shoot her? The picture that formed from that idea— she could see herself against the wall, a blindfold over her eyes, a last cigarette dangling from her lips—was ludicrous. Valerie had to stifle a giggle. She didn't even smoke! A hand flew to her mouth to muffle her nervous laughter.

"Val, what are you doing in there?"

Valerie's laughter dried along with all the moisture in her mouth and throat. Squaring her shoulders she went to face the firing squad.

The first volley hit her as she walked into the bedroom.

"Does he look like Etienne?"

Valerie paused, controlling the urge to step back. "No, not much," she answered truthfully. "His voice and eyes are almost the same, though." Why, she wondered, had he waited till now to ask questions?

"You obviously got to know him very well."

Valerie didn't trust his tone. It was much too silky. Surely he hadn't taken Lynn's sick remark seriously? "What do you mean?" she bristled.

"You called him darling when he arrived. You flew to his defense tonight." He shrugged. "You're very fond of him?"

"Yes, very," Valerie admitted. Her voice grew husky. "He— Jean-Paul was very kind to me when— when…"

"Never mind," Jonas cut into her throaty explanation. "I get the picture." He turned away, then swung back to face her, his mouth grim. "You must not let Lynn get to you. She loves shocking people." He shook his head. "I sometimes think she is less mature than Mary Beth."

"I'm sorry your birthday dinner was spoiled," Valerie said softly.

"Are you?" he asked with equal softness. "Well,

in that case, we could celebrate the occasion right here.''

Walking to her, he slid his arms around her and drew her close to his long frame. ''Say, happy birthday, Jonas,'' he ordered in a near growl.

''Happy birthday, Jonas,'' Valerie repeated, smiling.

''Very good,'' he murmured close to her ear. ''Now say, take me to bed, Jonas.'' His tongue, teasing the side of her neck, sent expectant shivers down through her body. His hands, tormentingly caressing the very outer curve of her breasts, removed her inhibitions.

''Take me to bed, darling.'' Valerie gasped when his fingers dug into the soft flesh of her breast.

''Do you call all your lovers darling?'' he demanded harshly.

''Jonas, you're hurting me,'' Valerie cried, holding her breath in an effort to relieve the pressure.

''I know.'' His fingers loosened but his arms tightened. ''You make me *want* to hurt you.'' His lips brushed hers, the tip of his tongue urging them apart. ''Say it again, Val, I want to hear it, even if it means nothing.''

Nothing. Valerie closed her eyes against the rush of hot tears. It means nothing to him. Which means *I* mean nothing to him. Nothing deep, nothing lasting. I'm a convenience, a warm body that's nearby whenever the need arises. Dear God, I love him, and all he wants from me is an heir and the moaning, feverish words that attend the begetting of that heir. Meaningless. Nothing.

''Val.''

Jonas's urgent groan pierced her mind, and her heart. Why not, she thought wildly. His teeth nipped her lower lip and she shuddered in response. Why not give him what he wants? It's his birthday. Curling her arms around his neck, she returned his playful bite. Happy birthday, Jonas, she cried silently, you're going to be a father. Her voice, when she spoke, was thick from unshed tears.

"Take me to bed, darling."

It was late when Valerie woke, which was not surprising. Jonas had not let her sleep till near dawn. Groaning aloud, she stretched aching muscles. Lord, where did that man get his energy? He was gone. Hours earlier, she had been vaguely aware of his movements as he showered and dressed to go to the office. Had he invented some kind of machine that kept him charged electrically? Valerie would not have been in the least surprised to find that he had. And during the night he had transmitted some of that electricity to her. It had been like a charge running between them. Jonas had generated fresh sparks with each new impassioned endearment she had moaned against his mouth or skin.

Sliding her fingers into her tangled hair, Valerie swallowed against the tightness in her throat. Was this the way the rest of her life was going to be? Hours and hours of indifference followed by moments of sweet, hot passion? Shaking her head to banish the chilling thought, she jumped out of bed. She had to do something, anything that would keep her from thinking.

Two weeks later, Valerie visited a doctor. During those two weeks she had seen more of Jean-Paul and

Mary Beth than of Jonas. In an effort to avoid Lynn, Valerie had spent more time away from home than Jonas had. Dear, gentle Jean-Paul, what would she have done without him? He had not only become her shield against Lynn, he had, in effect, given her Mary Beth.

Mary Beth had felt a natural resentment on coming home to find a stepmother in residence. Jonas's flat announcement about his hopes for another heir hadn't exactly endeared Valerie to her. But Jean-Paul's love had enabled Mary Beth to let her guard down enough to get to know her new stepmother. By the time Jonas celebrated his thirty-ninth birthday, Mary Beth and Valerie were friends—a fact that Jonas had not yet come to recognize.

Not having the slightest idea of which doctor to see, Valerie made an appointment with Dr. Milton Abramowitz, simply because Marge had mentioned having to see him for her six-month checkup soon after Valerie and Jonas had married.

It was not until after she was ushered into Dr. Abramowitz's office that Valerie learned he was a member of Jonas's small circle of close friends. By the time she left his office, Valerie was calling him Milt—at his request—and glowing at his confirmation of her condition.

Her euphoria lasted all the way home. Lynn burst her rosy bubble as soon as she entered the house by announcing, in a self-satisfied tone, that Jonas would not be home for dinner. Valerie had her foot on the bottom step of the stairs when Lynn added, sweetly, that she also would not be there.

For several seconds Valerie felt nothing but devastating disappointment. Then, suddenly, anger engulfed her. Who, she seethed, did this woman think she was? And for that matter, who the hell did Jonas Thorne think *he* was? Lifting her head regally, Valerie stared coldly at Lynn.

"Let me assure you," she said icily, praying she could back up what she was about to say, "Jonas *will* be home for dinner. As for you," she went on scathingly, "I couldn't care less if you *never* came back."

"Indeed?" Lynn sneered. "Well, *darling,*" she simpered sweetly, "We'll see about that! When Jonas hears about this you just might find that you're the one who goes and never comes back. I've put up with this situation long enough," she snapped. "I think it's time Jonas put an end to this farce of a marriage."

Valerie, shaken by Lynn's complacency, hesitated a moment, and then, with far more confidence than she was feeling, she went to the phone.

"I'm afraid you are riding for a fall, young lady. A bad fall," Lynn opined condescendingly as Valerie punched out the number of Jonas's private line. Steeling herself against rejection and subsequent humiliation, Valerie forced her voice to a cool calmness as she replied to Jonas's impatient "Thorne."

"Jonas, this is Valerie," she said unnecessarily. "Lynn tells me you won't be home for dinner and I…"

"That's right," Jonas cut in harshly. "I called to tell you I had some work I wanted to finish up here, but Lynn told me you were out…again. Strangely, Jean-Paul had to be out of the office today also."

There was something disturbing in the way he emphasized his last statement, but, filled with the importance of her news and the fear that he would refuse the request she was about to make, Valerie shrugged aside her feeling of unease and plowed on.

"Jonas, I would—" She paused, searching for the right word. "I would appreciate it if you *could* get home. There's something I must t…" She almost said "tell," but quickly changed her phrasing. "There is something I must discuss with you."

Valerie held her breath through the moment of silence that followed her request, letting it out slowly and soundlessly when Jonas finally spoke.

"Is this discussion—important?" he asked somewhat grimly.

"Yes," Valerie said quietly.

"All right, Val, I'll be home in time for dinner," Jonas said as quietly and then, without a good-bye, he hung up.

Schooling her features into an expressionless mask, Valerie turned to face Lynn. "Jonas *will* be home for dinner." She looked Lynn straight in the eye. "Perhaps *you* are the one riding for a fall."

"We'll see, little girl," Lynn spat, pure hate glittering in her eyes. With a dramatically sweeping motion she walked to the door. Pulling the door open she cast a withering glance over Valerie. "Oh, yes, we will see."

Suddenly exhausted, Valerie walked tiredly up the stairs and into the bedroom to drop limply onto the bed. Hours later the slamming of the bedroom door startled her awake. Jonas was standing just inside the door, his narrowed eyes fixed on her.

"You said there was something you had to discuss with me?" he prompted without preamble.

"Yes," Valerie whispered through parched lips. Why, she thought wildly, should telling him be so difficult? She was going to give him what he had wanted from her, wasn't she?

"I'm pregnant," she blurted out, then held her breath. She held it a long time, finally releasing it when he didn't respond. Why was he so still and quiet? Why didn't he say something? He *had* claimed he wanted an heir, so why was he so silent, so taut? When he finally did reply his voice had an odd, tense inflection.

"You're positive? It's been confirmed?"

"Yes, I saw Dr. Abramowitz this afternoon."

"This afternoon," he repeated softly. "I see."

What did he see? Valerie asked herself blankly. What was there for him to see? She was going to have his child and all he seemed capable of saying was "I see." Where was the tender concern she had hoped for? Where was the joy? Glancing up at him, Valerie stopped breathing altogether. Joy? His eyes were slate gray with rage, his body stiff with the emotion. As she cringed, Jonas strode to the bed to stand over her menacingly.

"And did you really believe I'd support your fun and games?"

"Fun and games?" Valerie shook her head in confusion. "Jonas, what are you talking about?"

"You," he rasped. "And that damned Frenchman."

Frenchman? Jean-Paul? Me and Jean-Paul? No! She cried silently, he can't believe that Jean-Paul and

I are... The idea was insupportable, and in an effort to deny it she began, "Jonas, you can't—"

"*And* the burden you're carrying inside your body," he interrupted nastily.

His words, his tone, were shocking. His crudeness insulting. Enraged, Valerie flung herself off the bed with such force that Jonas was startled into backing up. "Burden!" she screamed. "How dare you! Why are you talking like this?"

"Very simple, Val," Jonas retorted. "What exactly are you carrying? A young Thorne—or another DeBron?"

Another DeBron? The words echoed inside her head as Valerie felt the color drain out of her face. Wide-eyed with shock, she stared at him in disbelief. He actually thought...?

"I don't believe what I just heard." Although her voice was a rough whisper when she began, it rose steadily. "You...you think that I've been...like that? With Jean-Paul?" Gasping for breath, she controlled her voice enough to say, "You're nothing but a gutter-minded..." she raked her mind for the most stinging condemnation she could think of, "bastard!" Valerie flung the word at him.

"Exactly," Jonas agreed quietly. "In every sense of the word." Valerie stared anew at the unfamiliar sound of contrition in his tone. "I'm sorry, Val." Turning away from her abruptly, he strode out of the room.

He was on the stairs before Valerie came out of her shock. She couldn't let him go like this!

"Jonas!" Galvanized into action, she ran after him. She heard his car start up as she reached the bottom of the stairs and in an effort to intercept him she ran out of the front door. Jonas was backing the silver Cadillac out of the drive alongside the house.

''Jonas!'' Without pausing to think, she flew down the steps and along the front of the house toward the car just as he swung it back in her direction onto the curving drive.

The anguished shout was heard an instant before the car's back fender brushed her hip and spun her off her feet to land with a thud in a large privet hedge bordering the drive.

''Valerie!''

Chapter 11

Etienne's brother. Millions of Frenchmen in the world, and Barres sends me Etienne's brother. Oh, Lord.

What will I do if she dies?

Dammit, why did I listen to Lynn? Jonas could almost hear her voice purring cattily—was it only yesterday? He could still see her wide blue innocent eyes.

"Jonas, really," Lynn had sighed. "If you don't care for yourself, will you consider your daughter?"

"Lynn, I haven't the vaguest idea what you're talking about," he'd snapped, asking himself why he'd let her into his office in the first place. "I don't have time for your innuendos. Either explain or get out of here."

"You know, there are times I wonder what any woman would want with you," Lynn retorted. "You are…"

"Out," he'd cut in impatiently.

"All right," Lynn purred, as if satisfied with herself for making him angry. "I'm talking about your lovely *young* wife and the fact that she's been seen, by mutual friends, not only *with* Jean-Paul, but coming out of his apartment as well." Her purr became silky. "The apartment, I might add, that *you* pay for."

Why had he listened?

Face it, Thorne, you no more listened to Lynn than you would any other idiot who might presume to advise you. The questions, the suspicions were there long before Lynn injected her dose of poison. In point of fact, the feeling of unease he'd been living with for weeks had begun when Etienne's brother walked into the house and Valerie called him darling.

Lord God, what will I do if she dies?

Had Valerie ever had the courage to ask him, Jonas could have—but probably would not have—told her he did not only swear when he was mad, but when he was upset, as well. And now, at 6:03 on a rain-swept June morning, Jonas was not only upset; he was terrified.

The baby was lost. Jonas had faced that at once. He winced as he recalled her last faint words:

"Jonas, please, tell them to save my baby."

What he had told them was:

"You had damned well better save my wife."

He knew he couldn't back up his threats. Yet he'd made them, thereby straining the long friendship between himself and Valerie's obstetrician, Milton Abramowitz.

Jonas's clenched fist came down lightly against the

windowsill, the very lightness of the blow betraying the self-control he was exerting over himself.

Had he really threatened Milt with a malpractice suit? Jonas shook his head in disbelief. For a few minutes there, right after they'd arrived at the hospital, he'd gone slightly mad.

A soft, steady stream of expletives rolled off his tongue, each more colorful than the last, before Jonas pulled himself up short. Hell, he was still slightly crazy. But it was the waiting that did it. The waiting, and the wondering, and the pure, stark fear.

God, how long have I been in love with her?

In an effort to escape the fear clutching at his guts, Jonas played a game in his mind, trying to pinpoint *the* day.

Was it the evening Etienne's brother came to the house that first time? Without even considering it, Jonas shook his head. No, it must have been before that—he'd reacted too strongly when she'd called Jean-Paul darling.

What would I give to hear her call me darling? And really mean it? All my money? Without question. My immortal soul? In a second.

What has that got to do with it anyway, you arrogant fool? Jonas derided himself. *She hasn't asked you to give up anything. She doesn't want your money, or your soul, or your love either.* His sigh sounded loud and harsh in the small, quiet room.

Not even Lynn's arrival had had much of an impact on her. The fist resting on the windowsill tightened until the knuckles turned white. Oh, she'd been angry, sure, but her anger had been swiftly forgotten with the advent of Jean-Paul. Etienne's brother, for God's sake. His lips twisting bitterly, Jonas remembered the way Valerie had gone after Lynn when she'd attacked Jean-Paul.

Suddenly realizing he was beginning to think in circles, Jonas turned away from the window impatiently. What was taking so long? Crossing the room in a few long strides, he dropped wearily onto the plastic covered torture-rack they dared to call a couch, and picked up the March issue of *Time*. Jonas had skimmed through the issue the week it came out, but that didn't matter, he wasn't reading anyway.

Was it on their wedding night? The day after? Musingly, Jonas continued with his game. No, he gave a brief shake of his head. Not then. That he had been both eager and determined to consummate the marriage—and equally determined that she be fully aware of who was doing the consummating—pointed to his having been in love before that night.

The day he proposed to her in the office? He remembered how tense he'd become while waiting for her answer. And later that day, after he'd sent her home, he'd grown still more nervous, afraid she'd change her mind.

Did that nervousness indicate the presence of love? Jonas didn't know for sure, but he had a strong suspicion it did. Never having been in love before, he wasn't quite sure of the components that went into the emotion. Not knowing the language, how was a man supposed to read the signs? If those components included the desire to protect, possess and pamper a woman, well then, he was definitely in love.

Under better circumstances it might even be enjoyable. Jonas grimaced. Damn Jean-Paul! Jonas's grimace changed to a half smile of self-mockery. There was no earthly reason to damn Jean-Paul, and Jonas knew it. Jean-Paul was innocent—at least as far as Valerie was concerned. And Valerie was innocent as well. Why had he let his suspicions and his mouth run away from him like that? He had known the child was his from the moment the words "I'm pregnant" came out of her mouth.

His last thought propelled him out of the couch and back across the tiled floor to the window. He knew the child *had* been his, he amended thoughtfully.

That the child was lost he was certain. Jonas shuddered as his mind replayed the events of the evening before. God, would he ever completely forget the fear that had gripped him when he had glanced in the rear-view mirror and seen Val running into the back of his car? Jonas shuddered, remembering how he'd slammed on the brakes and flung open the car door to run to her and lift her, white and shaken, out of that hedge. Why was it, he fumed now, that doctors were never available when you really needed them? After carrying Val inside he had called Milt, only to be told the doctor was in the delivery room. By the time Milt returned the call, Valerie was ensconced in their bed, her color restored, insisting that but for a few minor scratches she was fine. Now, twelve hours later, Jonas asked himself why he'd allowed her to dissuade him from taking her to the hospital at once.

"Really, Jonas," she had pleaded. "I'm feeling much better. I promise I won't get out of this bed before tomorrow, and then only to go see Dr. Abramowitz."

And both he and Milt had listened! That was what

bothered him now. But, she *had* seemed all right! Until, less than three hours ago, she'd called out for him, wakening him from the light doze he'd fallen into on a living room chair. Just thinking about it created that same tightness inside that he'd experienced at the panicky sound of her voice, and the same gripping fear he'd felt on entering the bedroom to find her standing beside the bed, white-faced with pain. If he lived another hundred years he'd never forget the terror that had momentarily frozen his entire mind and body at the sight of all that blood! Her blood! In that frozen instant he had been certain that the life was flowing out of her. He was also certain that if she died, life would never again hold any real value for him. Not even his work could fill the void losing her would leave inside him.

She can't die! Dammit, I won't let her die! I can't give her up. I won't give her up! Not even to death. Why doesn't Milt come? What *is* taking so long?

Val, don't leave me!

Jonas stood very still by the window, shocked motionless by the intensity of his thoughts. Never had he experienced such agony of mind. Not even at the vulnerable age of seventeen when, for two months, he'd carried the anguish of uncertainty about whether or not he'd fathered the child Lynn was carrying.

The child! Once again his large, bony hands balled into fists. Had she lost his son? Jonas swallowed against an unfamiliar tightness in his throat. Valerie hadn't *lost* the child, *he* had robbed her of it!

No, his head moved in sharp denial. It had not been his fault. It had not been her fault either. It had been one of those stupid accidents that happen at times. And it *had* happened. No point in casting blame now.

Jonas was not a man to wallow in guilt or regret. What was done could not be undone. All he could do now was hope Valerie could have another child. *His* child.

If she lives.

She has to live, dammit. She has *got* to live!

What is taking so long?

Was this what *she* had gone through while Etienne had teetered between life and death? This sudden, new insight made him go still again. No wonder you withdrew, love, Jonas at last sympathized. The pain is close to unbearable.

Don't leave me, love. Mentally Jonas did what he would never be able to do aloud; he pleaded. Please, fight to hang on to your precious life, for if you die, living will be hell, but I cannot withdraw from it. Once again the words Jonas could not voice aloud screamed through his mind:

What will I do if she dies?

In an effort to escape the merry-go-round of his thoughts, Jonas jerked back the sleeve of his jacket to expose his watch. Had he really been here two hours? It seemed impossible, yet even as he gazed at the small face of the slim gold disc, the digital number changed from one to two. Six-twenty-two, and he had dashed out of the house with Val in his arms at around four-thirty.

It was a wide-awake nightmare. How often had he heard that phrase and dismissed it as exaggeration? Jonas shrugged. Live and learn. That's what life is all about, isn't it? What point in living if you *never* learn? And what have you learned, Thorne? That you are as capable as the next guy of feeling very deep pain and very real fear.

Your mind's meandering, Thorne. Jonas pulled his rambling thoughts together. You had better go back to the game.

Why bother? he asked himself scathingly. You *know* that what began as desire for her very quickly became love. What purpose in pinpointing the exact day, hour and minute? You love her. But *she* still loves a dead man—or his memory. She doesn't love you.

Impatience riding him, Jonas strode to the door and into the corridor. It was eerily quiet. Hadn't he always heard about how noisy hospitals were when the patients were sleeping? Where was everyone? Where was Milt?

He swung around and strode back into the waiting room. Reaching into the slash pocket of his jacket, he yanked out a crumpled cigarette pack, grimacing as he withdrew the last cigarette in the package. For an instant he contemplated going in search of the lunchroom or a cigarette machine. Then, with a shake of his head he decided to stay put. Surely Milt would come soon?

Some ten or fifteen minutes later, Jonas stood staring out at the lashing rain, his long fingers drumming a staccato beat on the windowsill, when a soft voice interrupted his thoughts.

"Dad."

Jonas turned to sweep his gaze over his daughter and frowned darkly.

"What are you doing here?" Jonas's tone betrayed his surprise.

"I came to be with you," Mary Beth answered quietly. "And to bring you some coffee." She held a stainless steel thermos bottle aloft. "Gram sent it."

"The coffee I could use," Jonas growled, walking to her. "The company I can do without." He plucked the bottle out of her hand.

"Dad!"

"What do you want here, anyway? Did you come to gloat?"

"How could you think something like that?" Mary Beth reproached him softly.

"I can think that, because you have given me good reason to think it," Jonas retorted. "You would have resented the child, the same as you resent her. Very likely you resent *me* for marrying her in the first place." Turning away, he walked back to the window, opened the thermos and poured the steaming brew into the steel cup.

"That's not true," Mary Beth denied.

Gripping the cup as if he'd like to crush it, Jonas turned to face her, controlling his anger with difficulty. "Isn't it? Can you honestly tell me you're sorry the baby's gone?"

"I *am* sorry," she choked, her eyes pleading for him to believe her.

"Are you? Why?" Studying her intently, Jonas sipped tentatively at the hot coffee, apparently unmoved by her stricken expression.

Her eyes swimming, Mary Beth bit down on her lip. "Daddy, please," she cried, "don't be like this. I—I know I was cool to the possibility of a baby at first, but—well, I'm twenty, for heaven's sake. How did you expect me to react?'' Jonas opened his mouth but before he could answer she went on, earnestly, ''I've had *all* your love for those twenty years. I...I guess I thought of you as my exclusive property. But Valerie can tell you that over these last few weeks we have become friends, and, well, I was kind of hoping for a brother or sister.'' When he didn't reply, Mary Beth reached out to grasp his arm. No longer even trying to contain her tears she sobbed, ''Daddy, you *have* to believe me. I never, never wanted anything like this to happen.''

What she said was true, he realized. She *had* had his love exclusively—with the exception of Marge—for the entire time she had been on this earth. Her reaction to his remarriage, and to his statement about another heir, had been completely normal. You're lashing out in fear, Thorne, he told himself wryly. Placing the cup on the windowsill with one hand, Jonas reached out with the other to draw his daughter to him. ''Okay, okay, honey, don't cry. I'm sorry I snapped at you, I'm a little worried and not thinking too clearly.''

Her arms clasped tightly around his waist, her forehead resting against his knit shirt, Mary Beth was just beginning to feel secure again when his words registered. Swallowing a half sob, she looked up at him wide-eyed. ''What do you mean? Why are you worried? Valerie *is* going to be all right, isn't she?''

''I don't know, honey.'' Unconsciously his arms tightened around her slim form. ''It's taking so damned long.'' Jonas sighed. ''I just don't know.''

Her eyes wide with amazement, Mary Beth stared

up at her father in astonishment. "You're in love with her!" she exclaimed softly. "You really are in love with her!"

Jonas fully understood her astonishment; he had been acting like anything but a man in love. But that didn't mean he was going to share his thoughts with Mary Beth. Arching his oddly dark brows, he asked, "Had you thought I wasn't?"

"Well…" She paused, then went on quickly. "Mother said that you were getting scared."

"Scared?" His brows went up further.

"About," Mary Beth bit her lip, suddenly sorry she'd mentioned her mother. "Well, about losing your youth."

"She said *what?*" Jonas laughed without humor.

"She said that you were probably getting edgy about getting close to forty, and that's why you married a woman so much younger than yourself. She said it happens to a lot of men, and that the marriages seldom work."

"And of course your mother's an expert on what it takes to make a marriage work." Jonas again laughed without humor.

"Well, kid, I've got a news flash for your mother. The threat of reaching forty bothers me not at all, and the difference between Val's age and mine never even entered my mind. And as far as our marriage goes, let me assure you, it will work." Brave words, Thorne, he chided himself. Yet he knew that if it was at all up to him the marriage would survive. If *she* does, he amended.

"Dad?" Mary Beth's soft voice broke into his

thoughts. "Do you think we should call Gram? She's concerned too, you know. She really likes Val."

"I know." Releasing her he turned to pour more coffee into the steel cup. "I think we'll wait until I've talked to Milt. There's no point in getting your grandmother upset needlessly. For all I know about this sort of thing, *I* may be worrying needlessly." He raked his hand through already disheveled hair, then asked, "Do me a favor, honey, and go see if you can find me a pack of cigarettes."

As she swung out of the room Jonas drained the cup of coffee Marge had laced with whiskey and poured what was left in the thermos into the cup. Taking a sip he silently thanked Marge for the whiskey. It helped, but not much. What *was* taking so long? If he didn't hear something soon he'd start raising some hell. No, Thorne, he advised himself sternly, raising hell won't help a bit. And if she does die nothing is going to help.

Jonas moved uncomfortably, not liking the sensation of fear that gripped his insides at this last thought. He was making his fourteenth circuit of the room when Mary Beth came back.

"Still no word?" she asked unnecessarily.

"No," Jonas shook his head. "Nothing."

"I'm sorry I took so long," she apologized as he brought the flame of his lighter to the end of a cigarette. "But I took a minute to call Jean-Paul."

The sharp click of the lighter sounded loud in the quiet room. "You did what?" Jonas asked in an ominously soft voice.

"I said I called Jean-Paul," Mary Beth repeated,

missing the edge in his tone. "He loves her too, you know."

"I had an idea he did." Jonas's voice had become raspy. Drawing deeply on the cigarette, he thought of all the times she had been with the Frenchman during the last weeks. Had she, he wondered, transferred her love for Etienne to the brother whose voice and manner were like his?

Jean-Paul can't have her. The thought seared into his mind like a hot flame, only to be followed by one that chilled him: Can I keep her if she decides to go to him? A wave of fierce possessiveness swept over him and he dragged deeply on the cigarette to hide his reaction from Mary Beth. Lord, just thinking about her leaving gave him the shakes. She isn't only under my skin, he thought hollowly, she's in my blood.

"Dad?" Mary Beth's sharp tone broke into his circling thoughts.

"Are you listening to me? I said Jean-Paul asked if one of us would call as soon as we hear anything."

Jonas swore to himself savagely. I could strangle the idiot and he calmly requests that I call him. Call him? I'll fire him.

"Dad?" Mary Beth repeated worriedly, obviously thinking he had not heard her the first time.

Deciding to leave her in the dark, Jonas looked at her blankly. "What did you say?"

"I said Jean-Paul is very concerned and he asked if we'd call him when we hear something."

"Yeah, okay, if we ever do hear anything." Swinging away from her he strode to the door and shouldered his way into the hall. He was just in time to catch sight of a nurse as she disappeared into an office. Lord, the place was as quiet as a morgue. That thought sent him back into the waiting room.

"Dad, you're making me nervous with your prowling back and forth. Sit down and talk to me," Mary Beth coaxed.

"What do you want me to talk about?" Jonas grimaced as he lowered his long frame into a molded plastic chair.

"You, and Valerie." Jonas stiffened visibly and she went on hurriedly, "Don't close me out, Dad, please."

"What, exactly, do you want to know," Jonas sighed.

"Well, for one, why didn't you make it plain from the beginning how you felt about Val?" Jonas moved to get up and she placed a staying hand on his tautly held arm. "Don't you see that if you had, I very probably would have accepted the news of your marriage a lot more easily?"

"Perhaps," Jonas conceded.

"And surely you realize that Mother would not have built up her hopes of a reconciliation with you if…"

"Wait a minute," Jonas cut in sharply. "Are you telling me that's why she came to the States?"

"Yes, of course," Mary Beth insisted. "When she found out that you sent Maria Cinelli packing she…"

"How did she find that out?" Jonas again interrupted.

"She said that a friend had mentioned it in a letter," Mary Beth explained. "Anyway, when she found out, she canceled our plans to go cruising. She told me she thought you were probably tired of the swinging life and were ready to settle down.'' At that point Jonas attempted to cut in again, but she held up her hand in a silent bid to be allowed to finish. ''I guess I had myself convinced she was right and was all set for an announcement of your remarriage. That's why I was so shocked when you introduced Val as your wife.''

''You should have known better,'' Jonas snapped in exasperation. ''You know I don't love Lynn. If you want the truth, I never did love her. You're old enough to count. You know why I married her in the first place.'' At her pained expression he stood up and pulled her into his arms. ''Honey, I've never been sorry you were conceived. But that doesn't change the facts. I never would have considered marrying her otherwise. I tolerate her for you and your grand-mother.''

''I suppose I always knew that.'' Mary Beth smiled tremulously. ''And I'm really not sorry you married Val. I've come to like her very much these last few weeks.''

Dropping his arms Jonas walked to take his place at the window. ''I'm glad you like her, but it wouldn't have made any difference whether you did or not, I hope you realize that.''

Mary Beth smiled ruefully. ''I've known you a long time, remember? I've always known that you do exactly as you please, no matter what I, or anyone else, thinks.'' She hesitated a moment, then decided to brave his anger by asking, ''Does she love you, Dad?''

''No.'' Jonas said bluntly, grimly. ''But I knew that

when I asked her to marry me." A teasing smile curled up the corners of his mouth. "Any other questions, nosey kid?"

"No." Mary Beth shook her head. "And I'm sorry, Dad, I wasn't prying, honestly."

Jonas smoked one cigarette after the other as the minutes dragged slowly by.

"Why don't you go on home, sweetheart," he told Mary Beth as he crushed out his fourth. Then, immediately lighting another, he rasped, "Where the hell is Milt?"

And at that moment, as if in answer to his question, Milt Abramowitz pushed open the waiting room door.

"She's all right," he said at once. "But we lost the baby. I'm sorry, Jonas."

Expelling his breath slowly, Jonas nodded. "I am too. Are you sure Valerie's going to be all right?"

Even though Milt heard the anxious edge in Jonas's tone, he snapped, "Do I question your knowledge of electronics? She is weak, but she will be fine."

"Okay, Milt, I'm sorry. But what took so long?"

"I work slow, but I work neat," Milt drawled in a tone that had infuriated more than one of his patients' husbands.

Jonas was not infuriated. Like Milt, he didn't like his judgment questioned by a layman either. "I said I was sorry, Milt. May I see her?"

"In a few minutes. And I'm sorry too," Milt sighed. "I sometimes get frustrated when I can't do anything to save a baby a woman wants very badly." He sighed again. "At least there was no permanent damage."

"She can have more children?"

"Yes," Milt assured Jonas, then cautioned. "But not right away. Be careful for a while."

He turned to leave and Jonas said softly, "Thanks, Milt."

Turning back, Milt threw him a wide, crooked-toothed grin. "You'll get my bill."

Chapter 12

Valerie lay unmoving on the bed ignoring the tears that rolled down her face. Her baby was gone, leaving in its stead an emptiness; not only in her body, but in her mind, as well. She didn't move an inch when the door to her room opened, but a spark of recognition entered her eyes when Jonas crossed her line of vision.

"Valerie, why are you crying? Are you in pain?" Jonas asked sharply.

His tone was too sharp; the flow of tears doubled.

"Valerie, answer me!" he ordered. "If you're in pain I'll get Milt."

"What's wrong with me, Jonas?" Valerie whispered as he reached for the button to ring for the nurse.

"Wrong?" Jonas repeated confusedly; surely she knew that the baby was gone? "Nothing's *wrong* Val.

Milt assured me, not ten minutes ago, that you will be fine. All you need is rest.''

"No," her head moved restlessly on the pillow. "What's wrong with *me?* Why do I lose everyone I love?"

"Valerie, stop," Jonas said softly. Bending over he clasped her upper arms gently. "You can have ano…''

"First my father," she cried over his quiet, unheard voice. Then my mother. Then my grandparents. Then…then Etienne," she sobbed, unmindful of the tightening of his fingers. "And now my baby." Gazing up at his blurred features, she cried, "Why, Jonas, why? What have I done that I must be punished this way?"

"That's nonsense," he said in a crooning tone. "You aren't being punished."

"Then why do I lose everyone I love?" she choked. "Even y—" Valerie caught back the word "you" just in time; she was distraught, but not *that* distraught. *He* had never been hers *to* lose. "Even my b-baby," she wailed.

"It was an accident," he soothed. "A stupid accident." Sitting down on the side of the bed he gathered her into his arms and held her shaking body close to his chest.

"Jonas, I'm never going to hold my baby in my arms," Valerie sobbed.

"*Our* baby," he admonished softly. His meaning was lost on Valerie, who was now sobbing uncontrollably. For a fleeting moment Jonas hesitated, then, kicking off his handmade loafers, he slid onto the bed beside her and pulled her tightly against him.

"Hush," he crooned. "I'm here. Rest, Val. I'll hold you while you rest."

Slowly, comforted by his crooning voice and his hand gently smoothing back her hair, Valerie stopped crying. Secure in his arms, lulled by his even breathing, she was beginning to drift into sleep when the door opened and she heard a nurse exclaim:

"What do you think you're doing?"

"Get out of here, nurse," Jonas growled softly.

The nurse gasped then sputtered, "But you...you can't lie on the bed like that. If you don't get up—at once—I'll have to call security and have you removed."

Stirring fitfully, Valerie felt tears come to her eyes again. It was childish, she knew, but right now his arms were a haven she needed very badly, a haven she was not yet ready to leave.

"Don't go away." Valerie's plea sounded every bit as insecure as the need that prompted it.

"I'm not going anywhere," Jonas assured her softly. Then he said with hard authority, "Nurse, call Doctor Abramowitz and tell your tale of woe to him. You can also tell him that I said I'm not moving. Now get out of here."

"But..." the nurse got no further, for Jonas was not about to argue.

"Out."

His bark sent the nurse into retreat with a rustle of her starched skirt and a grumble about arrogant men. That she *would* call Milt, Valerie had very little doubt. That Milt would more than likely tell her to keep out of the room, *Jonas* had very little doubt.

Loosening his hold on her, he murmured, "Move

over,'' and when she had done so he settled his long
length more comfortably in the narrow bed. Then,
drawing her close to him again, he ordered softly,
''Now go to sleep, Val. I'll be here.''

When she woke, some three hours later, she was
alone in the bed. Jonas was gone, leaving her to wonder if, perhaps, in her sedated, befuddled state, she
had imagined he'd been there in the first place. Her
mind now clear and alert, she found it hard to believe
he had chosen to defy convention to the point of
crawling into a hospital bed with her. Still weary in
body, if not in mind, she pushed the speculation aside
and rang for a nurse. She felt grubby; she wanted a
bath and a hairbrush.

Determined to get well, if only to get away from
the antiseptic smell of the hospital, Valerie recovered
swiftly. Surrounded by an entourage consisting of
Jonas, Mary Beth, Marge, and Lyle, Valerie left the
confines of the hospital on a bright, warm morning in
late June, eagerly breathing in the scent of flowers in
the fresh air.

Buoyant with renewed energy, she breezed into the
house with a confidence that was immediately shattered by the drawling voice of Lynn Varga.

''Well, the little near-mother is back. How—ah—
nice.''

''That's enough, Lynn.'' Jonas's voice, sounding
at once both tired and indifferent, slashed across the
gasps from Mary Beth and Marge and the muttered
curse from Lyle. Turning his back on the elegant form
of his first wife, he bent and scooped the now
stricken-faced Valerie effortlessly into his arms. As

he started up the steps he shot over his shoulder, "If you haven't enough manners to be pleasant to your hostess, then you'd better leave. Go spend some more of my money on something you don't need." He came to a full stop on the landing at the top of the short flight of stairs and stared down into Valerie's hurt-filled eyes, whispering for her eyes alone, "My—*wife*—has no use for my money."

With those words, all the hope Valerie had allowed herself to begin harboring rushed out of her, leaving her feeling defeated and tired. When she looked away from him without response, Jonas sighed and continued into their bedroom to place her gently on top of the bed. "You'd do well to stay there," he cautioned, "at least for a day or two." With that he turned and left.

They were back to square one, Valerie decided morosely as she listened to the fading sound of his car's engine. By the end of her first full week at home she was forced to face the fact that things between them were worse now than they had been before her stay in the hospital. At least then they had shared a bed. Now, with her health restored and all physical restrictions removed, Jonas treated her like a guest in the house that was supposedly her home. He was polite. He was considerate. He was a stranger.

For two weeks Valerie tormented herself with thoughts of what she had thrown away. Over and over she relived the events of that afternoon. Repeatedly she heard his cold voice demanding, "What are you carrying? A young Thorne or another DeBron?" Another DeBron. Valerie shivered. He actually believed that she would...she shivered again. And over and

over, the thought growing stronger each time it occurred, Valerie came to the decision that she could
not stay with a man who believed her capable of that
kind of deceit.

As the days changed from pleasantly warm to uncomfortably hot Valerie withdrew to the air-
conditioned comfort of what was now *her* bedroom.
Jonas had moved into the guest room on the day he
brought her home from the hospital, saying he didn't
want to disturb her rest with his comings and goings.

By the middle of July, feeling rejected, useless and
defeated, Valerie seldom came out of her bedroom.
And then Jonas announced that he was leaving for
Houston the following Monday and had no idea how
long he would be gone. Her nails digging into her
palm, Valerie turned away from him with a shrug,
missing the expression of hopelessness that washed
over his face.

The next morning Janet breezed into Valerie's bedroom without bothering to knock.

"Janet!" Valerie exclaimed, "What are you..."

"Val, honey," Janet cut her off impatiently. "I
know losing this baby was a shock for you, but you
absolutely cannot do this to yourself again."

Again? Do what again? Valerie, not thinking too
clearly, didn't have the vaguest idea what Janet was
talking about. "What do you mean?" she frowned.

"You know perfectly well what I mean," Janet
retorted. "It's Paris all over again, isn't it? I knew it
when Mary Beth called me and said you weren't seeing anyone, not even her and Jean-Paul." She sighed
with exasperation. "Honey, I know how you must

feel, but it's not the same as losing Etienne. You *can* have another baby."

Not by sleeping alone! Valerie thought bitterly. So, they all believed her to be in mourning for her lost child! Did Jonas believe the same? Did it matter anymore?

"Valerie, talk to me," Janet demanded. "Don't close yourself away like this."

"It's not only my baby," Valerie murmured, groping for a plausible reason for her attitude. Then a germ of an idea stirred. "I...I'm concerned for my mother. She's due any time now, and, well, she's not a young woman."

"Well, for heaven's sake!" Janet cried. "If that's what's bothering you, go see her. I'm sure Jonas would understand."

I'm sure Jonas couldn't care less, Valerie retorted silently. But Janet's suggestion was a good one. She *would* go to Australia, and maybe she'd just forget to come back.

"If I go now," Valerie said slowly, "I could be with her when the baby comes."

"And it would be the perfect time to go." Janet smiled, satisfied with Valerie's show of animation. "I mean, since Jonas will be in Houston for at least a week."

When Janet left, obviously much easier in her mind about her friend, Valerie coolly picked up the phone and punched out the number to Jonas's private line.

"Are you all right?" he said urgently the minute she said hello.

"Yes, I'm fine," Valerie replied, wondering if his

show of concern was genuine. "I...I was wondering if you would be home for dinner tonight?"

"Are you eating dinner tonight?" he asked quietly. The question was not as strange as it might have seemed. Valerie's eating habits lately had been erratic and she and Jonas had not shared a meal in nearly two weeks.

"Yes," she sighed. "And, if you have time, there's something I'd like to discuss with you."

"I'll make time," Jonas promised. "In fact, I'll come home early."

As she hung up the receiver, Valerie smiled sadly at the thought that she actually had to make an appointment to talk to her husband.

As she waited uneasily for dinnertime to arrive, Valerie was prey to all sorts of doubts and regrets: What if she had carried the child full term, would his cool manner toward her have warmed? What if she had told him, straight out, that she was in love with him, would he have treated her less like the secretary she had been and more like the wife she supposedly was? If they had discussed the loss of the child and what had precipitated it, would the strain between them have been eased? It was all a pointless exercise in frustration, as there was no way Valerie could answer any of her own questions. Only Jonas himself could do that.

Thoroughly sick of her own thoughts, Valerie heaved a deep sigh of relief when she heard his car come to a stop in front of the garage. Her pulse beginning to flutter with apprehension, she listened as he took the outside stairs two at a time and strode along the deck to their private entrance. Through the glass his form was bathed in a golden glow from the afternoon sun and she caught her breath in appreciation of the tall, deceptively slim-looking magnificence of him.

Was she completely out of her mind? she asked herself in wonder. He was a part of her now; the largest part. How could she face a life that did not include the sight of him each day? Oh, wasn't there some way she could remain with him?

Jonas began speaking even as he closed the door behind him.

"If you've called me home to tell me that you are pregnant again, I swear I'll strangle you, Valerie."

"That I'm..." Valerie gasped, totally missing the underlying note of fear in his voice. "Jonas, you know that isn't possible, we haven't even..." She came to an abrupt halt, her eyes widening. He had done it again! Not as crudely this time, but every bit as hurtfully. What did he hope to gain with these groundless accusations? Good Lord, she had only left the hospital a little over a month ago! She had not even been out of the house except to have lunch with Mary Beth and Jean-Paul at the end of her first week home. Jean-Paul! He still believed that she and Jean-Paul... Valerie shuddered, refusing even to finish the thought. Biting back the outraged protest she longed to fling at him, she forced her tone into cool unconcern.

"The reason I requested a moment of your precious time," she managed acidly, "was to inform you of my plans."

"Plans?" Jonas repeated warily. "What plans?"

"I—" Valerie hesitated, then plunged. "I'm going

to Australia to be with my mother when she delivers.''

''You're worried about her?''

Why, she wondered, did he have to voice even the most simple of questions in such an arrogant, demanding tone? ''Of course I'm worried,'' she snapped, refusing to let him see how his tone had hurt her. ''She's past the *safe* childbearing age. If,'' she swallowed against the sudden tightness in her throat, ''there *is* a safe childbearing age. She put on a good act the last time I talked to her on the phone, but she's scared, I know it, and I want to be with her.''

''All right, Val.'' Jonas surprised her by agreeing. ''You may go. I'll give you one month longer.''

I may? Valerie seethed. I may? Big deal! Would this man never stop treating her like one of the employees? ''I didn't ask for your permission, Jonas,'' Valerie flared. ''I have reservations to fly to San Francisco tomorrow afternoon whether you approve or...'' Valerie's voice faded as his last statement registered. ''What do you mean, you'll give me one month longer?''

''Exactly what I say,'' Jonas retorted grimly. ''One month to the day that you walk out of this house I will expect you to walk back in again.''

''But—'' Valerie paused, searching for words. What was he up to now? They had barely spoken to each other in weeks. Was he attempting to exercise his authority over her now? The very idea angered her. ''Why do you persist in speaking to me as though I was still your secretary?'' she demanded. ''I am leaving this house tomorrow. I will come back when

I'm ready...if at all." Head up, back straight, she started for the door.

Long, hard fingers curled around her upper arm to bring her to a stumbling halt. Pulling her to him he slid the fingers and palm of his other hand along her jaw, holding her head still. "If you know what's good for you, you will do as you're told," he murmured menacingly, his fingers spearing into the hair behind her ear. "I said you have one month and that is exactly what I meant." Using the heel of his hand, he jerked her head up so he could see her eyes. "Do you understand?"

"You don't frighten me," Valerie lied, trying to pull her head away from his hand.

"No?" Jonas smiled humorlessly. Slowly, deliberately, he dug his fingers into her scalp, pressing against the side of her face with his palm. "You'd be wise to be a little frightened, Val." His hand exerted more pressure.

Sucking in a quick gasp, Valerie stared at him mutely, disbelievingly. Never before had Jonas used his superior strength to deliberately hurt her. Angry, stubbornly refusing to cry out against the pain, Valerie glared at him rebelliously. Jonas was obviously unimpressed.

"One month, Valerie," Jonas growled as he lowered his head to hers. "And if you are not here at the end of that month, I will come after you."

His mouth came down onto hers, driving the breath back into her throat. For a second, panicked, Valerie struggled to tear her lips from under his. Releasing her arm, he slid his freed hand around her waist as he turned his body to hers. Spreading his fingers, he moved his hand down to the base of her spine, then, drawing her body against his, he coiled his long fingers around her neck.

His hand was still hurtful, but in a new, strangely sensuous way. The deep core of passion that only this man could tap answered the demand his hardened, aroused body was making on hers. Moaning softly, deep in her throat, she encircled his waist with her arms and arched herself to him.

"You will come back in a month, won't you?" Jonas demanded, dropping biting kisses on her lips as he spoke.

"Jonas, stop," Valerie moaned, not even believing the command herself. Wildfire raced through her veins. Her arms tightened convulsively when his tongue caressed the spots his teeth had so recently bitten.

"Wh—why are you doing this—now?" Valerie gasped, her breath coming unevenly.

"I have given you time repeatedly, and still you ask for more," Jonas muttered. "This additional month has a price tag, a high one. If you want to go badly enough you'll pay it."

Her mind cloudy with the devastation his mouth was inflicting, Valerie didn't understand a word he said, but, at the moment, she didn't care either. Greedily, she opened her mouth to his tongue as her hands slid down his back to grasp his buttocks and pull him tightly against her.

"You must want to go very badly," Jonas murmured thickly, confusing her even more. But then all thought fled at the electrifying thrust he made with his hips.

She had to have him. Nothing else mattered, nothing else had any importance. Valerie's hands slipped between their fused bodies to fumble shakily with his belt buckle. He liked that. Keeping his mouth clamped onto hers, he took a half step back to allow her hands freedom of motion. Loosening his grip on her neck, he moved his hand slowly down the front of her body, wringing soft moans from her as he did so.

"Can you wait to undress?" he growled into her mouth. Valerie answered him by outlining his lips with her tongue. "Neither can I," he groaned, drawing her with him onto the floor. Always before he had come to her with a slowness that drew out the moment to exquisite torture. Now, he took her with a voracious hunger born of his overwhelming need. Somewhere in the depths of her consciousness Valerie knew she should protest his violence. Instead, she met it with an answering violence of her own.

"Remember, Val," Jonas warned softly as he lay spent beside her. "You have one month."

Lying wakeful and restless in the spare room in her mother's house in Sydney, one day before that month was up, Valerie could hear again Jonas's whispered warning, could feel his lips brush her skin as he spoke. A shiver feathered her shoulders and she pulled the blankets closer around her. But it wasn't the air from the cold night that had caused the chill, and she knew it. The memory of the near savage way Jonas had made love to her, drawing her to him again and again long into the early hours of the morning, had caused repeated shivers during the last four weeks.

Edwin and her mother, looking radiant with happiness, had welcomed Valerie with open arms as she staggered from the plane after the seemingly endless flight. Three days after her daughter's arrival in Australia, Celia had given birth to a squalling, healthy son.

Even though Valerie had filled her days to the limit getting reacquainted with her mother, helping to care for her captivating new brother, and sightseeing, the hours and days and weeks seemed to drag by. She missed Jonas more than she would have believed possible.

He had sent flowers in response to Valerie's telegram about the arrival of the baby, but she had heard nothing more from him.

Unable to sleep, Valerie fought a silent battle with herself. When she had driven away from Jonas's house, it had been with the intention of never returning. Yet, as each day passed without a word from him, her resolve wavered. Impatiently, she told herself she was a fool to even consider going back. Jonas was arrogant, infuriating, domineering. He was also straightforward, honest, generous, and, at times, gentle. And, whether she wanted to or not, she loved him.

Suddenly Valerie could see herself, years from now, drifting from man to man in the hope of finding one who could blot Jonas out of her memory. Shuddering at the vivid images her restless mind projected, she scrambled out of bed to stare out the window.

By the time she slid tiredly back into bed over two hours later, Valerie's mind was made up. She was going home. Jonas had told her, months ago, to face reality. For Valerie, Jonas *was* reality, and she was going to face him, be honest with him, and find out, once and for all, if there was a marriage between them.

Chapter 13

She's not coming back.

The words rang inside Jonas's head like a death knell. As he had months previously, Jonas stood, taut and tense, staring out the window behind his desk. And, in just the same manner, his fingers dug into the tight muscles in his thighs.

She is not going to come back, and I don't know what to do about it. Should I go after her? He knew the answer to that. *No.* If she was coming back at all, she was coming back because she wanted to, not because he had forced her. But, sweet Lord, he ached to bring her home.

Valerie was already two days over the one-month time limit he had given her, and every nerve in his body felt drawn to the breaking point.

Absentmindedly he slid his right hand out of his pocket and lifted it to his midsection, where he unconsciously began to knead the area over his stomach. Jonas became aware of the action of his hand at the same moment he became aware of the burning sensation in his stomach.

"Damn."

Muttering the word aloud, he spun about and yanked open the top drawer of his desk. Taking out a small bottle, he unscrewed the cap, shook out two tablets, and popped them into his mouth.

All he needed at this point was an ulcer, he thought, chewing methodically. Grimacing, he turned back to his perusal of the parking lot. He really could not afford to waste time staring blankly out the window. He knew it, and yet he made no attempt to move.

As the tablets began to have an effect and the burning sensation eased, Jonas let his hand drop to his side. There was no ulcer yet, but the doctor had warned him he was on the right track. Jonas's lips twisted wryly as he remembered the doctor's exact words.

"Jonas, the nerves in your stomach are working overtime. If you don't slow down they are going to work a hole in the lining of your guts." Mike Slater, internist, had always thought he was something of a comedian. "The rest of your body's not faring a whole lot better, either. Lord, you high-powered types are going to make me a very rich man some day."

Jonas had agreed to watch his diet and take the medication Mike prescribed. He refused to cut down on his working hours. That had been two weeks ago. No one, not even Mary Beth or Marge, knew that Jonas had had cause to see a doctor, and, as far as Jonas was concerned, no one need ever know.

If Valerie had been home he might have told her. The thought stiffened his back. Never in all his thirty-nine years had he considered confiding in someone else that way.

The pain was completely gone now, and still he made no move. Good going, Thorne, he charged himself scathingly. Every move you made was wrong, starting with that blundering excuse of a proposal, and ending with that stupid ultimatum. No, scratch that, ending with the hell you put her through the last night.

A shudder of sexual excitement rippled through the entire length of his body and Jonas cursed softly. Lord, just thinking about that night brought him to aching arousal. The mere *memory* of her had the power to affect him more than the actuality of any other woman; Jonas had proof of that.

Lips twisting in self-mockery, Jonas called forth the memory of Maria's last day as his secretary. In his mind's eye he could see the confident smile she'd displayed when she'd strolled into his office. Had he given her reason to think he was ready for some extramarital fun and games? Jonas shook his head sharply; he had not. What was it with women, he wondered, that they insisted in living in realms all of their own creation? Again his head moved sharply. Valerie's fantasyland was populated by only one man, Etienne DeBron, the faceless enemy Jonas did not know how to fight.

Feeling his fingers curling into tight fists, Jonas forced his thoughts back to that last encounter with Maria just three days earlier. He had dictated several letters, and when he was through, Maria had caught her heel in the carpet on the way out of the office. Jumping out of his chair, he'd hurried over to her. With his arm supporting her, he'd helped her to the long white couch.

"Let's get that shoe off and have a look," he'd said, dropping to one knee in front of her and reaching for her left foot.

"Jonas, darling."

His name had whispered from her lips while her hand stole caressingly into his hair. Caught completely off guard, he'd glanced up in surprise as she bent to him. Not even to himself would he deny the stirring of response he'd felt at the touch of her hot, red mouth, her probing tongue. Yet, even as his body moved toward hers and his hands reached for her, an image of Val flashed through his mind. When his hands grasped her shoulders it was to push her away instead of pulling her close. It had been more than a month since he'd made love to Val and he had need of a woman, but, strangely, any woman would not do. He wanted just one woman, and that one was surely not Maria. He wanted Val, and only Val. What he would do if she never came back to him, he couldn't begin to imagine. Maybe, in time…Jonas closed his eyes against the jolt of fear his own thoughts caused.

Dammit, it was an impossible situation. Opening his eyes to narrow slits, he stared in disbelief at his trembling hands. Why, he berated himself, why hadn't he taken Maria right then and there? You know why, you fool. Because that couch is reserved for one woman only. And you love that woman with every inch of your body, and every cell of your mind. Forcing his thoughts away from the vision of his black-haired, violet-eyed tormenter, Jonas recreated the scene that had followed his rejection of Maria.

"What's the matter with you?" Maria had demanded in a stunned tone. "It was always good for us, wasn't it?"

"The operative word is *was* Maria," he'd replied quietly. "I'm a married man now."

"Really?" she'd sneered. "So where's your bride? Down under playing footsie with some rugged Aussie?"

Getting to his feet, Jonas had stepped back to run his eyes over her in cold appraisal. What had he ever seen in her? The answer was obvious. Maria was a good-looking woman, intelligent, clever, sometimes witty, in a biting sort of way, and a regular wildwoman in bed—which Jonas admitted without shame, had been her biggest attraction. What the hell, he was a man.

He was also fully aware of the fact that she had destroyed what little they had had going for them when she'd walked out on him. She had wanted the position of secretary *and* lover. Her mistake had been in thinking she could call the tune simply because he danced with her. She had not been the first woman to make that mistake. Jonas had *never* needed her. He didn't need her now.

"Clean our your desk and get out of here," he'd ordered her with deadly quiet.

"But—I..." Maria had sputtered in disbelief, then her red lips twisted nastily. "Oh, I get it. You don't need me *or* your little bride, do you? Not as long as you have Lynn living in your house. No wonder sweet Valerie ran for her life." Before she walked out the door, Maria paused to fire a parting shot. "You're a fool, Jonas. Don't you know that every one of your friends has slept with Lynn? She's not at all particular where she finds her loving." Then she added pityingly, "What was the problem, Jonas? Did little miss innocent Valerie object to your *ménage à trois?*"

"Out."

Jonas had not raised his voice, but the cold disgust he felt for her was evident in his tone. That had been three days ago, and yet the memory of the scene still rankled. Still more unpleasant was the scene that had happened that same night after he finally got home around ten-thirty. Mary Beth was out, again. Marge had already retired, and Lynn was waiting for him— like a spider waiting for a fly, Jonas had thought at the time.

"You look tired," she'd begun innocently enough. "Why don't you sit down while I get you a drink?" Rising with studied grace, she'd gone to the portable bar. "There is something we'd better discuss."

"Yeah?" Jonas had been tired, and certainly not in the mood for more problems. Dropping into a chair, he'd eyed the mother of his daughter disdainfully. Was she really sleeping with *every* one of his friends? he wondered disinterestedly. He hadn't realized they were all that hard up.

"It's about our daughter," Lynn said sharply, obviously aware that his thoughts had drifted.

At once alert, Jonas had straightened in his chair. "What about her?" he asked warily.

"You mean you really don't know?" She'd arched her brows. "She's sleeping with the hired help."

Lynn had smiled at the shock her statement caused. "Your *wife's* friend to be exact."

"Jean-Paul?" he'd asked very, very softly.

"Of course, Jean-Paul," she'd purred. "While you've been sleeping all alone in your empty bed, your daughter has been sleeping with your wife's lover." Her voice had then dropped to a whispered taunt. "One wonders, who is Valerie sleeping with?"

Furious, fighting the desire to slap her smirking face, Jonas had not answered. After several breathless moments, Lynn had offered, "You don't *have* to sleep alone, Jonas."

"You?" he'd asked quietly.

"Yes, of course. There's no reason why we shouldn't enjoy one another."

Come into my parlor said the spider to the fly. "You're out of your twisted mind," he'd laughed aloud. "I wouldn't touch you if you begged me for it." Getting up lazily, he'd smiled mockingly at her outraged expression.

"Where are you going?" she'd demanded as he sauntered to the door.

"Back to my office," he'd tossed over his shoulder. "At least there I don't have to worry about being disturbed by your lies."

Jonas blinked, refocusing his gaze out the window where the dusk-to-dawn lights were just beginning to dim as the pink light of morning touched the parking lot, empty of cars save for the lone silver Cadillac. He'd been right here in the office ever since, except to take his daughter to dinner the evening before.

As usual, he had come directly to the point. "Your

mother tells me you have—ah—become involved with Jean-Paul. Is it true?''

''If you mean by involved, am I going to bed with him, then the answer is yes,'' Mary Beth answered with refreshing honesty.

''I see,'' Jonas murmured, noncommittally.

''I don't think you do, Dad.'' Mary Beth shook her head. ''I love him and I'm going to marry him.''

''Does he know?'' he'd asked roughly, shocked by the mixed emotions her statement had stirred in him.

''Oh, that's cute, Dad!'' Mary Beth's voice revealed the hurt his tone had inflicted. ''Jean-Paul asked me to marry him weeks ago.'' She drew a shaky breath, then went on accusingly, ''He wanted to speak to you about it at once, but, knowing the trouble you're having with Trans Electric, I asked him to wait.'' She held up a silencing hand when he would have responded. ''Besides, I wanted to wait until Val came home...if she ever does.''

''What do you mean, *if* she comes home?'' he demanded harshly. ''Did she leave you with the impression she was not coming back?''

''No,'' she denied at once. ''But, well, it was pretty obvious to everyone that you weren't getting along. You...you do have a way of making your displeasure with someone felt without opening your mouth.''

''What is that supposed to mean?'' Jonas snapped.

''Dad, I...I...''

''Tell me,'' Jonas ordered.

''Well, you *were* giving her the cold shoulder,'' she said hesitatingly. Then she rushed on. ''Were you punishing her for losing the baby?''

Mary Beth's question had literally struck him

speechless. Was that what Val had been thinking when she'd decided to go to her mother? Had she run from his condemnation? Jonas had not answered Mary Beth's query. Instead he'd told her to ask Jean-Paul to come to his office in the morning.

Now, at six o'clock on a deceptively cool-looking summer morning, Jonas shook his head at the blunder he'd made in his campaign to awaken Valerie to reality. Totally unaware that at that very minute Valerie was landing at Philadelphia International Airport, Jonas mentally reviewed the debacle he'd made of his marriage. What had Mary Beth said? "You were giving her the cold shoulder." *He'd* thought he was being tactful and sensitive.

Sighing deeply, Jonas turned from the glare of the red sun and sat down wearily at his desk. He'd had very little sleep during the preceding two nights. He hadn't been able to sleep.

You've got to put her out of your mind, Thorne, and get to work. That is, if you can still find anything in the mess that last girl left. Loretta had not yet been able to find a replacement for Maria and a different girl had occupied the outer office every day, each more incompetent than the last.

Valerie had been very competent. Jonas groaned aloud. Always it came back to Valerie. God, he missed her. Would she ever come back? Sliding down in his chair, he rested his head against the leather back. What should he have done differently? Everything, the answer came at once. But worst of all had been his attitude toward Etienne. Why had he taunted her about him? Because he had been afraid. And he still was.

Yes, he finally admitted to himself, he was afraid of the hold Etienne's memory had on her emotions. He could still hear her asking him why she lost every-one she came to love, his own name conspicuously absent from her list. He had known from the begin-ning, of course, that she did not love him. But he had honestly thought that he could make her aware of him as a husband in every sense of the word, not just in bed.

And sexually, their relationship had been extremely satisfying. Again the memory of their last night to-gether rose in his mind to torment him. God, he had used her without compunction, and he had loved every minute of it. A sudden thought sent a thrill of excitement through his mind. What if he had made her pregnant again? Would that bring her home? Hope burned fiercely for a few moments before he recalled the agony of waiting for word of her condi-tion when she'd miscarried. Milt had warned him about not getting her pregnant too soon! A cold sweat sprang out on his upper lip. God! I hope she's all right! Moving uncomfortably, Jonas heard her voice crying to him, felt her body trembling in his arms as she sobbed out her grief.

There's a reason your plan didn't work, Thorne. You are by far too damned arrogant. While *you* thought you were giving her time to get over the mis-carriage, everyone else, very likely Val included, thought you were punishing her. While *you* assumed that, given time, she would welcome you back into her bed, she probably thought you had washed your hands of the marriage. Would she even consent to speak to him if he called her? Jonas doubted it. And he really couldn't blame her. Should he go after her? Try to make some kind of a deal?

Jonas shook his head in wonder at himself. He was actually thinking as though she were a corporation instead of a woman. Well, an errant grin slashed his thin lips, he wanted to merge, didn't he?

You're walking pretty close to the edge, Thorne, he advised himself seriously. Think about something else. But what? Mary Beth. Jean-Paul.

What would he say to the Frenchman when he came to his office later this morning? What *could* he say? Mary Beth was an adult; she didn't need his approval if she chose to marry a man he did not like. But then, he didn't dislike Jean-Paul. That had been part of his problem. Even when he had thought there was a liaison between Val and Jean-Paul he could not dislike the man. Lord, but he had wanted to.

So, you caution the man about the care of your daughter, and then you shake his hand and wish him well. Nothing hard about that. And if he presumes to ask questions about Val and your own marriage? Simple, you control the urge to rap him in the mouth, and tell him nothing.

Beginning to fear for his sanity, Jonas pulled a folder to the center of his desk and opened it. Within minutes, the technical jargon had caught his attention. When he closed the folder over an hour and a half later his eyes ached with fatigue. Still mulling over the information he'd read, he rested his head against the soft leather back of his chair. Less than five minutes later he was sound asleep.

Jonas had had the dream several times over the last month. Sweating, his head moving restlessly, he fought to free himself from the coils of unwanted sleep. The dream persisted, and once again he stood at the window in the hospital waiting room, sick with fear for Valerie. At his feet was a large pool of blood and at the door Milt stared at him accusingly, while behind him a nurse screamed, "She's dead, and it's your fault. You should have left her in Paris. Then she'd still be alive." His eyes wide with horror, Jonas watched, unable to move as a stretcher was wheeled down the hall, and although the form on it was shrouded, he knew it was Valerie.

A brisk tapping sound brought him awake with a jerk. His body was damp with a coating of cold sweat, and his hands had a death grip on the soft leather covering of the chair arms. Ignoring the renewed tapping at his office door, Jonas pushed himself out of the chair and went into the bathroom. Grabbing a small towel, he wiped his sweat-sheened face, tossed the towel in the sink, then walked back into his office with a growled, "Come."

At his command, Charlie's secretary opened the door a few inches and poked her small face around it.

"I'm sorry if I woke you, Jonas, but there's a call for you on line one. I wouldn't have disturbed you," she hurried on at his frown, "but it's Caradin in Washington."

"All right, Eileen." Jonas smiled an apology for his frown. As the door closed he picked up the receiver and punched the first button. "All right, George, let's have it," he said without preamble.

"You've won again, Jonas." George Caradin's

usually calm voice held a note of exaltation. "They're backing off."

A long, soundless sigh escaped through Jonas's lips before he rasped, "It's permanent this time? I don't relish the idea of having to play these games every couple of months."

"No." George's tone was confident. "I'm sure they realize the game is definitely over."

"Okay, George, thanks for the hours you put into this. Now it's back to business as usual."

"I was only doing what I get paid for, but you're welcome, Jonas." George chuckled, "I know it held you up, but I rather enjoyed the fight." He paused, then said seriously, "I'm glad I'm on your team, Jonas. You really know how to fight dirty when it comes down to the clinch."

Jonas's tone was dry as dust when he replied. "They grow them tough in the coal regions. Talk to you later, George."

George's news had completely banished the nightmare and a smile of satisfaction curved his lips as he hung up the phone. Then he went still, his hand still on the receiver. For several seconds he fought a silent battle within himself. The temptation to lift the receiver and make flight arrangements to Australia fought with his need to get back to work. Australia won. He lifted the receiver, then replaced it, sighing softly. He couldn't force her to come back. He'd tried to force her into facing life again, and instead he'd driven her away from him. He'd give her a little more time, he decided, and then, if she still had not returned, he'd go after her.

But a moment later he was snatching up the receiver and calling the airport. When he hung up again some fifteen minutes later he was booked on the late-night flight to San Francisco. The hell with it, he thought grimly, I'm bringing her home.

Jonas was still staring pensively at the phone when Eileen tapped at the door again.

"Do you want to dictate now, Jonas, or can I go take Charlie's?" she asked brightly.

"Go back to Charlie and catch up on some of your work there." Jonas waved her away. "I'm sorry about running you back and forth like this, Eileen." He smiled ruefully. "I don't know why Loretta's having such a hard time replacing Maria, but until she finds someone you're going to have to do double duty." Then he favored her with a rare grin. "I'll make it up to you in your paycheck."

"I don't mind, Jonas, really. I just hate to see everything get backed up like this." Eileen sighed over the mess the files were in. "I'll come back after lunch." With that she closed the door again.

Jonas picked up a sheaf of blue-line sheets and was engrossed in checking over them when there was another tap on the door. Wondering how he was supposed to get any work done with all the interruptions, he called, "Come in."

This time it was Jean-Paul who poked his head around the door. "You wanted to see me, *monsieur?*"

"Yes, Jean-Paul, come in." Jonas waited until he was inside the room and seated before continuing bluntly, "Mary Beth tells me you have asked her to marry you."

"Yes, sir," Jean-Paul responded at once. "I wanted to speak to you at once, but she thought it best to wait until this business with Trans Electric was cleared up.'' Jean-Paul gave a very Gallic shrug of his shoulders. ''I...I did not like seeing her without your knowledge but,'' again his shoulders lifted, ''I also did not wish to lose her.''

''Well, don't lose any sleep over it.'' Jonas smiled. ''My daughter knows exactly what she wants, and apparently, that is you. Oh, by the way,'' he added, ''that business with Trans *is* cleared up. We can get down to some serious work again.''

''But that is wonderful news!'' Jean-Paul exclaimed. ''And I get your—ah—drift?'' His eyebrows inched up his forehead. ''I will get out of here and get to work.''

''DeBron,'' Jonas said softly as the younger man reached for the doorknob.

''Monsieur?''

Jonas walked to within a foot of him. ''You *do* love her, don't you?'' he asked in the same soft tone.

''Mary Beth has become my life,'' Jean-Paul answered quietly, his eyes steady on Jonas's watchful blue-gray ones.

''Good enough.'' Jonas extended his right hand. ''You may tell her she can set the date.'' He liked Jean-Paul's strong grip. ''I hope you will be happy...Jean-Paul.''

Jonas's concession was duly noted by Jean-Paul, who grinned and assured him, ''As long as I have her, I will be...Jonas.''

What is the news of their engagement going to do to Valerie? The thought jumped into his mind as the door closed behind the Frenchman. Valerie had seemed to cling to Etienne's brother. Would she, he wondered, resent Mary Beth now? Telling himself he'd find out soon enough, he headed for the bathroom.

Uncomfortable from the fine film of sweat his dream had drawn from his body, Jonas stripped down for a shower. Stark naked, he stood in front of the medicine cabinet mirror to shave off his overnight growth of beard and brush his teeth. The pre-shower ritual completed, he stepped into the shower stall.

After a quick scrub down in hot water, Jonas slowly turned the hot water tap off. The tepid, then cool water cascaded over his body, bringing him to tingling life and sensuous awareness. Closing his eyes, Jonas had a wide-awake dream of Valerie, equally naked, stepping into the stall with him. With very little imagination, he could feel the silky touch of her skin against his own, could see her wet lips lifting to meet his hungry kiss. The low groan that was torn from his throat startled him and he turned the water off with a violent motion. Grabbing a large towel, he dried himself from head to toe as he walked into the adjoining dressing room.

Fifteen minutes later, dressed in a pristine white shirt, charcoal gray suit, and a very conservative blue-and-silver-striped tie, Jonas took one step into his office and came to a dead stop.

At the doorway to the front office, looking crisp and bright, and incredibly beautiful, stood the black-haired, violet-eyed temptress who tormented his every thought. Jonas was barely aware of the raspy sound of his own voice.

"Valerie."

Chapter 14

What would she say to him? Valerie had considered and discarded at least a dozen different opening lines. Now, with her hand raised to knock on his office door, she still had no idea what she *could* say. Somehow a simple "Hello" wasn't enough. She had been away over a month, and they had barely spoken to each other for weeks before she left. No, "Hello" was not nearly enough. Hoping that something brilliant would pop into her mind at the sight of him, Valerie rapped her knuckles against the door. Nothing. No growled "Come," no softly muttered curse, nothing.

Janet had spent hours convincing her that coming to the office was the right thing to do and he wasn't even in! Her hand falling limply to her side, Valerie made a half-turn away, then stopped. Could there possibly be a clue to his whereabouts on his desk? Before she could change her mind, she turned the knob and pushed the door open. She took two hesitant steps inside the room and came to an abrupt halt. Either he had left the water running or he was in the shower— and Valerie knew he had not left the water running. Mortals did dumb things like that, not Jonas Thorne.

He was here. In that bathroom. And she still did not know what she would say to him. For a delirious instant Valerie had the wild urge to rip off her clothes and join him under the spray. The urge died as quickly as it had sprung to life. Supposing he didn't want her, or worse yet, supposing he was not alone! Valerie did a quick inventory of the large room. The desk was in its usual state of disarray, cluttered with loose papers, folders, and blue-line drawings. Nothing significant there. Compared to the desk, the rest of the room looked stark in its neatness. Her sharp-eyed perusal found no sign of a woman, which still did not prove there was none.

Well, she thought, at least I'm prepared for a surprise, *he* isn't. Then, in self-disgust, she took herself to task; it is not yet nine o'clock in the morning—of course he's alone. The urge to retreat subsided, but she did not move out of the doorway. Glancing over her shoulder she gave the front office a quick survey. It looked neat enough, yet Janet had said it was in a mess. Had she lied to get her to come in?

Leaning back against the door frame, Valerie recalled the events of her morning from the time she'd left the airport around six.

Unsure of her welcome at home, she had decided while still on the plane that she would go to Janet's apartment first. After the long flight the cab ride to

Janet's had seemed amazingly short. Janet welcomed her with a delighted smile and open arms.

"Val, honey!" she'd exclaimed, after hugging the breath out of her. "Why didn't you let me know you were coming home? When did you get in?" But before Valerie could answer, Janet saw the suitcases in the hall. "Good grief! Haven't you been home?"

"No." Valerie shook her head. "I...I don't know yet if I'm going back h...to the house."

"Get in here at once," Janet ordered. When the door was closed she said grimly, "What do you mean you aren't sure? You aren't thinking of leaving Jonas, are you?" But again she didn't give Valerie time to answer as she drew her into the kitchen with another question. "Would you like some breakfast?"

"Just coffee, please, I had breakfast on the plane. And, to answer your question, I don't know what to think about Jonas," Valerie said steadily.

Placing a cup of steaming coffee in front of Valerie, Janet frowned. "I don't understand, why don't you know what to think about Jonas?"

"Just that." Valerie shrugged. "I don't know if he *wants* me to come back to the house. I haven't heard a word from him since I left, Janet."

"Nothing?" Janet asked sharply.

"Oh, he sent flowers to my mother after I telegraphed the news of the baby's arrival, but he never wrote or called."

"You telegraphed!" Janet exclaimed. "Why in the world didn't you call?"

"Because I didn't know what to say," Valerie replied calmly.

Janet was far from calm. "Val, that doesn't make

sense. Jonas is your husband. He…'' Her voice faded, then came back in a whisper. "Had you left him? I mean, for good?"

"I…" Valerie hesitated before admitting, "Yes."

"Oh, boy," Janet sighed. "Do you want to tell me why?"

"It just wasn't working," Valerie answered defeatedly. "We were barely speaking to each other when I left. I…I had to get away, Janet."

"And now?" she probed.

"Oh, I don't know." Valerie sipped at the hot drink. "I had some wild idea about trying to talk things out but—"

"Go on," Janet insisted. "But…what?"

"But I guess I'm afraid of what he might say." Valerie shook her head.

"You won't know, though, unless you do talk to him," Janet urged. "Go see him, tell him how you feel." A crafty smile curved her lips. "And I have the perfect plan of action for you to follow."

"What plan?" Valerie asked warily.

"He needs a secretary." Janet grinned.

"Why do I get the feeling that this is where I came in?" Valerie groaned. "What do you mean he needs a secretary? What happened to Maria?"

"She's gone." Holding up a silencing hand, she added, "I don't know why or how but she is gone. She took off a couple of days ago." Her grin widened. "Jonas has scared away two or three stand-ins since then. The way I hear it, the front office is a shambles. Added to that, Trans Electric is pushing again."

"He's in the middle of another go-round with Trans and he hasn't got a secretary?" Valerie cried.

"No secretary," Janet murmured complacently, her eyes correctly reading Valerie's outrage.

"How is the fight with Trans going?" she demanded.

"Who knows?" Janet shrugged. "With no regular secretary in the office, the information from the high-rent district is pretty sketchy."

"Jonas must be unbearable by now," Valerie muttered. "Remember how awful he was the first time Maria left?"

"How could I forget?" Janet smiled, watching her closely. "And, as I said, he has already scared a couple of girls into running for cover, so I can imagine how unbearable he is by now." She paused to let her words sink in, before adding, "Valerie, he needs you."

"In the office." Valerie laughed bitterly.

Janet sighed in exasperation. "You don't know that, and anyway, that's as good a place to start as any other. Better, actually, because he spends more time there than anywhere else."

"Oh, Janet, I don't know." Valerie sighed. "Before I left Mother's I'd decided to have it out with him. Find out exactly what, if anything, I meant to him. Somehow that prospect seemed relatively easy from a distance of thousands of miles. But the closer I get to him, the more difficult facing him becomes."

"Do you love him, honey?" Janet eyed her consideringly.

"Do you think I'd be here if I didn't?"

"Well, then what are we doing sitting here?" Janet asked. "Let's go."

"Now?" Valerie asked nervously.

Janet smiled in understanding. "Putting it off won't make it any easier, Val."

"But...I feel grubby, I need a shower and clean clothes," Valerie hedged. "You go on, I'll come in after I've changed."

"I'll wait." Janet grinned.

"But you'll be late and..."

"If I'm late, I'm late." Janet cut her off decisively. "I'm an executive, remember?" Lazily waving her hand in a shooing motion, she drawled, "Run along, I'll wait."

"Valerie."

The raspy sound of her name shattered her reverie. Glancing up, Valerie felt her breath catch in her throat and her legs go weak. He looked clean, and handsome, and sexy as the devil, and she had to bite her lip to keep from crying his name aloud.

Swallowing the lump in her throat, she managed a steady, if somewhat whispery tone. "I hear you have an opening for an experienced secretary."

"When did you get home?" Jonas asked in that same raspy voice.

"Early this morning."

"Why didn't you let me know you were coming?" Jonas demanded in sudden, relieved impatience. "I'd have been at the airport to pick you up."

"You mean you'd have sent Lyle," Valerie snapped, first hurt, then angered by his tone. What had I hoped for, she despaired, that he would welcome me with open arms? Yes, she knew that was exactly what she'd been hoping for. Disappointed, she added, "Exactly as you sent Lyle to take me to the airport."

"Val, you know—" Jonas began, feeling his elation deflate.

"Do you want my help or not?" she interrupted with a soft sigh.

"Yes." Jonas also sighed. You irascible idiot, he berated himself, are you trying to drive her away again? Moving slowly, he walked across the room to her. "I can't find a damned thing." He indicated the room behind her. "Those kids Loretta sent to me just messed everything up in there. And that phone never stops ringing."

Just then, as if to prove the truth of his complaint, the phone rang shrilly. Without a word Valerie walked to his desk and lifted the receiver.

"Jonas Thorne's office," she said briskly.

There was a pause, and then, "Valerie?" Charlie McAndrew exclaimed into her ear. "Is that you?"

"Yes, Charlie, it's me." Valerie smiled.

"Thank God," Charlie said fervently. "Maybe now the cracker will calm down and put the whip away."

She laughed wryly. "Don't hold your breath, Charles."

"I think I could," he returned seriously. "Does Janet know you're back?" he asked.

"Yes, as a matter of fact she drove me in this morning." Valerie could feel Jonas hovering behind her. "I'll see you later, Charlie, here's Jonas," she said, handing the receiver to him.

"What is it, Charlie?" Jonas asked, then paused to listen.

Valerie closed the door quietly and went to the desk that had once been hers. Everything was indeed a mess, and the files were in a positive shambles. With a sigh of acceptance, she got to work on the confusion of papers on top of the desk. Where, she asked herself two hours later, had Loretta found the girls she'd sent up—in a nursery?

Jonas had been on the phone for the majority of those two hours, with long distance as well as local calls. As yet he had not called her back into his office, either for dictation or anything else. Valerie couldn't decide if that was a good or bad sign.

She was working on the last of the file drawers when Janet sauntered into the office.

"Is Legree going to let you go for lunch, or should I bring you a sandwich?" she drawled.

The dry voice that answered came from the doorway to Jonas's office. "You can have someone in the cafeteria bring up two sandwiches, and a pot of coffee," Jonas ordered quietly. "And two pieces of apple pie, if there is any."

"What kind of sandwiches?" Janet glanced from Jonas to Valerie.

A wry smile curving her lips, Valerie attempted to let Janet know she had not yet found the courage to do any straight talking with Jonas. "Chicken salad," she murmured tonelessly. The matching smile she received from Janet told her her meaning was taken.

"I'll have the same," Jonas said in answer to Janet's questioningly raised brows. The slant of his own brows made Valerie uneasy. Could he possibly have read her meaning? Valerie glanced at him quickly, but his expression was unreadable. "Come in and take a break," he invited after Janet had sauntered out again. "We could both use one."

Valerie followed nervously at his heels, wondering if she had the courage to confront him. What was she going to say to him? Everything had seemed so clear-cut way down in Australia, but now that she was here, well, this was for real. Valerie suddenly felt actually sick. Positive she would not be able to handle it if he told her there was no hope for their marriage, Valerie went weak with relief when the phone rang again.

"Oh, hell," Jonas muttered, indicating that she should answer it on his phone. "I'm not in," he added tersely.

Valerie answered the phone, then, placing her hand over the mouthpiece, said softly, "It's Edouard Barres."

Jonas cursed again but took the receiver from her to say in a surprisingly pleasant tone, "Hello, Edouard, what can I do for you?"

Once again Valerie retreated to the front office. Jonas was still on the phone when the girl from the cafeteria brought a tray bearing their food. Relieving her of her burden, Valerie carried it to his desk just as he was saying, "Right, Edouard, within the week. Of course, hold on and I'll have the call switched to his office. You bet, good-bye." He punched out the numbers to transfer the call, then said, "I have the boss on the line, Jean-Paul. He wants to talk to you." He listened a moment, then hung up. Standing up, he took the tray out of her hands and strode to the white couch. "We may as well be comfortable while we eat.'' When she hadn't moved by the time he set the tray down he shot her a questioning glance. ''Are you coming over?'' he asked very softly.

''Y—yes, of course,'' Valerie answered nervously, running suddenly damp palms down over her hips.

''Relax, Val,'' Jonas advised softly. ''I'm not going to jump on you.'' You stupid fool, he accused himself at the nervous flicker of her lashes, now you've put her on guard. What would she do, he wondered, if I grabbed her and took her here and now? Although he would have liked to do just that, Jonas cautioned himself to go slowly. Don't spook her now, go easy, he told himself. She's showing signs of fright, and you don't want to put her on the run again. With cool deliberation he dropped his voice to a soothing tone. ''Come sit down, Val. I give you my word that I won't touch you.''

Eyeing him warily, Valerie crossed the luxuriously thick carpet and seated herself on the opposite end of the couch. Even with five feet of couch between them she didn't feel any too safe. There was silence for several minutes, as both of them discovered exactly how hungry they were. Glancing up to feast her eyes on him, her gaze collided with the sensually warm one he was casting at her, and Valerie felt every one of her senses go haywire. With sudden clarity she heard again Charlie's words of early that morning, ''Maybe now the cracker will calm down and put away the whip.'' Could it be possible that Jonas cared for her? The thought was a heady one, and her mind whirled with visions of what life with him would be like if he did. The ''if'' in her thinking was the only thing that kept her from sliding down the length of the couch and into his arms. If, if, if. How do I go about finding out? I can't just look him in the eye and say bluntly: Do you love me?

Meanwhile, Jonas was having similar thoughts about her. Why this sudden shy attitude? Even at the very beginning of their relationship she had revealed no shyness. Anger, disapproval, yes. And on their honeymoon, she had shown real fear—but shyness? Is it possible she feels something for me? Is that why she came home?

During the long afternoon the air in the two offices was heavy with tension. As the day wore on Valerie became more and more edgy, certain that something was about to happen. And while she sat beside him taking dictation the atmosphere was so heavy she felt stifled and breathless.

What was going through his mind? That question plagued her all afternoon. His voice was cool, his manner quietly polite, and yet his eyes were telling her things she was afraid to believe. It was nerve-racking…but it was also exciting.

Late in the afternoon Janet called her and asked with absolutely no tact at all, "Has he cornered you yet?"

"Of course not!" Valerie exclaimed indignantly. "This is a business office!" Her indignation was completely false. Actually, the idea of him seducing her held an inordinate appeal. "Jonas wouldn't dream of doing that." Darn it.

"Oh, no?" Janet laughed. "If Thorne decided he wanted to badly enough, he'd take you anywhere he pleased."

Sounds interesting. Valerie shocked herself with

her own suddenly erotic thoughts. Reminding herself that this was indeed a business office, she said, coolly, "Look, Janet, I'm very busy, why did you call?"

"I already told you," Janet teased. "I was curious as to whether you were still dancing around each other, or if you had decided to waltz together."

"Good-bye, Janet," Valerie said repressively. As she hung up the receiver she heard Janet chuckle.

Unknown to Janet, her call had achieved her intended purpose—it made Valerie wonder if both she and Jonas weren't behaving a little childishly. Why couldn't they discuss their relationship, past and present, rationally? Why couldn't *she* make the first move? What did she have to lose? Pride? What good was salvaging her pride, if she lost him?

Quitting time came, and went, and Jonas kept working. By seven o'clock Valerie decided enough was enough, and gathering all the courage she possessed, she covered her typewriter, straightened her desk and strolled into his office.

"Are you going to buy me dinner or not?" she asked, dropping into one of the chairs in front of his desk.

Jonas glanced up sharply at her aggressive tone, his eyes narrowing on her tiredly slouched body. "Of course I'll buy you dinner...if that's what you want."

"Am I to infer from that that you are willing to buy me *anything* I want?" Valerie asked softly.

"Yes." Jonas's tone was equally soft. "If you're willing to provide me with what I want."

"A...and that is?"

"You know damned well what *that* is." His eyes

raked the length of her body. "I want you, now, on that couch."

Straightening her shoulders Valerie stood up slowly. "It'll cost you," she murmured, starting to unbutton her blouse.

"You're serious!" A small smile tugged the corners of his mouth, changing his rather harsh expression to one of devilment. "You're willing to take all your clothes off here—and now?"

"It'll cost you more," Valerie warned, an answering smile pulling at her own lips. She had never indulged in this kind of sexual teasing, and excitement made her feel a little light-headed.

"I can afford it," he assured her, beginning to loosen his tie. "Name your price." The tie dropped onto his desk and his fingers went to work on his shirt buttons.

Valerie went cold. Name your price! What was she doing? This wouldn't solve anything! Would it?

"Val?" Jonas's voice, sounding strangely strained, drew her startled eyes to his equally strained face.

"Jonas…I…"

"Name it," he ordered tersely.

"Lynn has got to go," Valerie blurted out, her eyes pleading with him to stop this farce.

"You've got it," he promised. Swinging away, he strode to the desk. "She'll be gone by tomorrow morning." Snatching up the phone, he began punching out a number.

"Jonas! Darling, stop!" Valerie ordered frantically. She couldn't go on with this game! She just couldn't. To her surprise, Jonas froze in place. Then, very slowly, he turned to her.

"What did you say?" he whispered.

"I...I said..." Valerie faltered at the expectant look on his face. What had she said? "You don't have to call her now, I mean..."

"Not *that*," Jonas's hand sliced the air, silencing her as he walked to stand mere inches from her. "What did you *call* me?"

"Dar...darling?" Valerie murmured, wetting her lips.

"Yes, darling." Lifting his hands, he grasped her waist. "You called me that once before, at my command. I decided then that I didn't want to hear it again unless you meant it." Valerie bit back a gasp as his fingers dug into her flesh. "Do you mean it?" Jonas demanded harshly.

"Yes!" Valerie released that gasp on a strangled note. "I meant it then, Jonas!"

"Oh, God, Val." Burying his face in the side of her neck, he slid his arms around her to enclose her in a rib-jarring embrace. "If you knew..." His groaning words were lost as his mouth came down on hers.

Which one of them made the first move? Valerie didn't know, nor did she care. Within minutes, divested of her clothes, she found herself beneath him on the couch, wildly responding to his driving urgency.

"Darling...darling...darling!"

Later, when they lay entwined in one another's arms, Jonas whispered, "Lord, that was good. It was never that good with any other woman." She stiffened and his lips brushed her shoulder. "Easy, my love," he murmured. Lifting his head, he smiled down at her. "And that's the reason it was never as good. I didn't love any one of them."

"Oh, Jonas," Valerie choked, clasping his face in her hands. "Do you love me, really? Because, if you don't then don't say you do. I couldn't bear it if…"

"Will you shut up?" He grinned. Jonas could no more stop grinning than he could stop breathing. It was either grin, he thought wryly, or laugh like an idiot. With her big violet eyes staring up at me all misty with tears, I could easily whoop like a demented wildman.

"Yes, I love you." The grin was gone, replaced by a look so intent Valerie shivered. "God, how I love you."

As he lowered his mouth to hers, Valerie slipped her arms around his neck. His kiss was so gentle, so tender, that the hovering tears spilled over her lids and trickled down her cheeks.

"Now it's your turn," Jonas prompted as his mouth reluctantly released hers.

"I love you, Jonas Thorne. I didn't want to, but I do."

"You're not sorry are you, Val?" Jonas frowned. "I mean that I forced you to leave the dead alone and join me in living?"

"No." She smiled, then gasped. "Are you telling me every move you made was planned?"

"Most of them," he admitted, shifting his weight so that he lay beside her. He drew her into his arms. "Of course, I hadn't planned on your leaving me to go to Australia, or…" He became quiet.

"Or what?"

"Or for you to lose our child."

"Jonas, I'm so sorry about…"

"Stop!" he ordered roughly. "It wasn't your fault." His arms tightened protectively. "Dear, God, you had me worried there, love. I was scared to death I was going to lose you."

"But you didn't, and you won't." Valerie drew a quick breath, then rushed on. "When can we start another baby? Did you have that planned?"

"How about in the next couple of minutes?" he teased.

"What's wrong with right now?" she challenged.

"Right now, my love—" Jonas heaved his long frame off the couch "—I'm going to call and cancel my plane reservations to Australia."

"Australia!" Valerie exclaimed, wide-eyed. "Jonas, you were coming after me?" A sensation of pure delight shot through her at his disclosure.

"You're damned right I was coming after you," Jonas growled softly, bending over to take a nip at her lower lip. "And if you ever take off to visit anyone again you'd better keep a sharp lookout over your shoulder, because I'll be right behind you."

The playful nip turned into a lingering kiss. Straightening slowly, he drew Valerie up with him.

"Why don't you get dressed while I make my phone call?" The smile Jonas gave her set her pulses pounding. "Then we'll go home to bed."

THORNE'S WIFE

Finally:
Pat Smith and Vivian Stephens;
Nag, nag, nag.

Chapter 1

"This time I'll kill her!"

The solid thud of the slammed car door punctuated the angry mutter. Settling his long frame behind the steering wheel, Jonas Thorne jabbed the car key into the ignition with an impatient flick of his wrist. The powerful engine under the gleaming black hood of the big Lincoln came to life with a well-tuned purr.

Breathing slowly, deeply, Jonas backed the car out of the space marked for his exclusive use, and with a sweeping movement of one broad hand on the wheel swung the vehicle around on the large lot that surrounded the office complex of J.T. Electronics. Consumed by fury, Jonas didn't spare a glance for the tall building that was the result of his labor. At that moment, every molecule of his body was centered on reaching home and the woman he felt he could happily throttle.

Long months leading into longer years had gone into the making of the taut expression on Jonas's strong, sharply delineated face. Strangely, over the previous three years and until a few hours ago, his face had apparently reversed the aging process, growing younger-looking instead of older. That very morning, one month shy of his forty-second birthday, Jonas had looked younger than he had at thirty-five. Now, ten hours later, he looked every one of his years on earth, and more. For both the young and the old look Jonas had his wife to thank.

His wife. Valerie.

A vision of her captured his imagination and flooded his senses. Valerie—small, delicate and wafer-thin. Valerie—with the elusively haunting beauty of a heart-shaped face, large violet eyes and long, gleaming black hair. Valerie....

Jonas sighed. God! How he loved her!

And, damn! How she infuriated him at times!

Harshly expelling his breath, Jonas drove off the lot and into the flow of early-evening traffic. Handling the car with automatic expertise, he mentally replayed the telephone conversation he'd had earlier that afternoon with Val. His teeth clenched now as they had then.

"Darling," Val had greeted him as always. "I thought I'd better call and tell you not to make any business or social plans that would include me for the week of the twenty-fourth of next month. I'll be in California."

"What?" His mind still assimilating the information in the business report he'd been studying when

her call came in, Jonas frowned, positive he'd mis-
understood her.

"Jonas, really!" Exasperation was sharp in Val's
tone. "Do you ever pay the slightest attention to a
word I say?"

"I heard the bit about California." A smile lurked
in his deep voice; Val accused him of not listening to
her on an average of once a week.

"Yes, Cal-i-for-nia," Val said distinctly.

"Where in California?" he'd asked immediately.
"And why, for God's sake?" Jonas had had to strive
for the note of indulgence in his voice; Val *had* involved herself in the damnedest projects since the accident that had caused her to miscarry with their child
almost three years ago.

Val sighed loudly. "I'm going to attend a rally of
the Protect Artistic Individuality group in San Francisco," she'd explained with lessening patience.

Though Jonas snorted at the first part of her reply,
he responded to the last in a carefully controlled tone.
"San Francisco?" Merely repeating the name of the
city evoked the memory of their short honeymoon
trip.

"Yes, San Francisco!" Val's tone was edged with
suspicion now. "Jonas, are you reading something
and talking to me at the same time again?"

Jonas could picture the indignation flushing his
wife's lovely face. He grimaced. With a flash of guilt,
he acknowledged Val's right to be indignant; he had
taken to paying only partial attention whenever she
started on the latest of her varied and—at least to
him—confusing interests.

"No, Val, I'm not reading."

"You're angry?" Val was never deceived by his even replies. "Again?" she'd snapped.

Up to that point, Jonas had been more confused than angry. Val's barb had further shortened a fuse that had already grown extremely short the past few months. "Forgive me if I'm wrong," he'd retorted sarcastically, "but hadn't we planned to visit San Francisco together?"

There were fully thirty seconds of utter silence before Val exploded. Warned by the lull, Jonas had tilted the receiver away from his ear.

"I absolutely do not believe you have the gall to say that to me, Jonas Thorne! It has been three years...three years!" Val had actually sputtered. "You...you promised to take me back there! Yet not at any time since then have you as much as mentioned returning!" The sound of her erratic breathing came clearly over the connecting wire. "I—I— How dare you say we *planned* to go back together?"

Jonas winced, because every incoherent word was true. "I'll take you in a couple of months," he'd responded, trying to smooth her ruffled feathers.

"I will take myself next month, thank you!" Val slammed her receiver onto the cradle, and Jonas yanked his farther away from his ear.

"Damn it!" he'd growled. "This positively does it!" His own receiver crashed onto the phone console.

Shoving back his desk chair, Jonas had jumped to his feet and marched to the door with every intention of rushing home to straighten out his infuriating wife. He had grasped the door handle, then remembered the meeting he had called with his executives. He had frowned at the slim gold watch on his wrist. He had set up the meeting for four sharp; it was already three minutes after the hour....

Later that afternoon, while adeptly maneuvering the Lincoln from one crowded lane of the bypass to another, Jonas now merely simmered at the memory of his inattention at that meeting. Though he should have been concentrating on new uses of the electrical components under discussion, he'd been reevaluating his marital situation. And with each successive mental step, his frustration had escalated into cold fury. By the time he'd ended the meeting a half hour ago, he had primed himself for a fight.

If only Val had conceived again.

As the still-painful memory of that terrible night unwound in his mind, Jonas's fingers tightened around the leather-covered steering wheel in reaction.

God! What a mess he had made of everything! he recalled, shuddering reflexively. He didn't want to remember that night, yet was powerless to withstand the force of memory's flow.

They had been married two months; two months, during which all hell had seemed to have broken loose, both at home and in the office. Jonas remembered clearly—too clearly—that it had begun the day after the wedding with a phone call from his assistant, Charlie McAndrew.

If he and Valerie had only had some time together, Jonas reflected with a sigh. After the thrilling wedding night they'd shared...if they had only had some private time together. But they had not had that time. Their private time had ended with Charlie's phone call.

Because of a breakthrough Jonas had made in the field of communication systems for space exploration, J.T. Electronics was about to become embroiled in an industry fight with another, failing company, whose president just happened to have friends in very high places in Washington, D.C. The president of this firm had decided to save his floundering company by grabbing a piece of Jonas's action.... But Jonas wasn't about to share his action with anyone.

As he had told Valerie during their rushed return flight from San Francisco to Philadelphia, "No one picks *my* brain."

That had been three years and one month ago. The industrial fight had lasted four weeks but, though Jonas had won the professional battle, he had at the same time apparently lost the personal war. For although their nights together had been sheer heaven for Jonas, he had been too involved with the business battle to devote any of his daytime hours to getting to know his new wife in any way other than physically.

A sharp curl of sensual arousal broke through Jonas's reverie. A wry smile skipped over his thin lips as, savoring the physical discomfort, he noticed that he was almost home. And home, to Jonas, meant Valerie.

Valerie, who had coolly announced that she was going to San Francisco next month without him.

Next month.

June.

Jonas cursed as he remembered the anger and anguish he had lived through three years ago during his birthday month.

Jonas had turned thirty-nine that June. He hadn't cared a damn about that fact. What he had cared about was Valerie's apparent interest in Jean-Paul DeBron, the man his French associate had sent to Jonas as a liaison for the special project they were collaborating on.

The Frenchman had arrived the same day Jonas's daughter, Mary Beth, came home from the finishing school she had been attending in Switzerland. Lynn, Jonas's ex-wife, had returned to the States with her daughter. Marge, Jonas's beloved ex-mother-in-law, rounded out the group.

Even now, three years later, the memory of that day retained enough power to wrench a groan from Jonas. The entire day had proved to be a debacle. In retrospect, Jonas accepted the guilt not only for ruining his daughter's homecoming, but for having put his new bride at such a disadvantage.

Jealousy. Damn, Jonas hated the word. But what was more important, he hated what the emotion had done to him three years ago. His long fingers gripped the steering wheel so tightly that the skin paled over his broad knuckles. Grimacing, he forced himself to relax his grip.

The memory ate at his mind like acid.

If he hadn't been so damned jealous and so scared of losing Val, he wouldn't have been blind to the brother-sister affection between Val and Jean-Paul, or to the growing love between the Frenchman and his daughter.

But Jonas had been blinded by his own unreasonable jealousy to the extent that, when Val told him she was pregnant, he had actually accused her of being unfaithful.

The big car was air-conditioned, yet Jonas's brow was beaded with perspiration. Cursing beneath his breath, he carefully monitored his driving, while reliving the horror of the consequences of his accusation.

Knowing he was wrong to accuse her, Jonas had apologized almost at once, then had turned and left the house. Valerie had run after him. As he backed around in the driveway, Jonas hadn't seen her running toward his car. He could still hear the echo of his own cry of warning on catching her fleeting image in the rearview mirror. But his warning came too late. The back end of his car struck her a glancing blow, and Valerie had suffered a miscarriage later that night.

Jonas knew that he would go to his grave blaming himself for the accident.

Valerie wanted a child so very badly. How very different their life together would be today, if only she had conceived again.

Like Val, Jonas longed for a child from their union. He wanted a son.... Hadn't his desire for a son been the reason for proposing marriage to Val in the first place?

Oh, sure Thorne, you bet. The jeering voice of his conscience mocked Jonas. Desire had first, last and always been the reason for his proposal.

Recalling that far from romantic proposal, Jonas's lips tilted derisively. At the time he had in actual fact offered Val a business proposition. In exchange for his name, wealth and protection, all Val had to do was give him a son. Yet from the outset, Jonas had known full well that he had acted on the strength of the attraction he felt for her. Val, then his personal secretary, was simply playing havoc with his libido by showing up for work every day.

The jarring blare of a car horn, too close for comfort, jolted Jonas back into the present. If he wasn't careful, he advised himself scathingly, he wouldn't *live* to challenge Val's decision to go to California without him.

His thoughts centered once more on making it home in one piece, Jonas concentrated anew on the traffic weaving in and out and around him until he turned the car onto the private lane that ended in a circular driveway before the house he had had built over two years ago.

Pulling the Lincoln to a stop in front of the four-car garage, Jonas stepped out and slammed the door behind him. Anger simmering at near boiling point, he strode along the flagstone path to the front door of the trilevel glass and redwood house. Key at the ready, he shoved it into the lock, only to curse fluently when the door opened with the turn of the knob.

How many times had he cautioned Val about keeping the door locked when he wasn't at home? Jonas railed inwardly, marching into the house. And *she* had the temerity to accuse *him* of never paying attention!

Jonas paused in the black and white marble foyer, his nostrils flaring as he sniffed the air. Val was doing her thing again in the kitchen, he decided, noting the delicate aroma of cooking food. What was it this time? he mused. Stir-fry? Greek? Tex-Mex? Closing his eyes, he inhaled deeply and identified the mouth-watering scent of shrimp tempura.

The low rumble of Jonas's stomach reminded him that he'd forgotten to eat lunch—as usual. Moving with his normal long-legged, loose-limbed gait along the hallway to the kitchen, his eyes narrowed with suspicion.

Valerie knew how much he enjoyed her stir-fried meals. Had she hoped to avoid a confrontation by preparing his favorite rice and shrimp tempura dish? If that had been her plan, Jonas thought unmollified, Valerie Thorne was in for an unpleasant surprise.

But as he drew nearer to the kitchen, Jonas's appetite sharpened with the increasing strength of the tantalizing aroma. Damn! He was hungry, he grumbled to himself. Maybe he'd wait until after dinner to throttle her.

Pausing in the kitchen archway, Jonas propped one shoulder against the smooth wall and ran his narrow-eyed gaze over the small, slender form of his wife. She was standing at the stove, her back to him, humming softly as she busied herself with two long-handled utensils.

From the back, Valerie looked more like a teenager than a mature, thirty-one-year-old woman. A frothy, lace-trimmed apron was tied in a large bow at the back of her tiny waist, protecting her paisley cotton skirt. A leaf-green sleeveless blouse was neatly tucked into the waistband of the skirt. Slim-heeled sandals complemented her small, narrow feet. Her glorious mane of gleaming black hair was piled into a haphazard mass on top of her head, revealing her slender neck.

Jonas's teeth ached with a sudden overwhelming need to nip at her satiny skin. Compressing his lips, he swallowed a groan. The mere sight of her, even her back, aroused an appetite much sharper than the one tormenting his stomach. The hunger for food could easily be appeased by regular meals or even periodic snacks. Yet oddly, the hunger Jonas felt for Val had never truly been slaked, no matter how many times he availed himself of her ardently offered bounty. If anything, each and every physical encounter with Val left Jonas hungry for more. It had been that way between them from their very first time together on their wedding night.

Feeling himself beginning to weaken, Jonas straightened and squared his broad shoulders, reminding himself that this time Val had gone too far.

"You are *not* going to San Francisco next month, and that's final." Although his voice was low, it held steely conviction. If Jonas hoped to get the advantage by startling Val—and he had—he succeeded admirably.

Emitting a tiny screech, Val whipped around to face him. "Darn you, Jonas!" she exclaimed. "How dare you sneak up on me like that?" Still clutching her tools, Val planted her fists on her hips and glared at him. "Are you trying to give me heart failure?" she demanded, her eyes flashing angry warning signals.

"And rob myself of the pleasure of beating you?" Jonas retorted, arrogantly raising one ash-brown eyebrow.

Valerie mirrored his expression with a perfectly arched black brow. "You wouldn't dare," she taunted confidently.

"Don't make book on it, sweetheart." Jonas sauntered into the room as he offered the advice. "There is a limit to how much I'll put up with from you."

Valerie angled her chin defiantly. "Oh, heavens, please don't frighten me like this." She didn't sound frightened; she didn't look intimidated, either. "I'm going to California, Jonas, and there's nothing you can do about it." Casually turning her back on him, she attacked the large wok once more. "Dinner will be ready in a few minutes." Beginning to hum again, she gently stirred the shrimp.

"Damn it, Val!" Frustrated, Jonas grasped her by one arm and swung her around to face him, feigning retreat as one utensil flashed by his head.

"How would you like to be skewered?" Val brandished the two-pronged fork threateningly.

"How would you like to be—?"

"Jonas!" Val's sharp exclamation covered his words. "Don't be crude," she admonished, lips twitching with her attempt to contain a smile. "At least not before dinner."

Jonas wanted to maintain his anger.... An errant smile of his own defeated him. "I really should beat you, you know," he muttered. "But I won't." His tone thickened to the consistency of honey. "At least not before dinner."

"How magnanimous of you," Val drawled.

"Yeah, I know," Jonas retorted. Bending swiftly, he gave her a quick, hard kiss, then swung away before she could raise her culinary weapon. At the kitchen archway, he paused again to shoot a glance at her, a blatantly sexy smile curving his lips now. "On second thought, I don't believe I will beat you," he said slowly in a low, enticing tone. "I have other, infinitely more effective methods to change your mind." Whistling softly, he ambled from the room.

And those methods usually work too, darn it! Val acknowledged in silence as she returned her attention to her meal. While she stirred the contents of the wok, she absently skimmed the tip of her tongue over her lips, savoring the taste that was uniquely Jonas. Feeling desire uncurl deep inside her, Val sighed and shook herself free of the web of sensuality he had so effortlessly woven around her.

Not this time, she promised herself grimly. She was going to San Francisco, and nothing Jonas could say or do would dissuade her. Not because she was all that fervently dedicated to the cause of preserving artistic individuality. The individuality Val was dedicated to preserving was her own. Jonas's personality was so very strong that Val actively feared she'd be swallowed up by it if she didn't assert herself. San Francisco was Val's statement on the subject.

Dashing into the powder room off the front foyer, Val checked her makeup while removing the large butterfly hair clips that anchored her black mane. A quick attack with a brush, a shrug of her shoulders, and she was dashing back into the kitchen, her sharp-eyed gaze sweeping the table as she passed the archway that led into the dining room.

The oval cherry wood table was set for two with delicate china, lead crystal and sterling silver cutlery on wide, lacy place mats. An arrangement of spring blossoms with two tall slim candles rising from their midst stood in the center of the table.

Val was removing two wooden bowls of salad from the crisper drawer in the refrigerator when she caught sight of Jonas's tall figure entering the kitchen. He had removed his suit jacket and necktie, had opened the two top buttons of his pale blue shirt and had rolled up the sleeves, revealing his lightly haired forearms. The sight of him, so tall, muscularly slender and devastatingly handsome in his chiseled, rugged way, caused a tremor in Val's arms. The bowls tilted precariously, nearly dumping the salad onto the floor. With a sigh of acceptance, Val concentrated on steadying both her hands and the contents of the bowls.

It was always the same, Val mused, backing away from the fridge. Even after three years of marriage and the difficulties they had been through, Jonas didn't have to do anything but walk into a room to set her pulse racing.

"Is there something I can do to help?" he asked, offering assistance, as he never failed to do. Val had adamantly refused to hire a housekeeper.

"Yes." Val shut the fridge door with a sideways nudge of her hip. "You can take these in to the table." She handed him the bowls. "Oh, and light the candles, please," she called after him.

"What about wine?" Jonas asked a moment later from the dining-room archway, where he stood watching her transfer the food from the wok to serving dishes.

"You choose." Glancing up, Val frowned at the smile that was tugging at his sculpted mouth. She knew absolutely nothing about wine, which never failed to amuse Jonas. Sweeping by him with the large serving tray, Val promised herself that someday she'd enroll for a course on wine appreciation—if and when she ever found the time.

Jonas knew quite a lot about wine, and the one he chose had just the proper texture to complement their meal.

Sipping the pale gold liquid from the fragile flute, Val watched Jonas as he eagerly consumed three-quarters of the food she'd placed on the table. Meanwhile, she merely made a show of eating the small portion she'd taken.

After long months of hard work, Val had finally achieved her goal of getting into a size three dress again. She was almost frantic in her determination to maintain that size—and the weight of ninety-six pounds that she had not seen registered on the scales since before meeting Jonas.

On the other hand, Jonas seemed equally determined to see her eat her way back to the size six she'd attained after losing their baby. This evening, other than making the occasional pointed remark, he said nothing about her meager intake. But when she served a single dessert—his—he scowled in a familiar way that warned Val of an approaching argument.

"No dessert?" Jonas arched his brows into an exaggerated peak.

Val's sigh spoke of long endurance of this boring topic. "Jonas, I have not been eating desserts for months now." Her expression was a study in controlled patience. "One really does not require dessert to survive." Smiling serenely, she sipped at her wine. Her smile was a goad to his temper, and she knew it. Pondering on the urge that drove her to continually challenge him, she calmly observed the storm brewing in his gray-blue eyes.

"No, one doesn't need dessert to survive," Jonas agreed, returning her smile in a way that shot a thrill composed of equal parts of apprehension and excitement through Valerie. "But one might have to be very careful when speaking to one's husband. Do you get my drift?" he asked quietly—too quietly.

"Why, Mr. Thorne, sir!" Val fluttered her eyelashes flirtatiously. "Are you threatening little ol' me?" Her attempt at a Southern accent was appallingly bad—deliberately.

Jonas was not amused. "Keep pushing, sweetheart," he warned, an edge of annoyance in his tone now.

"And then what?" Val taunted, asking herself why she persisted when he was obviously becoming angry all over again. Of course, she knew full well why; she was damn tired of being treated like a second-class person—in other words like a wife!

"I'll be left with two choices," Jonas informed her smoothly. "I'll either have to ignore you," he said, "or make very rough love to you, which I'd enjoy immensely." His shrug was eloquent.

"Promises, promises," Val chanted, suddenly breathless and commending herself on the evenness of her tone. Sliding her chair away from the table, she rose with unstudied grace. Taking advantage of the opportunity to look down on the man who stood a good foot taller than she did, Val couldn't resist one last shot. "You're all talk and little action, Thorne." Scooping up the tray of now empty dishes, she beat a hasty retreat into the kitchen.

Valerie expected Jonas to stalk after her—and he did. Her excitement churning to near fever pitch, she shot a glance at the wall clock. A sigh that was a mixture of relief and disappointment whispered through her lips when the door chimes pealed, just as Jonas was reaching for her.

"Now who in hell...?" he began in a low growl.

"Oh! Did I forget to tell you?" Val managed a helpless look of confusion. "I expect it's your daughter and son-in-law." Swinging away from him, she smiled sweetly. "Mary Beth called earlier to ask if we'd mind if she and Jean-Paul stopped by tonight. She said they have something to tell us." She paused in the hallway to give him an arched glance. "Since I thought I might need their protection, I told them we wouldn't mind at all." Val grinned at the muttered curse that followed her to the front door.

Before Val set foot on the marble floor in the foyer, Jonas was by her side. "Having fun, are you?" he growled, striding past her to the door. "Make the most of it, my love," he murmured. As his hand grasped the brass latch, his glittering gaze swept her figure. "Mary Beth and Jean-Paul will have to go home sometime." Not giving her time to respond, he pulled open the door.

"Hi, Dad." Mary Beth stepped into the foyer, grinning as if she'd just won the lottery. At twenty-three, Mary Beth was a lovely young woman. Tall and clear-featured like her father and golden-skinned like her mother, she had a look uniquely her own with her soft eyes and mouth and honey-blond hair...which was several shades darker than Jonas's ash blond. "I

hope you don't mind us dropping in on the spur of
the moment like this?'' she asked, grinning impishly.

"Not at all," Jonas assured her with what Val considered commendable aplomb for a man on the verge
of going up in smoke. "We had no plans for this
evening." Reaching out, he accepted the hand his
son-in-law offered—thinking it slightly comical, considering he'd left Jean-Paul in the conference room at
J.T. Electronics less than two hours ago. "Jean-
Paul," he drawled, quietly shutting the door.

"Jonas." The handsome Frenchman smiled in appreciation of the irony in the formality of the hand-
shake.

"Jean-Paul, will you look at the figure on this
woman!" Mary Beth exclaimed dramatically, motioning toward Valerie. "What are you living on, Val,
cottage cheese and low cal air?"

"Just about," Jonas muttered as he led the way
into the spacious living room.

"Oh, Jonas, really!" Val protested, frowning at his
expression of disapproval.

Coming up beside her, Jean-Paul slipped an arm
around Val's tiny waist. "You look *magnifique, ma
petite*," he said, brushing her soft cheek with his lips.
"Quite like the young woman I met in France over
four years ago."

Val smiled gratefully and returned his kiss. "*Merci*,
Jean-Paul."

"And I feel like a cow in comparison!" Mary Beth
wailed, running her palms over her own slender
curves.

Jean-Paul sent her a smoldering look. "If you
would care to return home, my sweet, I would be

delighted to demonstrate how very much I adore little blond cows.''

Laughing softly, Val gave Jean-Paul a quick, fierce hug; she would always love Jean-Paul, who had come within two weeks of being her brother-in-law, love him in a very special way. And it was obvious to everyone who knew them that Jean-Paul returned her affection.

Hands on hips, Mary Beth glared at her husband before rolling her beautiful blue eyes at Valerie. "I swear, Val, do men ever think of *anything* other than bedroom games?''

"Your father does," Val replied, sliding a glance at Jonas. "He thinks mainly about electrical components and computers and such." Moving easily but purposefully, she headed for the hallway and escape. "Now if you'll excuse me, I must finish clearing the dinner table.''

The laughter that erupted from Mary Beth and Jean-Paul didn't drown the ominous tone of Jonas's voice.

"Valerie, come back here.''

"In a few minutes." She called the response over her shoulder from her relatively safe position in the hall. "I'll bring a tray of coffee with me." Smiling to herself, Val returned to the dining room and the dishes cluttering the table.

Mary Beth joined her in the kitchen as she was stacking the dishes in the dishwasher. "Can I help with anything?''

Val smiled at her stepdaughter, who was only seven years her junior. "Yes. You can start the coffee if you like." She raised her eyebrows. "Don't tell me, let me guess. Your father and Jean-Paul are talking business?"

"What else?" Mary Beth shrugged. As she ran water into the glass coffeepot, she slanted a contemplative glance at Valerie. "Are you and Dad having problems, Val?"

"Problems?" Val repeated, frowning as she switched on the machine before turning to look at the younger woman. "What do you mean?"

"Oh, come on, Val!" Mary Beth grimaced. "Don't pull that blank confusion act with me. I thought... believed...we were friends."

"We are!" Val exclaimed. "But—"

"But nothing!" Mary Beth interrupted. "I've been married long enough to read the signals, and both you and Dad are sending them out. Good grief! You two have been taking verbal potshots at each other for months now. I don't want to pry, really, but I'm concerned. Jean-Paul's concerned, too."

Val felt trapped. What could she say? She and Jonas were having problems, personality problems, but she certainly wasn't about to confide in his daughter—regardless of how fond of the young woman she'd become.

"I suspect all married couples have their off moments," Val replied vaguely. "Your father and I are no different than most." Avoiding Mary Beth's skeptical look, she turned to the kitchen cabinet to remove cups and saucers.

"There...ah..." Mary Beth hesitated. "There isn't another woman involved.... Is there, Val?"

The fragile china rattled in Valerie's hands as she spun to face a frowning Mary Beth. "Another woman?'' Sheer amazement raised her natural soft tone several decibels. "No!" she exclaimed. "Of course there's no other woman! Why would you even think—?"

"I don't!" Mary Beth interjected forcefully. "Not really. It's just...well..." Her shoulders lifted and fell in a helpless movement. "Suddenly you and Dad seem to be drifting apart, and I was afraid that..." Her voice trailed away on a sigh.

So it was beginning to show. Hiding her thoughts, Val busied her hands by arranging the china on a tray. How many others had noticed the strain between Jonas and herself? Val wondered tiredly. And how long would it be before she found herself in the position of fielding polite inquiries from other curious, well-meaning friends? She stifled a groan. The prospect was daunting. Giving up the pretense of busywork, she raised her eyes to meet Mary Beth's concerned gaze.

"There is no other woman, Mary Beth." Solid conviction underlined Val's tone, conviction instilled by her absolute trust in Jonas. While it was true that they were having some marital trouble, Val was positive the problems weren't of the *other woman* variety.

Mary Beth was visibly relieved. "I'm glad. You've been so very good for Dad, Val," she said earnestly.

She had? A startled laugh burst from Val. "Do you really think so?" Privately she had doubts—many, many doubts.

"Yes, of course." Mary Beth's response was flatteringly prompt. "All I have to do is look at him. Dad looks five years younger than he did five years ago."

Val's violet eyes darkened with memory. "Your

father was always a dynamic, attractive man.'' Her voice had softened.

''And he is even more dynamic and attractive than before.'' Mary Beth grinned. ''He smiles more, and Dad always did have one fantastic smile.''

''I'll say!'' Val exclaimed. For an instant she felt again the heady, stunned reaction she'd experienced the very first time she saw Jonas smile; and he'd smiled at another woman on that occasion! ''I couldn't begin to explain the effect his first smile had on me.''

''Like being poleaxed?'' Mary Beth teased.

Val pretended to consider. ''That comes pretty close,'' she agreed, grinning when the younger girl giggled. ''It also comes pretty close to what he'll do to us,'' she went on brusquely, ''if we don't get this coffee in to him.'' Reaching around the grinning Mary Beth, Val drew a white coffee thermos from the countertop. ''I'll pour the coffee into this. You can get the cream and sugar.''

''What, no cake or cookies?'' Mary Beth's brows arched. ''Dad loves desserts.''

''And he's had his.'' A smile eased Val's adamant tone. ''I'm watching his weight for him.''

Mary Beth was still smiling when she carried the tray into the living room. As her husband leaped from his chair to take the tray from her, her father challenged her smile.

''I know that particular smirk, kid.'' Jonas's tone smacked of parental indulgence. ''What have you and Val been up to?''

Mary Beth burst out laughing. ''Not dessert, that's

for sure. Val assures me that *she*'s watching *your* weight.''

''Val would do better to provide the dessert,'' Jonas retorted. ''And then eat it herself.'' He raked his wife's ultraslim figure with a hard-eyed glance. ''If she gets much thinner,'' he added, ''I'll have to tether her to something, to prevent her from blowing away with the slightest breeze.''

''But, Jonas! I think Valerie looks wonderful.'' Jean-Paul ran an appreciative look over her. ''She looks exactly as she did when I first met her.''

Jonas shifted his narrowed gaze to his son-in-law. ''So you said before,'' he replied evenly. ''Personally, I prefer her the way she looked when *I* first met her.''

Yes; overweight, undernourished, scared and submissive. Val prudently kept the response to herself, but felt positive that this attitude of his lay behind their inability to communicate. Jonas insisted on casting her in the role of *his* wife, *his* hostess, *his* ornament, and altogether submissive—whereas she was determined to become *her* own person.

Raising her cup to her lips, Val sighed into the dark brew. It had been an uphill battle all the way and, as the remark Jonas had just made proved, she wasn't even near the top of her particular goal-mountain.

Evidently not in the least put off by Jonas's cool attitude, Jean-Paul shrugged in the way only a Frenchman can. ''Then we shall have to agree to disagree, eh?'' His teeth were a flash of white against his dark skin.

Jonas didn't smile. ''If we must.''

''Oh, for the sake of harmony, I think we must.''

Jean-Paul's eyes crinkled with inner amusement as he shot a sparkling glance at his wife.

Jonas was alert at once. Shifting his sharp gaze from Mary Beth to Jean-Paul, then to Val, he slowly replaced his cup on its matching saucer. "What's going on?" he demanded of Val.

Since she was asking herself the same question, Val shrugged. "I haven't the vaguest idea." Her eyes moved in unison with his to the couple seated side by side on the long sofa.

"Well?" Jonas prompted, when it appeared that all the two were capable of was smiling smugly.

Their smiles widening still more, Mary Beth and Jean-Paul glanced at each other, then back to Val and Jonas—who by this time was showing distinct signs of thinning patience. Then they rushed into speech simultaneously.

"I'm pregnant!"

"We're going to have a child."

There was an instant of utter silence, then Val and Jonas responded in unison.

"How wonderful for you both!" Val exclaimed.

"Honey, I'm delighted for you." Springing from his chair, Jonas crossed to the sofa, pulled up Mary Beth and gathered her into his arms, while extending his right hand to Jean-Paul. "I'm delighted for you, too," he added with a grin.

Following at her husband's heels, Val took her turn at bestowing excited hugs on the glowing pair. Then her eyes flashed at Jonas as Mary Beth stated what would soon be obvious to everyone.

"You're going to be a grandfather, Dad!"

Chapter 2

A *grandfather*. He was going to be a grandfather.

His mouth curved in a wry smile, Jonas turned off the shower spray and stepped out of the ceramic tile stall. His Mary Beth, his baby, was going to have a baby.

Suddenly tired, Jonas muffled a yawn with one hand, reaching with the other for a brown-and-white-striped oversize towel that was neatly folded over a long gleaming chrome rack mounted on the wall.

Though he seldom retired much before midnight, tonight it was even later than usual. It had been after one before Mary Beth and Jean-Paul departed for home, thanks to the impromptu celebration they'd put on—complete with a snack Val and Mary Beth had prepared and the bottle of imported champagne Jonas had provided for the occasion.

Where had all the years gone? Jonas mused, drying

his body with absentminded sweeps of the thick bath sheet. By his reckoning, Mary Beth still seemed little more than a baby herself. And yet in seven months or so his little girl, his baby, would make him a grandfather.

Jonas couldn't decide whether he liked the idea or not. It wasn't so much the fact of being a grandfather as the word's connotations of age. Though there were days when Jonas felt a hundred and twelve, usually he didn't yet feel old enough to be a grandfather.

His Mary Beth. Picturing the sweet-natured, golden-haired little girl who had run into his arms whenever he'd managed to make it home from the office before her bedtime, Jonas sighed. His baby. Feeling the pressure of time, he glanced into the full-length mirror on the door.

Was he getting old? He'd be forty-two next month. Was forty-two old? His lids narrowed over his gray-blue eyes, Jonas studied his reflection, searching for telltale signs of encroaching age. He didn't have to look very hard. The sprinkling of gray that had merely peppered the thick, abundant ash-blond hair at his temples a few years ago had grown into wings of solid silver. The lines radiating from his eyes and bracketing his mouth had deepened into permanent grooves. His brow was creased. He acknowledged with a vague sense of dissatisfaction that all these signs were definite indications of middle age.

On the other hand, his face and form still retained vestiges of youth and vigor, Jonas decided with wry humor, as he scanned his reflected image.

There was a sheen of health in the skin that stretched tautly over his big-boned, sharply defined facial features. His eyes were clear, shrewd, intelligent. His tall form still had the flat, angular look of youth, the musculature long and steel-hard rather than bunched and flabby. His hips and waist were still narrow, his belly flat to slightly concave.

Turning away from his reflection, Jonas tossed the towel into the clothes hamper and shrugged into the black silk robe Val had given him the previous Christmas. Recalling his initial reaction to the gift, Jonas smiled with self-mockery.

Jonas had never considered himself a robe type; he was either dressed or undressed. That being the case, he knew his expression had been one of consternation when he opened the elaborately wrapped package on Christmas morning. Not wanting to hurt Val, he'd infused a note of enthusiasm into his voice as he thanked her for the present.

Proving she knew him better than he had suspected, Val had laughed and said, "I know you're thinking that it's too sybaritic for you."

She was correct.

Jonas had concurred with a grunted, "Damn right."

"But you're wrong," Val had continued, ignoring his mutter of agreement. "I knew it was for you the moment I saw it." Leaning over him, she had curled her arms around his neck and nibbled delicately on his earlobe. "Please, darling, try it on for me. I just know you're going to look as sexy as the devil in it."

Since it was very early on Christmas morning, hours before Mary Beth, Jean-Paul and Marge were due to arrive for the traditional meal and exchange of gifts, Jonas and Val had been sitting on their huge bed to exchange their personal gifts.

"Sexy, hmm?" Though Jonas had laughed, he had modeled the robe for her—after a mutually exciting interlude—and had worn it nearly every evening since then.

Feeling the silk glide against his skin brought back the fiery excitement of that holiday morning. Desire, hot and swift, flared through Jonas, burning away his sleepiness, searing his tired body into taut revival. Suddenly needing the sensations only Val could arouse in him, he raked a brush through his hair and pulled open the bathroom door.

Maybe he wasn't quite as old as he had almost convinced himself he was.

The sight that met his eyes as he walked into the bedroom drew from him a sigh made up of equal parts of amusement and frustration.

Her only covering a minuscule scrap of white satin panties, Val was on the floor in a hatha-yoga shoulder stand. Her slim body rose into the air, straight as an arrow from the base of her neck and the edge of her shoulders. Her arms lay relaxed and limp on the carpet. Her eyes were closed. Her breathing was measured, even and regular. Her small, rose-tipped breasts shivered with each breath.

Jonas had become so accustomed to observing Val in a variety of exercise positions that he was no longer fazed. Yet, seeing her this time in that particular upside-down position for some inexplicable reason added fuel to the fire raging in his body.

Obeying an impulse, Jonas padded toward her across the lush carpet. Halting mere inches from her raised legs, he reached out and stroked his broad hands over her slender, shapely calves. Fire licked through his veins when he felt her muscles quiver in reaction and heard the catch in her breathing pattern.

"Jonas." Val didn't open her eyes as she murmured his name in a tone of admonition.

Ignoring the warning, Jonas curled his long fingers around her ankles. Gently applying pressure, he drew down her body until her weight was resting on the upper part of her back. Then, parting her legs, he stepped forward and tucked them neatly around his waist.

Val's eyes flew open. "Jonas! What are you—? Oh!" She gasped aloud as he slid one palm down the inside of her thigh. "What are you thinking of?"

"I'm thinking that this position you're in has very definite possibilities," Jonas murmured, stroking the underside of her knees with his fingertips.

So delicately balanced, Val couldn't move. Jonas knew she couldn't move. She knew that he knew she couldn't move. His smile was slow, sexy and incredibly exciting. Val shivered with anticipation.

Jonas didn't disappoint her. Savoring the tightness coiling inside him, he let his hand drift with excruciating slowness to the satin barrier at the apex of her thighs.

Valerie didn't disappoint *him*. Murmuring low in her throat, she moved her body against his tingling palm. Jonas shuddered in reaction to the sensation that streaked like lightning from his hand to every nerve ending in his body. The intensity of the desire clamoring inside him was slightly shocking…

considering that they had slept side by side for three years.

Would he never get enough of her? Jonas asked himself, responding to her sensuous movements by stroking his long fingers over the heated satin beneath his hand.

The query was the last cohesive thought to form in Jonas's head for some time. Moaning his name, Valerie moved against him in invitation. Her action cleared his mind of all considerations except the overpowering need that was storming his senses and converging on the center of his masculinity.

Forgetting the comfort of the enormous bed behind him, Jonas continued to stroke her through the warm satin while he slowly sank to his knees. Within seconds both his robe and the scrap of fabric swathing Valerie's hips lay in a shimmering heap on the carpet beside him.

Old? Middle-aged? Ha!

Silent laughter rippled through Jonas as he slid his taut aroused body between her silky thighs. The encroaching years were meaningless, powerless against the surge of vigor now quickening his body. Valerie and his unquenchable hunger for her kept him young, vital…hot.

Sliding his hands beneath her, Jonas held Val's undulating hips still. Denying the urgency shuddering through him, he entered her slowly, savoring the thrill of burying the strongest and most vulnerable part of himself deeply within the velvet softness of her body. Excitement took a quantum leap inside him when Val grasped his thighs and sank her nails reflexively into his quivering muscles.

"Jonas." Valerie's husky whisper contained both a plea and a command.

He granted both. Bending to her, Jonas captured her mouth with his in a hard, hungry kiss. Then, spurred by her throaty murmurs, he speared his tongue into the depths of her sweetness, initiating a rhythm of complete possession that was reflected by the movement of his body. Impelled by a need beyond his comprehension, Jonas drove his body relentlessly toward the goal of utter ecstasy. Gritting his teeth, he denied himself until he felt the first of the cascading shudders that began pulsating through Val. Then, releasing his restraint, Jonas made the final thrust, crying her name in a hoarse groan as he was swept into the vortex with her.

Valerie couldn't breathe. She couldn't think. She could only feel. Her entire body sensitized, she gloried in the tension coiling ever tighter inside with each stroke and thrust of Jonas's hard body. Quivering, she abandoned herself to sensation. It was always the same, yet ever different. Clutching his taut flanks, Val strained to draw him deeper within herself, at that instant needing the fullness of him more than she needed breath to survive.

Forgotten was the discord between them. There had never been discord while they were locked together, united in the most intimate embrace of lovers. And Valerie loved Jonas with every part of her being. The clawing need robbing her of thought and inhibition was a direct response to the depth of the love she felt for him. In three years, Valerie had never had enough of his lovemaking, and never felt completely satiated.

She always craved more, more, and still more of Jonas.

Valerie made a strangled sound of surprised pleasure when release caught her, and gasped in appreciation of his final driving thrust. Fusing together, clinging to each other, they rode the wave of completion.

"You know I love you." Jonas's voice was ragged from his uneven breathing.

"Yes." Val smiled. Jonas never spoke the words of love while performing the act of love. He always waited until they had attained the heights of passion before speaking aloud his innermost feelings, complimenting her with his declaration after sharing his pleasure with her. "As you know I love you," she murmured, returning the compliment.

"Do you?" Levering his body away from her, Jonas stared into her eyes as he stretched his length on the carpet beside her.

"Jonas!" Val didn't try to conceal the confusion and hurt his question caused her. "You know I do."

"Then why in hell are you going to San Francisco without me?" Jonas demanded, ruthlessly searching her shadowed violet eyes.

The discord between them was back, weighing Val down with disappointment and depression. She escaped his piercing stare by closing her eyes. "I've explained why I'm going," she answered in a weary tone. "I'm going in support of the—"

Jonas cut her off impatiently. "I don't believe you."

Was she so very transparent? Val asked herself, trembling in reaction to the harshness of his tone.

Could Jonas see through her so easily? Did he know, understand or even care that she was fighting an up-hill battle to move out of the shade of his protective, smothering shadow and establish her own identity? Didn't he realize that she couldn't be a true mate or partner to him until she became all she could be as a woman?

Anger dried the tears gathering in Valerie's eyes. Opening them, she gave him a glittering look. "Are you calling me a liar, Jonas?"

"No." His denial held conviction.

"But you just said that you don't believe me," she reminded him pointedly.

"I don't believe that you're that concerned with protecting artistic individuality." As usual, Jonas swore when he was mad. "Damn it, Val, you've been involving yourself in one pursuit after another for months." His eyes narrowed; his harsh voice lashed at her once more. "Are you bored with this mar-riage?" He paused, then added in a dangerously soft tone, "Or are you bored with me?"

"Bored?" Her expression incredulous, Val jerked into a sitting position. "You can ask me that after what just happened here?" She indicated their carpet-bed with a sweep of her small hand.

Obviously uncomfortable with having her glare down at him, Jonas sprang up beside her. "Well, damn it, Val, you must be dissatisfied with some-thing," he insisted, grinding out the words.

"For your information, dissatisfied is not synony-mous with bored," Val said, scrambling to her feet so that she could look down at him again, even while admitting to herself that her action was childish.

As if not to be bested, and revealing a streak of immaturity himself, Jonas rose to tower over her. "Then you admit to being dissatisfied?" Accusation colored his tone; a ruddy hue tinged his prominent cheekbones.

Tamping down an urge to climb onto the bed to gain additional height, Valerie tilted her chin defiantly and glared up into his stormy steel-blue eyes. "Yes," she said distinctly. "I am dissatisfied."

Her boldness seemed to stop him cold for an instant. Then, his movement calculated, Jonas turned to rake a gaze over the carpet. "You didn't appear to be dissatisfied a few minutes ago," he said as he returned his gaze to hers. "Or was your response an act, put on to appease me?" His eyes were the icy color of the Atlantic Ocean in the dead of winter.

Valerie might have shivered in the face of his cold stare, if it hadn't been for the flash of hot fury that seared through her. Angrier with him than she had ever been, she reacted to his accusation without thought or consideration or even instinctive self-preservation. Val's arm flew up and out. Her palm connected with his cheek with a stinging, resounding whack. Valerie felt the rippling force of the blow from her palm to her shoulder and all the way down to the base of her spine.

"How dare you accuse me of putting on that kind of act?" she cried, snatching her burning palm away from his face. A sinking sensation invaded her stomach as she watched a fiery imprint of her palm form on his pale skin.

Jonas had gone deathly still, for long moments not even appearing to breathe. The only living things about him were his eyes, and the expression in them nearly scared the life out of Valerie. In their sea-tossed depths she could see the inner battle he was fighting against the need to lash out and strike back at her.

Until that moment, Val had never felt an instant of physical fear of Jonas. Now, fear crawled through her veins like a cold-blooded viper. If Jonas lost his inner battle and struck her, she would go down like a felled tree, and she knew it. What was more, Val also knew she'd deserve it.

But she wouldn't run. She couldn't run! She could barely breathe.... Her spine rigid, Val endured his chilling stare, awaiting the outcome. The breath eased from her constricted chest a heartbeat after Jonas exhaled harshly.

"That was a close call, Valerie." His voice was tight with strain.

Relief brought a sheen of tears to her eyes. "I'm sorry, Jonas," she whispered.

"Don't ever dare to hit me again."

Val bristled. "And don't you ever again dare to accuse me of putting on an act to appease you."

Jonas had the grace to back down. "I'm sorry for that. I knew it wasn't true when I said it."

"I shouldn't have allowed it to hurt me." She sighed. "You've accused me unjustly before." Val was immediately sorry for the indictment.

Jonas winced, revealing the pain he had refused to acknowledge from her physical blow. His eyes grew dark, betraying the unceasing inner torment. With her unbridled tongue, she had sliced through the fabric of their past three years together, exposing the wound still open and bleeding in his soul. He *had* accused her unjustly before, knowing while he did so that it wasn't true. In consequence, an accident had caused Val to miscarry with their child. Jonas was still paying the price.

"Jonas." Hurting for him, Val reached out to him. It was when her palm touched his warm bare skin that she remembered that they were both still naked. It didn't matter. In comparison to the exposure of lingering pain in the soul, naked skin was of little importance. With a mental shrug, she stepped forward to slide her arms around his waist. Tears running freely down her face, she held him close, offering compassion and comfort, gratefully accepting the same from him when Jonas enclosed her within his crushing embrace.

"I'm sorry, Val." His voice was low and unsteady, and Valerie knew he was apologizing for his past as well as his present unfounded accusations.

"It's all right, Jonas." Val smoothed her hands over the tightly bunched muscles in his back, trying to ease the tension that was gripping him.

His arms contracted convulsively. She could hardly breathe. She didn't care.

"I'm going to be a grandfather," he murmured against her temple.

"I know." Val's smile was tender.

"I wanted to be a father again." Longing was woven through his whisper.

"I know." Val closed her eyes against a stinging surge of tears. The moisture clung to the springy hair on his chest. Jonas felt her tears and groaned.

"I love you, Val."

The memory was riding him, terrorizing him; Val could hear it in the tremor in his low voice. "I love you, Jonas." Turning her head, she pressed her parted lips to his moist chest.

"You're a part of me now," he said, responding to her caress with a shiver. "I don't know if I could survive without you. I don't think I'd want to survive." His shiver intensified. "Don't leave me, Val. Don't ever leave me."

"I won't. You know I won't." Val tightened her arms around his waist. "I couldn't."

Jonas was quiet for a moment, his strong arms crushing her softness to him. Val could feel the tension ease out of his taut muscles. A few moments later, she felt a different kind of tension ripple through him. She wasn't at all surprised when he backed her into, then onto, their king-size bed.

This time there was no sense of urgency to Jonas's lovemaking. His kiss was warm, sweet, seductive. Clinging to him, Val returned his kiss fervently. And after three years he knew exactly how to draw passion from her.

His broad hands encased her small, tip-tilted breasts, long fingers stroking the dusky peaks into quivering arousal. The touch of his tongue made her cry out with pleasure and with need. Val arched her back when he drew her into his mouth, and shuddered in response to his hungry suckling.

When Jonas brought his mouth back to hers, Val wrenched a receptive moan and shudder from him by gliding her palms down his torso and encasing him in her hands.

"Oh, Lord, Val, don't stop!" Jonas groaned, as she

lightly danced her fingers along his length. His breathing rough, erratic, he endured her ministrations for as long as possible before whispering, "Bring me to you, love."

Once again the tension coiled inside Valerie. And when at last it snapped, she clung to Jonas's solid form to keep from being swept away in the flood of ecstatic release.

Feeling warm and replete, Valerie burrowed close to Jonas as she drifted back to reality. She made a purrlike sound and arched luxuriously in response to the hand that was stroking her from shoulder to hip.

"We're fantastic together," Jonas murmured, gliding his palm to the base of her spine. "Aren't we?"

"Yes." Val smiled in appreciation of the soothing care he never failed to give to her in the afterglow of their lovemaking.

"And you love me?" he asked in a low-pitched voice, continuing his ministrations.

"Yes," Val breathed, again moving luxuriously against him, basking in his attention.

"And you promise never to leave me?" Jonas whispered, trailing his fingers slowly up her body to capture and tease one quivering breast.

"Yes." Val shivered in response to the tormenting stroke of his fingers.

"And you'll forget this nonsense about going to San Francisco without me?" he asked softly.

Floating on the sensuous web Jonas had woven around her, Val was about to murmur one more yes, when his question registered. Another fact registered, as well. Jonas had set out with calculated intent to bemuse and confuse her into capitulating to his wishes!

"No!" Forgetting his warning and her own contrition of a short time ago, Val administered a smart smack to his exposed flank. "Darn you, Jonas!" she exclaimed. Ignoring his grunt of pain, she scrambled away from him. He reached for her, but she avoided his hands by rolling off the side of the bed. "You're trying to manipulate me, and I don't like it."

"Valerie, come back here," Jonas barked, as she stormed toward the bathroom.

Unaware of the alluring picture she made standing framed in the doorway, Val spun around and planted her hands on her hips. "Is that an order, Mr. Thorne, sir?" Arching her raven's-wing eyebrows disdainfully, Val raised her chin and glared at him with outraged defiance.

With the agility of a much younger man, Jonas leaped from the bed and stalked after her. "Damn it, Val, will you wait a minute?" he growled when she turned and dashed into the bathroom.

"For what?" she retorted. "To give you time to think up some other method of persuasive control?" She swung the door closed, but was a heartbeat too slow. The palm of Jonas's hand caught the door a hairbreadth from the frame.

"I'm not trying to control you," he said, forcing her to retreat before the pressure he was applying to the door.

"Ha!" Val exclaimed in ridicule. "In one manner or another, you've exerted control over me from the day we met." She gave a sharp shake of her head, then corrected herself. "No. You were in control long before we actually met."

Jonas sliced one hand through the air with a gesture of dismissal. "I was your employer. The control I had then was minimal."

"Yes, when I first came to work for you, and when I worked in your Paris office," Val conceded. "But you have been in control, in one form or another, ever since you brought me back to the States with you three years ago."

Jonas had the look of a man teetering on the brink of losing his patience. "You needed someone to take control when I brought you back from France," he retorted. "At the time, you were barely able to think straight, let alone make the simplest decision for yourself."

Stung, because his harsh assertion was true, and she hated being reminded of the state she'd been in back then, Valerie was forced to take several deep, calming breaths to keep from shouting at him.

Her heaving chest drew his narrowed gaze and kindled a flame of renewed arousal in his flinty eyes. "If I've imposed my will over you or exerted control, it has been for your own welfare." A revealing tightness strained his voice.

Valerie was not flattered; she was furious. "How diligent and thoughtful of you," she said with exaggerated sweetness. Quivering in reaction to the anger searing through her, she drew herself up to her full height and glared directly into his eyes. "Well, Mr. Thorne, sir," she continued in a scathing tone, "your diligence is no longer required. I am now able to think as straight as the next person—man or woman—and

I am fully capable of making my own decisions, thank you.''

"Damn it, Val!" Jonas raked his hand through his hair. "I never said you weren't capable."

"I'm delighted to hear it," she said grittily. "Because my decision is made. I am going to San Francisco next month...*with* or *without* your approval!"

Jonas stared at her in cold fury, his expression frozen, his mouth tight. Val returned his stare until she thought she'd scream, just to break the tension crackling in the small space that separated them. When at last he broke the silence, his voice was hard, dismissive, hurtful.

"Do what the hell you want." Turning, Jonas stormed from the room, slamming the door behind him with deliberate force.

Val had to bite her lip to stop herself calling out after him. She took a step forward, then stopped. Not this time, she thought, shaking her head sharply. She would not run after Jonas this time. She had been that route before...almost exactly three years before. That time, her impulsive action had cost her the life of her child. This time it might cost her the budding life of her individuality.

But he had looked so alone in his fierceness.

Stop it, Val ordered herself. Just stop it right there. If Jonas now felt alone, it was because he had withdrawn, removed himself from the trials and tribulations of everyday life. If he didn't see the pain and striving of those closest to him, it was because he refused to look, observe, become involved.

It hurt to become involved. Val sighed. She was living proof of how very much it hurt to become involved. She had gone through the process not once, but twice.

Strange how the memory of her first experience with pain had paled into insignificance with the advent of her love for Jonas, Val mused, as she turned on the taps and adjusted the water temperature. Stepping into the stall, she stood directly under the shower spray. The warm water cascaded over her tired body, easing the tension from her mind and muscles.

Her first involvement.

Etienne.

The name whispered through her mind, bringing a bittersweet smile to Val's lips. Absently lathering shampoo into her hair, she slipped into a reverie about the man she had almost married.

Val had loved the gentle, elegant Frenchman, handsome brother of the equally handsome Jean-Paul. And Etienne had died. Val had watched him die. At the time, she had truly believed that all her hopes and dreams for the future had died with him.

Despondent, Val had wallowed in her grief for nearly a year, listless, without interest in the world around her, not caring either for herself or for the effect her carelessness was having on the Paris office of J.T. Electronics.

Then Jonas Thorne himself had flown into Paris, bringing with him Janet Peterson—and the winds of change. When he'd flown out again, back to Philadelphia, Jonas had taken with him a very unwilling Valerie.

And Valerie had felt an immediate and surprising antipathy toward Jonas Thorne.

Val's bittersweet smile curved wryly as she turned

off the water and stepped from the shower. How she had resented the man's dynamic personality. His arrogance. His impatience. And his indifference. Even in the numbed state her mind had been in, Val had experienced an unprecedented surge of resentment for her cold-eyed employer.

Now, three years later, Val could smile with amused remembrance of how those feelings had quickly evolved, first into respect, then into admiration for Jonas. It had been because of her growing respect that she had allowed him to talk her into a mutually convenient proposition of marriage.

Smoothing a delicately scented lotion into every inch of skin she could reach, Val winced as she recalled the spineless twit she had been. But then, she mused thoughtfully, even a strong-willed woman wouldn't have stood much of a chance against the determined Jonas. Not three years ago. Not today, either, come to think of it.

Val laughed softly to herself as she recapped the bottle, then wiped the excess lotion from her hands. In her now expert opinion, holding out against Jonas was like trying to halt the incoming tide or attempting to stop a tank with your bare hands.

When Jonas Thorne set his sights on something, be it a business deal or a woman, he played hardball. And when he was in high gear, both the weak and the strong had better head for the hills.

In high gear, Jonas Thorne was a sight to behold. Nobody knew it better than the woman he slept with.

And, having slept with Jonas for over three years, Valerie knew him very well—not completely, not entirely, and definitely not as well as she'd like, but very well indeed.

Val had thought Jonas was operating in high gear when he had unceremoniously whisked her back to the States from France. She had thought the same when he had overridden all her objections and talked her into marrying him. In retrospect, Val realized that in both endeavors Jonas had been merely coasting. Valerie had only seen Jonas shift into high gear the morning after she had slept with him for the first time.

They had been married less than twenty-four hours and were ostensibly on their honeymoon. Jonas had received an early-morning phone call, informing him of an impending business fight. The phone call had catapulted him into high gear and had put an end to their honeymoon.

Val had always believed that if they had had more time alone together, away from the pressures and stress of Jonas's work, they might have avoided the disastrous results of misunderstanding. But they hadn't had that time.

The business battle had raged for over a month, and Jonas had revealed a new facet of his character. When he was mad, really mad, Jonas was a power-house of energy, and he swore like a dockworker.

In awe and a little fearful of him, Valerie had kept her suspicions of being pregnant to herself. He had enough to contend with, she'd reasoned, without the added distraction of wondering about a possibility that might prove false with her very next normal cycle.

But then, immediately following his triumph in the business war, Jonas sprang the news on Val that his daughter would be returning home from the school she had been attending in Switzerland…on the same day that he was expecting the arrival of a liaison from the offices of a French business associate.

Even now, three years later, Valerie cringed inwardly at the memory of that disastrous day. For when Jonas returned to the house from collecting Mary Beth at the airport, he had with him her mother Lynn, his former wife. And as Val swiftly realized, the still-beautiful Lynn was a certified witch. She was also furious that Jonas had remarried, since she had clearly hoped to remarry him herself.

As if the confusion of meeting both Mary Beth and her acid-tongued mother wasn't enough, the French liaison arrived, and just happened to be Etienne's brother, Jean-Paul.

If they had had time alone together! Val had to laugh at the thought. She had known that Jonas had offered to house the liaison until he could secure a place of his own. But she had been stunned to discover that Lynn would be staying at the house during her visit, as well.

Large though Jonas's home was, Val had suddenly felt that she could hardly move without tripping over somebody. For, besides Jonas, Mary Beth, Lynn, Jean-Paul and Val, there was also Lynn's mother, Marge, who had shared Jonas's home since Mary Beth was an infant.

The mere memory of those tension-filled weeks boggled Val's mind. A chill feathered her naked skin, jolting her out of her introspection.

After slipping a lace and satin nightgown over her head, Val picked up her brush and dryer and turned to face the image reflected in the long mirror above the vanity.

The sodden mass of her black hair was daunting. With a sigh, Val set to work brushing the tangles from the long strands. For years she had worn her naturally curly hair short. But Jonas preferred it long.

The below-shoulder length her hair had attained said reams about how effectively she held out against Jonas, when it came to the crunch.

Not this time, Val vowed to her tight-lipped reflection.

She and Jonas had spent their one-night honeymoon in San Francisco. She had conceived her baby there. Jonas had promised to take her back. He had never mentioned it again.

With a final flip of the brush to her gleaming dry hair, Val set brush and dryer on the vanity. Tilting her chin, she gazed into the mirror and made a promise to herself.

She was going to San Francisco.

Chapter 3

"You did what?"

Valerie smiled at the look of astonishment on her companion's face. Janet Peterson had been Val's friend for over ten years, but she had known and worked for Jonas a lot longer. "I said I slapped him," Val repeated.

"Jonas!" Janet exclaimed in a shocked whisper that blended into the muted buzz of the lunchtime conversation from the other patrons, primarily female, in the small suburban Philadelphia restaurant, located within minutes of the home office of J.T. Electronics.

"Twice," Val confessed, omitting to add that the second slap had been to his naked flank.

"Incredible."

"Yes, I know." Val sighed. "I'm still having difficulty believing it myself." Her shoulders moved in a brief, helpless shrug. "I, ah, lost my temper."

"Well, that explains everything." Janet's expression was wry. "You really have changed," she observed, studying Valerie over the rim of the wineglass she'd raised to her lips.

"Have I?" Val frowned.

Janet rolled her eyes. "Are you kidding? Good grief, Val. Two years ago you wouldn't have dreamed of slapping anybody." She gave an abrupt laugh and shook her head. "Now you've slapped Jonas? Yes, I'd say you have changed quite a bit."

Valerie gnawed on her lower lip while contemplating her friend's opinion. She had suffered pangs of remorse and regret for striking Jonas through every one of the four days since that night. She had also suffered stabs from her conscience. Was she becoming too independent and aggressive in her determination to be her own person? More importantly, would she run the risk of losing Jonas if she continued toward the goal of equality that she had set for herself?

On the other hand, Val's emerging assertiveness had countered with the stark declaration that she couldn't revert to the pliable lump of clay she'd been when Jonas had literally taken over her life.

This inner conflict had been Val's primary reason for inviting Janet to lunch. Of all the women Val knew, Janet was the most liberated and sensible. So, if Janet thought she was going too far, Val figured she'd better rethink her game plan.

Of course, Janet hadn't actually said she thought Val was overdoing the feminist bit—only that Val had changed. Deciding to find out how Janet felt, Val went directly to the point.

"In what way have I changed?" she asked. "For the better? Worse? How?"

Janet, being Janet, laughed at Val's blunt demand for answers. "Oh, definitely for the better," she said with conviction. "I'd say you've come pretty much into your own." Her grin was purely feline. "By thinking for yourself, you've not only shaken Jonas up, you've given him something to think about—I mean besides electronics."

Though she felt a measure of relief, Val murmured, "But I shouldn't have hit him."

Janet shrugged. "Probably not...since striking out physically never solves anything." Her expression grew thoughtful. "Did he provoke it?"

"Yes," Val answered without hesitation.

Janet responded with a shrug. "Then don't worry about it. It's not the end of the world, you know."

Val sighed. "But it was rather childish."

"Maybe." Janet eyed her speculatively. "Nevertheless, you have definitely matured."

"I guess everyone needs to grow up sometime, Janet." Val's voice took on a defensive edge. "And, in my case, I'd say it's long overdue. I'm going to be thirty-one years old."

Janet was noticeably unimpressed, but then, it took a great deal to impress Janet. She had often said that her insouciance was a result of Jonas's influence. "Getting brave in your old age, too, are you?" She arched one eyebrow.

Valerie made a sour face, which was unrelated to the taste of her wine. "No," she admitted.

"Yet you slugged him."

"It was pure reflex." Val set her glass on the table

beside her half-eaten salad. "I didn't think... I re-acted."

"May one ask what provocation you reacted to?"

A spark of amusement lighted Valerie's eyes. "You mean you can't guess?"

"You told Jonas about your decision to attend that rally or whatever in San Francisco?" Janet asked.

"Yes." Valerie was not about to tell Janet the in-timate details, but she felt no compunction at reveal-ing the reason for the argument.

"And might I ask if you're still planning to go?"

"Yes." Val lifted her small chin in defiance.

"Uh-huh." Janet took another sip of her wine, ap-parently unconcerned. "Then may the bride ask what the chances are of the matron of honor and the best man being on speaking terms on the day of the wed-ding?" Her smile revealed a tiny crack in her outward composure. "Just curious, you know, since the wed-ding is only two weeks from tomorrow."

Val's defiance gave way to concern. A tired-sounding sigh whispered through her soft lips. "Oh, Janet, of course we'll be on speaking terms." Val sent up a silent prayer that she could make good on the promise. "You know neither one of us would do any-thing to ruin your wedding day."

"I sincerely hope not—" Janet's smile was tinged with self-mockery "—considering how long it's taken me to work up the courage to face the altar and the idea of spending each and every one of my re-maining days with a man."

"Charlie loves you," Val said with utter convic-tion.

Janet smiled. "I know. And I love him. But loving

each other and living together in holy wedlock are two entirely different concepts.''

"Tell me about it," Val rejoined wryly. "But at least you won't need to work through a drastic change of image," she added. "Charlie fell in love with a strong-willed woman. Jonas believed he had married a marshmallow.''

"Jonas did marry a marshmallow. Poor Jonas." Janet's grin belied her words.

Valerie made a face. "Poor Jonas my foot. I think poor, arrogant Jonas is long overdue for a mental shaking. I love the man to distraction," she readily admitted. "But I'm tired of playing the boring echo to his voice of authority.''

"Love him to distraction?" Janet laughed. "I think you just might *drive* him to distraction.''

Val shrugged. "It'll do him good. He's never been there. He might even learn what all the rest of us mortals have to contend with day after day.''

"I wouldn't make book on it," Janet drawled, unconsciously echoing one of Jonas's stock expressions. "But meanwhile," she said, glancing at her wristwatch, "I have to get back to the office and contend with the meeting Jonas scheduled for two o'clock this afternoon.'' She reached for the check, then smiled when Val scooped it from beneath her fingers. "Thanks for lunch," she said as she slid her chair away from the table. "Where are you headed to from here? One of your classes?''

"Nope.'' Val set her black hair swirling with a brief shake of her head. "I'm armed with plastic and I'm going shopping for some new clothes to take with me to California. I saw a gown in Bloomingdale's that I'm considering for the formal reception that's being held on the last night of the rally. It's a trifle daring.'' Her smile was sweet. ''Jonas will probably blow a fuse when I show it to him.''

Janet's ripple of delighted laughter turned heads in the elegant restaurant. ''You are living dangerously, aren't you?'' she said as they left the establishment.

''It adds spice to life,'' Val replied. It had certainly spiced up her love life, she thought, recalling Jonas's ardor on the night of their confrontation. To be sure, Jonas hadn't touched her since that night, but...

''Will you be at class tonight?'' Janet asked, interrupting Val's thoughts.

''Yes, of course.''

''Okay, see you then. But right now, I've got to run.'' With a flashing smile Janet dashed for her car, which she'd parked beside Val's on the restaurant's parking lot.

Despite her protests at the time against his extravagance, Val loved the silver Cadillac Jonas had given her on their first Christmas together. A soft, faintly sad smile curved her mouth as she slid onto the plush leather seat behind the steering wheel.

She had been infinitely more amenable then, Val mused, recalling that holiday morning. Jonas had made hot, sweet love to her that morning, in quite the same way as he had four nights ago, Val remembered with a shiver.

Forgetting where she was for a moment, Val stared through the windshield, reliving the promise of hope she had felt then, two and a half years ago.

Val had been happy then. She and Jonas had weathered the first stormy months of marriage and the loss of their unborn child. Since their marriage had begun as an unromantic business deal, Val had naturally felt uncertainty and doubt about Jonas's feelings for her. With the intention of ending their union, Val had left him a few weeks after suffering her miscarriage.

But she couldn't stay away.

A reminiscent smile shadowed Val's eyes and mouth. Even then, confused and unsure of the feelings, if any, Jonas had for her, Val had loved him to the exclusion of all else, even her own sense of self-protection. Giving in to her own needs, she had returned to Jonas, determined to salvage their marriage if at all possible. Jonas's reaction to her return and her own willingness to make the union work had made the possibilities for their future together seem endless.

Jonas had said he loved her. His declaration was all that Val required...at that point in time.

And Val had been happy.

But as the months passed, and she failed to conceive again, Val's happiness began to dissipate, to be replaced by feelings of inadequacy and discontent.

A wealthy man, Jonas showered luxuries on her, beginning with the silver Cadillac and culminating, but certainly not ending, with the house they now occupied. What Jonas didn't understand, couldn't seem to understand, was that although she appreciated and enjoyed every one of his generous gifts, Val didn't need *things*. She needed a sense of purpose, of contribution, of partnership.

Since she had fulfilled the very demanding duties as Jonas's private secretary before their marriage, and was qualified to be the assistant to almost any CEO,

Val decided to go back to work. But when she told him about her plans, Jonas swiftly scotched her aspirations.

His objections were valid; Jonas's objections, as well as his objectives, were always valid. He reminded her, unnecessarily, that he himself put in long hours of work each and every day of the week...in addition to quite a few nights. He pointed out to Val that their time together was precious, because it was limited.

Furthermore, although Jonas believed in and supported the principle of equal opportunity for women, and had proved his support by placing several women, Janet included, in executive positions within his company, he stated arrogantly and unconditionally that he wanted his wife in his home. Period. And, as far as Jonas was concerned, the subject was closed.

Acceding to his wishes, Val drifted through life month after endless month, playing the role of housewife and hostess, while plaguing her obstetrician with questions about her seeming inability to conceive a child.

The harried physician ran test after test, all of which proved negative. He then had her doing the morning temperature routine, also to no avail. When he ran out of tests and other ideas, the doctor finally offered the opinion that Val was too tense and too stressed about the whole thing, and advised her to find something to concentrate on other than her inability to become pregnant.

That had been nearly a year ago. Since then, Val had followed the doctor's advice with the fervor born of desperation. It had been a hit-or-miss endeavor.

And her first attempt had turned out to be an unmitigated disaster.

Val laughed aloud as she turned the key in the ignition, firing the engine into a well-tuned purr.

She had joined the community garden club, only to learn that she had a thumb as black as her hair, capable of knocking off the heartiest of plants within days of purchase.

Switching on the car radio, Val hummed along with the music as she drove off the parking lot and onto the highway leading to a nearby shopping mall. Along with the soothing melody, memories wafted through her mind as she drove.

Undaunted after the garden club fiasco, Val had enrolled in an eclectic cooking course being offered by a local department store. She was more talented in cooking and, as a result, Jonas suddenly discovered better fare at the dinner table.

He didn't object, Val recalled. On the contrary, Jonas was lavish with his praise. Of course, she mused wryly, preparing excellent meals went hand in glove with housewifery...not to mention with his healthy appetite.

Jonas's objections came later.

Had his initial grumblings of disapproval begun with the course she had taken on emerging female supremacy? Or had they started with the first overnight trip she'd taken away from home as a new member of the local chapter of the Ideas for a Saner World Society?

Val couldn't remember, but she did recall Jonas's opinion of the society in general.

"I think the whole idea is insane," he'd growled.

"I'd bet a year of the company's profits that the society was founded by bored women looking for something to do and an excuse to travel while they're doing it."

He was right, of course. Val quickly lost interest in the disorganized organization and the petty squabbling the women indulged in. But while admitting that Jonas was right about the society, Val realized his reasoning on the subject of women was faulty.

In truth, most of the women Valerie had come into contact with in the course of her varied pursuits *were* bored. But, she reflected, had anyone ever bothered to delve into the reason why they were bored? As far as Val could ascertain, no one had…most especially not the women's own husbands.

Although Val had met women who were plainly just malcontents, the majority was happily married to men with high incomes, men who took pride in their ability to support and maintain their families, men who preferred their wives not to have careers. In other words, Valerie met housewives who needed something more, women exactly like herself.

A blast of rock and roll from the radio jolted Val out of her reverie just as she was about to drive by the last entrance lane into the mall.

Cursing under her breath at her inattention, Val made the turn in the nick of time, telling herself to get her head together and keep it that way.

At midafternoon on a Friday, the mall was full, mainly of women with small children. Dodging the baby strollers, Val concentrated on her business. The reason she had given Janet for her expedition was true…up to a point. Val did intend to shop for a few things to take to California. But her main objective was to pick up the engraved sterling silver service she had ordered as a wedding gift for Janet and Charlie.

Leaving the gift for last, Val browsed through several of the stores, vacillating in her mind over the gown she had mentioned to Janet. After forty-odd minutes of indecision, and telling herself Jonas really would explode if she came home with the dress, Val straightened her shoulders and marched into the large department store. Some thirty or so minutes later she left the mall, the silver, several accessory items and the gown in hand.

The phone was ringing when Val let herself into the house through the garage entrance. Dumping her handbag, car keys and packages onto the table, she dashed across the room and grabbed the kitchen extension.

"Hello," she panted in a breathless voice.

"Where did I chase you from?" Marge, Jonas's former mother-in-law, asked in her usual down-to-earth manner.

"Oh, hi, Marge," Val said, in between taking deep breaths. "I just came in from shopping."

"Did you buy yourself some goodies?" the older woman asked, bringing a smile to Val's mouth. Marge, as Val well knew, was a dedicated window shopper.

"A gown to die for," Val answered, her smile growing into an impish grin. "Jonas will likely need to hire a roofer after he gets a look at it."

"Go through the ceiling, will he?" Marge said with a laugh.

"I'm afraid so," Val replied in a dry tone.

"Good," Marge snorted. "The cracker needs to be jostled out of his rut every now and again."

Val chuckled at the older woman's use of the nickname the people closest to Jonas used to describe him. Having originally come from Tamaqua in the Pennsylvania coal region, Jonas had acquired the appellation of "coal cracker" somewhere along the way from bastard orphan to business titan.

Reminded of him, Val slanted a glance at the clock. "And, speaking of the cracker," she drawled. "I'd better get cracking with dinner."

"And speaking of dinner," Marge echoed. "That's the reason I called. Tomorrow night. Seven-thirty."

"I hadn't forgotten, Marge." Val groaned silently. Excited about becoming a great-grandmother in the near future, Marge had insisted on preparing a family celebration dinner, which by itself didn't bother Val. The hitch was that Marge had also insisted on including Lynn in the party. "Is there something I can do to help?" she asked, resigned to the ordeal.

"No, thank you. I have everything under control."

Val had to laugh. "You always do. But if you find you need some help, give me a call."

"Under the circumstances, that's very generous of you." The older woman's voice was thick with emotion. "You're a real lady, Valerie."

"Thank you," Val said, then blurted out without thinking, "That's nice, but can you tell me why it seems that the real ladies of this world have to fight for everything twice as hard as the real bitches?"

"No, I can't," Marge replied. "But remember, you have Jonas, Val."

And Lynn doesn't. The unspoken rider hummed along the line connecting the two phones.

"Yes, I have Jonas," Val said. The problem is to hold the marriage together without surrendering unconditionally, she reflected with wry humor. Keeping her thoughts to herself, she continued smoothly, "And Jonas and I will be there tomorrow evening."

"I do understand how difficult this will be for you, Val," Marge said, making it clear that she saw through Val's smooth tone. "And I want you to know how much I appreciate it. Some women…a lot of women…would have raised a fuss, if not flat out refused to show up."

"Well," Val said, "I won't promise that I'll be there with bells on, but I will be there."

"Because you're nice," Marge said.

Or stupid, Val thought. Or a coward. Or both. Aloud she merely said, "It's nice to know you think I'm nice, but right now, I have to get a move on. See you tomorrow, Marge."

Val shot another glance at the clock as she hung up. Time was gaining on her, and she had a lot to do before leaving for the exercise class she attended twice a week with Janet. As it was, she probably wouldn't have time to eat dinner, especially if Jonas was late getting home, which he was more often than not.

Being careful of the large white bow on the elaborately wrapped gift, Val collected her packages, carried them to the bedroom and deposited them on the bed. After changing into lightweight slacks and a tailored shirt, she returned to the kitchen to prepare dinner.

Jonas was late. He was tired. He was in a concili-
atory mood. But, as luck would have it, he had, as
usual, forgotten that it was Val's night for exercise
class.

"What's the rush?" he asked idly, observing her
hurried activity from the doorway.

Val continued to stir the cheese sauce for the vegetables as she cast a look at him. "I hope you don't
mind sitting at the breakfast counter to eat," she said,
avoiding his eyes and his question.

"I don't." Jonas strolled to the stove. Looming
over her, he sniffed appreciatively. "Smells good."
Dipping his head, he nuzzled the curve of her shoulder. "So do you."

While Val's senses soared, her spirits plummeted.
Why now? she groaned inwardly. During the past
four days she had been waiting and hoping for his
mood to improve. By why did it have to be now? She
trembled visibly when his teeth gently raked her soft
skin. Feeling her tremor, he murmured her name and
slid his arms around her waist.

"Jonas." Forgetting the sauce, Val turned into his
arms and raised her mouth for his kiss.

His mouth was hotter than the burners on the stove.
His kiss gave silent testimony to the hunger raging
inside his body. "I need you, Val," he groaned
against her mouth. "It's been four days, and that's
three and a half too many. Let's postpone dinner for
an hour or so."

"Oh, Jonas, I can't," Val cried, pulling away from
him.

"Why not?" Jonas inquired with a frown.

"I have to leave in a few minutes to meet Janet," Val replied.

"For what?" he demanded.

Anger born of impatience sharpened Val's voice. "It's Friday, Jonas. My exercise class... Remember?"

"Oh, hell," he muttered. Frustration scored his strong features. "I was looking forward to a quiet evening alone with you."

Weakening, Val glanced at the clock. If she could catch Janet at home, Val was positive she wouldn't mind if—

"Why don't you give the class a skip?" Jonas muttered, interrupting her thoughts. "You don't need the damned exercise, anyway. You're thin as a rail now."

Thin as a rail! That did it, Val thought, moving away from the stove. "No, Jonas, I can't give it a skip. I told Janet I'd be there." Stiff with anger, Val walked to the closet to get her purse and gym bag.

"Hey!" Jonas exclaimed. "What about dinner?"

Val paused at the door to level a cool look at him. She was tempted to tell him precisely what he could do with the meal. Instead she said, "Since you're going to eat it, you can damn well finish cooking it yourself."

As a rule, Val enjoyed the exercise class. Tonight was the exception. Seething with anger and resentment at Jonas's lack of interest for practically everything unconnected to electronics, she performed the routines automatically, stretching and flexing her mind more than her body as she inwardly raged against his attitude. By the time the class was over, Val was physically exhausted and mentally depleted.

"God, I hate this class," Janet grumbled as they changed from their leotards into street clothes. "I keep wondering why I do this to myself two nights a week."

"To stay trim, supple and young looking," Val replied in a tired mutter.

"Right." Janet grimaced. "You know, Val, there are days, many in number, when I feel like saying to hell with all this silliness." She raked a brush through the hair she had allowed to grow to shoulder length because Charlie liked long hair on a woman. "I mean," she added, tossing the brush into her nylon carryall, "do you ever get the feeling that what you have to go through to stay trim, supple and young looking is rather ridiculous...considering that in the end you lose the battle to old age, anyway?"

Some of Val's resentment seeped through her guard. "Why, Janet Peterson, surely you're not suggesting we let ourselves go to pot and simply enjoy life?"

Janet eyed her shrewdly as they left the building and headed for the parking lot. "You're tired of it, too, huh?"

Val sighed. "Not the exercises. I usually enjoy the workout. I suppose I'm just in a bad mood tonight."

Janet stopped beside Val's car. "And I suppose I'm just having pre-wedding jitters." Her grin was unrepentant. "But I still hate the exercises." She started to move toward her own car, then paused to ask, "By the way, did you buy that gown you were telling me about?"

"Yes."

"What did Jonas say?"

"Nothing."

"Really!" Janet exclaimed. "Incredible."

"He hasn't seen it yet," Val admitted.

"Well, good luck, with Jonas and with Lynn tomorrow night." With a grin and a wave, Janet turned away. "If the witch gives you a hard time, haul off and belt her. No one deserves it more." Her laughter wafted back to Val on the warm spring air.

Valerie mulled over Janet's parting sally all the way home. And the more she mulled it over, the madder she got.

Without a shadow of a doubt, Val knew that Jonas would have a fit when she showed him the dress. The realization rankled.

Why shouldn't she buy any damn dress she wanted? she asked herself irritably. Why shouldn't any woman, come to that? Men bought and wore whatever they chose, didn't they?

So the dress was a little daring, she railed. So what. It certainly didn't overstep the bounds of decency, and she looked pretty terrific in it, if she did say so herself.

Oh, but she knew, knew too well what Jonas would say, Val thought, kicking her anger into high gear. He'd very likely give her that cold, arrogant look of his and ask her what kind of game she was planning to stalk.

What was it with the male of the species, anyway? Val fumed. What was it in their thinking process that prevented them from affording the female the same rights as they demanded for themselves?

And why, when he devoted the majority of his energy and time to his professional pursuits, did Jonas object so strenuously to his wife wanting to plumb the depths of her own capabilities? Now Val carried her furious stream of consciousness to the personal level. Why couldn't he see or understand her need to feel his equal in situations and circumstances other than those requiring a prone position in a bed?

And why should she be expected to endure his former wife's waspish remarks? Val asked herself in outrage. Everyone, from Janet and the rest of Jonas's employees to Jonas himself, knew that Lynn derived pleasure from baiting Val. And, though Jonas generally ignored Lynn and had advised Val to do likewise, she was thoroughly fed up with the tiresome woman.

By the time she made a sharp turn into the driveway, Val had whipped herself into a righteous fury and was spoiling for a fight.

One was waiting for her.

Standing at the bedroom window, Jonas narrowed his eyes as he watched the car's headlights precede the silver Cadillac into the driveway. Behind him, Val's new gown lay in a crumpled heap on the bed, where he had flung it in unbridled anger.

Val had been gone less than three hours, but that was enough time for Jonas to work himself into a jealous rage.

And all because of an innocent, if marginally daring, chiffon confection in the exact same shade of violet as his wife's hauntingly beautiful eyes.

He had discovered the dress while seeking to relieve his boredom. Not that it had been hidden away;

it hadn't been. It had been on the bed, still in the distinctive department store box, where Val had obviously placed it on her return from shopping.

Restless after finishing the delicious meal Val had prepared for him, which he had no more than picked at, Jonas had wandered upstairs. His intention had been to work until Val came home, but he never made it into the office. On entering the bedroom, Jonas couldn't help but notice the packages strewed across the bed.

Wryly wishing that he and Val were cluttering the spread instead of the parcels, he idly crossed to the bed and curiously began examining the contents of the assortment of bags and boxes. The wrapped wedding gift brought a grunt of satisfaction from his throat. The skimpy pieces of satin and lace he uncovered in another package brought a smile to his lips and an ache to his loins. The low-cut bodice on the shimmering gown, on the other hand, sent a quiver of uncertainty shafting through him.

The gown was beautiful, and would look even more so draped on Val's sylphlike body. A frown drew Jonas's brows together. Val had never before bought or worn anything quite so suggestive, at least not to his knowledge, and not for him. Why had she purchased this particular gown now? Had she bought it to take with her to San Francisco? Jonas felt positive that she had. The gown was obviously expensive. The price didn't upset Jonas, but Val's reason for buying it did bother him.

With little effort, Jonas could imagine how Val would look with the shimmering dress floating around her ankles and her gorgeous hair swirling around her bared shoulders. The image was so sharp, so appealing that he caught his breath.

But why had she bought the gown to wear when he wouldn't be with her? Jonas asked himself, feeling anger stir. The question repeated itself throughout the hours Val was away.

Intellectually, Jonas knew his anger was unwarranted. But his emotions were running close to the surface. Jonas wasn't feeling intellectual or even logical. He was feeling the sharp claws of jealousy.

Was Val tired of competing with his obsession for his work? Tired enough to seek solace in the attentions of another man? Jonas didn't want to believe that Val would deceive him. But jealousy clouded his thinking and ignited his temper.

All because he had opened a box and found a gown seemingly made for seduction.

Responding to his own unsettling thoughts, Jonas crushed the filmy material in his clenched fists, then flung it away from him.

Jonas was still standing at the window, his expression frozen, when Val entered the bedroom. He didn't turn around until he heard her startled gasp.

"Jonas, what…?" Val's voice trailed away as she ran to the bed.

"What did you buy it for?" he asked, turning to watch her carefully lift the gown from the bed.

The look she sent him held dawning comprehension. Without having to hear him admit to the act, she knew he had deliberately tossed the gown into a heap. "I bought it to wear to the dinner and reception being held the last night of the rally," she replied angrily, examining the dress for possible damage.

"If it's still in one piece," he said, as she held the garment aloft and gently shook it, "take it back."

Val raised her chin in a familiar gesture of defiance. "I most certainly will not take it back. I am taking it to California." Her tone was tight with determination. Crossing to the walk-in closet, she disappeared inside. When she emerged, her hands were empty, and planted on her narrow hips. "And I am going to wear it to the reception." The glitter in her eyes defied him to forbid her to do either.

"Are you planning to come back from California?" Jonas asked, not even certain he wanted to hear her answer to the question that had just occurred to him.

Val's expression went blank an instant, then her eyes flew wide with surprise. "Yes, of course I'm coming back!" she exclaimed. "Why would you even dream that I wouldn't?"

The breath Jonas hadn't realized he was holding eased from his constricted chest. "That dress." He flicked his hand at the closet. "It's the kind of thing a woman wears when she's trying to attract male attention."

Val looked astonished. The next moment, her eyes flashed with anger. Then she exploded. "Jonas Thorne, that is the most ridiculous statement you've ever made! It ranks right up there with the blanket condemnations made by the idiots who maintain that a woman is inviting physical attack by the way she dresses." Moving slowly, she walked to within inches of him. Her voice was soft, but held a steel thread of warning. "Watch yourself, mister. You're getting fast and loose with your accusations…and I'm getting pretty damn tired of hearing them.''

She was right. Jonas knew she was right. His remark wasn't merely ridiculous, it was stupid. Jonas didn't like feeling ridiculous and stupid. He didn't like feeling jealous, either. But, since he'd never experienced any of these feelings before falling in love with Val, Jonas didn't know quite how to back out of the corner he'd talked himself into.

Besides, there was his pride to contend with.

''I haven't accused you of anything,'' he finally replied. ''But you can't blame a man for objecting to his wife parading around half-naked in front of other men when he's not with her.'' The instant the words were out of his mouth, Jonas knew he was in even deeper trouble.

''Half-naked!'' Val erupted like a volcano. ''Parade! How dare you! I never parade around in front of men…naked or otherwise.'' She raised her hand, and Jonas's eyes narrowed in warning. But all she did was tap him on the chest, hard, with her small index finger. ''And, for your information, Mr. Thorne, the only reason my husband won't be around is simply because he refuses to accompany his wife.''

She scored a bull's-eye. Jonas felt it, but wasn't about to concede the bout. ''You never said a word about the damned rally until you called to inform me that you were going to San Francisco. I didn't refuse to accompany you,'' he shot back. ''I wasn't invited along.'' But Jonas had to admit to himself that had she asked him to go with her, he would have refused, all the while assuming that with his refusal, Val would not go by herself. All the same, when it came to confessing to Val what he admitted to himself, pride got in the way.

"Because I knew you wouldn't go," Val countered.

"Someone has to work to pay for things like cars and jewelry and expensive gowns that are only half there," he retaliated without thinking.

Val literally bristled. "Some*one* wouldn't have to, if he weren't so dead set against his wife working!"

"Don't start that again," Jonas growled, his anger renewed by that old bone of contention. "Why can't you be content just being my wife?"

"Would you be?" Val demanded.

"What?"

"Reverse our positions, Jonas," she said patiently. "Then ask yourself if you'd be content to stay home, twiddling your thumbs and vegetating."

Jonas was outflanked and knew it. He was a fair man and had never treated any woman with less than equality. But he had a blind spot about Val. It had been that way from the beginning. She was exclusively his. He wanted to maintain the status quo.

So, even though he knew intellectually that he was being unfair, Jonas was caught in an emotional web that had been reinforced by ego and pride. By rights, he knew he should back down. Hell, by rights he knew he owed Val an apology. But pride, ego and emotional entanglement dominated. Instead of backing down, Jonas attacked.

"But our positions aren't reversed. I'm not a woman. You are." Lifting his hand, Jonas caught her delicate chin with hard fingers. His voice was harsh with warning. "You are *my* woman. And don't you ever forget it."

Chapter 4

Valerie lay beside Jonas in the big bed, separated from him physically by mere inches, but emotionally by miles. Her body was taut, quivering in reaction to the anger simmering inside her tired mind.

His woman.

The taunt sprang into her mind every time she began to relax, releasing a fresh onslaught of anger. Half an hour had passed since Jonas had coldly informed Val that she belonged to him. The scene following his pronouncement had been replayed inside her head repeatedly during that tense span of time.

"I'm not a thing, Jonas!" Val had cried.

"I didn't say you were. I said you were a woman."

"You said I was *your* woman."

"Well, aren't you?"

"Yes, but…"

Jonas's smile was maddeningly triumphant. "End of argument. I'm tired and I'm going to bed."

The memory of the frustration she had experienced, was still experiencing, had Val grinding her teeth. Turning away from her without another word, Jonas had proceeded to undress. Then, sweeping the packages off the bed and dropping them into one of the easy chairs by the window, he crawled between the sheets, leaving her fuming. She had no option but to follow suit.

Val had considered sleeping in the guest room, but rejected the notion out of pure stubbornness. Jonas had had his way once too often, she'd decided, beginning with his insistence that they marry, and ending with his insistence that she remain at home, playing the role of dutiful wife. She had retreated before his commanding personality for the last time. She would not retreat again.

Tossing off her clothes, Val had climbed onto the very edge of the king-size mattress. She had literally clung there, seething, ever since.

"Val?"

His soft voice alerted her an instant before his arm curled around her waist to haul her against his naked body. His *aroused* naked body. Val went stiff with outrage and disbelief. Surely he didn't think she'd...? But of course he did, she thought, incensed. She was *his* woman, wasn't she?

"I love you, Val." Looming over her, Jonas lowered his head to hers.

Val pulled her head away as his mouth brushed hers. "Let me go, Jonas," she ordered through gritted teeth.

Ignoring her command, Jonas slowly glided his palm from her waist to her hip and over her flat belly, taking possession of the soft mound below as he planned to take possession of her whole body...as if by right of ownership.

Passion unfurled deep inside Val, strong and urgent. Fighting her response to his nearness, his touch, she clenched her teeth. She couldn't allow him to do this again, she told herself. She would not! Stiff muscles beginning to grow warm and pliant, she strained against his hold.

Jonas tested her resistance by caressing the corner of her mouth with his parted lips. "The argument's over, ended." A smile hovered on his lips. "Come, love, kiss me, make love with me, it's not like you to sulk," he murmured, inadvertently freeing her from the sensuous spell he alone could induce.

"I'm not sulking." Val's voice was soft, raspy from her effort to control the urge to shout at him.

Mistaking the husky sound for passion, Jonas worked his long fingers between her tightly closed thighs. "Then why don't you relax? Why won't you kiss me?"

"Because I'm mad, Jonas," Val said angrily. "And when I'm mad, I'm mad all over." Clasping his wrist, she pushed his hand away. "Now get your hands off me."

His surprise and shock apparent, Jonas grew absolutely still. Val saw the color seep from his face, then rush back, flaring darkly under the taut skin over his jutting cheekbones.

Staring at him, Val lay rigid and shivering, waiting for his reaction. When it came, it was abrupt and violent. Muttering a string of curses that singed her ears, Jonas threw back the covers and leaped from the bed.

Every muscle in his trim, magnificent body taut with tension, he stared down at her from narrowed eyes.

"I'm sorry if my touch is repulsive to you," he said with unrelenting harshness.

Although his set features were devoid of expression, Val could sense the pain of rejection and humiliation he was suffering. Jolting upright, she reached out to him. "Jonas, I didn't say or mean that I find your touch repulsive. I don't. You know I don't. But I can't go on—"

"Spare me the excuses," Jonas interrupted her in a hard tone. "I don't need them." Spinning on his heel, he strode from the room, slamming the door after him.

Val's extended arm fell limply to her thigh and she stared at the door until the tears filling her eyes blurred her vision. She had started to say that she couldn't go on acting as if nothing had happened, while the dissension between them remained unresolved. Why hadn't Jonas listened? More importantly, why didn't he ever *hear* her, even when he did listen?

Chilled on the inside and outside, Val lay down again, this time on Jonas's side of the bed. Suddenly it seemed enormous. Feeling the warmth left from his body, inhaling the masculine scent of him, she curled into a ball of misery beneath the covers. Val rarely gave way to tears. But now she was alone, with no one to see her submit to despair. Burying her face in the indentation made by his head, Val sobbed into Jonas's pillow.

His muscles locked with tension, Jonas lay in the unfamiliar bed, alternately cursing and berating himself for his uncivilized behavior. But though he was disgusted, he was not surprised. He always wound up losing his temper when he and Val argued. Jonas even knew why he always lost his temper with her; the possibility of losing her scared him stupid.

She had rejected him, and that had both scared and hurt Jonas. So he'd reacted true to form by lashing out at her. Then when she had tried to explain her feelings she had scared him even more, because he'd been afraid she was going to say she couldn't go on with him any longer. So he'd cut her off.

He had been hurt, and he'd wanted to hurt her back. Yet now, alone in a strange bed, aching for her in every cell of his body, Jonas was hurting as much for Val as for himself.

Val had ordered him to take his hands off her.

That had been his problem from the first time he saw her. Jonas groaned. He just couldn't keep his hands off her.

Rolling onto his side, Jonas curled into a ball and punched the pillow.

Damn it! Why did being in love have to hurt so much?

The question kept Jonas awake most of the night.

Val awoke early Saturday morning with a hangover from the crying jag in the form of a blasting headache. Feeling as though she'd been on a three-day binge, she dragged her tired body from the bed. She had slept a total of three hours. Her eyes were red-rimmed, her mind was dull and her spirits were not merely low but down for the count.

Other than leave her body clean and wet, a stinging shower had little effect upon her condition. After pulling on her regular Saturday attire of jeans, a T-shirt and flat shoes, Val took a few listless swipes at her disheveled hair with a brush before heading downstairs.

The house was quiet. Valerie had become accustomed to the silence. The house was always quiet. Jonas seldom stayed home from the office on Saturday. As a rule, Val woke when he left the bed, then got up to make him breakfast. This morning, she hadn't even heard him moving around.

Val sniffed as she made her way to the kitchen. The aroma was tantalizing. Obviously Jonas had made breakfast for himself before leaving for the office. The scent of coffee drew her like a magnet. Val took a step into the room and came to an abrupt halt, a startled "Oh!" bursting from her parched throat.

Jonas was seated at the breakfast counter, a steaming cup of coffee cradled in his hands. He glanced around at her as she began to move again.

"There's coffee," he said brusquely, jerking his head to indicate the nearly full pot.

"Yes, I see." Val's voice was strained. She wet her dry lips. "Thank you."

"You're welcome," her husband replied.

Like strangers, Val thought, grasping the handle of the coffeepot with trembling fingers. They were acting like strangers, making polite, stilted conversation.

"What would you like for breakfast?" Val tried to infuse some warmth into her voice, and winced when the sound came out flat and dull.

"It doesn't matter." Jonas's tone betrayed a lack of interest.

"I don't know how to cook that." She winced again; her attempt at wry humor was falling as flat as she felt.

"I think you use a frying pan." Instead of teasing, Jonas's voice sounded chiding.

"Right." Val sighed. She was tired, and it was going to be a very long day.

In silence she cooked him scrambled eggs. Jonas ate them in silence. He read the morning paper. She listened to the kitchen clock tick. When he finally spoke, she started.

"I've ordered a half dozen bottles of champagne to be delivered to Marge for tonight."

"That was thoughtful of you."

More silence. Heavy. Oppressive. When Val couldn't stand it another moment, she spoke again. "I picked up the gift for Janet and Charlie yesterday."

"I saw it."

Silence.

When Val had had enough, she decided to fill the quiet with some productive noise. Pushing back her chair, she got up and carried her cup to the sink.

"Where are you going?"

Val's head whipped around at the sharp note in Jonas's voice. "To collect the laundry." She frowned. "Why?"

His shrug looked more stiff than casual. "Would you mind refilling my cup?" As if in afterthought, he picked up the cup and held it out to her. She filled the cup for him, then left the room.

* * *

It was a very long day, peppered by awkward attempts at innocuous conversation and obvious avoidance of meaningful discussion.

It was a trying day, at least for Val. Every time she turned around, she nearly ran smack into Jonas, who seemed to be trailing her from room to room as she went about her normal Saturday routine of straightening the house, while the laundry went through the wash and dry cycles.

Lunch proved to be a reenactment of breakfast—silence, intermittently broken by stilted remarks. Val had never faced the cleaning up with such relief.

Late in the afternoon, Jonas suggested a nap. Val told him to go right ahead. After staring at her for tautly strung seconds, Jonas turned away from her.

Watching him with pain-filled eyes, Val fought against the clamoring desire to run after him, burrow into the secure haven of his strong arms and agree to any demands he might make of her, be they for then or the future.

Her eyes closed in time with the bedroom door. She had won the inner battle. But had she lost the marriage war?

Val felt beat. Three hours of sleep followed by ten hours of busywork, tension and dodging the issues were not conducive to a party mood. The last thing she felt like doing was getting ready to go out. Nevertheless, get ready she did, and with attention to detail, at that.

Faced with the unavoidable necessity of socializing with the acid-tongued Lynn, Val donned full battle array. Her tiny-flower-strewed, crinkle silk dress enhanced the color of her eyes, displayed her slender figure to best advantage, and was in perfect taste for the occasion. Her narrow, three-inch heels increased her height, added length to her slim legs and drew the eye to her delicate ankles. Employing the expertise she had acquired in Paris, Val deftly highlighted her eyes, cheekbones and mouth. Her gold filigree necklace and earrings had been custom made to Jonas's design. The elusive scent surrounding her sold for over two hundred dollars an ounce.

When she had finished, Jonas's expression alone was worth every minute of the time she'd invested. By the same token, Val felt certain her own expression of admiration mirrored his. Attired in a business suit, Jonas didn't merely look terrific. In semiformal midnight blue against a stark white knife-pleated shirt, he was nothing short of devastating.

"New dress?" Jonas asked, in what sounded like a croak.

"Yes." Val raised her arms to swirl the matching stole around her shoulders; his narrowed gaze followed the gentle lift and sway of her silk-draped breasts.

"I like it." His voice grew low. "It looks beautiful...on you."

Val told herself that she couldn't care less whether he approved of her choice or not, but knew she was lying. She told herself she didn't care if he thought she looked beautiful, but knew she did. The proof was in the sudden lack of strength in her entire body.

Silence filled the car throughout the five-mile drive to the house Valerie had entered as a bride, which Jonas had signed over to Mary Beth and Jean-Paul when their residence he had had built for Val and himself was completed.

Tension crackled in the air between them. Val's mind wandered into deep, dark waters.

He looked good. She looked good. They were good together in a social situation. They were even better together in bed. So what were they doing driving in emotion-fraught silence to a dinner that obviously neither of them wanted to eat? Why weren't they at home, in bed, feasting on each other?

"Hungry?"

Val started. Warmth suffused her cheeks. Had she spoken her longing? Jonas's voice had been too soft for her to detect any inflection…or insinuation. She would have to look at him to know. Slowly Val turned to gaze at his profile. A sigh of relief whispered through her lips; the stern expression he had worn all day was still in place. Jonas was once more making polite conversation.

"Ah…a little." Val's voice was barely there. "You?"

Jonas was at least honest. "Not particularly."

Silence. Again. And for what seemed like forever….

Jonas shattered the quiet as he brought the car to a stop in the driveway of their destination. "Marge did tell you that Lynn would be here this evening?" he asked, rather belatedly, Val thought.

"Yes, she told me."

He killed the engine and turned to look at her. "I'd appreciate it if you'd try to ignore Lynn if she runs to type with her sugar-coated barbs," he said, in a way that had the overtones of an order. Bristling, Val was on the verge of telling him what he could do with his appreciation, when he saved himself by adding,

"I don't want Mary Beth upset at this stage of her pregnancy." The dark specter of memory shaded his tone. "Do you?"

Val felt a stab of pain deep in her womb. "No," she answered in a tight murmur.

"Good." Jonas pulled at the car door handle, then paused to shoot a hard look at her. "Do you think you could manage a smile and pretend that you're happy being married to me?" A cynical smile tugged at one corner of his mouth. "I'd hate it like hell if Lynn suspected we were anything but deliriously happy." The smile struggled across his mouth. "She'd laugh her brainless head off." Without waiting for her to respond, Jonas shoved the door open and stepped out of the car.

By the time Jonas circled the car, Val had opened her own door and was about to get out. Accepting the hand he extended to help her, she stepped out and spoke out at the same time. "Are you planning on joining in on this pretense?"

Careful of her dress, Jonas shut the door before answering. "Of course."

"Very well." Slipping her arm through his, Val moved with him to the house. An instant before the front door was swung open for them, she glanced up to give him a brilliant smile. "Let's go bamboozle Lynn."

As he entered the house Jonas was laughing, the rich, warm laughter that never failed to dissolve Val's bones. She clung to his arm in reaction to the melting sensation.

"Hi, Dad," Mary Beth called as they strolled into the spacious living room. "What's the joke?"

The look Jonas gave Val could have sizzled bacon. "It's a private...personal joke, honey," he replied to his daughter, while gazing at his wife.

"Jonas," Val murmured, following his lead.

"Hmm?" Jonas murmured.

"We're not alone." Val had difficulty in keeping her voice husky and her laughter contained. To her amazement, she was enjoying their charade.

"Ain't it a bitch?"

"He always did swear like a seasoned marine," Lynn said in a scathing tone.

Thinking the words applied better to Lynn, Val turned her head to offer the still-beautiful, voluptuous woman a sweet smile. "At times," she said, her lashes sweeping down as she cast a sideways glance at Jonas, "he even makes love like a seasoned marine."

Jonas's burst of laughter was echoed by everyone in the room except Lynn. She narrowed her eyes.

"Perhaps you should get a scrap of paper and take notes, my pet," Jean-Paul advised Mary Beth. "It would appear that Valerie could give lessons on the exquisite art of stroking a husband's fragile ego."

Mary Beth looked at her husband, at Val, then she frowned. "Why is it," she mused aloud, "that everything a Frenchman says sounds so much sexier than even the most seductive whispers of other men?"

Pretending to consider the question, Val moved to sit in the corner of the long sofa. "I don't know," she said, primly folding her hands in her lap.

Jean-Paul was chuckling as only a Frenchman can.

Lynn was scowling.

Marge was grinning.

Sauntering to the sofa, Jonas sat down next to Val and cocked a brow at his daughter. "Forget the scrap of paper, kid," he drawled. "You require no lessons on the art of stroking your husband's ego."

"Or anything else, come to think of it," Jean-Paul said, sharing a secret smile with his wife.

"Disgusting!" Lynn said, grimacing.

"Disgusting, *madame*?" Jean-Paul raised his eyebrows, his expression betraying the disdain he normally kept scrupulously concealed.

"Mother, really." Mary Beth sighed.

"They're only teasing, Lynn," Marge chided.

Biting back a retort, Val remained silent.

His expression cool, Jonas turned his head to look at his former wife. "There is never anything disgusting about love, or the expression of it," he rebuked her in a voice threaded with steel.

There was a moment of tension while Lynn tried to outstare Jonas. The moment ended when she glanced away. In an odd way, Val sympathized with the other woman. Val had experienced the freezing effect of a quelling stare from Jonas's icy eyes.

"May I offer you a drink, Valerie, Jonas?" Jean-Paul's smoothly inserted question banished the chill. "A glass of your generous gift, perhaps?"

Jonas shifted to glance at Marge. "When were you planning to serve dinner?"

Marge smiled, revealing the affection and respect she held for him. "Ten minutes after you arrived," she replied.

Jonas grinned, and turned his attention back to his son-in-law. "Since dinner is about to be announced, I'll wait." He raised a brow at Val. "Darling?"

Jonas had called her darling many times over the previous three years, but the sound of the endearment still had the power to interfere with her normal heartbeat. "No, thank you." She smiled at Jean-Paul as she stood up. "I'm going to help Marge serve dinner."

"How sweet." Lynn's sour expression betrayed her feelings only too well. "You play your role very well, don't you, dear?"

Valerie froze, and checked an urge to look at Jonas. Had Lynn somehow seen through their pretense? Holding on to her outward composure, Val met the other woman's envy-ridden eyes. "I beg your pardon?"

"Your role of devoted housewife," Lynn said disparagingly. "The little woman who keeps her husband's house, and cooks his meals, and washes his dirty laundry."

Relief shivered through Val. "I'm not playing a role, Lynn, I'm living a life," she said with pride. "And I consider being Jonas's wife a lifetime commitment." Val refrained from adding that it was too bad that Lynn hadn't felt the same while she was married to Jonas.

Minutes later, while she was carrying the meat platter to the table, Val caught Jonas staring at her with eyes that revealed both longing and reproach. Her boast to Lynn resounded in her mind, and her feelings of relief and pride changed to remorse and shame. Averting her eyes, she placed the platter on the table and returned to the kitchen.

While chatting with Marge and generally making herself useful, Val suffered the relentless stabs of her conscience. She had spent months pursuing self-understanding and rebelling against being considered nothing more than a wife and homemaker. Yet she had defended that very position to Lynn only moments ago.

Telling herself that she was only keeping her promise to Jonas didn't ease her sense of guilt. Val knew that the sincerity in her tone when she'd made the statement was genuine; she had believed every word she'd uttered.

For most of the meal Val was distracted. Although she heard every word spoken around the table, and responded when someone spoke directly to her, inside her head Val was struggling with her thoughts.

Was it possible to believe that accepting the position of wife and making that lifetime commitment could coexist with a woman's right to grow and expand to her full potential? Didn't the latter cancel out the former, or vice versa?

But she wanted it both ways! The realization jolted through Val, shedding light on her confusion. Raising her flute, she sipped her champagne and slanted a surreptitious glance at her husband's face. As always, merely looking at his rugged, harshly chiseled face caused a flutter of excitement in her midsection.

Jonas Thorne was one exciting man, Val mused. He was formidable but exciting. And she loved him so much that it scared her at times. But it wasn't only a matter of loving Jonas, she concluded. She loved being his wife, with all the responsibilities that entailed.

Val dredged up the memory of Lynn's cynical taunt for a closer examination.

Devoted housewife. The little woman who keeps her husband's house, and cooks his meals, and washes his dirty laundry.

Yes, Val acknowledged, the description fitted her to a capital *T* and in truth, she enjoyed keeping his house, cooking his meals, and even washing his dirty laundry. Val knew that while she told herself she didn't want a housekeeper because she needed to feel that she was contributing something to the marriage, she was deluding herself. She kept house simply because she enjoyed keeping house for Jonas.

On the other hand, Val admitted to herself that she also enjoyed the outside activities she'd become involved with in her determination to discover the limits of her own capabilities as a mature individual.

So she wanted both... Her position as a wife and as an equal individual.

Val sighed into her glass, then took another sip of the wine. Were the two facets irrevocably opposed? she wondered. Or was there a middle ground, where the best of both could not only meet but merge?

Yes, with the right man, Val decided. But was Jonas that man? Not the Jonas she knew. But could Jonas become that man? A tiny smile brushed Val's lips. Maybe, if she gently nudged him in the right direction. He'd resist, she knew that, but...

"Aren't you feeling well, Valerie?" The concerned sound of Marge's voice drew Val from her reverie. "You've barely touched your food."

"I'm fine," Val said. "I'm just not very hungry."

"Val's watching her weight, Marge," Jonas drawled, in an indulgent tone that surprised Val, until she recalled their pact for the evening.

"A bit too stringently, I'd say," Lynn interjected. "I can remember when Jonas preferred a more curvaceous woman." Her voice was silky, and the look she gave Jonas was blatantly suggestive. "Didn't you, darling?"

Val steeled herself for the twinge of jealousy she always experienced whenever Lynn made a remark designed to remind her of Jonas's previous attraction. The twinge didn't...twinge. Surprised, she looked at Jonas and murmured, "Really?"

"Yes, when I was young and green." His smile was sardonic. "My taste in women has improved with age and experience." Jonas raised his glass and tilted it at Val in a silent salute. "I'd say my taste has been refined, as well."

Flushed with pleasure, Val returned his salute. "Thank you, my love." She deliberately emphasized the endearment. "I'd say my taste is even more refined than yours."

"Love." Lynn's tone made the word sound dirty. She sneered at Jonas. "For you it's love of a pretty, fawning woman." Her glittering gaze shot to Val. "And for you it's love of money and position."

Val gasped, appalled by the woman's viciousness.

"Mother!" Mary Beth exclaimed in shock.

"*Mon Dieu!*" Jean-Paul exploded.

"That's enough, Lynn!" Marge ordered.

"The checkbook is closed." Jonas's frigid voice cut through the uproar.

Checkbook? Val frowned. Confused, she shifted her gaze to Lynn. The woman's stricken expression startled her. Val didn't understand. Since Jonas had obtained his divorce from Lynn on the grounds of desertion, he had not been required to pay her any alimony or support. Yet from what he had just said, it was obvious Jonas had been supporting Lynn on a voluntary basis, and his coldly stated decision to cease writing checks had shaken the woman considerably.

"Jonas, you wouldn't!" Lynn cried.

"You think not?" Jonas's eyes were as cold as his voice. "Watch me."

Val knew that expression. Jonas used it whenever he was dead set on a course of action. When Jonas said "Watch me" in that tone of voice, everyone around him searched for cover.

"But, Jonas," Lynn said. "What will I do for money? How will I live?"

Jonas had been supporting Lynn! Shock jolted through Val. All these years. She had never so much as suspected....

"You could go to work," Jonas suggested dryly.

The color drained from Lynn's face. "But I have no training! I could never earn enough—"

"To provide the luxuries my money has afforded you," he finished for her. Lynn turned pleading eyes to her daughter, but before she could utter a word, Jonas said, "And don't look to Mary Beth for support, because I'll stop her allowance and convince Jean-Paul to withhold his money."

Lynn's lovely mouth curled into an ugly twist, and she lashed out at him nastily, "You really are a bastard."

Val gasped and pushed back her chair. Jonas clasped her arm to hold her still.

"Sit down," he said to Mary Beth, who had cried out in protest and jumped to her feet.

"But, Dad…" she began.

Jonas gently cut her off. "It's all right, honey."

"It's not all right," Marge argued, glaring at Lynn.

"It's unforgivable," Jean-Paul muttered.

"It's true," Jonas said flatly.

"Jonas," Val murmured, sliding her palm over the back of his hand. Jonas didn't look at her, but continued to glare at Lynn.

"I'll sell the house in the South of France," Lynn threatened.

Jonas laughed in her face. "You really should pay closer attention to details, Lynn."

"What do you mean?" Lynn was looking scared again.

"The house in France isn't yours to sell." His smile was devoid of humor. "It never was."

The tension was palpable. In silence, everyone waited to hear Lynn's response.

Lynn glared down the length of the table at Jonas for several long, drawn-out seconds, then caved in. "I'll make a bargain with you, Jonas," she said in a strangled-sounding, subdued voice.

Jonas arched one eyebrow in mockery. "You're not in a position to bargain," he reminded her.

"Will you just listen?" Lynn pleaded.

Unmoved, Jonas continued to stare at her. The very air in the room seemed to stretch and quiver.

Mary Beth was the first to break. "Dad, please, listen to what she has to say!" she cried.

Still Jonas continued to observe his former wife with his hard, unyielding stare.

"Jonas," Val whispered, growing concerned at the paleness of his daughter's face.

At her murmur Jonas's eyes flickered, then he relented. "All right, Lynn, I'll hear you out." His tone was chilling. "But it'd better be good."

Lynn wet her lips, swallowed, then said in a rush, "If you'll continue with my allowance as before, I'll return to the South of France."

"Forever?"

"Jonas, I want to be with Mary Beth when the baby's due!" Lynn protested.

Jonas sneered. "A little late in the game for maternal instincts, isn't it?" He waved a hand to silence her when she started to object. "All right, Lynn. I'll maintain you in the life-style you've become accustomed to," he said.

Val had not taken her eyes off Jonas throughout the exchange. When the tension eased, she stole a glance at Lynn. This time she did feel a twinge of pity for the older woman. Failure, not only in this one instance, but the failure of an entire life lurked in the depths of Lynn's eyes. Lynn was vanquished, silenced.

Val suspected that Lynn would eventually regroup to strike again, but at least until Mary Beth's child arrived, her viperous tongue had been stilled.

To Val's relief, the remainder of the evening passed without further incident. Lynn excused herself and retired after the first of the belated toasts that were raised to the expectant couple. The natural soft pink color returned to Mary Beth's cheeks. Jean-Paul was amusing in his pride of accomplishment. Marge was obviously eager for her first great-grandchild. Even

Jonas managed to laugh, despite the evidence of anger still smoldering in his eyes.

Val was grateful that the party broke up early. She was exhausted and had a raging headache. The effort she was expending to keep up the pretense of being happy with Jonas was beginning to wear on her nerves.

At that moment, Val wasn't at all happy with Jonas. She had been hurt, deeply hurt by the discovery that he was supporting Lynn. But it wasn't the knowledge that he was making regular payments to Lynn that bothered Val. What Jonas did with his money was his business. No, what had wounded her was the realization that Jonas had not told her that he had been keeping Lynn for years.

And Val felt certain his failure to tell her had been deliberate, for it was obvious the other members of his family knew, including Jean-Paul.

What did his secrecy say about their marriage? Val asked herself, sitting stiff and unresponsive beside her husband in the car as they drove home. In her opinion, it certainly didn't indicate trust or openness or communication. And without those elements, a marriage wasn't a marriage at all. It was a sham, a farce, a convenience.... His.

In brooding silence, Val preceded Jonas into the house. Feeling humiliated, sick, used, she mounted the stairs. She didn't go to their bedroom. Ignoring the purposeful sound of his tread behind her, she went into the guest room and shut the door in his face. She had taken two steps into the room when the door rebounded off the wall.

"What the hell do you think you're doing?" Jonas

demanded. Storming after her, he grasped her by the arm and spun her around to face him.

Though his hold wasn't painful, Val stared pointedly at his hand. When he released her, she raised her eyes to his. "I'm going to sleep here."

"You're still angry." It was not a question.

Val sighed. "No, Jonas, I'm not still angry. I'm angry again. Angry and hurt and—" she raised a hand to massage a throbbing temple "—and tired, so tired."

"Of me?" he asked tersely.

She lifted a hand, then let it fall to her side. "At this moment, yes. Of you, of everything." Her eyes were bright with tears she refused to let fall, her shoulders drooped. Defeat lay on her like an immense weight.

"This is about Lynn, isn't it?"

Val gave a short, humorless laugh. She knew by the sound of his voice, that arrogant note, that his back was up. If there was one thing Jonas detested, it was having his actions questioned. By anyone.

"You're angry because I've been supporting her," he persisted. "Aren't you?"

Val longed to curl up in a corner and weep. Instead she straightened her spine and lifted her small chin in defiance. "And shouldn't I be?"

Jonas reflected her action with the thrust of his hard jaw. "It's my money, Val. I earned it. And I'll do with it as I damn well please."

His tone broke the last thread of her composure. "I don't care about your damned money!" she shouted. "Give it away," she said wildly. "Throw it away. Burn it. I don't care!" Fighting to regain control, she spun away. A startled gasp burst from her throat when he grabbed her arm and swung her around once more to face the building anger in his eyes.

"Then what the hell is this all about?" he demanded. "What's biting at you?"

"Trust, Jonas!" Val said. "A solid marriage is built on trust. Yet you didn't trust me enough to tell me that you've been keeping Lynn all this time." She drew a quick harsh breath. "It was obvious that everyone else knew—Marge, Mary Beth, Jean-Paul, and God knows how many others."

"Val...I—" Jonas began, but she wasn't finished. Her voice cut across his.

"You've been keeping Lynn for years. And you've hidden it from me," she accused heatedly. "Exactly as you would keep a mistress."

"Mistress!" Jonas barked. "Is that what this is really about?" Grasping her by the shoulders, he shook her, not roughly, but as if trying to shake sense into her. "Damn it, Val, I wouldn't touch Lynn with a dirty stick, and you know it. Or at least you should. I love you, damn it!" he shouted. "And you should know that, too."

"You really don't understand, do you?" Weighed down by defeat, Val's body sagged, and was literally held erect by his strong hands.

"Understand what, for God's sake?"

"You don't love, you possess," she replied dully. "I'm *your* wife, *your* possession, your *thing*." Her voice grew thin. "Your woman." Shaking off his hands with her last bit of strength, Val moved away from him. "I'm very tired, Jonas," she said, turning to look at him. "If you don't mind..."

"I do mind." Though his voice revealed the strain and anger he was feeling, Jonas made no attempt to close the distance separating them. His frustration was evident by the way he raked his hand through his hair. "What do you want that I haven't given you, Val?"

"Full partnership," she answered at once.

"In the company?" Jonas looked genuinely confused.

"No, you blockhead!" Val retorted, stung by the very fact that he had thought immediately of his business. "I don't want half of your company. I want half of your personal life!" She laughed; the sound held a hint of encroaching hysteria. "Hell," she cried. "I'd be satisfied with the consideration you extend to your female executives!"

"Val, calm down." Jonas took a step toward her.

Val took two steps back and held up her hand. "Go away, Jonas." Her short, choppy words betrayed her crumbling inner resources. "It's late. I'm exhausted. I don't want to argue anymore."

"Val..." Jonas took another step.

Val broke completely. "Jonas, please!"

He hesitated, his expression stark with concern. "I don't want to leave you like this. Come with me," he coaxed, as if placating an overwrought child. "Come to bed with me. Let me hold you."

Because she was so very tired, and because, despite everything, she loved him so very much, Val was sorely tempted to chuck it all—all her needs as a woman, all her principles, all her ambitions for a true union with him—to give up and surrender to him. Jonas himself saved her by murmuring four inflammatory words.

"Let me love you."

A sad smile skipped over Val's mouth. "That's your answer, your cure-all for everything. Make love, and the problem will go away."

"No, but—" Jonas began.

Val silenced him with a sharp shake of her head. "Not this time, Jonas. I thought I made that clear last night."

"We need to talk, Val," he said adamantly.

"Yes." Val nodded. "But first we need to think, long and hard, about what we want as individuals. Because you see, Jonas, whether you approve or not, I *am* an individual. Not your shadow. Not your echo. But a real, live person. But for now I'm tired," she said, unconsciously echoing his words of the night before. "I'm going to bed."

Chapter 5

Estrangement. Jonas hated the word and all the pain that it entailed: becoming distant, unfriendly, the denial of feeling. Jonas hated it. Yet the word precisely described his relationship with Val.

Two weeks, he thought, kneading the tight muscles at the back of his neck. Almost two full weeks had elapsed since the night of Marge's celebration dinner.

Some celebration. The noise Jonas made sounded like a snort.

Pushing his chair away from his large, cluttered desk, he strode to the wide window of his office. It was late. It was dark. Artificial light illuminated the company parking lot, empty except for the small cluster of vehicles belonging to the office cleaning service and the night security personnel, and for his own car, parked directly beneath his office window, looking oddly abandoned.

Did Val's car look abandoned, sitting alone in the four-car garage attached to the house? Jonas wondered, sightlessly staring at the gleaming Lincoln six floors below.

No. Of course it didn't. Val's car wasn't even in the garage, Jonas thought derisively, turning back to his desk. Val wasn't at home, nor would she be, he recalled. It was Friday, the night before the wedding. Val had informed him that she'd be spending the entire night with Janet, doing whatever it was women did the night before a wedding.

Jonas smiled wryly as he settled into his chair. Considering her present attitude toward the institution, Val was probably trying to talk Janet into changing her mind about getting married, before it was too late.

Suddenly needing to hear Val's voice, even if it was the distant one she had used through every conversation of the previous two weeks, Jonas reached for the no-nonsense black console phone set close at hand at the right side of his desk. His fingers grasped the receiver, but he didn't pick it up. Exhaling impatiently, he drew back his hand.

He had work to do, and he wouldn't get it done chatting on the phone. The admonition to himself might have been funny under normal circumstances. Tonight it merely served to drive home the truth of the situation: he and his wife were barely speaking. The idea of the two of them chatting was ludicrous.

But then, had he and Val ever relaxed enough with each other to engage in a simple chat?

The thought made Jonas uncomfortable. Although he didn't like admitting it, he knew they had seldom shared a meaningful conversation, let alone a friendly chat. Feeling suddenly prickly all over, Jonas shifted in his chair, and was grateful for the distraction presented by the abrupt intrusion of his assistant, who entered the room without his usual polite knock.

"What are you doing here?" Jonas demanded. "Aren't you supposed to be out somewhere, getting drunk or something on your last night of freedom?"

Charlie McAndrew grinned at his employer. "The bachelor party was last week, remember?"

Jonas groaned. "How can I forget?" He motioned the younger man into a chair with a flick of his hand. "You have some wild friends, Charlie," he observed, remembering with distaste the drunken revelry the other men had indulged in the previous week. Jonas had never met any one of the five men before, all of whom had been college buddies of Charlie's. Jonas wasn't thrilled about spending the entire day with them tomorrow, either. "I can only hope they'll all be sober enough to seat the guests and stand up through the wedding ceremony."

Charlie dropped into the chair with a tired-sounding sigh and an even more tired-sounding excuse. "They don't get out alone all that often."

Jonas arched a skeptical brow. "Are they caged?"

"Close," Charlie replied with a laugh. "They are all very much married."

"Which you will be in less than twenty-four hours," Jonas reminded him. "Is that how you view the state of matrimony?" he asked with interest. "As being caged?"

"No, of course not!" Charlie exclaimed.

"There's no of course about it," Jonas said.

"You'll be as very much married as they are," he pointed out reasonably. "Where's the difference?"

Instead of answering, Charlie responded with a question. "You're married. Do you feel caged?"

Though Jonas stiffened, he considered the question before giving a reply. Did he feel caged by marriage? Without looking, Jonas could see the plain gold band encircling the third finger of his left hand. Had he ever felt constricted by the binding band of metal? He slowly shook his head from side to side. Frustrated, yes, but... "No," Jonas answered both Charlie and himself.

"And there's the difference." Charlie shrugged.

Jonas frowned. "You lost me."

"It's the woman," Charlie explained. "Brad's married to a grind, and he hears nothing but nag, nag, nag. Ted's wife is a spender. She wants everything yesterday. George's wife is house-proud, makes him go outside to smoke his pipe. Jeff's wife is cold, and starves him for sexual warmth. And Randy's wife is a clinging vine, which bolstered his ego at the beginning, but is strangling him now."

Jonas frowned in disapproval. "They discuss their marital problems with you and each other?"

"We've all been friends for a long time, Jonas. I don't know—" he shrugged "—I guess it helps to talk about it. Maybe it's either that or explode."

"Maybe." Jonas didn't sound convinced. "But don't you think they'd be better advised to talk about it with their wives, rather than each other?"

"Sure," Charlie agreed. "But I gather that they have tried that and failed. In any case, do you understand what I mean about the difference being in the woman?'' he asked. ''You and I are the lucky ones. We both found exceptional women.''

Jonas thought about the conversation long after he had thrown Charlie out of the office with a growled order to go home and get some rest.

In what way were Val and Janet exceptional? he mused, once again wandering to the wide window. With respect to Janet, the answer was simple. She was exceptionally bright, exceptionally talented, exceptionally well-balanced and even-tempered. Jonas felt certain Janet would make a terrific wife for the ambitious, yet basically shy Charlie...or any other man.

But Val? In what way was his wife exceptional? Jonas frowned, and recalled the complaints of Charlie's friends. Val was certainly not a shrew. She never nagged him about anything. She wasn't a spender, either, even though he had given her several credit cards and had set up a large household account for her at his bank. She didn't cling like a smothering vine and, thank heaven, Val was definitely not cold in bed.

At least, she hadn't been cold while she was still sharing his bed. A deep sigh was wrenched from his throat. Hearing the longing underlying his sigh, Jonas dragged his attention back to the subject under consideration.

In what way was Val exceptional and different from all the other women he had known? In many ways, Jonas acknowledged. Then he laughed, softly. Hell, the Val of today was even more different and more exceptional than the Val he had first come to know over three years ago.

Casting his mind back in time, Jonas recalled her

as she had been when they'd met. She'd had an elusive, wistful look. Her fantastic violet eyes had revealed the grief she was still suffering from after the tragic death of her fiancé just two weeks before their scheduled wedding day. She had an uninterested look, as if she no longer cared what happened to her. She had been breathtakingly beautiful, soft and extremely vulnerable, and instilled in most men the urge to care for and protect.

But her vulnerability hadn't been the snare that had captured Jonas's interest. He had worked too hard, had come too far on his journey from bastard orphan to the owner of one of the largest electronics firms in the world, to be moved to anything other than impatience with her vulnerability. Jonas had no time for anyone, male or female, who retired from the battlefield of life. No, what had initially caught his attention and interest was the spark of angry defiance Val had shown during their very first verbal exchange. Within hours, his interest had changed to desire, and within the few weeks she had worked as his private secretary, that desire had expanded to fill his waking and sleeping hours.

Jonas could remember how he'd wanted her as if it were yesterday. He had stood at this same window, his muscles aching, his body taut, his mind centered on one thought.

God, he wanted her.

He still did.

Feeling his body tighten in response to his memories, Jonas turned away from the window and forced his thought into safer channels.

Yes, the Val of today was vastly different from the

woman he had met three years ago. Although she was still breathtakingly beautiful—no, more so—still soft, still gentle, her spark of defiance had blossomed into a determination that nearly equaled his own.

I am not a thing.

The echo of Val's voice whispered through his mind. His anger flaring anew, Jonas strode to the door, past the work he had planned on finishing that evening. The work would still be waiting for him when he returned.

Val was not waiting for him. The house was dark when he got home. Dark and empty. It seemed too big, too spacious without Val's presence to lend welcoming warmth.

Trailing through to the kitchen, Jonas opened the refrigerator, looking for something to appease his protesting, empty stomach. As usual he had skipped lunch. A covered baking dish sat at the front of the center shelf. Jonas was reaching for the casserole when the phone rang. Leaving the refrigerator door open, he crossed to the kitchen phone.

"Thorne," he said into the receiver, in exactly the same way he answered his office phone.

"Surprise, surprise," Val drawled, causing the emptiness inside Jonas to expand into aching need. "Have you found your dinner?" she went on to ask.

Jonas shot a glance at the open refrigerator and casserole on the center shelf. "I think so. The baking dish?"

"The same," Val said in a dry tone.

"What is it?" Jonas really didn't care; he just wanted to keep her talking.

''Macaroni and ham casserole.''

''What do I do with it?''

Val's impatient sigh sang along the line to him. ''You heat it in the microwave and eat it, Jonas.''

''I know that,'' he retorted. ''But you know I never use the micro, Val. What setting do I use?''

''You're the electronic wizard,'' Val said sweetly. ''You figure it out.'' With that, she hung up.

Naturally, Jonas did figure it out. It required thirty seconds of his time to read the instruction manual that came with the appliance. The steam rising from the bubbling mixture of macaroni and chunks of ham smothered in a creamy cheese sauce sharpened his appetite when he removed the dish from the microwave a few minutes later.

Jonas ate his dinner perched on a stool at the breakfast counter. Under normal conditions he would have relished the food. Tonight he simply ate it to appease the hungry growl of his stomach. But then he wasn't dining under normal conditions, he reminded himself.

As if he needed reminding, Jonas thought, staring at the phone. He wanted to talk to Val. Not true. He wanted to see her. Wrong. What Jonas really wanted was to hold her, love her, never let her go.

With one emptiness filled, the deeper emptiness was fully exposed. It had been exactly two full weeks since Jonas had held Valerie in his arms, kissed her with his mouth, loved her with his body. Two weeks of stilted conversation, meaningless words, thick, heavy constraint. How he had longed to break through the cloak of reserve Val had drawn around herself, her emotions, he reflected, automatically scraping and rinsing the dishes before stacking them in the dishwasher.

As he returned the untouched portion of the meal to the refrigerator, a consideration struck Jonas. It was strange, but although Val was barely speaking to him, she continued to keep the house spotless, do the laundry and grocery shopping, and cook for him, not just any old thrown-together meals, but some of his favorites.

Val confused him, and Jonas didn't appreciate the feeling. He had never understood her adamant refusal to have help in the house, other than the woman who came in once a month to do the heavy cleaning. He was a wealthy man; he could easily afford to have live-in help for Val. Yet she insisted on doing it all, or the majority of it, herself, claiming that since Jonas rarely entertained on a lavish scale, she didn't require or want additional help.

Shaking his head, Jonas wandered through the empty house and up the stairs. A sigh whispered from his throat as he passed the closed door to the guest room.

After a quick shower, Jonas grimaced and slid between the freshly laundered sheets. He didn't appreciate the sudden emptiness of the king-size bed any more than he valued his state of confusion. And he knew that if Val went through with her plans to fly to the West Coast at the end of the coming week, the house, the bed and he himself would feel not only empty, but deserted as well.

Why was Val being so damn stubborn? Jonas railed in silent frustration. What did she want or expect from him? Damn it, he was faithful to her and honest with her. He had happily provided for her not only the necessities, but luxuries beyond the wildest imaginings of many other women. And he loved her to the marrow of his bones. What more could he offer her? Why was she so restless and dissatisfied with their life together? Even as Jonas asked the silent question, the memory of their bitter argument tormented his tired mind.

Trust. Val had accused him of not according her the trust necessary to a successful marriage.

But he did trust Val, Jonas defended himself. It was other men he didn't trust. And in the sorry case of Lynn, Jonas had believed he was right in keeping the fact that he was supporting Lynn to himself. It had nothing to do with Val. Well, at least the question of Lynn was now resolved. With her usual flair for the dramatic, Lynn had departed Philadelphia for France the previous Monday.

Partnership. Val had insisted upon being a complete and equal part of his life.

But didn't she know how very much a part of his life she was? Jonas wondered. *Equal?* Hell, she *was* his life. Didn't she know that? Then again, how could she know? he mused. When was the last time they'd talked, not just about trivial matters, but really talked to each other? When had they ever communicated, understood, touched base intellectually and emotionally?

Jonas shifted beneath the light weight of the smooth sheet. He had been too busy with the company, he excused himself—or attempted to. There had never been enough time. Three years of being too busy and not having enough time? Jonas jeered at himself. And through every one of those too busy years without enough time he had refused her pleas to return to work. She was his wife. And Jonas Thorne's wife did not work outside the home.

His wife.

His possession.

His woman.

Jonas winced. Was it any wonder Val had attempted to fill the lonely hours of her days with courses and causes? And had he, in his superior wisdom, understood, or better yet, encouraged Val in her quest for fulfillment?

Not he, Jonas derided himself. Not the electronic genius. Not the strong, fiercely independent and individualistic man who had fought his way from the stigma of bastard and the brutality of a foster home to a position of wealth and respect. No, instead of helping his wife realize her full potential as a woman, he had demanded she stay home and play house.

When had he stopped thinking in matters concerning Val?

When had he ever started?

Rolling onto his back, Jonas stared into the middle distance. He knew the answer to his own question. He had never done any rational thinking about Val, simply because his emotions always got in the way.

Val had told him that they both needed to do some thinking about their relationship. She had been thinking about it for two weeks at least, and very probably much longer. It had taken him nearly two weeks to work his way up to thinking about it. She had said that when they were finished thinking, they'd talk. Jonas was ready to talk now.

Flinging back the sheet, he sat up and reached for the phone. His hand fell away before it touched the plastic receiver. He couldn't force the issue, couldn't take the chance of having her accusing him of once again trying to assert his will over her. He had no other option than to wait until she was ready.

I am an individual.

The echo of Val's voice whispered through his mind. And though Jonas was aching for her, longing to go after her, bring her home and enclose her in his arms forever, he contented himself with sending her a silent reply.

In spades, sweetheart.

While Jonas had his mind full of questions, Val had her hands full trying to keep the nervous bride calm.

"Oh, God, am I doing the right thing?" Janet wailed, pacing up and down her living room.

"Yes, Janet," Val said in a soothing tone.

"But I'm nearly forty years old!"

"What does that have to do with anything?"

Janet came to an abrupt halt at the low coffee table, picked up her glass and took a sip of champagne Valerie had brought with her. "Nothing, I suppose," she mumbled into the glass. When she looked at Val there was fear in her eyes. "Do you think I'm too old to have a child?"

Val was taken aback. "Are you pregnant?"

"No!" Janet exclaimed. Then, more quietly, "No, I'm not pregnant. But suppose I should get pregnant. What then?"

"You'll have a baby?" Val asked in wide-eyed innocence.

Janet frowned. Then she laughed. "I'm acting rather silly, aren't I?"

Val smiled. "You're acting like a bride on the eve of her big day."

"You didn't get crazy the night before your wedding," Janet pointed out. And, since Val had stayed with her at the time, Janet was in a position to know.

"Yes, well," Val murmured, "Jonas didn't give me time to get really crazy. You've had months of planning and preparation to help you along," she said, hoping to divert Janet from the topic of Jonas. Her ploy failed.

"No, Jonas didn't give you much time," Janet said, her tone full of musing remembrance. "About two weeks, wasn't it?"

"Mmm." Val nodded, concealing a wince behind the glass she raised to her lips.

"It seems so long ago now."

Val arched her eyebrows.

"I mean, it seems now that you and Jonas have been together forever," Janet explained.

"Does it?" Val asked vaguely, thinking that the past two weeks had seemed like forever.

"Yes," Janet replied, taking off again, this time in the direction of the kitchen. "I've got to get something to eat. I'm famished."

"Nerves," Val said with authority.

"Do you want something?"

"Yes." Standing, Val carried her glass into the kitchen, thinking that she had nerves to feed herself.

* * *

Tears trickled down Val's face. She didn't try to check the flow. After months of frantic activity, and the morning's confusion of getting dressed, then to the church with a bride and six attendants, all with nerves on the brink of twanging out of control, the procession went off like clockwork. The solemn ceremony was touching in its beauty and serenity.

Val's tears were for the lovely bride and the endearingly attractive bridegroom, to be sure, but mostly for the devastatingly handsome best man.

Jonas.

As she preceded Janet down the aisle, Val's heart had contracted at the sight of him, standing tall and composed at Charlie's right side. The wedding guests packing the church faded as her vision focused on Jonas's imposing form. Her steps correctly measured, Val closed the distance between them. Then he was momentarily lost to her sight as she stepped to the left and turned to watch Janet take the remaining steps to her bridegroom's side.

Her tears began to fall halfway through the ceremony. Under cover of the cascading bouquet she carried, Val rubbed her thumb over her marriage rings. The words of the service were muted by her thoughts.

How very different this service was from the one that had united her with Jonas. Valerie had had a similar thought on the day Mary Beth and Jean-Paul were married. Val had not had the round of showers and parties both Janet and Mary Beth had been treated to. She had not had the excitement and the hassles of fittings and shopping and last-minute details to be seen to, either. Val had not been decked out like a fairy princess in yards and yards of China silk and imported lace, as Mary Beth had been. Nor had she been dressed in skillfully cut shimmering satin, as Janet now was.

With the clarity of her inner eye, Val could see the suit she'd worn for the occasion. It was nice, but not spectacular. Jonas had not worn a tuxedo. He had been attired in a three-piece suit, attractive, but not special. They had not been married in a church. There had not been a note of music. They had recited their vows before a judge in his chambers.

Yet Valerie had never felt any less married than any other woman.

And now, standing beside her friend, two bodies away from her husband, Valerie ached with the need to touch the man she had married under such inauspicious, mundane circumstances.

Two weeks. It seemed like forever.

She came into his arms in a swirling cloud of warm satin and heady perfume.

Lord, she was beautiful, Jonas thought, his pulse quickening as he enfolded Val in his arms for the wedding party dance. She looked good. She smelled good. She felt...wonderful.

Jonas and Valerie had not danced together very often over the past three years, yet they moved as one, in perfect timing to the haunting music of a current love song.

"I missed you last night." Jonas startled himself with the unplanned, open admission. The surprise in the eyes Val raised to his indicated he had startled her also.

"Did you?" Her tone indicated that though she was startled, she was equally skeptical.

"Of course I did," Jonas said in an impatient whisper. "The house felt empty."

Val met his impatience with cool reserve. "I'm well acquainted with the feeling."

Her shot hit home. Ignoring the hint of warning, Jonas persisted. "It's going to feel even emptier after you leave for California next week."

"I'll only be away for four days, Jonas," Val reminded him. "You've often been away twice as long."

"That was business," Jonas said defensively.

"I know." Val smiled at the couple dancing by. "The house was just as empty. I was just as alone."

"Val…"

The music ended. Val danced out of his arms.

Had he heard what she'd said? Had he understood? Val's thinking process was unaffected by the male arms that had caught her as she spun away from Jonas. The arms belonged to Ted, one of Charlie's friends and groomsmen. He was a pleasant enough young man, good-looking and well built. But when compared to Jonas, he paled into insignificance.

Had he heard a word she'd said? Did he give a damn? Val gave the large reception hall of the country club a casual scan, her eyes searching for the tall, imposing figure of her husband. She spotted Jonas at the edge of the dance floor, conversing with a plump, matronly woman, whom Val recognized as the wife of an important business associate of his.

Business. Val smothered a sigh, and smiled at whatever it was Ted had said to her. With Jonas it was always business. Val didn't actually resent Jonas's devotion to his company. She understood the force of the ambition that drove him. He was a self-made man. Jonas was on top in his particular field and fully intended to remain there.

But there were times, more and more frequent in number, when she wished Jonas would delegate more and work less. He had not taken a vacation, a real getaway vacation, since she'd met him. They spent very little "quality time" together. They had never played together with the abandonment of other couples, married or single, on a carefree holiday. The work was a joy to him, Val knew. She also knew that his work was a growing strain on their relationship. If only...

The music ended. Val murmured the appropriate inanities, then turned toward the spot where she had last seen Jonas. He wasn't there. Wandering aimlessly around the room, her restless gaze skimming the faces of some of the over three hundred guests, Val stalked her husband.

She eventually found him leaning against a decorative Grecian pillar while he observed the gathering with an aloof, contemplative expression. He'd been watching her progress, and his eyes narrowed as she approached him.

"You're the best man," Val reminded him as she came to a stop in front of him.

"I know." Jonas smiled.

Val chose to ignore his wry humor. "You should be mingling with the guests." She knew what was coming when his smile grew.

"If I'm going to mingle, sweetheart, I'll..."

"Jonas." Val silenced him with that single warning murmur. "This is hardly the time or the place."

Supremely unconcerned with the laughter and conversation rippling around them, Jonas rooted her to the floor with an intense stare. "When is the time?" he asked softly. "Where is the place?

The room was suddenly too warm. Val's gown was suddenly too tight across her breasts. She couldn't think. She didn't want to. In that instant, all the discord between them dissolved in the achingly familiar heat that was rushing to her head, plunging to the depths of her femininity. Val was unaware that her feelings were clearly revealed in her violet eyes. All she knew was that she longed to drown in the blue-gray depths of his eyes.

Normally a man of few words, Jonas didn't speak; he acted. Pushing away from the ornate pillar, he grasped her hand and led her around the fringes of the crowd and through the open doors that led to the spacious patio and extensive country club gardens.

The intoxicating scent of roses permeated the soft summer air. The velvet night sky sparkled with the light of millions of stars and the nearly full moon. A thrilling sensation of strangely illicit excitement trembled through Val's overwarm body.

She came to her senses when Jonas came to a stop, midway along one of the graveled walkways. Val had to smile at the first coherent thought that swam into her head. She was literally being led down the garden path. The low, terse sound of his voice jolted her back to reality.

"When are you coming home?"

"I was only away one night, Jonas."

Jonas released his grasp on her hand and then, catching her off guard, pulled her into his arms. His voice was a low, hungry growl near her ear. "I mean, when are you really coming home, back to our bed, where you belong?"

Resistance flowed along Val's spine. Always the same, she thought. It was always the same. For Jonas, the cure to any personal problem could be found in bed. Working a hand free, she pressed it against his shoulder.

"Jonas, don't."

"Don't?" he repeated in an incredulous tone. "Val, I need you so much I can hardly think straight." Sliding a hand up her spine to her nape, he tangled his fingers in her hair and tugged her head back. "And you tell me 'Don't'? You might as well tell me to stop breathing." Lowering his head, he fastened his mouth onto hers.

His kiss was heaven. His kiss was hell. And it was all the levels of sensation quivering between the two extremes. It was always the same...yet always different. His mouth was hard, yet warm. His lips were demanding, yet tender. His tongue was piercing, yet gentle.

Needing the feel of Jonas, the taste of him, every bit as much as his taut body told her that he needed her, Val stole a moment out of their time of discord and surrendered to the sweet forgetfulness of his kiss.

Her spine bowed in response to the tightening of his arm around her waist. Her soft, trembling body was fused to the rigid strength of his. Plundering her mouth, Jonas arched protectively, possessively, over her slight form.

Her gown was being crushed; Valerie didn't care. The curve of her spine was being strained; Valerie didn't feel it. For the length of his kiss, her mind abdicated, her senses rejoiced, her passion reigned.

His breath was a harsh sound on the still night when Jonas lifted his mouth from hers. "You want me as much as I want you." His voice was low, raspy, intense. "Come home with me, Val. Come home and make love with me."

With the despairing thought that lovely dreams always seemed to end in rude awakenings, Val brought her hand from his shoulder and laid her palm against his cheek.

Disarmed and heartened, Jonas combed his fingers through the silky strands of her hair, gleaming ebony in the wash of moonlight, and eased his grip around her waist. "Val," he murmured, lowering his head for another kiss.

Her small hand stroked his cheek, then she nimbly slipped out of his loosened embrace. "It would solve nothing, Jonas," she said from a safe distance of several feet. "Except to alleviate the obvious, immediate discomfort."

Stiff with anger and frustration, Jonas cursed under his breath. Watching him warily, prepared to make a run for it if he took one step toward her, Val listened to him swear in mounting surprise, amazed at his extensive vocabulary.

When he at last fell silent, after having not once used the same word twice, Val asked, "Are you quite finished?"

Jonas had the grace to be embarrassed. "I'm sorry," he said, raking a hand through his neatly brushed hair. "But you have a positive talent for making me mad."

"That's my line," Val quipped, in a weak attempt to defuse his explosive temper.

His burst of laughter was harsh, short, involuntary. But it did the trick. Jonas exhaled, easing the stiffness from his body. "And you've been using it a lot lately." He took a step toward her; Val took a step back. In the bright moonlight she could see the cynical smile that curved his thin lips. "You can relax, sweetheart," he said, slowly moving toward her. "I won't pounce on you again."

Ignoring the twinge of disappointment she felt, Val gave him a considering look. "I'd like your word on it."

"You have it."

Val relaxed, and unwittingly offered him the compliment of physically displaying utter belief and trust in his given word. His smile tearing her poise into ribbons of shivering expectancy, Jonas closed the space that separated them.

"We must go back inside," Val said, clenching her hands into fists to combat the effects of his nearness on her senses. "As the best man and matron of honor, we are expected to mingle and be charming to the guests."

"I want to kiss you again."

"No, Jonas." Now she was denying herself as well as him.

"Just once more," he murmured seductively.

"No, Jonas." Refusing him hurt her.

"You're my wife."

Val lifted her chin. "Are you issuing a veiled ultimatum?" she challenged.

Jonas pinned her for an instant with an angry stare. Then he shook his head in sharp denial. "You know better."

Relief shivered through Val, for, although she thought Jonas would never force an issue with her, she wasn't absolutely sure. "Then I suggest we go back inside. In case you've forgotten, our friends are celebrating their wedding." Displaying a confidence she was light-years from feeling, Val turned and began walking toward the lights and sounds of music and laughter that were pouring from the open doors of the country club.

"I haven't forgotten a thing, Val," Jonas muttered, falling into step beside her.

You never do, Val acknowledged, but only to herself. To him she raised one delicately arched eyebrow. "Do we present a show of unity or dissension?" Her nod indicated the building they were approaching and the people inside.

"Unity." Marginally smiling, Jonas angled his arm in invitation.

Faintly returning his smile, Val slid her arm through his. She glanced up at him in startled surprise when he came to a halt mere inches from the open doors. "Jonas?"

"This is ridiculous." His tone was adamant. "We don't have time for socializing, Val. We must talk."

"Not here, Jonas." Her tone betrayed her impatience. It succeeded in igniting his own.

"When?" he demanded. He shouldn't have.

"When I return from California," she answered in

a fierce whisper as they crossed the threshold. The arm beneath her hand grew taut, revealing the control Jonas was exerting over his temper.

"What?" Impervious to the startled looks sent their way from the guests who had overheard him, Jonas stared at her in furious disbelief.

Smiling sweetly for the benefit of the onlookers, Val repeated her answer, but this time succinctly and through her sparkling, gritted teeth. "I said when I get back from California, Jonas."

a mixture consists as they walked the corridor to the
soundless air-conditioned family suite that Gomael
kept for his private employee use.

"Where," Gomael went on smoothly, "Or I mean who
is Jenna the ghost who has overheard this joint
motion at this minute conference.

Stella, cross by the demand of the Sky Gods
who removed his cellular in the corridor daily as
he sat and gained format levels "I don't think I
can talk about anything else."

Chapter 6

The weather in San Francisco was miserable. It had
rained, at times in pouring sheets, at others in light
drizzles, throughout every one of the seemingly endless four days Val had been on the West Coast.

Val's mood was in perfect harmony with the prevailing weather conditions. The rally for the protection of artistic individuality, over which she had
fought with Jonas to attend, was, at least for Val, a
complete farce.

Bright-eyed and eager, Val had set out the morning
after her arrival in San Francisco to be a part of the
opening event. Disillusionment had set in minutes after she entered the designated display room.

The garish, childishly executed paintings on the sit-
ting-room walls in the elegant home of one of the
rally sponsors had nothing whatever to do with individuality, and even less with artistry. In Val's opinion,

the general public deserved protection from the crude, overbearing idiot who had the temerity to refer to himself as a working artist.

Nevertheless, reserving judgment, Val sought out the sponsors she had corresponded with. They were not difficult to identify. Never before in her life had she encountered such a group of dilettantes, sycophants, pseudointellectuals and just plain phonies.

Edging away from the group, she unobtrusively drifted toward the front door. Slipping out of the house, Val went sightseeing in the rain.

When she got back to the hotel late in the afternoon of that first day, Val considered returning home. She felt foolish for making the trip in the first place. She was discouraged and depressed. Not even sight-seeing in the city she had longed to explore had managed to lift her spirits.

And, irascible as he often was, Val missed Jonas even more than she had three years before, when she'd left him, ostensibly to visit her mother in Australia, but with every intention of not returning. After only one day away, Val ached for the sight of Jonas. Yet she knew that if she went home, she would have to explain to him why she had cut short the trip. There was no way she could lie to him about it. And, though Jonas might not say "I told you so," Val knew he would definitely think it. Unwilling to admit he'd been right, Val decided to remain in California.

During the remaining three days of her stay, Val followed the same routine. After breakfast, she made her way to the first scheduled rally event of the day, each of which grew successively worse. Then, having put in an appearance, she escaped to spend the day on her own.

By the end of the third day, Val concluded that being on her own, even in a city as interesting and varied as San Francisco, was not her idea of a fun time. If only she and Jonas had resolved their differences...

But they hadn't. Trudging along the sidewalks, all of which seemed either straight up or straight down, Val chastised herself for the aloof, withdrawn attitude she'd maintained with Jonas during the week between the wedding and her departure for the coast.

And all because of stupid pride...hers as well as his, Val acknowledged. But, stupid or not, Val's pride had still been smarting over the revelation that Jonas had been supporting Lynn financially. And Val knew that she had stung Jonas's pride by rejecting his advances the night of Janet and Charlie's wedding.

By spiriting her away from the reception, Jonas had initially excited, then angered Val. The setting of a moon-washed garden drenched with the heady scent of early summer roses had been conducive to romance. Jonas had not only ruined the mood with his blatant sexual overtures, he had thrown away the perfect opportunity to effect a reconciliation.

Why were married men so incredibly dense? Val railed in silent frustration, panting as she climbed yet another steep hill. She had often heard married men deride women, married as well as single, for being gullible enough to fall for a smooth line pitched by a glib-tongued male. Whenever she had overheard remarks of that nature, Val had had to bite back the urge to upbraid the speaker for his own lack of insight. Why, she'd asked herself, couldn't the poor fools—Jonas included—figure out that, if they gave even half as much attention to their wives or lady friends as they paid to their work, the glib-tongued men would be out of business?

And so, since Jonas had made Val angry by wasting the romantic setting of the garden, she had determined to let him cool his heels, waiting for the "talk" he'd insisted upon, until after she had returned from the coast.

There was one final event for her to attend—a large formal gala, to be held in the ballroom of one of the oldest, most prestigious hotels in the city. Val wasn't looking forward to the event, but since she had shelled out a bundle for two tickets in the vain hope that Jonas would condescend to join her, she was determined on going, alone or not…maybe because, though she was on her own, she was never completely alone.

Sitting in a cable car as it screeched down the paved face of a hill, Jonas was with her.

Wandering in and out of the stalls on Fisherman's Wharf, examining the ordinary and the exotic merchandise proffered there, Jonas was with her.

Standing on the bay shore, the wind whipping her hair around her head, watching the fog shroud the Golden Gate Bridge and the island of Alcatraz, Jonas was with her.

And as she dressed for the gala in the gown Jonas had so violently disapproved of, he was definitely with her, scowling in spirit, if not in person.

For three days after Val's departure for California, the employees of J.T. Electronics took great care to avoid their employer. To put it in their words: the cracker was on the warpath. In fact, Jonas was mad.

He was mad at the world, he was mad at Val, but most of all he was mad at himself. Being human and male, Jonas didn't like facing his own failings. But he had failed, and knew it. He had failed Val and, in so doing, had ultimately failed himself.

Frustrated, agitated, impatient, Jonas prowled the confines of his office just as he had three years previously, the first time Val had left him alone.

He and Val had been estranged then, too, Jonas recalled with painful clarity.

Come to that, Val had withdrawn from him at that time, too, in much the same way she'd withdrawn into herself after the wedding reception for Janet and Charlie.

Jonas came to a halt at his brooding spot before the wide window that overlooked the rear parking lot. A derisive smile curved his thin lips. He had spent an inordinate amount of time on this spot during the past three days, he reflected, fighting an inner battle with himself—one that he'd been waging in silence throughout every one of those three days.

Three years ago, Jonas had allowed Valerie a month. Now she had told him she would be gone four days.

Jonas made a rude sound. His assistant was off on a romantic honeymoon with one of his executives. Charlie and Janet were very likely making love at that very minute, Jonas thought with envy, while he, the boss, stood like a statue, staring out a window, aching in every inch of his being for his woman.

It's only two nights and one more day, Jonas told himself, staring bleakly at the golden glow of the sunset. He could wait one more day.

"Like hell."

Fully aware of growling the decision aloud, Jonas turned away from the window and strode to his desk. Stabbing the intercom with his long index finger, Jonas issued terse instructions to his secretary.

"Linda, I want the Lear made ready to depart for San Francisco tomorrow morning. Take care of it."

"At once, Jonas."

Even in this edgy mood, Jonas had to smile, if faintly, at the woman's immediate response. Linda wasn't a good secretary, she was damn near perfect. And at thirty-two she wasn't merely attractive, she was gorgeous.

When Jonas thought about it, which wasn't often, he invariably smiled. Linda had been handpicked and scrupulously trained by his former secretary, his wife, Valerie. If nothing else, Linda's presence in the outer office bespoke Val's trust in him.

It was something. Jonas hung on to that something like an invisible talisman.

The elegantly appointed hotel ballroom was packed. Tuxedoed men and exquisitely gowned and bejeweled women stood in small groups conversing with the cadre of "artists" for whom the benefit was being held.

If nothing else, the normally scruffy self-declared artists had cleaned up well, Val thought wryly as she drifted from one group to another. Even the obnoxious young man she'd had the misfortune to meet at the first day's event looked reasonably presentable, having made the supreme sacrifice of trimming his shaggy beard and having his too long, lank hair shampooed.

Quiet, composed, reserved, Valerie chose to sit at a table near the back of the room for dinner. The food was excellent. Val barely tasted it. The speeches were blessedly short. Val didn't hear them. Behind a facade of interest, she asked herself what in hell she was doing there, allowing herself to be bored to numbness, when she could be at home, fighting with her blockhead of a husband.

Steeped in her loneliness for the only man who possessed the power to make her pulse race and her heartbeat play leapfrog with itself, Val was immune to the blatantly overt looks sent her way by many of the men present.

When the dinner was at last concluded, Val followed the lead of the other guests and mingled, listening to bits of a discussion here, adding her voice to bits of conversation there, then moving on, restless, yet unwilling to return to her hotel room to be alone with her own thoughts and fears.

In her preoccupation, Val was as unaware of the speculative glances sweeping her face and form as she was of the impact of her appearance and the challenge presented by her cool, untouchable attitude.

She was repeatedly invited onto the dance floor. She politely, but repeatedly declined.

The evening dragged on. Beginning to wonder if the interminable reception would ever come to an end, Val was standing with a small group of women, sipping at a glass of champagne she really didn't want, when her wandering attention was snared by the throaty low exclamation made by the beautiful, thirtyish, self-admittedly bored woman standing beside her.

"Oh, my! Yes," the woman murmured. "Please, Santa, bring me that for Christmas!"

"I beg your pardon?" Val responded, frowning at the staring, avaricious expression on her companion's face.

"Him," the woman said, nodding to indicate someone behind Val. "I'll take him as is, no gift wrap necessary."

A chorus of avid agreement was raised by the other women in the group, all of whom had their glittering eyes glued to the person in question.

Mildly curious, and grateful for the interruption of the rather dull discussion, Val turned to see the paragon who had called forth a sheen of pure lust on the other women's faces. A spasm of shock quaked through her at the sight that met her eyes.

He was attired in an expertly tailored tuxedo that molded and defined his broad shoulders and long, rawboned frame. A knife-pleated, sparkling white shirt gave sharp contrast to the unrelieved black. His chiseled jaw held at an arrogant angle, spine straight, shoulders squared, the man stood framed in the wide ballroom doorway, his narrow-eyed gaze slowly taking inventory of the guests, who were staring at him in gaping curiosity.

"Who is he?" The awed question came from a gaunt middle-aged woman directly opposite Valerie.

"I don't know," the woman who had first spotted

him responded in a husky, thought-revealing tone. "But I intend to find out."

Turning her back on the unexpected late arrival, Val took a sip of her wine, then said casually, "His name is Jonas Thorne."

"He looks important," one woman observed.

"He looks powerful," another woman opined.

"He looks like he'd be great in bed," the woman who'd first noticed him said bluntly.

Valerie concealed a smile behind the glass she raised to her lips. She had been through a scene like this before. At that time, the obvious sexual interest in Jonas revealed by other women had both shocked and dismayed her. After three years, all Val experienced was amusement and pity.

"I understand that he's married to a very possessive, jealous woman," she murmured.

"Aren't the terrific-looking ones always married?" the gaunt woman wailed.

"It's the story of my life." The other woman sighed.

"He may be married, but he's alone now," the original speaker noted in a tone of sheer calculation. "And," she continued, smiling with smug satisfaction, "he's heading my way."

Val nearly choked over the woman's capacity for self-deception. Besides herself, there were three women in the group, yet this one was convinced she had snared his attention. Refusing to turn, Val sipped her wine and waited. She knew when he came to a stop beside her; a thrill trickled along her spine.

"Valerie." His voice was low, controlled, sexy.

Val could actually feel the collective shudder of

response that swept through her companions. Tilting her head, she gave him a distant smile. "Jonas. Let me introduce you to a few of the patrons of the rally." Val felt grateful for her excellent memory as she rattled off their names.

"Ladies," he said smoothly, inclining his head.

"Ladies," Val echoed, her tone dry, "I'd like you to meet my husband, Jonas Thorne."

"Cute." Jonas made the observation from the corner of the limousine. "When did you decide you enjoyed creating uncomfortable little scenes?" he asked, referring to the gasps of surprise Val had drawn from the women by introducing him as her husband, and the furious spate of questions that had followed, which he had saved her from enduring by whisking her from the ballroom. Before Val had a chance to interpret his actions, he had swept her from the hotel and into the long gray car.

Val shrugged. "I couldn't resist," she defended herself. "Those female barracudas were sizing you up like a side of beef on the auction block."

"And that bothered you?"

Since his voice was free of inflection, and his face was shadowed so that she couldn't read his expression, Val couldn't tell whether Jonas was pleased or annoyed. Nervous, but determined not to let him see it, she carefully kept her own tone bland. "As a member of their sex, their behavior demeaned me." She casually glanced out the side window and drew in a deep, calming breath. "May I ask where you're taking me?" she inquired as she turned back to him.

"My hotel."

Val felt a quick flash of irritation. "I have my own room, Jonas," she said grittily.

"I have an entire suite, Valerie," Jonas retorted.

"But my clothes are in my room!"

"Give me your key," he said, holding out his hand, palm up. "I'll send the driver to collect your things."

"But…"

Jonas's control snapped. "Damn it, Val, you're my wife! And though we've been sleeping in separate beds, I'll be damned if I'll tolerate sleeping in separate hotels." He paused to draw an exasperated-sounding breath. "I know the driver. He'll be careful packing your things.…"

"I packed nearly everything this afternoon," Val informed him.

Jonas's shrug was a blur of movement in the shadows. "So, no big deal. He'll finish the packing, then deliver your cases to my hotel." His tone took on an edge of steel. "Now, give me your key…please."

Although his outburst had ignited Val's anger, she subsided and flipped the catch on her evening bag. Unwilling to argue with him in the car, she withdrew the key and handed it to him. Tension crackled in the air between them during the remainder of the drive to his hotel. Sitting in frozen silence beside him, Val seethed with impotent rage. Jonas was spoiling for a fight. She could feel the vibrations radiating from him.

Val had witnessed Jonas in a fight. She knew that, when geared for battle, Jonas was darned near invincible. Steeling herself for the coming confrontation, Val vowed that he would not win, at least not without knowing he'd been in the fight of his life.

Valerie had expected to be delivered to the stately old hotel where she and Jonas had spent their wedding night. Instead, the limo glided to a stop in front of a fairly new building. As she stepped from the car, Valerie glanced up at the clean, straight lines of the tower, rising majestically above the surrounding structures. In a way she was disappointed, as she had decided it would be fitting to conduct their argument in the same suite in which they had spent their aborted honeymoon.

Head high, her purpose firm, Val entered the hotel at Jonas's side. The suite that Jonas ushered her into was lavish, if not steeped in the elegance of the suite they had shared three years ago. It consisted of four rooms, a spacious sitting room, two large bedrooms and a connecting bathroom. The floor-to-ceiling draperies were drawn in the sitting room and the largest of the bedrooms, revealing floor-to-ceiling walls of glass. The night view of the lights of the city below and the bay beyond the windows was spectacular.

Dropping onto the settee the stole she'd worn against the evening damp and chill, Val walked to the wide expanse of window as if drawn by a magnet. "Beautiful," she whispered, transfixed by the panorama before her.

"Yes."

Val turned at the odd note in Jonas's voice. His expression puzzled her. What was he thinking? she wondered, experiencing an inexplicable thrill of anticipation.

"Beautiful" seemed barely adequate to describe her, Jonas thought, feeling his insides tighten. Val was stunning, breathtaking. In the setting of the night view behind her, Val stood out like a rare gem in a collection of unpolished stones.

She was wearing the off-the-shoulder, violet-hued chiffon gown she'd purchased for the occasion—the gown Jonas had decided had been designed to arouse male interest and admiration. The enticing way the chiffon draped her breasts, revealing just a hint of the gentle curves beneath, certainly succeeded in arousing him. Jonas felt his stomach clench at the thought of other men experiencing the same response to her fragile-looking beauty. Her only adornments were the filigree necklace and drop earrings he'd given her...and the rings encircling the third finger of her small left hand.

A flash of possessiveness streaked through Jonas as his gaze lingered on the gold band nestled beside the large solitaire diamond that appeared too heavy for her slender finger. Slowly he trailed his gaze up her body to confront her. Val was his, and he'd be damned if he'd let her get away from him. But this time he'd play it smart, Jonas decided. He'd blown his chance to make things right with her the night of the reception, while they were in the garden. He wouldn't make the same mistake again.

Val stood poised in front of the window wall, her facade of composure concealing a growing uneasiness. Jonas was so quiet, too quiet. A curl of excitement combined with her uneasiness to make an explosive mixture when he slowly examined her with his narrowed eyes. The silence lengthened, tearing at her nerves. Val was afraid that if Jonas didn't say something, and soon, she'd begin to unravel.

"It's time for us to talk."

Valerie started at the soft sound of his voice. Expecting him to attack with anger and impatience, she was confused by his reticence. Was she imagining things, or had she detected a hint of uncertainty underlying his quiet tone? Valerie hoped so, because she didn't like the idea of being the only uncertain person in the room. "I know," Val replied softly.

He didn't move for long seconds. Then, when he did, she jumped again. A wry smile twitched the corners of his lips. "Relax, sweetheart," he drawled. "I'm not going to pounce on you." Instead of walking toward her, Jonas strode to the small dining table that stood in one corner of the room. Picking up a large folder, he flipped it open. "I don't know about you, but I didn't have dinner and I'm hungry." He gave her an inquisitive look.

Not quite sure what to make of his mild manner, Val simply stared at him, trying to gauge his mood.

"Val, are you hungry?"

Now Val was really confused. Rather than impatient, Jonas actually seemed amused. Relieved, yet still suspicious, she answered, "Yes, a little. I didn't eat very much of my dinner."

Jonas grinned, and thoroughly rattled Val in the process. "The usual tasteless banquet chicken, huh?"

Stunned by his show of good humor, Val replied without thinking. "No, I think it was some sort of beef, but I really don't remember."

"Whatever." Jonas shrugged, and glanced down at

the folder. "Let's see what room service has to offer."

"Jonas, it's nearly midnight," Val reminded him. "Isn't it too late for room service?"

"No," he murmured, intent on the menu. "This hotel offers twenty-four-hour room service. But it is too late for dinner. After eleven it's mostly snack foods, but they do have a selection of basket meals." Once again he glanced up to give her a questioning look.

Perfect, Val thought. A basket meal for a basket case. Distracted, she asked, "What's the basket meal?"

Jonas kept a straight face. "A basket meal, Valerie, is a meal contained in a basket."

"I know that!" Val flashed a quick, tremulous smile, and felt a spark of warmth flutter inside when Jonas inhaled sharply in response. "Ah..." She paused, trying to recall the subject. Food! Right. "What I'm asking is: what does the meal in the basket contain?"

Jonas laughed, spreading the warmth inside Val. "We have our choice of several," he answered, the low sexiness of his voice at variance with the mundane topic. "There are chicken fingers, burgers and their version of a Philly cheese steak," he recited, referring to the menu. "They all come with French fries and slaw on the side." Jonas raised his head and one eyebrow simultaneously. "You want to try the steak?"

"No thanks." Val gave him a knowing look and a brief shake of her head. "I've tried other places' versions of a Philly cheese steak. I'll wait till I get back to Philly and have the real thing.'' She thought it over for a moment, then decided, "I think I'll have a burger.''

"Okay." Jonas reached for the phone.

"With cheese."

"Fine." He punched the room service number.

"And bacon."

He shot her a droll look. "Right."

"And lettuce and tomato and mayo."

Jonas lost control. Holding his palm over the receiver, he roared with laughter. "I thought you said you were only a little hungry?" he gasped as his laughter subsided.

With a nonchalance that belied the melting sensation his amusement induced within her, Val strolled to the settee. "That was fifteen minutes ago," she informed him with a regal air. "My appetite has sharpened since then."

"My appetite's pretty sharp, too," Jonas muttered before he responded to the prompting from room service.

His double-edged remark stole Val's breath and increased the melting sensation. Feeling suddenly lightheaded, boneless, she sank onto the settee. She didn't know what kind of game Jonas was playing, but then she didn't much care, either. Experiencing an odd, exciting sense of adventure, Val waited expectantly for whatever might develop.

After placing their order, Jonas circled the table to the long cabinet set against the wall. "The person in room service said it'll be about fifteen minutes. Would you like a drink while we wait?" He swung one cabinet door open to reveal two fully stocked shelves of bottles.

"Is there any white wine?" Val asked, smoothing the long chiffon skirt over her knees with trembling fingers.

Jonas gave her a dry look. "Of course. Had you seriously thought I'd forgotten that you never drink anything other than white wine?"

"No...." She hesitated, then confessed. "At least, I had hoped you hadn't forgotten." The issue was minor, yet Val was amazed how very important it was to her to hear that he had remembered.

"Hoped?" Jonas asked with a sigh. "Have I been so neglectful of you, Val, that you would even doubt?"

Tension slammed back into Val, robbing her of the heady sense of adventure and excitement. Disappointed, she lowered her eyes. "Jonas...I..."

"Never mind." Jonas spoke, not impatiently, but in a surprising, almost supplicating tone. "You don't have to say it, I know the answer." Then his voice changed, becoming brusque. "There's a bottle of champagne chilling in the fridge."

Val glanced up to see him swing open the door on the other side of the cabinet to reveal a small refrigerator, complete with ice trays and bottles of mixers, seltzers and mineral water. Reaching down, he removed a dark foil-capped bottle from the wine rack mounted on the door. After closing the door, he turned, smiling wryly as he held up the bottle for her inspection.

"Impressive," Val murmured at the sight of the imported label. "A meal of burgers served with champagne that costs one hundred and fifty dollars a bottle?''

Jonas shrugged. ''Well, it's not the best,'' he said, turning to pick up two long-stemmed tulip glasses from the tray on top of the cabinet. ''But it'll have to do.'' He removed the foil wrap and wire guard, then with a deft twist of his hand eased the cork from the bottle with a muted pop, without losing a drop of the bubbling contents.

He poured the golden liquid into the glasses and had started toward her when a light knock sounded on the door.

''Dinner?'' Val guessed, holding out her hands in a silent offer to relieve him of the glasses.

Stepping to her, Jonas handed her the tulips, then turned toward the door. ''Could be the driver with your cases.''

It was. After the man had departed, Jonas carried the two suitcases into the bedroom…his bedroom. Setting the glasses on the low table in front of the settee, Val rose and trailed into the room after him. Jonas shot her a narrowed, challenging look as she entered.

''I, ah, think I'll change into something more casual,'' she said, hoping to keep the atmosphere between them defused by removing the gown that seemed to have an explosive effect on Jonas.

''No, don't,'' he said quickly, then continued with a suggestive smile. ''At least, not until after dinner.''

Val frowned in confusion. ''But I thought you didn't like the gown, Jonas!''

Leaving the cases where he'd dropped them, Jonas came to her. Raising a hand, he caught a bit of the filmy material capping her shoulders and slid it between his fingers. "It's a beautiful gown, and even more beautiful on you, Val," he murmured. "What I didn't particularly like was having you wear it for anyone else but me."

Val went weak and swayed toward him. "Oh, Jonas."

Jonas brought up his other hand to grasp her shoulder as he slowly lowered his head to hers. Val could feel his moist breath against her mouth. The mood was shattered by another knock on the door and a muffled voice announcing: "Room service."

Jonas froze. He frowned. Then he swore.

Laughing softly, Val raised one hand and silenced him with a finger over his lips. "You get the door," she instructed, moving away from him. "I'll get the wine."

Glasses in her hands, Val stood patiently by as the waiter transferred the food and utensils from the serving cart to the table.

"I'll leave the cart by the door," he said, as Jonas ushered him from the room. "Just roll it into the hallway when you're finished."

"Fine," Jonas replied, bringing a wide smile to the man's face with a large tip. "And thank *you*." He shut the door firmly, cutting off the waiter's profuse thanks.

"You weren't very polite to the poor man," Val chastised Jonas laughingly, as he slid into the chair opposite her at the small table.

"But I was generous," Jonas retorted, raising his glass to her in a silent salute. "Now eat your dinner before it gets stone-cold."

Val accepted his salute by taking a sip of the wine, then murmured in obvious amusement, "Yes, sir, Mr. Thorne, sir."

Jonas grew still, the burger in his hands poised midway between the basket and his mouth.

"Jonas?" Val asked hesitantly, suddenly nervous again. "What is it? What's wrong?"

A faint smile, partly sad, partly reflective, played over his firm mouth. "Do you have any idea how long it's been since you've called me that in that irreverent, teasing tone?"

The nervous sensation changing to an altogether different feeling, Val took a deep breath and a hopeful guess. "Too long?"

Jonas sighed. "Much too long."

Val assumed guilt without question—like most wives? she wondered. "I'm sorry, Jonas."

"Yeah, so am I." He smiled derisively. "You're angry that I didn't tell you about the monthly payments to Lynn." It wasn't a question; he knew the answer.

"Yes," Val answered anyway. "Angry and hurt."

Jonas exhaled deeply. "I've thought it over, and finally realized that you have every right to be angry," he admitted, surprising Val. But before she could respond, he surprised her even more. "I'm sorry, too, Val," he continued. "I have no excuse. I honestly never even considered how it might concern you. It's meaningless." He offered her a wry smile. "I want you to believe that. I support Lynn for one reason and one reason only, and that is to keep her out of my hair."

Val was silent for a moment, during which she

could see that Jonas looked strained and decidedly uncomfortable. Then, delighted to discover that she had the singular power to make the otherwise impervious Jonas Thorne squirm, she drew out the silence a little longer.

It was a battle of nerves; Jonas surrendered first, turning Val's surprise to utter amazement. "I wish you'd say something, anything," he muttered. "Even if it's only to give me hell."

"I believe I've tried that in the past," Val replied in a dry drawl. "It never did me much good."

Jonas actually winced. "I know I haven't been the easiest man to live with, but—"

Val's spontaneous burst of laughter cut him off. "The easiest?" she taunted. "Try the most difficult."

"Yeah." Jonas suddenly looked tired, and a little afraid. "You're bored, aren't you, Val?"

"Not with you!" Val cried at once, frightened by the defeated look on his strong face. "Never with you, Jonas."

"But with our life together?" he persisted. "With our life-style?"

Val broke the end off a golden-brown fry, then looked at it as though she'd never before seen its like. "Jonas, our life-style is..." Her voice trailed away, and she idly played with the bit of potato as she raked her mind for a way to express her feelings of inadequacy and frustration.

"Confining," Jonas finished for her.

Val lifted her head. She had entered the suite expecting an argument. When Jonas appeared intent on avoiding one, she had begun to hope they could discuss their problems without rancor or raised voices.

But Val could not, would not back down from her position simply to fulfill that hope. "Yes, Jonas," she answered clearly. "I find our life-style confining."

Jonas had said he was starving, yet he had barely touched his food. As if suddenly becoming aware of the large burger he was holding, he raised it to his mouth. "Okay." After murmuring the single word, he nodded once and bit into the sandwich.

Okay? Val frowned. What did that mean? she asked herself. Okay...what? Okay, they'd change their life-style or...? Val felt a flash of sheer panic. Surely he hadn't meant to imply that he'd be willing to end the marriage. Her thoughts darting here and there, Val absently picked up her burger and followed his example. He couldn't have meant that, she assured herself, chewing, swallowing, but not tasting anything except fear. Jonas was too possessive, too—

His terse voice sliced across her fractured thoughts. "Did you hear me, Val?"

"Y-yes." Val couldn't have controlled the tremor in her voice if her life had depended on it. "I heard. I—I'm just not sure I understand what you meant."

"I meant... Okay, I'll free you from the exclusive, confining role of being my housewife."

Panic ballooned inside Val, and she rushed to explain. "I don't mind the housework, Jonas, really I don't. It's just that it's not enough. I mean, I want to do more. I need to—"

Once again Jonas cut her off. "But if you're coming back to work, even if only on a part-time basis, I insist you hire someone to help with the housework."

"Coming back to work?" Val repeated, unable to believe she'd heard him correctly. "Jonas, I—"

Jonas interrupted her for the third time. "You don't think I'd allow you to work for a competitor, do you?" Picking up his glass, he tilted it at her. "I could use another assistant." Bringing the glass to his lips, he drank to her. "Do you want the job or not?"

"Want it?" Val stared at him in stunned amazement. "Jonas, you know I'd adore working with you again."

Jonas raised his eyebrows mockingly. "Really? I have it on good authority that I'm a bas—"

"Jonas," Val's warning voice overrode his.

He grinned. "A devil to work for," he finished, biting with relish into his sandwich.

This time Val deliberately followed his lead, and this time she tasted the burger. It was rather good. "What authority?" she asked after swallowing the morsel.

"The best," Jonas replied blandly, popping a fry into his mouth. "You."

"Did I say that?" Val asked in feigned innocence, beginning to enjoy herself. In fact, she realized, she was beginning to feel wonderful.

"Mmm." Jonas nodded, his eyes teasing her over the burger he'd just bitten into.

"Fancy that."

"I fancy you."

Val melted. "Oh, Jonas, I fancy you, too. You'll never know how unhappy and depressed I've been from all the discord and bitterness between us."

His smile was wry. "I have a pretty good idea." He reached a hand across the table, palm up. An audible sigh of relief whispered through his lips when she slid her hand into his. "Oh, God, I've missed you, Val."

"I missed you, too." Val could barely speak around the emotion gripping her throat.

"The house was empty." Jonas shuddered. "I was empty."

"I know." Val blinked.

"Can you forgive me for being such an arrogant, unsympathetic ass the past three years?"

"Yes." Val smiled mistily. "If you can forgive me for driving you crazy with all my courses and projects."

Jonas grimaced. "You did have me going around in circles."

"I'm sorry."

Jonas gave a quick bark of laughter. "No, you're not."

Val's grin was shaky, but there. "I did manage to get your attention."

"You did at that." His hand tightened convulsively around hers. "I love you, Val."

"I love you, Jonas."

"Finish your dinner, Val." Jonas's voice grew low, sensuous, enticing. "You're going to need your strength for the dessert I have in mind."

"Yes, sir, Mr. Thorne," Val whispered. "Anything you say, anything you want, sir."

His smile was beautiful.

Chapter 7

Inspired by Jonas's smile, Val managed to finish most of her food, and all of the wine in the glass he kept refilling until the bottle was empty.

But it wasn't the wine that went to Val's senses, it was the man seated opposite her, devouring her with his eyes every bit as thoroughly as he devoured every bite of his burger, French fries and slaw.

Jonas had opened his bow tie and the two top buttons of his shirt midway through the meal. Although Val had lived with him for three years, had seen him naked nearly every night of those years, for some inexplicable reason she found the sight of those two strips of black silk lying against the pristine white of his dress shirt as sexy as the devil he had earlier said he was reputed to be.

If Jonas was a devil in the office, Val mused, watching him polish off her fries as well as his own, he was an even more effective devil in bed. A thrill glided from her nape to the base of her spine. And it had all begun for them here in San Francisco, three years ago. Then she had shivered for a different reason, Val reflected.

Though she had worked in the office with him as his secretary, Val hadn't known Jonas very well. And what she did know of him—his arrogance, his impatience—hadn't endeared him to her. Jonas had bargained with her over their marriage, but when it came to the crunch on their wedding night, Val had been more than nervous. She'd been scared witless.

A smile lurked at the corners of Val's mouth as she remembered the delaying tactics she had tried to employ to escape the inevitable...all to no avail. Jonas had humored her for a time, then he had reached his limit. He had taken a wife, and had every intention of taking her as his wife.

What had she expected? Val's smile was shaded with self-mockery. She knew full well, had known that night, what she'd expected. She had both feared and expected that he would take her arrogantly, impatiently.

Foolish woman, Val silently chided her younger self. In an elegant hotel suite, less than a mile away from where she now sat sipping her wine and drinking in the exciting sight of her husband, that younger Val had stood shivering in fear of the man she now loved more than her own life.

Oh, Jonas had taken her as his wife, Val reminisced. But he had taken her gently, sensuously, caressing her with exquisite torture until she had grown wild with the hungry need to be one with him.

Even after three years and all the problems they'd encountered in simply living together, the memory of that night retained the power to turn Valerie's insides to the consistency of melting cream.

Observing him over the rim of her glass with betraying, smoldering eyes, Val acknowledged that she still was wild with a hungry need to be one with him.

"What's going on inside that beautiful head of yours, I wonder?" Jonas murmured, scattering her thoughts, intensifying the thrill in her body. "You're wearing the most intriguing, sexy little smile on your inviting mouth."

"Is my mouth inviting, Jonas?"

His lips curved in appreciative amusement. "Don't change the subject. What were you thinking about?"

Val swept her eyelashes downward, demurely, enticingly. "I was remembering our wedding night." The thrill spread up to the back of her head, making her scalp tingle, and she heard him catch his breath.

"It was a fantastic night."

"You said we'd come back to San Francisco someday for a repeat performance," she reminded him.

Jonas's voice was low, sensuous. "We're here now."

"Yes."

A teasing note enhanced his tone. "Is it time for dessert, Val?"

Val raised her eyes to his. "Yes."

"Since we're in the state of make-believe, should I sweep you up into my arms in true Hollywood fashion and carry you into our bedroom?"

"Good Lord, no!" Val exclaimed with a laugh. "I think you should help me clear the table and roll the room service cart into the corridor. Then we'll walk into the bedroom together, in true husband and wife fashion.''

Jonas shoved back his chair. "Then let's get to it." He grinned suggestively. "So we can get to it."

With the reward of pleasure as incentive, Val and Jonas made quick work of clearing away the dishes. Then, while he rolled the cart into the hallway, Val drifted into the bedroom, drawn once more by the expanse of windows overlooking the sleeping city. It was late, very late, and considering how tired she'd been earlier, Val should have felt exhausted. She didn't. Quite the contrary, she felt wide-awake and elated.

Spread out before her, the gold-toned city lights appeared muted and dimmed by the billowing shroud of fog rolling in from the bay. Rather than feeling chilled by the sight of the creeping mist, Val felt removed from the damp and the cold, warm and protected, not by the heated suite, but by Jonas's indomitable presence.

"I thought the plan was for us to walk into the bedroom together." The direct cause of Val's feeling of comfort spoke from the bedroom doorway.

Her expression dreamy, her smile alluring, Val slowly turned to look at him. "I stood before a window overlooking San Francisco on a night three years ago," she murmured. "Remember, Jonas?"

"Yes." Though Jonas didn't move, his soft voice crept across the room to envelop Val in warm sensuality, clouding her mind as completely as the fog clouded the city. "You were wearing a chiffon gown then, too. You stole my breath and my heart, and infuriated me by trying to superimpose another man's form over mine.'' His voice grew softer with compassion. "Do you remember, Valerie?''

"Yes." Val's smile was tinged with remembered sadness and gratitude. "I told you I had loved him... and I begged you to understand. You did.''

"I tried. It wasn't easy." Jonas shrugged and moved into the room. "I wanted you so much," he whispered as he came to her. "And I wanted you to want me, too.''

"It didn't take you long to achieve that goal," Val confessed with a shiver of remembrance.

Jonas trailed his fingers over her cheek. "And then having you want me wasn't enough. I wanted you to love me.''

"I do." With a sense of awe, Val felt the tremor that rippled through his body to his fingertips.

"And then," Jonas went on in a voice rough with self-condemnation, "like a fool, I ran the risk of losing what I value most—you and your love for me.''

"No, Jonas," Val denied with soft vehemence. "Never, *never* that.''

"Oh, God, Val," Jonas groaned, pulling her into his arms. "Hold me. Don't ever let me go.''

Sliding her arms around his neck, Val clung to him fiercely as he bent over her. "I won't, darling," she promised, lifting her face to his.

Jonas shuddered at the sound of the endearment, then crushed her mouth with his. His lips were hard. His kiss tasted of desperation. Clinging to him, Val answered to his need.

Without haste, between lingering kisses and inflaming caresses, they undressed each other, pausing to kiss, stroke, adore each newly exposed area of heated flesh.

And then, when his elegant tuxedo lay where Jonas had tossed it, on the floor atop the delicate violet chiffon of Val's gown, and they were both trembling with desire, Jonas did sweep Val into his arms, Thorne fashion, and carried her to the bed. He stared down at her for several seconds after settling her on the mattress, then whispering of his love for her, his need of her, Jonas covered his wifc's shivering form with the blanketing warmth of his body.

Murmuring his name, Val welcomed Jonas into the haven of her silken embrace and cradling thighs. His possession was swift and hard and complete. Val wouldn't have had it any other way. Enticing him with biting kisses, raking fingernails and mewing moans deep in her throat, she arched into his thrusting body, not merely accepting but demanding the shattering joy of release and completion.

"Was I too rough, my love?" Jonas asked, stroking one broad palm over the satiny skin of her hip.

Val smiled and moved her body luxuriously against the length of his. "You were more than rough. You were magnificent," she responded, almost purring, undulating her hips in time with the motions of his caressing hand.

His low laughter had the exciting dark sound of satisfaction and pleasure. "And you were the perfect match for me," he murmured, sparking a delicious new shiver inside her. "I'm positive I'll carry your branding claw marks to my grave."

The shiver turned to ice and Val jolted back to stare at him with concern-widened eyes. "Did I hurt you?"

"Hurt?" His laughter whispered into a sigh. "Oh, sweetheart, the only way you could ever hurt me is by holding back, denying me the passion commanding your response."

Her fear eased, Val shimmied her body along the angular length of his, her parted lips reaching for his mouth. "Was I good for you, Jonas?" she whispered, dropping tiny kisses over his collarbone.

"No," he growled, skimming his hands from her hips to her hair. "You were deliciously bad."

Her soft laughter ended on a gasp as he tangled his fingers in her hair and tugged back her head, exposing her throat to his searching mouth.

"You like that?" Jonas asked, probing the hollow at the base of her throat with the tip of his tongue.

"Yesss." The response hissed through her lips on a sigh.

Arching her back, he trailed his tongue to the valley between her breasts. "And that?"

"Yes." This time her response was short, a mere puff of breath.

Continuing his exploration, Jonas slid his tongue to the crest of one arching breast. "I guess I don't have to ask if you like that," he said with a chuckle, feeling the shudder that quaked through her.

"Jonas...Jonas..." Val chanted, gripping his shoulders convulsively. "Please..."

"No, not yet," he murmured. Releasing her hair, he eased her onto her back. "Lie still, darling. Don't move. Let me show you how much I love you."

Holding her delicate wrists in one large hand, he drew out her arms straight over her head.

"Jonas?" Val flexed her fingers, revealing her need, her desire to touch him.

"Relax, love." His crooning voice slowed the urgency racing through her body. "This is for you."

Jonas began by touching his lips to the pulse that was hammering in her wrist. Then, murmuring new endearments, he strung soft kisses down her arm. Within seconds, Val drifted into a state of liquid warmth. Her thundering heartbeat slowly decreased its rate, her breathing grew regular, her eyes closed, the fire inside her body burned low. Her mind floated, dancing to the rhythms of his downy kisses and the feather-light caresses of his hands.

It was incredible. Val ached, but the ache was sweet. She hungered, but the hunger was teasing. She yearned, but the yearning held promise. Val had never before experienced anything quite like this sedating seduction. Jonas didn't make love to her, he worshiped her. He didn't caress her, he adored her. With his mouth, his hands and his low, intense murmurs, Jonas cherished Val's body, mind and soul.

When he came to her, into her, Val enfolded Jonas within the living beauty of her love for him.

When Val awoke, the sun was shining. Her world was beautiful, because Jonas was there, stroking her, soothing her, loving her. His power over her was complete; she was his to command. In the light of that acknowledgement, his very first words to her were enslaving.

"Good morning. I adore you."

Tears brightened her eyes and clung to her inky lashes. "Oh, Jonas, I love you so very much." She gazed at him, her love shining from her eyes as brightly as the sunlight sparkling outside. "And I'm so sorry."

"Sorry?" Jonas narrowed his eyes. "Sorry for what?"

"I accused you of being possessive," she answered. "And now I'm sorry for not realizing that in your own way you were caring for me."

His smile was a little tender, a little self-derisive. "I didn't realize it, either."

"That you were caring for me?"

"No. That in your own way *you* were caring for me." He shook his head. "I didn't really appreciate the care you took, keeping me well fed and comfortable, armored to face each and every day, good, bad or indifferent." He gave her a chiding smile. "Now that I do realize it, I'm almost sorry I offered you the job of part-time assistant."

"But that's the beauty of it, my love!" Val exclaimed. "Don't you see that now I can care for you in the office, as well as at home?"

Jonas laughed and hugged her to him. "At the risk of repeating myself, I adore you, Valerie Thorne."

Val planted a smacking kiss somewhere in the vicinity of his laughing mouth. "And I love you, Jonas Thorne, sir."

"That's all I want," he said, lifting a hand to gently stroke away a teardrop lingering on her lashes. "Having your love is all I need to survive."

"And that's all?" she asked in teasing awe.

"Well," Jonas drawled. "Maybe that…and some

breakfast.'' Grinning wickedly, he hauled her on top of him. ''But let's have the loving first, then the breakfast.''

Valerie and Jonas spent one laughter-filled, love-drenched week in San Francisco, enjoying the honeymoon they had never had, the honeymoon they would have been too uncertain of each other to enjoy if they had had it three years ago.

Valerie gained four pounds. Jonas lost the lines of strain around his mouth. She looked sleek and content. He appeared vital and energized. They turned heads wherever they went. They went just about everywhere.

Jonas took her dancing. Val took him shopping along the wharf. He escorted her through Chinatown. She guided him through art galleries. They rented a car and drove down the coast, through Big Sur and into Los Angeles. There they boarded a flight back to San Francisco.

And for the first time in three years of marriage, they took the time to talk…and talk…and talk.

''She's like a child, you know,'' Jonas said at one point, when Lynn's name was mentioned. ''A selfish, greedy child. In intellect, if not in years, she is younger than Mary Beth. But Lynn is her mother, and for Mary Beth I'll tolerate her.''

''Of course,'' Val replied, at last fully understanding his position. ''And so will I.''

''Oh, Jonas, the exhibitions were dreadful,'' Val confessed at another point, when he asked about the rally. "I knew I had wasted my time after five minutes of the first event."

"So why didn't you come home?" Jonas growled.

"I was being independent," Val admitted. "Besides, I didn't want to face an 'I told you so' look from you."

Jonas laughed. "You should've braved my expression. You could have saved the office from the beast."

"Were you being a brute, love?" Val inquired, delighted by the idea of him being as miserable without her as she had been without him.

"No, I was being a regular bas—"

"Jonas."

"Basket case," he finished with an unrepentant grin at the warning in her tone.

"Where am I going to work?" Val asked, cuddling as close as she could get to him in the seat of the plane as the Lear jet streaked eastward.

Without ceremony, Jonas hauled her from her seat and settled her on his lap. "I was thinking about the room separating my office from Charlie's."

"The one used for storage?"

"Mmm." Jonas nodded. "Would that be big enough?"

Thrilled at the prospect of being situated just a few steps down the hall from him, Val said eagerly, "That'll be fine. When can I start?"

"It'll have to be cleared out and decorated," Jonas said, weighing the possibilities. "How about, say, a month?"

Fully aware of how quickly Jonas could get a job

accomplished if he was determined to have it done, Val gave him an arched look. "How about one week?"

"Two." Jonas grinned, obviously enjoying the new sensation of bargaining with her.

"Ten days," Val said, returning his grin, telling him she was enjoying herself as much as he was.

"You win." Then, just as her grin slipped into laughter, he added, "This time."

It was Friday. It was late. It was quiet. The weather was warm and fine. Eager to commence their summer weekend, the employees of J.T. Electronics had left the building over an hour before. The place was deserted except for the security personnel...and the boss.

A smile of satisfaction easing the firm line of his mouth, Jonas stood in the doorway of the newly refurbished office. Thanks to the generous bonus he had offered the work crew he'd hired to renovate the storage room, the office was finished, five days ahead of schedule.

Jonas felt a surge of anticipation as he slowly ran his gaze over the interior of the room.

Taking precious time from his schedule, Jonas had personally chosen the decor. Now he couldn't wait to tell Val about *her* office.

Why should he wait? Jonas asked himself. Both his smile and feeling of anticipation growing, he turned away and strode the few steps to his own office suite. Using his private line he punched out his home number and drummed his long fingers impatiently on the desk top while the connection was made. The phone at home rang and rang. On the fourth ring, Jonas curled his fingers into his palm in frustration.

Damn it! Where was she? Even as he fired the question at himself there came a click. At the breathless sound of Val's voice, he redirected the question at her.

"Where the hell were you?"

"Right here," Val replied, unruffled by his impatient tone. "Where the hell are you?"

Jonas suppressed an urge to laugh. His wife was picking up his bad habits...and his language. "I'm still in the office," he said in a much milder tone.

"Why?"

Jonas shot a glance at his watch, the new one Val had given him for his birthday. It had been a belated gift, arriving the day after they'd returned from the West Coast. It was fashioned in mat gold, elegant in its simplicity. In that flashing instant, Jonas could see with his mind's eye the message Val had had inscribed on the back. There were two dates, those of their wedding and of that memorable first night they'd spent together in San Francisco. Jonas treasured the gift, as he treasured its giver.

It wasn't past his usual time for leaving the office. He frowned and replied, "Why what?"

"Why aren't you here with me?" Val asked softly. "When the phone rang, I was in the shower—" her voice dropped even lower "—and missing you."

The image that sprang into Jonas's mind displaced every other thought. He forgot his intention of asking her to come to the complex to see her new office. He forgot the report he had planned to skim over before calling it a day. All he could think about was Val with her hair pinned up, water cascading over her slender form.

"I'll be home in fifteen minutes," he promised, the huskiness in his voice betraying the sudden tightness in his body. "Keep the water running."

"It'll get cold."

"I won't."

"Drive carefully, darling," Val cautioned. "I want you in one piece."

Jonas groaned. "No comment."

Jonas walked away from his desk without a second thought or backward glance. He drove his car into the driveway exactly fourteen minutes after hanging up the phone.

Val was waiting. She swung the door open as he loped along the flagstone walk to the front of the house. Her hair was not, as he'd imagined, pinned up. It tumbled in a mass of loose curls on her shoulders. From neck to ankles she was covered in a belted robe, the picture of modesty. But the toes peeping out from beneath the hem of her robe were bare. Jonas fervently hoped the rest of her body was the same.

Stepping over the threshold, he pulled her to him with one arm and shut the door with the other. When her soft curves conformed pliantly to the hard angles of his body, Jonas knew he was home. He didn't bother with a verbal greeting. Lowering his head, he said hello by crushing her raised mouth with his own.

"What are you wearing under your robe?" he murmured, ending the kiss, but maintaining contact by brushing his mouth over her lips.

"Expectations," Val breathed, bringing her hands up to frame his face.

Jonas's blood raced, he was immediately hot and tight and more than ready to fulfill her slightest whim. "And what are they?" he asked, teasing her by holding his mouth a sigh away from hers.

"I'll tell you after dinner," Val promised, teasing him in return.

"The hell with dinner." Sweeping her into his arms, Jonas mounted the stairs. "I'll have 'dessert' first."

Jonas groaned a sigh as he slid into her satin warmth. For a moment he didn't move, savoring the sensations streaking through his body. Making love with Val had always been better than good. Since San Francisco, it was better than fantastic.

"Jonas."

He shivered, both at the enticing sound of her voice and the inflaming caress of her silken thighs gliding slowly around his hips. Obeying her plea, Jonas began to move, stoking her passion and his own as he drove deeper and yet deeper into the heart of her desire.

Jonas was trembling outside, quaking inside from the intensity of need consuming his body. His teeth were clenched and the tendons in his neck were rigid from the strain he was exerting on his control. Conflicting desires warred inside him. While part of him screamed to let go, to surrender to the blazing joy of release, another part of him fought to hang on, drawing out the sweetness of pleasure to the point of pain.

Strong tremors rippled through his muscles wherever Val's restless hands paused to stroke and caress. His breathing grew ragged; his skin grew moist. Still he held on to his control, wringing delicious agony from the pleasure.

When, at Val's moaning plea, Jonas relinquished control, he cried out her name as he was flung into the fiery center of his exploding senses.

"Are you ready for dinner now?" Val murmured teasingly a while later, as she smoothed back his hair from his damp brow.

"Do I have to get up?" he muttered, groaning as he heaved himself onto the mattress beside her. At that moment, Jonas felt positive he'd never move again.

"No, of course not." Val's tone of unconcern had him prying one eyelid open. "I'll serve you dinner in bed," she said agreeably, sliding off the side of the bed. "But first I'll take a shower." She sighed and glanced over her shoulder at him as she went toward the bathroom. "All by myself."

Jonas was off the bed and after her as if he'd been shot from a cannon. "Vixen," he growled when she evaded his hands. But his growl turned to a purr beneath the soothing shower spray and the gentle ministrations of his laughing wife.

"Did we ruin dinner by lingering over dessert?" Jonas asked, tucking a short-sleeved sport shirt into his pants.

"No." Val's voice was muffled by the silky knit top she was pulling over her head. "Since it's Friday," she continued, smoothing the blouse over her skirt, "I was hoping to beguile you into taking me out for dinner." Tossing him a coaxing smile, she slipped onto the velvet padded stool in front of her vanity table.

Jonas fastened his watchband before crossing to her. "Lady," he said to her reflection in the lighted mirror, "You are one expert beguiler." He didn't mention that her suggestion fitted in neatly with his plans for the evening. "Where would you like to go to eat...and do I have to change again?"

Val paused, one hand raised, her fingers gripping a mascara wand, and ran a comprehensive look over his image in the glass. "No." She shook her head and smiled. "You look devastating in casual clothes."

"Devastating?" Jonas laughed. "After that work-out a few minutes ago," he drawled, "don't you mean devastated?"

Finished applying her makeup, Val set down the wand and picked up a hair brush. "It was rather invigorating, wasn't it?" She stroked the brush through the strands Jonas had tangled with his fingers. "I'm starving."

Jonas grinned and plucked the brush from her hand. "Let me," he murmured, gently drawing the brush through the long strands, still damp and gleaming from the shower.

"Mmm." Val sighed with pleasure. "That feels lovely. You're spoiling me, Jonas."

"I'm working at it, darling," he murmured, sliding her hair to one side to expose her nape to his mouth.

"Heavenly," Val breathed, shivering in response.

"Dinner," Jonas said decisively, backing away from her while he still could.

They dined on broiled seafood and icy mugs of beer in a local tavern with a reputation for excellent meals and a friendly atmosphere. While they ate, Jonas asked Val about her day and told her some of the details of his own, which in itself said reams about the increasing depth of their relationship. Never before had he discussed anything other than the most trivial things about his business.

"I'm going to stop by the office before we go home," he said casually over coffee. "I want to pick up a report to read—" he grinned "—sometime over the weekend."

Val looked stunned. "You're not going into the office this weekend?"

Jonas smiled with wry humor. He understood her amazement; he had always gone into the office on the weekend, if only on Saturday, both before and since their marriage. But since returning from San Francisco the previous Sunday, he had reorganized his thinking. Jonas was still dedicated—no, addicted—to his work. He had simply decided that from now on, if there was work to be done over the weekend, as he knew there invariably would be, he'd do it at home at the convenience of his wife. He told her so, enjoying the changing expressions on her face, which ranged from amazement to sheer delight.

Val bombarded Jonas with questions during the short drive to the office building. Since she barely paused for breath, never mind waiting for an answer from him, he kept his responses to murmurs and grunts laced with amusement.

"Does this mean I can actually look forward to tripping over you in the house on weekends?"

"Mmm."

"Jonas! Do you think we might steal a whole weekend away every so often?"

"Sure."

In love with her, enthralled with her, Jonas smiled and listened as Val went on and on with questions in the same vein, until they arrived at their destination.

"Want to come along and see how the work's progressing on your office?" he asked casually as he brought the car to a stop.

"Of course!" Val exclaimed, jumping out of the vehicle. "I can't wait for it to be finished," she went on as the elevator swept them to the sixth floor.

Jonas smiled and ushered her along the carpeted corridor to the closed door a few steps down the hall from his suite. "Let me go first," he said, stepping in front of her to block her view. "There might be ladders left standing or something." He opened the door, reached inside to flick the light switch, then stepped aside to watch her reaction. It was immediate, vocal and extremely satisfying.

"Oh, Jonas, it's finished." Val's cry came out in a choked whisper. "And it's beautiful! How did you manage it? I mean, you've only had five days and...oh, Jonas, thank you!" Spinning around, she flung herself into his arms. For Jonas, that was even more satisfying.

Later that night, satisfied now in body as well as in spirit, Jonas lay awake, cradling his sleeping wife in his arms. He was relaxed and thoughtful. Val had been more thrilled with her office than she'd been with any of the luxuries he'd given her. And all because he had finally agreed to share a portion of his working life with her.

Incredible. Val loved him, truly, honestly, unconditionally loved him. Jonas closed his eyes and
thanked God for the inner wisdom that had sent him
to California. He had thought he had been happy before, but only now did he realize the magnitude of
true happiness.

Val loved him.

The work was demanding. The boss was at times
a tyrant. Val loved it…and him. It was the end of her
second week in her new office. After the expected
interval of confusion, Val was settling in, getting back
into the swing of the electronics business.

Although her job description was different than
when she'd manned the desk as Jonas's secretary, and
the work more involved, she was beginning to get a
handle on it.

Val had received invaluable help from Charlie, Janet and Jean-Paul, but the biggest and best assistance
had come from her employer and husband.

Val was so happy that sometimes, if she allowed
herself to think about it, it scared her. So she seldom
allowed herself to think about it. She simply felt and
rejoiced in the feeling.

Living with Jonas, sleeping with Jonas, had been
wonderful, even when it wasn't so great. But living,
sleeping and working with Jonas was as close to perfection as Val could ever hope to get, and so far it
had all been great. A day didn't pass that Val didn't
thank God for the defiant determination that had sent
her to San Francisco.

Val was holding a prayer close to her heart. She
had missed her normal cycle the week before. Hope

bubbled like champagne inside her—hope that, as she had on their wedding night, she had conceived Jonas's child on the night of their reconciliation in San Francisco.

But Val was being cautious, rational. Her life had changed dramatically over the previous three weeks, in numerous ways. Any one of those changes could have tipped the balance of her inner clock. Val hadn't said a word to Jonas. She felt it would be cruel to build his hopes, only to dash them again if she was wrong. She decided to wait and pray.

It was Friday again—the end of Val's third week on the job. She was tired, but that wasn't unusual. Lately Val was always tired. She didn't mind. She knew excessive weariness was one of the first symptoms of pregnancy. She wanted to sleep a lot, which was the reason she had switched from working mornings to coming into the office after lunch.

The weekend beckoned with the alluring promise of rest. Pushing aside the contract she'd been studying, Val stretched her cramped back muscles and glanced at her watch. It was six-twenty. Collecting her purse and the attaché case Jonas had given her at breakfast on the morning of her first day of work, Val slid her chair away from her desk.

Her step firm, her small jaw set with purpose, Val walked through the empty outer office and into the private domain of the boss. Jonas was bent over the design table near the large window, poring over computer spread sheets.

"Okay, warden, how much?"

Jonas looked up, a distracted frown tugging together his ash-blond brows. "Warden? How much? Val, what in the world are you talking about?"

Val kept a straight, stern face. "The bond," she explained, tapping her foot impatiently. "How much will it cost me to spring my husband from this electronic prison?"

Jonas's brow cleared. Obviously fighting a smile, he worked his chiseled features into stern lines that were much more intimidating than hers. "You do realize, madam, that I can only issue a weekend pass for your husband?" he intoned severely. "You will have to return him to this cell by eight o'clock on Monday morning."

Val fought a bubble of delighted laughter but lost the battle. A Jonas who was not only willing to be interrupted from his work, but ready to contribute to as well as participate in her silly games, was too new an experience for her. Laughing, she dropped her purse and case and ran across the room into his open arms.

"What time is it?" Jonas asked, rubbing his cheek against her silky hair.

Raising her left arm, Val glanced at her wristwatch. "Six thirty-two exactly."

"That's right!" Jonas said in exaggerated exclamation. "And for giving the correct answer, you, Mrs. Valerie Thorne, of Philadelphia, Pennsylvania, have won the grand prize!"

"Which is?" Val laughed as she posed the question.

"A kiss from the boss." Dipping his head, Jonas covered her open mouth with his.

As prizes went, Val thought fuzzily, his kiss *was*

pretty grand. The sensuous play of his tongue, however, was evocative of a different, grander prize.

"Mmm," Val murmured when he raised his head a fraction, ending the kiss but maintaining contact by nibbling on her lower lip. "That tasted like more."

Jonas lifted his head to look at her. "More leads to more," he said in teasing warning.

"That's okay." Val smiled and pressed herself to his tautening body. "It's after business hours."

"Watch it, sweetheart," he growled. "Or you might suddenly find yourself on your back on that couch over there. It's happened before.... If you remember?"

Remember! How could she forget? Val thought, shivering with the memory. It had happened in the early evening of the day she'd returned from Australia. Because the secretary who had replaced Val had quit without notice, a competent replacement hadn't been found. Since Val had not returned by the promised date, Jonas had been in a foul mood.

Acting on Janet's advice, Valerie had offered her assistance. She and Jonas had worked throughout the day in an atmosphere of tense truce. Somewhere around seven Val had had enough. She was tired and hungry. Marching into his office, she had demanded to know if he was planning to buy her dinner. Jonas had replied that he would, if that was what she wanted. Suddenly cautiously excited, Val had responded by asking him if he was inferring that he would be willing to give her anything she wanted. Jonas had softly countered by saying he would...if she would give him the single thing *he* wanted. When Val asked him what it was, Jonas had indicated the long white couch that still stood against the wall in his office.

"I want you, now, on that couch."

His words seemed to echo in Valerie's mind as if Jonas had just said them to her. His low laughter interrupted her reverie, and Val realized with a jolt that he had repeated aloud the demand he'd made three years before.

The effect of Val's scandalized expression was ruined by the twitch of amusement at the corners of her mouth. "Jonas, really," she scolded. "Aren't you ashamed?"

"No more than I was the other time." Jonas grinned. "But as a matter of fact, I'm even hotter and more ready to…"

"Jonas!" Val laughed as she spoke his name and slipped away from him. She held up a hand when he started after her. "Have you forgotten that we are due at your daughter's at eight?"

His only response was to scowl and utter a muttered curse.

"Tsk, tsk." Val clicked her tongue. "If I recall correctly, you were the one who agreed to join Mary Beth and Jean-Paul this evening for a friendly game of penny ante poker."

Jonas's scowl gave way to a wicked smile. "I'd much sooner stay home and play strip poker with you."

"So would I," Val admitted, a responsive shiver going through her. He took a step toward her, she took a step back. "But we can't. Mary Beth, Jean-Paul and Marge are expecting us."

Jonas exhaled a deep, exaggerated sigh and slanted

a mournful glance at the white couch. Laughing at him, Val took his hand to lead him from the office.

"Come on, Jonas, I'll let you buy me dinner."

Jonas stopped in his tracks. His eyes glittered with devilry as he echoed the words she'd said to him that same evening over three years ago. "It'll cost you."

Val proved how good her own memory was by repeating the response he'd given to her. "Name your price."

Jonas managed to keep a straight face. "I want your promise that no matter how late it is when we get home tonight, you and I will have a little game of strip poker." He destroyed the effect of his somber look by wiggling his eyebrows at her.

Laughing, Val quoted his final words of long ago, "You've got it."

Val and Jonas didn't bother going home. They stopped for dinner at an out-of-the-way restaurant located less than a mile from their former home. The establishment had been in existence for over a hundred years. The decor was early American, warm and homey. Val couldn't help but recall that, close though they had lived to the place, the only time they had ever been there had been for a birthday dinner for Marge.

They dined on game pie prepared from an original recipe, a full-bodied burgundy and apple cobbler. And while they fed the hunger of their bodies, they replenished the deeper need of the soul with soft, intimate conversation.

Finally replete, they reluctantly left the restaurant, Val's hand securely clasped inside Jonas's, and went on to spend a laughter-filled evening with Mary Beth, Jean-Paul and Marge.

It was late before the penny ante game broke up. Pleased with herself for having won two dollars and fourteen cents, Val cheerfully pitched in with the cleaning up. The look of smoldering promise in the eyes Jonas swept over her was all the incentive Val needed to work swiftly.

Marge went into the kitchen to stack the glasses and snack food bowls in the dishwasher, while Val and Mary Beth replaced the lacy cloth and flower centerpiece on the dining-room table, at which the games had been played.

The phone rang, and Mary Beth and Jean-Paul exchanged frowning expressions.

"Now, who in the world...?" Mary Beth began, turning away to answer the call on the phone in the living room, but at that moment it stopped ringing.

"I suppose Marge answered it," Jean-Paul observed with a shrug. "We'll soon know...."

Suddenly they heard a scream from the kitchen.

"Oh, God! Jonas!" Marge called in a cry of agony. "Pick up the extension! Lynn was injured in an automobile accident! She's in critical condition in a hospital in Paris!"

Chapter 8

Jonas was going to Paris. They were all going to Paris—Marge, Mary Beth and Jean-Paul. Only Val was staying at home.

"This shouldn't take very long." Jonas tossed a couple of shirts onto the bed near the open suitcase. "I figure two, three days at the most."

It was late, or early, depending on how one viewed it. At 4:00 a.m. on a Saturday morning, with weariness dragging down her spirit, Val didn't view it at all.... She endured it.

"Okay." The exhaustion in her voice was at odds with the competence of her movements as she neatly folded each shirt before placing it in the case.

"You're not angry?" Jonas came to a stop beside her, three neckties dangling from his fingers. Val could actually feel the tension in him.

"Angry?" Val looked up to offer him a faint smile. "No, Jonas, I'm not angry."

"But you do understand why I feel I must go?"

Val caught her lower lip between her teeth. She thought she understood. She was trying to understand. But she was so tired. A soft sigh escaped her guard. "I think so." She blinked against the hot sting of tears in her eyes. Tears of weariness, she told herself. That was all they were. "I want to understand, Jonas. It's just that—" The tears crested the barrier of her eyelids. "Why you?" she cried. "Why is it always you?" She lifted her hands, then let them fall. "I didn't miss the fact that Marge called out for you… not Mary Beth or Jean-Paul, but you. Whenever there's a crisis or even a minor problem, everyone turns to you to solve whatever it is."

"I have to go, Val."

"But why in this instance? Lynn is not your responsibility, Jonas," she argued. "Why must you go? Can't Jean-Paul handle whatever must be handled, if…?" Val couldn't force herself to say *if Lynn dies*.

Jonas had no problem saying it. "You mean if Lynn doesn't make it?"

Val nodded in response.

Jonas's nod reflected hers. "In that event, Jean-Paul could handle it. But that possibility isn't the only consideration. Whether Lynn lives or dies, there will be arrangements to make and bills to pay." He grimaced. "More than likely, very large bills to pay."

"But Jean-Paul could—"

"Val," Jonas interrupted her. "I must go myself. My only child is pregnant. Her mother may be dying. Mary Beth is going to need the support of both her husband and me. Besides—" his tone took on an edge of determination "—this is a family matter. My family. And you're wrong. It is *my* responsibility, not Jean-Paul's. I'll take care of it myself.''

Of course. There it was, the secret vulnerability that Jonas took great pains to conceal. Val had had a hint of the presence of that sensitive area while they were in San Francisco, when he had told her that he continued to tolerate Lynn because she was Mary Beth's mother. Val now understood that his feelings ran much deeper than that.

Jonas was a bastard. He had never known either one of his parents, since his mother had died at his birth and his father's identity was a mystery. As a ward of the court, Jonas had been placed in a succession of foster homes, most of them bad. Until he met and married Lynn, and had been accepted wholeheartedly by her parents, Marge and Stosh Kowalski, Jonas had never had a family. Subsequently, even though his marriage began to disintegrate almost at once, the birth of his child had emphasized Jonas's need to maintain *his* family.

Staring at him with compassion, Val now acknowledged that she should have recognized or at least suspected the depth of that need in Jonas before they were married, when he'd told her that his former mother-in-law had lived with him since Mary Beth was an infant.

Jonas would take care of his own, his family, Val realized. With an unconscious gesture she slid one hand over her abdomen. Being the man he was, Jonas would naturally extend that care to all of them, even Lynn, a family member whom he merely tolerated.

The absentminded, protective movement of her splayed hand did not go unnoticed.

"Val, are you all right?" Jonas asked with quick concern, bringing up his hands to grasp her shoulders.

"Yes, I'm fine, just a little tired," she replied, dredging up a smile for him. "It's been a long day."

Jonas looked unconvinced. "You're pale," he said, frowning as he examined her colorless cheeks. "And now that I think about it, you've been tired a lot lately." His eyes narrowed. "And you look unnaturally fragile. I think you should call your doctor and make an appointment to have a complete checkup."

"Jonas, I am—" Val caught herself in time. She had planned to call their friend, her obstetrician Milton Abramowitz, that coming Monday. Catching her breath, she went on, "I am fine."

"You'd better get plenty of rest while I'm gone," he ordered, drawing her into his embrace with a show of tenderness that brought fresh tears to her eyes. "Because if you're still pale and tired when I get home, I'll personally escort you to the doctor." He buried his face in her hair and murmured, "Is that understood?"

Val sniffed and managed a strangled-sounding laugh. "Yes, sir, Mr. Thorne, sir."

"I want you to crawl into bed as soon as I leave," he said. "And stay there for the weekend, if you feel like it."

"Jonas!" Val exclaimed, pulling back her head to stare at him. "I'm going with you to the airfield!"

Jonas shook his head. "Val, it's after four now. You're already overtired. If you go with me, it'll be at least six by the time you get home. I don't think..."

Val lifted her small chin in a defiant manner that

was all too familiar to him. "I'm going with you, Jonas."

They drove through the hushed quiet of predawn, along streets empty except for an occasional car. There was more traffic on the highway, primarily tractor-trailers and delivery trucks. They didn't speak much; there was little left to say. Val began to miss Jonas even before they arrived at the small airstrip where Jonas rented hangar space for the Lear.

The others—Marge, Mary Beth and Jean-Paul— were already there, waiting beside Jean-Paul's elegant new Chrysler. Val heard the whine of the Lear's jets the moment Jonas brought the Lincoln to a stop alongside his son-in-law's car.

Stepping out of the vehicle, Val went directly to Mary Beth. The young woman looked as tired as Val felt.

"I sincerely hope Lynn will be all right," Val said, drawing the trembling girl into her arms. "And Mary Beth, try to get some sleep during the flight." Stepping back, Val smiled through her own tears. "Don't forget, you must take care of your father's—" she hesitated, then went on more strongly "—*our* grandchild."

"I'll be careful," Mary Beth promised, sniffing. "Thank you, Val."

"Come along, *chérie*," Jean-Paul murmured, slipping his arm around his wife's waist. "It's time to board." He turned to gaze solemnly at Val. "You take care of yourself, Valerie."

"I will." Val hugged Jean-Paul and Marge, then turned to Jonas. "And you take care of yourself."

"Come here," Jonas said, hauling her into his

arms. He kissed her hard, but fast, then released her and quickly stepped back, as if afraid he'd never let her go if he didn't leave at once. "Drive carefully on your way home," he ordered, as he bent to pick up his valise. "Rest. I'll call you tomorrow." He made a face and shook his head. "Later today." He stared at her longingly for an instant, then abruptly swung away. "Be good," he called back softly as he strode toward the plane.

Val felt an ominous sensation of fear as she watched him walk away from her. It was strange, for she had never before been anxious about Jonas flying. But now oppressive fear was clutching at her throat.

The others had boarded, and Jonas was nearing the plane, when suddenly Val broke into a run. "Jonas!" she cried, running to him and launching herself against his reassuring strength.

His free arm caught her to him and she clung, hugging him fiercely. "What it is? What's wrong, darling?" he demanded, searching her tear-streaked face.

"Nothing." Val shook her head, not understanding herself. "Only please remember that I love you."

"I'll remember." Jonas's arm tightened compulsively, crushing her softness to him. His mouth covered hers in a deep kiss. "If you'll remember that I only adore you," he murmured, smiling as he raised his head.

"I'll remember," she promised, returning his smile, if a little tremulously.

And then Jonas was gone.

Val stood alone on the airstrip, straining her eyes until the jet's wing lights flickered and disappeared into the muted glow of dawn.

* * *

She slept badly. Although she had dropped onto the bed like a stone when she got back to the house, Val only dozed in fits and starts, waking suddenly each time with the shakes. Around noon she gave up trying to sleep and dragged herself from the bed. A shower didn't go very far toward reviving her body or her spirits.

Val spent the day prowling around the house, back and forth like some wild creature, caged and edgy. She occupied herself by glancing at the clock, then at whatever phone was closest, then at the clock again.

She was at a loss to account for or pinpoint the reason for her uneasiness. Jonas traveled often for business purposes, and was often gone for as long as a week. But although she had always missed him, she had never reacted to his absence in this panicky way.

Telling herself that she was being ridiculous didn't help. Assuring herself that she'd have heard something by then, if there had been any difficulty during the flight, didn't help, either. The unsettling sensation persisted, filling her mind with terrifying thoughts of the direst catastrophes imaginable.

When at last the phone did ring, Val jumped, startled by the sound she had waited all day to hear. Running to the instrument, she snatched the receiver from its cradle.

"Hello. Jonas?" she blurted out.

"Yes, love," Jonas replied, in a steady voice. "How are you?"

"I'm fine," Val lied. "How are *you*?"

"Bushed," he replied with a tired laugh. "It's been a very long day."

"How was the flight?"

"Uneventful. Mary Beth, Marge and Jean-Paul slept through most of it."

"But not you." It wasn't a question; Val knew her husband. "You should have."

"I dozed a little."

As I did. Val didn't offer that information. "I'm glad Mary Beth got some rest. I was concerned."

"So was I," he admitted. "But she's okay now that she's seen her mother."

Val shivered. "How is Lynn, Jonas?"

Jonas sighed. "She was banged up pretty badly. She was in surgery when we arrived." He sighed again. "But she is conscious, or at least she was a short time ago when she spoke to Mary Beth. And the doctors are optimistic. They've downgraded her condition from critical to serious. But it'll be a while before she can travel."

Val felt a quiver of unease. "Travel?"

"Of course," Jonas replied. "We can't leave her here on her own. Neither Mary Beth nor Marge would have any rest if we did. So tomorrow—" he paused "—later today, I'm going to start making arrangements to fly her home as soon as her doctors give the okay for her to be moved."

"I understand." Val sighed in silent acceptance of what must be. "This means you're going to have to stay longer than the three or four days you'd planned on, doesn't it?"

"I'm afraid so." This time, Jonas's sigh was harsh with frustration. "Damn it, I miss you like hell already, and it hasn't even been twenty-four hours."

The endearingly familiar sound of him swearing

made Val feel a little better. Enough to smile. "I miss you like hell, too," she confessed.

"I've noticed lately that you're beginning to curse pretty often, Mrs. T.," Jonas said in a low, intimate drawl.

"It's the company I keep," Val explained.

Jonas laughed, then yawned. "Sorry."

"You're tired. You'd better hang up and go to bed, Jonas," she said, hating the thought of losing the verbal contract with him.

"I don't want to hang up," he murmured. "I don't want to lose the closeness of the sound of your voice."

"I don't want to hang up, either."

"But I must, love. I'm falling asleep on my feet."

Val's eyes smarted, and her voice was unsteady with the threat of tears. "Good night, darling. I love you."

"I remember. And I only adore you." Jonas's tone was tender. "Good night, love. I'll call you tomorrow."

Sniffling, and chiding herself for being a fool, Val hung up the phone and went straight to bed—straight to sleep. She slept around the clock and woke shortly after dawn spread its pink and mauve glow over the summer landscape. Rested and refreshed, she stood at the window, watching the golden glitter of morning illuminate the terrain, wishing Jonas was beside her, yearning inside to share the wonder of it all with him.

But he wasn't there, and no amount of wishing could whisk him magically across thousands of miles to her side, Val told herself, turning away from the window. And pacing the length and breadth of the house, as she had yesterday, wouldn't change the situation either, she continued in the same self-chastising vein. She had work to do…the work she should have taken care of with dispatch the day before, instead of prowling aimlessly.

"Serves you right for not hiring one of the women the domestic service agency sent out," Val muttered to herself as she went into the shower.

"You could've hired any one of those women," she went on a few minutes later, as she stepped into her cleaning attire of jeans and a T-shirt. "They all had excellent references."

Throughout the morning, as she went briskly about her chores, Val kept the encroaching silence at bay with the sound of her own scolding voice.

"That last woman…what was her name? Oh, yes, Grace…mmm, Grace…Vining! That's it." Val snapped her fingers. "Grace Vining. She was very nice, the motherly type. I could use a motherly type right now." Val sighed and murmured, "I wonder if she's still available?" Deciding to call the agency in the morning, Val finished folding the last of the laundry.

Val read the Sunday paper while she methodically chewed and swallowed the salad she'd tossed together for lunch. Prince Valiant was in the midst of a battle; Mandrake had everything under control, and Hagar brought a reluctant smile to her lips. She was puzzling over Doonesbury when the phone rang.

Since she wasn't expecting Jonas to call until much later, Val took her time answering. She knew from the underlying note of tension in his first words that Jonas was angry about something.

"What's the matter?" Val asked after the initial exchange of greetings. "Why are you angry?"

"It's obvious, huh?"

"I can practically see your teeth grinding together," Val said. "Is it bad?"

"Not so much bad as annoying," he answered. "Our Lynn has made the headlines.

Val frowned. "Because of the accident?"

"Because of who she was with at the time of the accident," Jonas explained.

Val waited a moment, then when he wasn't forthcoming, she exclaimed, "Jonas! Who was she with?"

Jonas rattled off a name that Val immediately recognized, simply because it appeared in print with almost boring regularity. She sifted through her memory to recall what she had read about the man. Memory stirred and Val exhaled a sigh of impatience with Lynn. The man in question was handsome, held the title of *comte* or something, and was impoverished.... At least he had been before his marriage two years ago to the very wealthy and reputedly insanely jealous daughter of one of the wealthiest men in Europe. The man was also some ten or so years younger than Lynn.

"Oh boy," Val breathed.

"Exactly." Jonas swore.

"Was he badly injured?"

"Yes," Jonas answered. "But not as badly as Lynn. We didn't get the details concerning the crash until this afternoon, and only then through Jean-Paul." He paused, and Val could almost see him massaging the back of his neck, as he habitually did when he was angry and frustrated.

"Jonas, calm down," she murmured into the silence.

"Yeah, okay." His harsh sigh sang over the transatlantic connection. "Anyway, it turns out that they had just left Paris to return to the South of France, after having spent a few days' *holiday* together in a friend's château on the outskirts of Paris. He was driving...thus totaled the Porsche his wife gave him just last month for his thirtieth birthday."

"This sounds like the scenario of a bad glitzy movie," Val observed.

"I wish to hell it was," Jonas retorted. "In her own inimitable way, Lynn has managed to create the juiciest scandal of the season. The newspapers are having a field day."

"Scandal sells."

"Tell me about it," he said in a dry tone. "And it'll probably get worse before it gets any better. The wife's outraged, and already making noises like..." Jonas hesitated, as if searching for a descriptive word.

"A wife?" Val interjected sweetly.

Jonas chuckled, and Val could hear the release of tension in the sound. "Purely theoretically, of course, but if it were me, would you make noises?"

"Of course not, darling," she purred. "I would very quietly kill you."

Jonas roared with laughter. "Love me that much, do you?" he asked when the laughter subsided.

"That much," Val confessed. "And more."

His laughter ceased, and was replaced by a low groan. "Oh, Val, what would I do without you?"

"Forget how to laugh?"

"Worse," he murmured. "I'd probably forget how to live."

"Jonas."

"Oh, hell." He groaned again. "I've got to get off this phone."

Val blinked. "Why?"

"Because I'm getting visions of you wearing a sexy black teddy."

"But I'm wearing faded jeans."

Jonas's voice grew low. "The tight ones?"

Were they? Frowning, Val looked down at herself. They were. "Yes, but how...?"

Jonas didn't let her finish. "I knew it. You look sexy wearing them, too."

Val absently slid her palm over her hip. "Do I?" She hardly recognized the sultry-sounding voice as her own.

"Mmm," Jonas murmured. "But you look even sexier not wearing them."

Her face grew warm, her limbs grew weak and her mind formed some erotic visions of him, too. "I miss you."

Jonas caught a quick breath. "I miss you, as well. And I want you...now. So you see, if I don't get off this phone, I'll be making love to you long-distance. And very likely melt the transcontinental wires in the process."

"Good night, Jonas," Val whispered. "I love you."

"I remember."

Val lived for the daily phone calls from Jonas through the days that followed. To fill the long hours between calls, she kept herself almost constantly occupied.

On Monday morning, Val made an appointment to see her obstetrician at the end of that week. Then she called the domestic service agency to inquire about the motherly-looking Grace Vining. On learning that Mrs. Vining was not only still available, but anxious to start working as soon as possible, Val asked the woman at the agency to send Grace right over.

Val liked Grace Vining even more after the second interview, and was prepared to hire her on the spot, if she would agree to one stipulation. Val had decided she would prefer a full-time, live-in housekeeper.

"Well, what do you say?" Val asked, after she finished showing Grace through the house and explaining what would be expected of her.

Grace Vining's rounded face creased with a wide smile. "I think you're the answer to all my prayers," she replied.

"In what way?" Val asked, intrigued.

The woman sighed. "It's a long story."

Val shrugged. "Okay, come out to the kitchen and we'll heat some soup or make a couple sandwiches. You can tell me your story over lunch."

Grace gaped at her. "But, I can't do that, Mrs. Thorne!" she exclaimed in obvious shock.

"Why not?" Val asked with a frown. "Do you have another appointment?"

"Well, no, but—" Grace shook her head "—you're my employer and all—"

"And my name's not Legree," Val interjected, motioning Grace to follow her as she headed for the kitchen. "It's not Mrs. Thorne, either. It's Val or Valerie," she said, shrugging her shoulders. "Whichever you prefer."

"Valerie's a beautiful name," Grace said, trailing into the kitchen after Val. "I'd like to call you that.... If you're positive it's all right?"

"I insist." Val tossed her a grin from over the top of the open refrigerator door. "Jonas calls me Valerie only when he's exasperated with me."

"Mr. Thorne?"

"Yes," Val said, pulling the makings for sandwiches from the fridge.

"Will Mr. Thorne be here for lunch?" Grace asked timidly.

"Oh, no." Val backed away from the fridge and shut the door with a nudge of her hip. "Jonas never comes home for lunch during the week. And he won't be here for dinner, either. At least not for a while. He's out of town and—" Val's words were buried by the other woman's exclamation.

"What!" Grace cried in astonishment. "You're all alone in this big house?"

"Well, yes, until Jonas comes home, but—" That was as far as she got before Grace again interrupted her.

"That settles it then." Drawing herself up to her full, impressive height, which was a good six inches taller than Val, Grace planted her hands on her ample hips. "I can't in good conscience allow you to remain alone in this house. With your permission, I'll move in this afternoon."

"And she did," Val finished after relating the tale to Jonas when he called that evening. She had taken the call on the phone in their bedroom and was lying on the bed, the phone balanced on her stomach.

"She sounds intimidating," Jonas said, laughing softly.

"She's a cream puff," Val replied, laughing with him. "And she cooks like a dream."

"Stir-fry?" Jonas asked with interest.

"No, but I promised to teach her how to make your favorite dishes."

"Oh, stop, I'm getting hungry," he groaned. "As good as it is, I'm tired of rich French food."

Val kicked off her shoes and rubbed the soles of her feet over the spread. "I'll stir-fry shrimp and vegetables for dinner for you your first night home."

"On my first night home, I seriously doubt I'll be thinking much about food," Jonas drawled.

"Oh, Jonas." Val's toes curled into the spread's nap.

"Valerie, stop that."

"Stop what?"

"Stop saying 'Oh, Jonas' in that soft, seductive voice," he ordered. "The memory of it kept me up most of last night."

Val giggled at his phrasing. "Really?"

"Valerie," his voice was low with warning, "change the subject."

"To what?"

"Hell, I don't know!" Jonas growled. "Yes, I do. Did Mrs. Vining ever get around to telling you her long story?"

"Yes."

"Is it boring?" he asked, hopefully.

Val sighed. "It's sad."

"Lay it on me. Maybe it'll put me to sleep."

Val smiled. "I know it's very late there, so I'll make it short. Then you can go to bed. To begin, Grace is alone. I don't mean that she merely lives alone, she is alone. As she put it, she and her husband were never blessed with children. And so they lived for each other. Only had a few close friends. He died last year. And since she's not old enough to collect social security, money's getting a little tight."

"You were right," Jonas murmured. "That is sad."

"Yes." Val sighed. "At any rate, Grace said she was hoping to secure a live-in position and sell her house." She paused, then murmured, "Oh, Jonas, she said she couldn't bear to live with all the memories in the house."

Jonas was quiet a while, then he said, "You did say her references are good?"

"Impeccable," Val replied.

"And do you like her?"

"Oh, yes. And I know you'll like her, too."

"Okay, now Grace has a new house to live in," Jonas said. "And we'll give her some new memories to live with."

Val's eyes were misty. "Thank you, darling."

"For what?" he asked gruffly.

"For being you." She sniffed; he heard her.

"I'm going to hang up now. I think maybe I'll sleep better knowing you're not alone in the house." His voice lowered to a whisper-soft caress. "Good night, adored one."

"Good night, Jonas. I love you."

"I remember."

*   *   *

With the advent of Grace to hold down the home front, Val decided to work full-time rather than half days in the office. She honestly enjoyed her work, and keeping busy staved off the loneliness that enveloped her during the long hours between calls from Jonas.

On Tuesday, Jonas told her the scandal over Lynn's accident was beginning to die down in the newspapers. Val breathed a sigh of relief. They didn't talk long because the transatlantic connection was bad.

The minute Val heard his voice on Wednesday, Val knew he'd had good news.

"Lynn was moved from the constant care unit into a private room this afternoon," he told her at once. "And her doctors said that if she continues to improve at the rate she has been, we might be able to bring her back to the States by the middle of next week."

"Jonas, that's wonderful!" Val exclaimed, suddenly needing to be held by him. "I miss you so much."

"I know, love. I miss you as much. But at least now I have hope of getting home sooner than I had believed possible when I arrived here."

"But, darling," Val said, bringing up a consideration that threatened her elation, "will Lynn be well enough to endure a flight of that length?"

The sound of his soft laughter reassured her before he uttered another word. "She will now. I've managed to hire a plane from a business associate of Edouard Barrès's. I've also retained a private nurse. Lynn, the nurse, Marge and Mary Beth will be returning to the States in it."

Though she was reassured by his explanation, Val

was also confused. Of course she knew who Edouard Barrès was, for the Frenchman was not only an associate of Jonas's, but Jean-Paul's former employer, as well. What she didn't understand was why Jonas had found it necessary to hire another plane.

"Is there something wrong with the Lear, Jonas?" she asked, frowning as she realized that he hadn't included either his own name or that of Jean-Paul on the passenger list he had given to her.

"No," he answered. "Jean-Paul and I will be flying home in the Lear. But the plane I hired is a large executive jet, complete with a private bedroom. In a bed, sedated, with a trained professional in attendance, Lynn should have no difficulty making the trip."

"A bedroom, no less," Val murmured. "How tantalizingly decadent."

"Yeah," Jonas agreed. "It's a sight to behold. As a matter of fact, I'm thinking about buying one."

"Jonas Thorne!" Now Val could laugh again. "Are you considering membership in the Mile-High Club?"

"The idea has very erotic possibilities," Jonas responded in a low, sexy voice that sent a shower of tingles cascading down her spine. "Even though I must admit that I feel a mile high every time we make love in our bed on the ground."

"Why, Jonas," Val said in a teasing tone, "I do believe you're turning into a romantic."

"And if I don't soon get home to you," he returned in a soft growl, "I'm afraid I'll be turning into a raving sex-starved maniac."

* * *

Her flagging spirits bolstered both by Jonas's fervently expressed need for her and the expectation that he would be home in a week or so, Val cruised through her work on Thursday.

But her spirits plunged at the sound of rage in his voice when he called early that evening.

"It's hit the fan," Jonas snarled in tones of fury and outrage. "The scandal's been revived, and my name and photograph are plastered all over every newspaper and yellow journalism rag in Europe."

"But...how?" Val was stunned. "Why?"

"I'll tell you how," he snapped. "Some overeager news hound became curious about my visits to the hospital. He did some digging, added one and one, and managed to come up with four."

Val shivered at the sound of his voice. Jonas in a cold rage was not a pretty sight. And Jonas was definitely in a cold rage; Val could almost feel the chill emanating from the telephone wire. "Four?" she repeated blankly. "Jonas, please calm down and explain. I don't understand."

"It's simple enough," Jonas said. "The news hound sniffed along the trail Lynn has left littered with discarded lovers and ex-husbands over the years until he discovered the very first of the bunch...yours truly. He then apparently did his homework on me and decided I was news."

Val winced. She knew how much Jonas disliked personal publicity. He painstakingly worked at keeping a low profile. She knew also that he absolutely detested notoriety. Furthermore, she was very much afraid she knew the answer to her next question, but asked it just the same. "And the four you mentioned. Where does that come in?"

His low laughter had the sound of a feral growl. "Just where you'd suspect. The newspaper stories are loaded with speculation that instead of a triangle here, there might be the possibility of a quadrangle."

"But that's not true!" Val cried indignantly.

"Calm down, sweetheart," Jonas murmured. "It probably won't amount to more than a three-day wonder. I just wanted to warn you in case it hit the gossip columns in the States."

Had Val been able to look dispassionately at the situation, she might have concluded that it was almost funny. The conversation had begun with her attempt to calm him down, and ended with him soothing her. But Val was beyond viewing the debacle objectively. Upset and worried about him, she revealed the depth of her emotion when she wished him good-night.

"Please remember that I love you, Jonas," she whispered fiercely.

"I remember," he said, repeating his now habitual response. "Remembering that is what's keeping me going."

Val's spirits were dragging on the floor behind her when she left the office Friday morning to keep her appointment with her obstetrician. After a thorough examination, Milt Abramowitz offered his opinion that Val was, as she'd suspected, into her sixth week of pregnancy. To confirm his opinion, he had his nurse draw a blood sample for a pregnancy test.

Val spent the intervening hours in a fever of anxiety. When the doctor called later in the afternoon to inform her that the test results were positive, her lagging spirits took flight.

During the hours that followed the call from the doctor, Val became a dedicated clock-watcher. She couldn't wait to tell Jonas that within a few months of becoming a grandfather, he would become a father again.

It was only as the time drew nearer to his expected call that Val began to have second thoughts, admittedly selfish ones, about telling him over the phone. By telling him now, she'd be denying herself the thrill of seeing his expression, and of being swept into his arms and crushed to his chest in his exuberance. Besides, it was an event they should share, Val thought dreamily, when they could witness the joy shining in each other's eyes. It was not a moment to be squandered on a long-distance telephone call.

She would wait, Val decided, and hug the news secretly to her until Jonas came home. She almost dreaded his call, afraid her excitement might overrule her decision, so that she'd find herself blurting out the announcement to him.

The time for his call came, and passed. Another hour crawled by. Then another. As on the day he'd left, Val paced their bedroom, silently ordering the phone to ring. Where was Jonas? she asked herself countless times. Why didn't he call? Was he ill? Had an unexpected crisis arisen, a setback to Lynn's recovery?

Through the night and into the dawn, Val was plagued by fears, doubts and dozens of questions. She had no answers. She was exhausted but couldn't rest.

Something was wrong, she knew. Something had to be wrong or Jonas would call.

The phone rang just after six-thirty. Pouncing on the instrument, Val snatched up the receiver. Her voice was expelled from her throat on a gasping sigh.

"Jonas?"

"No, *ma chère*."

"Jean-Paul?" Panic dug its claws into Val's chest. "Jean-Paul, why are you calling? Where is Jonas?" she demanded, inwardly fighting a need to shout.

A tired sigh whispered through the connecting wires, then Jean-Paul said softly, urgently, "Valerie, you must now be brave."

"Brave?" Val whispered around the fear gathering in her throat. "Why must I be brave? Jean-Paul!" Now she did shout. "Where is Jonas?"

"I wanted…had to call you before…" His voice cracked, then he went on in a strangled tone, "You'll soon be receiving official notification, but I felt I had to—"

The words "official notification" wrenched a scream from Val's heart. "Where is Jonas?"

"He's been kidnapped."

Kidnapped? Kidnapped! Val's mind whirled. Her thoughts spun crazily. Kidnapped? No. It was ludicrous! Jonas? Ridiculous. It was a mistake. That was it! Someone had made a dreadful mistake. Jonas had not been kidnapped. Prominent men got kidnapped. Distinguished men, recognizable because their names and photographs were frequently seen in the newspa— Val's thoughts ground to a sudden stop. Names and photographs. Newspapers. Jonas.

"...Valerie, Valerie, are you there? Do you hear me? Valerie, answer me!"

Jean-Paul's loud imploring voice crashed through the stunned horror gripping Val's mind. "Jean-Paul, when did this happen?" she cried. "How did this happen?"

"He was...taken as he was leaving the hospital this morning. Witnesses said that three men grabbed him and flung him into a waiting car. The car...got away."

"Taken?" she repeated in a voice that was barely there. "Grabbed? Flung?"

"Valerie, I swear to you that every effort possible is being made to apprehend the kidnappers," Jean-Paul said reassuringly. "Not an avenue will be overlooked in the effort to get Jonas back safely."

Val was beyond being reassured; she was in a state of abject terror. After Jean-Paul said he must hang up, she replaced the receiver, then sat on the edge of the bed, waiting for the phone to ring again, dreading the sound.

Official notification duly came, along with more words of assurance. Val heard and responded to the disembodied voice, while inside her head she screamed his name in agony.

Jonas.

When the initial shock wore off, Val took herself to task. Falling apart would not help Jonas, she told herself. He would be found and returned to her, she assured herself. Val determined that when Jonas was returned, it would not be to find either his wife or his business in a shambles.

Val asked questions of the authorities. She received

evasive answers until Jean-Paul and the others came home a week later. It was some time before Val had an opportunity to talk to Jean-Paul in private. Mary Beth was a frightened wreck; Lynn had had a relapse; Marge had aged ten years.

"I want to know everything that you know," Val said to Jean-Paul when they were finally alone. "The authorities can't or won't tell me anything."

Faced with her defiantly lifted chin, Jean-Paul sighed. "All I've been able to garner from friends is that the authorities suspect the kidnappers were from Central America and that they fear he has been taken there."

Central America. Val fought a new, insidious fear. There was so much turmoil in some of the Central American countries. She had read accounts of terrible atrocities....

With sheer willpower, Val controlled her rioting imagination. She absolutely refused to fall apart. But Val did falter a little. "What do they want?" she cried. "They can have anything. They can have everything! If they'll only let Jonas go, set him free."

"As far as I know, no demands have yet been made," Jean-Paul said. He hesitated, then added with a Gallic shrug, "Valerie, I fear you must prepare yourself."

Val's heart thumped. "What do you mean?" she asked in a dry croak. "Prepare myself for what?"

Jean-Paul gripped her by her shoulders to support her trembling body. "I'm afraid, *ma petite*, that when demands are made, they will be political in nature, not financial." He paused again, as if gathering fortitude before continuing. "Valerie, you know the prevailing sentiment in this country about granting concessions of that sort.''

Val broke then. Sobbing, she collapsed against Jean-Paul. Cradling her in his arms in much the same way he had during his brother's funeral five years before, he let her cry until the wracking sobs dwindled. Stroking her hair, he comforted her.

"We must be strong, you and I, *ma mignonne*." He smiled when she raised her tear-drenched eyes to his. "We must be strong for Jonas, and for his family, because we love him." Jean-Paul's eyes were suspiciously bright. "And because he would wish us to be strong and responsible."

Recalling her own assessment of Jonas's sense of responsibility the morning he had left for France, Val nodded her head. "Yes," she agreed softly. "Jonas would want that."

Gaunt and silent, and to all appearances docile and resigned, Jonas stood in the midst of his captors. Head hanging in apparent exhaustion, his expression blank, he listened to the agitated discussion between the five kidnappers, straining to catch a word he understood in the rapid-fire Spanish.

Jonas was in fact exhausted. He was also hungry, thirsty and filthy. But, though his attitude of weary acceptance didn't reveal it, more than anything else Jonas was furious.

The anger had begun simmering inside him soon after he regained consciousness. Initially he'd felt confused. He was in a plane, a rather decrepit prop plane. And he was securely bound at the wrists and

ankles. A throbbing pain at the back of his head trig-
gered Jonas's memory.

Jonas recalled the sharp suspicion he'd felt when
four men had casually encircled him as he was leaving the hospital. Then, when he'd tried to step between two of them, his arms had been grasped on
either side. Jonas remembered demanding an explanation an instant before a brutal blow to his head
knocked him out cold.

Ignoring the thumping ache resulting from the
blow, Jonas glanced around the shabby interior of the
flying rattletrap. He was alone in the compartment.
He had remained alone until a few minutes prior to
landing.

At first, asking questions and demanding to know
where he was being taken, Jonas had resisted being
removed from the plane. All his efforts gained him
were more brutal blows to the body and the verbal
abuse of an angry spate of Spanish curses.

Jonas had not reached the pinnacle of success by
being stupid. Deciding to bide his time and save wear
and tear on his hide, at least until he could figure out
where he was, he gave every appearance of being
cowed. But inside him, simmering anger had grown
into cold rage.

By Jonas's reckoning, he had now been in captivity
nearly six full weeks. He had attempted to escape
twice. He had been beaten and starved for his trouble.
Having overheard mention of some city names, Jonas
speculated that the plane had landed somewhere in
South America and that he had been transported north
into Central America. Intellect and reason told him
that his ransom price was probably political in nature.

Reason also told Jonas that unless he could pull off an escape, he was probably one dead bastard.

Now, after six weeks of moving at night from one crummy shack to another, Jonas knew something was about to happen. He and his five watchdogs had been in their current location for over a week. It was not the Trump Plaza. Constructed primarily of sheets of rusting metal and wishful thinking, the place was a pigsty. Other than a single water pipe, there was no indoor plumbing.

An hour before, two men had joined their party of six. The discussion had been raging ever since. From the few words Jonas had been able to pick up, he knew something was going on. What he hadn't been able to figure out was whether that something was a deal or a raid. But whatever it was, it had sure managed to excite his captors and their two visitors. Every one of Jonas's senses was alert, quivering with an urgency for flight. It was now or never. Raising his head, Jonas added his voice to the babble of the others. He knew that at least two of the men understood English.

"Hey, I've got to relieve myself. Are one of you clowns going to take me out, or do I do my business in here?" He curled his lips into a sneer as he glanced around disdainfully. "Not that it'd make much difference in this cesspool."

As he'd expected, Jonas was rewarded for his sarcasm with a backhand rap across the face from the man nearest to him. But as he had hoped, the man snarled an order to one of the others to take Jonas to the "facility."

The other man made a gesture with the Uzi that

was cradled in the crook of one arm and, head meekly lowered, Jonas preceded him from the shack.

The "facility" was located at the edge of a thicket, some distance behind the shack. The reason for the distance became apparent yards before reaching the three-foot-wide trench. The stench was awful.

With the Uzi poking him in the back, Jonas held his breath and stepped to the edge of the trench. Before he was completely finished, the thug behind him gave Jonas a shove with the butt of the gun.

Cursing the man viciously, Jonas twisted and went sprawling backward into the filth in the trench. He heard the man laugh sadistically—an instant before an earsplitting explosion shook the earth and plunged him into unconsciousness.

The weeks slipped by. Two became four, then five, then six. Holding onto hope for all she was worth, Val persevered. She lost weight, but hung on. She told no one about her pregnancy.

Between them, Val and Jean-Paul soothed, encouraged, and literally held everything and everyone together...Jonas's family as well as his business and employees.

On the second day of the seventh week, Val got home from work to find two men waiting for her. At the sight of Grace's pale face, Val began to tremble. The men introduced themselves and proffered official-looking identification for her inspection. Feeling the world crashing in on her, Val swallowed convulsively as the older man began to speak.

"Mrs. Thorne, I regret that I must inform you of the death of your husband, Mr. Jonas Thorne." He held out a small manila envelope, which she hadn't noticed at first. ''I further regret that these two personal possessions of your husband's are all that we found at the scene of the devas—''

''No.'' Val's whisper silenced the man; the scream inside her head silenced her consciousness.

Jonas!

Chapter 9

Val fought through the last clinging webs of slumber. Confusion blurred the line between sleep and consciousness. A frown tugging her brows together, she blinked and glanced around the room.

Long fingers of late-afternoon sunlight speared through the filmy window curtains, creating patterns of gold and shadow on the opposite wall.

What time was it? Val wondered, striving for complete awareness. Late afternoon? Early evening? Shifting her head on the pillow, she stared at the bedside clock. Six thirty-four? What was she doing in bed at six thirty-four in the evening?

Reality returned with sudden clarity, piercing the numbness, restoring memory, stripping away the protective buffer that desensitized her mental anguish.

Jonas!

Val's thinking kicked into gear.

Those two official-looking men had said Jonas was... No, it wasn't true; it couldn't be true. Jonas couldn't be... But they had identification, and it looked genuine. They had said they were from some federal department. They had said Jonas was... They had brought a small tan envelope that held his personal possessions. No, it could not be true....

Val's eyes were now wide. Her gaze darted around the room, searching for a solid point of reference.

The mental wheels started to spin, and flung Val back seven weeks in time.

The bedroom! Of course! That was it. She had been pacing the bedroom, frantic with worry, waiting for Jonas to call. The last she remembered it was sunrise. She hadn't slept all night. That explained why she was in bed at six thirty-four in the evening. Exhausted, she must have finally fallen asleep, slept straight through the day. That was it. Had Jonas called? Had she missed Jonas's call?

Something stripped the gears, sending a shudder from Val's skull to her heels. Her thoughts stopped for a breath-catching instant. When her mind cranked up again, the rhythm was normal, unwinding regulated impulses of lucid thought.

Jonas hadn't called at all. Jean-Paul had called. And it had not been earlier that morning. The call from Jean-Paul had come seven weeks ago.

Jonas was dead. He would never call again.

"No!" Val sprang up and off the bed as the denial burst from her aching throat. Nausea invaded her stomach, her head whirled, darkness closed in on her and she flailed her arms around for something to hold on to.

There was nothing there. Val went down. She heard her body thud onto the cushioning carpet, felt a jolt of pain, and responded with a startled cry.

Val was pushing herself into a sitting position when the bedroom door was flung open.

"Mon Dieu!" Jean-Paul exclaimed, bursting into the room, Grace at his heels. "Valerie, what has happened?" he asked dropping to one knee beside her.

Raising a shaking hand, Val pushed her heavy, disheveled hair from her face. "I—I fell," she said in vague astonishment. "I must have gotten up too fast."

Grace bustled to her other side. "Are you all right?" she asked anxiously.

Her eyes dazed, Val glanced from one to the other. "Yes, I think so," she began, then her eyes flew wide and she cried, "Oh, my Lord! The baby!"

"Baby?" Jean-Paul repeated, frowning. "What baby? My baby? Mary Beth's baby?"

"I knew it!" Grace exclaimed.

Jean-Paul shot a blank look at the older woman. "I don't understand. What did you know?"

Val answered his question. "I'm pregnant." Swallowing convulsively, she gripped his arm. "Jean-Paul, please, will you call Dr. Abramowitz? I lost my first baby due to a fall. Dear God, I can't lose this one!"

After an instant of shocked stillness, Jean-Paul took command of the situation like a man who had been tutored by a dynamo…which he had been, of course. Scooping Val into his arms, he barked an order to Grace as he strode to the door. "I'm taking Valerie to the hospital. Call Dr. Abramowitz and ask him to meet us there."

* * *

The rain revived Jonas. Slowly he came to his senses. Through the fog he could feel a stabbing pain in the back of his head. As if echoing its pounding roar inside his skull, thunder rumbled overhead. The rain came down in torrents.

Where was he? Jonas winced; it hurt to think. Come to that, it hurt to breathe. Stifling a groan, he opened his eyes. He had to blink several times to clear his vision. The sight that met his gaze brought a frown to his brow.

"What the hell!"

There was a man lying above him, sprawled over what appeared to be the outer edges of a trough. Less than six inches separated the man's body from Jonas.

Startled, Jonas moved, intending to ease himself from beneath the man. Another groan escaped his throat as his head scraped against something hard. Rockets of pain exploded. Closing his eyes, Jonas drew in great gasping breaths. Then he gagged and his stomach heaved, protesting against the stench in the air. Ignoring the pounding in his head, he scrambled backward. It was only after he was clear of the other man that Jonas realized that his own head had been lying on a large rock. The pain he was suffering gave ample proof that his head had not struck the unlikely pillow gently. Dismissing the questions this realization activated, he heaved himself up and over the edge of the trough.

He was exhausted, but he was out of that disgusting hole. Lying on his back, Jonas closed his eyes and welcomed the cleansing beat of the rain against his filthy body. When the throbbing in his head subsided, and his breathing slowed to a near-normal rate, he carefully pushed himself up and opened his eyes once more.

Where was he? The question reverberated in Jonas's mind as his astonished eyes absorbed the scene of utter devastation around him. The area looked like a battlefield—a bombed-out battlefield. Twisted and burned pieces of debris cluttered the landscape. Wondering what the pieces used to be, Jonas shifted his gaze to the man lying suspended over the trench. The man's back was gone, as if literally torn away by a blast of enormous proportions.

Bile gushed into his throat. What in heaven's name had happened here? Jonas wondered sickly. And what was he doing here, wherever "here" might be? The questions were followed by another consideration, one that caused him to break into a cold sweat.

Who was he?

Sitting beside a stinking waste trench in the pouring rain, Jonas raked his mind for a memory...any memory. He found none. For an instant, stark terror gripped him. From the destruction around him, he appeared to be in the middle of a war zone, and he didn't know who he was, where he was, or where he belonged.

War zone. The thought unlocked the grip of fear on his mind. Immediately his senses picked up the muted sounds of movement in the distance. He had to get away.

Jonas jackknifed to his feet. His head reeled. Gritting his teeth, he fought back the wave of darkness that threatened to wash over him until his equilibrium was restored. When the world was again in focus, he began to move. Without a backward glance at the scene of destruction, he slipped into the dense thicket of evergreen and deciduous trees surrounding the leveled compound.

Jonas struggled through the thick growth of foliage until he felt far enough away to avoid detection. Then, standing exposed in a tiny clearing, he stripped to the skin and let the pouring rain sluice the filth from his body. When he felt relatively clean, he spread out his clothes and beat them clean with a stout stick. By the time he was satisfied with the combined efforts of the pouring rain and the pounding of the stick, he was exhausted and breathing heavily. Pulling on the sodden garments, he methodically searched the clothing for some form of identification. There was nothing— no billfold, no papers, no money, no clues at all. Shoulders drooping in weariness and resignation, he moved back into the undergrowth in search of a place to rest.

The best Jonas could find was a tall, full, broad-leafed plant. It afforded some protection from the heavy rain and concealed his curled-up body from casual observation. Jonas went to sleep hungry, but he was able to slake his thirst by catching rainwater in his cupped hands.

When Jonas awoke the sun was shining. It was early and already hot and humid. Water dripped from every tree and plant. Jonas didn't mind the dripping water, the heat or the humidity. He was famished, he still felt excessively tired, but the thumping inside his head had subsided to a dull ache. After standing and testing his strength, Jonas decided he'd survive until he found something to eat.

Since he had no idea who he was, where he was,

or where he came from, Jonas had no idea where he was going. Yet strangely, intuition or instinct—some inner something—urged him to move in a northerly direction. Judging direction by the position of the sun, he headed north without question or doubt.

Val half sat, half reclined against plumped pillows in the large bed. A brown envelope lay on her lap. Her small hand clutched the contents of the envelope close to her breast. Jean-Paul and Mary Beth were seated in the room's two easy chairs, which had been moved close to the bed. Jean-Paul looked grim; Mary Beth was weeping softly.

At Val's insistence, but against his better judgment, Milton Abramowitz had released her from the hospital after twenty-odd hours of close observation. He had urged her to stay, for although she had suffered no injuries from her fall, Val was in a deep state of emotional shock and depression. Unable to keep her in the hospital against her will, the doctor had relented on condition that Val have complete bed rest at home.

"It's true, isn't it?" Val said, her expression stark with the knowledge she could no longer deny. "Jonas really is dead, isn't he?"

"Yes, *ma chèrie*," Jean-Paul murmured, tightening the grip of his hand around his wife's cold fingers. "I'm afraid we must accept the truth that Jonas is dead. The information was released this morning. It is the headline story in all the afternoon newspapers."

"How…?" Val's voice failed, and she had to draw a breath before continuing. "How did he die? Was he murdered?"

Jean-Paul winced at the harsh sound of pain in her

voice. His hand gripped Mary Beth's trembling fingers. "Valerie, *ma petite*, believe me, you do not want to hear." He heaved a sigh. "It is an ugly story."

Val caught her breath, but determination was written on her pale face. "No, I don't want to hear about it," she said struggling for control. "But don't you understand that I must hear, Jean-Paul? I must know, or else I'll never be able to believe, accept...." Once again her voice failed. The expression in Val's eyes pleaded for understanding and compliance.

Sitting forward in her chair, Mary Beth supported Val's insistence in a quivering plea of her own. "Val's right, Jean-Paul. I keep thinking it's all a mistake, that any minute the phone will ring and—" she sobbed "—and it'll be Daddy, telling us it was all a horrible mistake." Shudders rippled through her body.

Releasing her hand, Jean-Paul put his arm around her violently shaking shoulders and drew her close to the protective strength of his own trembling body. "All right," he said on a sigh, relenting. "I will be brief. But perhaps I should relate to you what I was told unofficially by friends. It seems that Jonas was kidnapped by one of the newer, relatively small but apparently violent takeover groups to appear on the scene in an already strife-torn country in Central America. My informants told me the group consists mainly of malcontents and ex-mercenaries looking for the main chance."

"But what did these men hope to gain by kidnapping Jonas?" Val asked in a strained voice.

Jean-Paul moved his shoulders in a weary shrug. "Who knows? Recognition, political leverage...it's anyone's guess.'' His sigh conveyed a sense of futility. ''At any rate, the authorities here learned that Jonas was being held in a remote, heavily forested area and a rescue mission was activated. But meanwhile there was apparently friction within the group itself. I was given no details. All I know is that when the rescue contingent arrived at the location, they found complete and utter devastation. The place had been leveled, destroyed by bombing.'' He paused, as if dreading the need to continue.

Val sat as if frozen. Her lips barely moved as she prompted him. ''Go on, finish it.''

Jean-Paul shut his eyes. When he opened them again, they were dark, shadowed by horror. ''All the rescue team found in their search through the debris were bits and pieces, Valerie.''

Val flinched, as if from a hard physical blow. Jean-Paul's free hand shot out to steady her. Her control shattered. ''So this is all I'm to have of him?'' Val cried in anguished protest. Lowering her hand, she opened her fingers and stared at the two articles in her palm. ''This is all that's left of my husband?''

''And my father,'' Mary Beth whimpered, shuddering as a heart-wrenching sob was torn from her throat.

Springing from his chair, Jean-Paul gently drew his sobbing wife into his arms, consoling her with endearments murmured in French.

Tears running unheeded down her face, Val stared at the two objects in her hand. The metal was twisted and the edges blurred by melting from intense heat, yet the objects were identifiable as Jonas's wedding ring and the watch Val had purchased for him in San

Francisco for his birthday. Barely discernible, Val could still make out the inscription she'd had etched on the back of the watch.

"This isn't fair!" Val cried, closing her fingers and once more clutching her hand close to her breast. "It just isn't fair! Is this what I'm to show Jonas's child?" she demanded. "And all because of some demented, self-styled would-be rulers? Jean-Paul, Jonas never even knew that he was going to be a father again!" Sliding down on the bed, she curled into a ball and gave way to uncontrollable sobs.

His expression revealing his sense of helplessness in the face of two grief-stricken women, Jean-Paul heaved a sigh of relief when Grace came bustling into the room. "You take care of your little lady. Mr. DeBron," she said softly. "I'll take care of Valerie."

In truth, there was very little anyone could do to care for Valerie, other than see to her obvious physical needs. Desolate and inconsolable, Val withdrew into herself. She ate only enough to sustain the life and health of her child. She slept fitfully. She didn't leave the bedroom and rarely left her bed. Jonas was dead. Val's instinct for survival had died with him. She no longer wished to live.

Condolences poured in after Jonas's death was reported in the newspapers. The employees of the firm were devastated by the news. The evidence of the high esteem in which Jonas had been held by scores of people all over the world, as well as in the States, did not surprise Valerie, but it did little to alleviate her remorse or ease her sense of loss.

Cloistered in the bedroom she had shared with Jonas, existing primarily on her memories of him, Val

locked out the rest of the world. In much the same
way as she had after the death of her fiancé, Jean-
Paul's brother, Etienne, four and a half years before,
Val closed herself off from everyone. Only this time
it was worse, much worse. Etienne had been Val's
first love, and with his loss, she had suffered the death
of love's young dream. Losing Jonas was a deeper
anguish, like losing the most vital part of herself.

Val was bitter and she was angry. In an agony of
grief, she ranted in silent fury against a fate so cruel
as to rob her of newfound happiness, not once but
twice.

With the loss of Jonas, Val relived their time together over and over in her mind, especially their time
since their reconciliation in San Francisco. Listening
intently to the echo of Jonas's voice, Val was deaf to
the reasoning of other, living voices. Jean-Paul could
not reach her. Mary Beth could not reach her. Marge
could not reach her. Not even Janet could get through
to Val, as she had in Paris over three years before.

To all intents and purposes Valerie had abdicated
from life, shutting out the people who loved her. Inside her head, she heard and wept with the echoing
sound of Jonas's whispering voice.

I remember. I remember. I remember....

Because of his compelling inner determination to
trek in a northerly direction, it took Jonas only two
months to get across the border into Mexico. It would
have taken him longer, if it hadn't been for the occasional rides he picked up from friendly farmers
along the way. Jonas would probably also have faced
starvation, if it hadn't been for the food provided by

those same farmers. At other times, Jonas survived by applying the keen intelligence that had enabled him to work his way up from the status of penniless orphan to the ownership of one of the most prestigious electronics firms in the world.

Though his memory of past events was gone, Jonas possessed common sense, and knew that if he was apprehended without identification papers he could be in big trouble. Whenever possible, he traveled parallel to guiding roads, not close enough to be observed by any passing traffic, yet near enough to recognize the farm vehicles. He ate off the land, availing himself of a tiny portion of the farmers' crops of fruits and vegetables.

During the first month, the going was arduous because of the mountainous terrain. During the second month, the going was arduous because, skirting the mountains, he traveled through a section of the dense rain forest. Jonas grew gaunt, and since he was without the luxury of a razor or even a pocketknife, he grew a beard, which surprisingly came out red, liberally peppered with gray. When his clothes deteriorated to the point of falling in shreds from his thin body, Jonas stole others, which seldom fitted but at least covered and protected him.

The urge inside him to keep moving northward inexplicably grew stronger after he crossed the border into Mexico. Following that inner directive, he continued along the course he had intuitively adopted, avoiding towns and villages, eating off the land where possible, and accepting help from farmers whenever it was offered.

Dodging, wary and cautious, it took Jonas another

month and a half to reach the Mexico-Texas border. He crossed the line somewhere between Nuevo Laredo and Rio Bravo exactly as many others had before him, by getting his back wet.

When he crawled out of the water onto United States soil, Jonas drew a deep breath of relief. He still didn't know who he was, where he belonged, or where his inner urge was leading him. But deep inside, Jonas was certain of one thing. He knew he was in his own country. Armed with that knowledge, Jonas felt he could endure anything.

Val awoke with a start in the middle of a cold night in early November. Something had wakened her. But what? A dream? A sound? What? She frowned into the darkness. A moment passed, quiet, still, then Val's frown changed to a wide-eyed expression of sheer wonder.

She had been awakened by the one sensation powerful enough to rouse her from her lethargy—the tiny flutter of quickening life inside her body.

Her baby had moved! Jonas's child was alive and making his presence felt within her womb. Tears rushed to Val's eyes as she carefully slid her palm over her gently mounded belly. Motionless, barely breathing, she waited.

The flutter came again, stronger, more definite. Trembling, Val whispered into the shadowed room.

"Jonas, our baby, the child of our love is alive." A short bubble of laughter burst from her throat as the sensation was repeated. "Darling, I can feel him stretching his tiny limbs inside my body."

Her hand pressed protectively over her abdomen,

Val shuddered as sobs wrenched from her throat. She had often given way to her tears during the past two months, but this time Val wept tears of healing. Within minutes she was laughing and crying at the same time. Her baby had moved, and in so doing had restored to Val the desire to live.

Val did not go back to sleep. Lying in the darkness, she reviewed the self-indulgence of the past two months and found herself wanting. In retrospect, she realized that she had been so self-absorbed, so steeped in self-pity that she had barely noticed the passage of time, had been oblivious of the fact that the heat of summer had surrendered to the crisp air of autumn. Only now was she prepared to acknowledge the pain, suffering and anxiety of those around her, including those most important to Jonas...his family.

Jonas would not be proud of her, Val admitted to herself. Nor would he be pleased by her willful repudiation of life. Jonas had felt disdain for quitters, especially those who in his own words copped out on life.

Jonas Thorne had been more than a fighter in the battle of life; he had been a genuine scrapper. The insight gave Val's depleted spirits a shot of determination. Lifting her small chin, she whispered once more into the darkened room.

"From here on, my love, I promise that I will be a scrapper, too. Your responsibilities will be my responsibilities. And I will do more than fight and scrap for the welfare of our child; I will live for him."

Her energy renewed, Val waited impatiently for the dawn. Not for an instant did she doubt that the child quickening with life inside her was a son.

* * *

Jonas spent over ten weeks in Texas. Not a glimmer of his memory had returned. But, if nothing else, since entering the States he now knew the date, month and year. He also knew the value of a dollar. That particular bit of knowledge amused him, considering the fact that he didn't possess as much as a dime.

Though the urge to keep moving north grew stronger with each passing day, and he continued to obey that urge, he progressed with calculated slowness. He was exhausted, he was undernourished, he was emaciated, and he knew it. He also knew somehow that though the fall weather was mild in the Southwest, it would be growing cold in the Northeast.

Reason cautioned him to bide his time in the temperate climate before attempting to face the biting onset of winter to the north. He needed rest. He needed food. He needed to rebuild his flagging strength.

Without funds, and looking like a wild man who had just fought his way through a wilderness—which, in effect, he had—Jonas had few options available for seeing to his needs. The most obvious of those options was to seek assistance at the shelters that were operated for and utilized by the street people—the homeless, the rejected, the dropouts.

Drifting in a northeasterly direction, Jonas stayed a few days, at times an entire week, in small towns along his route.

In one of the first of those towns, Jonas was offered a bath by a kind but harried-looking man who was hard-pressed to keep from wrinkling his nose in distaste. Jonas accepted the offer with controlled eagerness. The man had shown him to the bathroom, then hurried away, telling Jonas he'd bring clean clothes for him to wear. The room had held a commode and an old, claw-footed, rust-stained porcelain tub. Jonas had luxuriated in both of the conveniences.

Jonas never knew what happened to the rags he'd torn from his skinny body, but then he didn't particularly want to know. The clothes the overworked man brought to him were used but had been well cared for and, luxury of luxuries, they fitted, as did the previously worn but still serviceable shoes and socks the man had placed atop the folded garments.

When he was clean and decently attired, Jonas was provided with a hot meal and his first cup of steaming coffee. Grateful for the man's kindness, Jonas savored every bite of food and every sip of the coffee. When he had finished eating, Jonas asked the man if there was some work he could do as a measure of repayment for the bath, clothing and food. Grateful for the offer of help in the understaffed shelter, the man assigned him the job of washing dishes.

Staggering with exhaustion, but determined, Jonas stood for some four hours washing and drying the seemingly never ending flow of dishes the man brought to him.

"You got a name, mister?" the man asked when he entered the large kitchen with the last load of dirty dishes.

Jonas hesitated, then spoke the first name to spring into his mind. "John. The name's John."

The man smiled with wry acceptance. "Isn't everybody's?" Not waiting or expecting a response, he thrust out his hand. "Mine's Hopkins, Ben Hopkins, and I appreciate the help. Flu goin' around and we're shorthanded." He indicated a shed off the back of the kitchen. "There's a cot in there. You can flop for the night if you've no place else to go."

"Thanks, Ben." Jonas strove to keep his voice steady; he nearly made it. "I have someplace to go, but I'm just too damned tired to keep moving."

Ben studied Jonas's eyes for several seconds, then nodded. "If you don't mind working, you can stay a few days, eat, rest up."

Jonas's throat worked and his voice cracked. "I don't mind working, and I appreciate the offer. Thanks again."

Ben shrugged and headed for the doorway. "It's nothing. Like I said, we're shorthanded."

Jonas stayed at the shelter until one of the volunteers returned to duty five days later. It was to be the first of many shelters. He was always given food, and sometimes a cot or pallet to sleep on, but either way, Jonas always insisted on doing some sort of work in payment for the bounty received.

Ten weeks after entering Texas, Jonas crossed the state line into Louisiana. With his constant moving and working, Jonas hadn't managed to gain any weight, but his strength was returning. He was ready to move on, still heading north.

Val was tired. Resting her head against the plush seat back, she closed her eyes and tried to relax. Being driven home from the office was a new experience for her; Val had always driven herself. But it had begun snowing around noon, and by quitting time the driving was hazardous. Not wanting to take unnecessary chances in her advanced state of pregnancy,

Val had placed a call to the company garage to ask Lyle Magesjski to drive her home.

"Sure thing, Mrs. Thorne," Lyle had said, as if genuinely pleased to be of service. "Tell me what time you'll be ready to leave, and I'll be at the door."

Lyle had been with Jonas for fifteen years. He'd been devoted to him. Now his devotion had been extended to Valerie.

Jonas.

Listening to the swish of the windshield wipers, Val sighed and conjured up an image of Jonas's strong, chiseled face. Late-winter snowstorm notwithstanding, it was almost spring. Her projected due date was only two weeks away. It was six months since she had received notification of Jonas's death. Four months had passed since she had awakened to the flutter of life inside her. Val's mouth curved into a tender smile. Jonas's child now at times appeared determined to kick and punch his way out of her body.

She missed Jonas terribly. There were moments when Val felt certain she could not bear to go on one second longer weighed down by the knowledge that she would never see her husband again. Her sense of loss, her anguish, had not lessened with the passing days and weeks and months. Val merely kept the loss, the anguish to herself, hidden behind the charge she'd assumed to care for his family and for the business Jonas had worked so very hard to make succeed.

Jonas had a granddaughter he would never see. Two months before, Mary Beth had given birth to a fiery red, squalling, beautiful baby girl. The baby was born with Jean-Paul's dark hair and coloring and her mother's bright blue eyes.

Val adored the baby and had secretly vowed to protect the heritage of both Jonas's granddaughter and that of his own child.

With inner amusement, Val recalled the expressions of skepticism and doubt she'd received when she had returned to the office the day after she had felt her baby's first tentative movements. Everyone, from Jean-Paul to Charlie to Janet and straight down the line of employees and family had been sympathetic; some, like Janet and Marge, even encouraging. But none of them believed she could actually run the company in Jonas's stead.

Satisfaction replaced her amusement as Val reflected on her own rather amazing accomplishments of the previous four months. She had moved into his office with bold decisiveness. By working night and day, she had studied and learned until she knew the business inside and out and even sideways. While certain that no one could replace, let alone match Jonas's genius, Val knew he had hired brilliant electronic engineers who, with the proper support and leadership, were fully capable of maintaining the company's excellent position.

Val had taken control, and she had succeeded. She was tired, but she had grown used to being tired. And on a snowy evening in mid-March, she was aching for Jonas. She knew she would never grow used to the ache. She would live with it. Val had no choice. She had his family, even Lynn who, upon full recovery from her injuries, had wisely decided to take her mother's advice to grow up, and was proving to be a surprisingly effective grandmother. Val had his company, whose employees had rallied around her to a man…and woman. And before too long, Val would have a part of Jonas himself, in the form of the child they had conceived in love.

Val was content…or as content as possible while silently screaming in agony.

Chapter 10

Two days after the official arrival of spring, Val sat propped up in a hospital bed, cradling her own spring arrival in her arms. Tears ran down her cheeks as she gazed into the face of Jonas's son and tiny image.

Her labor had been long and hard, but the advent of the infant Val had already named Jonas had been worth every minute of the pain it had involved.

"The likeness is incredible," Jean-Paul observed, staring in astonishment at the baby.

"Yes." Glancing up, Val smiled through her tears. "Isn't it wonderful?"

"It's...almost like having Dad back," Mary Beth murmured, reaching out to stroke a trembling finger over one downy pink cheek.

Val shifted her tear-bright violet eyes to the younger woman. "A part of him," she agreed softly.

"And we'll always have that part of him, won't

we?'' Mary Beth raised eyes shining with hope and happiness. ''As long as we have baby Jonas, we'll have a living part of Dad.''

Cradling the baby in one arm, Val reached out to grasp Mary Beth's hand. ''Yes, we'll always have a living memory of your father...of Jonas.''

Later that night, as Val coaxed her son to suckle nourishment from her breast, she stared into his new, yet endearingly familiar face and made a silent vow.

I remember, Jonas. I'll always remember.

The urge was stronger now inside Jonas, so strong that at times he had to fight against an overwhelming need to run.

Where did the inner pressure want him to run to?

The question was beginning to torment him. The urge had expanded in time with his slow movement north.

Jonas had planned to spend the winter months in the warmer climate of the southern states, but the urge persisted, overriding his common sense. Unable to rest after a stop of more than a few days in any one place, Jonas kept moving north, ever north.

He took refuge in shelters, and as he had in Texas, Jonas repaid every kindness with whatever work needed doing. He mopped floors, he washed dishes, he cleaned toilets. No task was too menial or beneath his dignity. The rewards of his labor were sustenance for his body, clothes to ward off the chill and a dry place to sleep. That was enough for Jonas.

In a church shelter in North Carolina, a soft-voiced, sad-eyed woman gave him a winter coat. It was worn and the sleeves were too short, exposing his flat bony wrists and long broad hands. But it was made of good wool, and the pockets were deep and lined with flannel. And that was enough for Jonas.

The distinctive scent of spring sweetened the air by the time Jonas reached Virginia. The wind was chill, but the sunlight was bright with the promise of coming warmth. The now bushy beard he had let grow to protect his face from the cold began to itch. Jonas decided that the beard would have to go within a month or so.

He was tired. Having been unsuccessful in picking up a ride, he had walked the last twenty-five miles. Locating a shelter run by the Salvation Army, Jonas introduced himself as John, the name he'd used since that first time in Texas, and offered himself for work in exchange for food and rest for a few days. After receiving a dissecting stare from the army captain, his offer was accepted and, defying the clamoring inner urge, Jonas settled in to rebuild his stamina.

Jonas had been at the shelter five days and was feeling surprisingly good when, on glancing up from the bowl of soup before him, he had the strangest experience.

There was a woman seated at another long table nearby. Her back was turned, so he couldn't see her face, but there was something about her that riveted his attention. She was small and slender and had shiny black hair that fell to her shoulders. While he stared in fascination at her hair, Jonas was startled and shocked to feel a tightness in his chest; his breathing had become labored, too.

Stunned by the reaction of his body, Jonas sat and stared at the woman until she had finished eating and stood up. The minute she turned and he saw her face, the tightness in his chest began to ebb. Before she had crossed to the door to leave, his pulse rate had returned to normal. But moments later, Jonas felt a sharp pain sear through his head. Then it was gone. But not for long. Through the following two weeks, as Jonas slowly made his way to Baltimore, the pain struck with increasing persistence and severity.

Val looked forward to warm weather with both anticipation and dread. The winter had been hard and bitterly cold and she was eager to see new, lush green grass and flowers blooming in colorful profusion in her garden. But the warmer months would also bring with them anniversaries, so many anniversaries.

Val's birthday was in May. Their wedding anniversary and Jonas's birthday fell in June. Also in June was the anniversary of their reconciliation in San Francisco. Four weeks later it would be one year since Jonas had been kidnapped. And in August she would have to face the anniversary of the day she'd received notification of his...

No! Spinning away from the long dining-room window, Val headed for the stairs. She would not think about it. Blaming her wandering thoughts on her inactivity, Val quietly entered the nursery. Walking softly to the side of the crib, she gazed in adoration at the sleeping cause of her leave of absence from the office.

Lying on his belly, his face turned toward her, his small chin thrust out and his tiny hands curled into fists, Val's little Jonas was a youthful miniature of his father.

No, Val decided, she would not think of the horror, would not allow herself to dwell on the pain. Jonas had left her a precious gift in their son. She would not squander her time on useless remorse. She had a son to raise, a company to run and a family to care for.

Touching her fingertips to her lips, Val brushed her fingers over his silky black hair, the single feature of hers he had inherited, then turned and left the room.

She had things to do; she had to confer with Grace about the meal they would serve that coming Sunday, when Jonas's daughter and son-in-law and grand-daughter were coming for dinner.

The trucker stopped to pick up Jonas on I-95 outside Baltimore.

"Thanks for the lift," Jonas said, panting as he pulled himself up into the high cab.

"Sure," the trucker drawled. "Where ya headed?"

"North," Jonas answered.

"Well, I'm running to Allentown." The trucker grinned. "That far enough north for you?"

Jonas returned his grin and slumped against the seat. "That'll do. Thanks again."

Jonas had considered resting a while at a shelter on the southern edge of the city, but the sense of urgency was a constant now, eating at him, pounding through his bloodstream. The searing pain in his head was another constant, at times causing an instant of darkness, at others moments of brilliant shards of flashing lights. The pain was what had driven him to the highway. Now he was almost grateful for it.

"You can grab some sleep if you like," the trucker

said, never taking his eyes from the roadway. "I won't mind. I'm not much of a gabber."

"I think I will," Jonas murmured on a sigh. "It's been a long haul." Somewhere in the neighborhood of six months, he added in weary silence.

Minutes after he shut his eyes, Jonas was deaf to the sound of grinding gears and the trucker cursing all Sunday drivers. Jonas dreamed of explosions and a dead man without a back, of hunger and thirst, of sweating as he trudged around a mountain and shivering as he walked along a backcountry road, and he dreamed of the back of a small, slender woman with shiny black hair.

The pain woke him. It was worse, intense, like knife blades stabbing into his skull. Jonas winced and sat up. He tried to read a road sign as the truck rumbled by it, but the lights were flashing inside his head and he couldn't focus.

"Where are we?" Jonas had to concentrate to articulate the question.

"Fifteen miles this side of Allentown," the trucker replied. "Give or take a mile."

Jonas felt sick. "If you don't mind pulling over, you could let me out here," he said between measured, pain-filled breaths.

"Makes no never-mind to me." Even as he spoke, the man sent the truck lumbering to the side of the highway.

"Thanks again," Jonas said, pushing the door open and jumping to the ground the instant the truck came to a halt.

"Sure. Have a good day."

The incongruity of the trucker's response didn't

strike Jonas. He was beyond registering anything but the pain and flashing lights inside his head. Disoriented, he began to walk, but had taken less than a dozen stumbling steps when the inside of his head seemed to explode. The world turned a glaring red, then went black. Unconscious, Jonas pitched forward and into a shallow gully off the soft shoulder of the highway.

He was cold when he regained consciousness. The pain and the flashing lights were gone. He was clearheaded. Rolling to his feet, he stood and glanced around to get his bearings. A smile curving his thin lips, he started walking again...south. He knew exactly who he was and exactly where he was going.

Jonas Thorne was going home to his wife.

Without a twinge of doubt or hesitation, Jonas stepped boldly onto the highway to flag down the first police car to come cruising by.

"What's your problem, buddy?" the officer asked, running a wary glance over Jonas's rumpled appearance.

Briefly, concisely, impatiently, Jonas explained his situation. The officer was patently skeptical.

"Thorne?" His brow creased in thought, then his eyebrows flew into an arch. "What are you trying to pull, fella?" he demanded. "Thorne's dead. It was in all the papers."

Jonas bit out a brief curse. Since regaining consciousness, his imagination had been busy with speculation about the possible effects his disappearance had had, both on Val and everyone else. Val! Jonas groaned. Val thought he was dead! A new sense of urgency ripped through him.

Flicking Jonas a look of dismissal, the officer turned away. Jonas placed a hand on his arm, detaining him. "I am Jonas Thorne, officer," he said tersely. "And I can prove it. But first I've got to get home."

Something in his voice convinced the officer. Jonas got a ride home...compliments of the Pennsylvania State Police.

Dusk shadowed the landscape when the police cruiser pulled into the driveway. Jonas's throat felt tight and his eyes smarted as he stared at the house. The windows were aglow with light. Only Jonas knew that the only light of any real value to him inside that house shone from the violet eyes of a small, dark-haired woman.

The officer loped behind Jonas as he strode to the front door. A frown touched Jonas's brow when he found the door unlocked. How many times had he cautioned Val about...? Jonas's thought splintered with the derisive laughter that lodged in his throat. Feeling suddenly light-headed, he turned the knob and pushed. The door noiselessly swung open on well-oiled hinges. Shaking and inexplicably scared, Jonas walked into the house. The sound of weeping drew him to the living-room archway. The scene that met his clouding vision was one of grief. Jonas absently noted the presence of his daughter and son-in-law, even that of the baby lying on a blue blanket on the floor. But his hungry gaze was riveted on the lovely, tear-streaked face of the small woman seated on the floor opposite his daughter, on the other side of the infant. Jonas felt odd, as if his head was floating. He had to work his throat several times before a sound emerged. And when it came, the droll sound of his voice amazed him.

"Is this a private wake, or can anybody cry along?"

The instant the words were out of his mouth, he knew he was losing it. But as the darkness closed in on his mind, he heard the sweetest sound imaginable, the sound that had fueled the inner urgency, driving him on for thousands of miles—the sound of Val calling his name.

"Jonas!"

Epilogue

Val sat by the bed in the quiet room, her eyes devouring the gaunt, hollow face of her husband. Jonas had slept through most of the nearly twenty-four hours that had passed since he'd fainted in the living-room archway. Except for checking periodically on the baby, who was in Grace's excellent care, Val had kept vigil by the bed throughout every one of those hours. She wasn't tired. Joyful energy hummed through her body, defeating weariness.

Her mind raced with images and impressions and Val knew that, should she live another hundred and thirty years, she would never forget a single detail of the scene in the living room and the hectic activity following it.

As they had seemed fated to do, Val and Mary Beth had once again been weeping over the uncanny resemblance of little Jonas to his father. Almost as if her unceasing grief had conjured it from the grave, the clear, dry sound of Jonas's voice had gone through Val like an electric shock.

Whipping her head around, Val had seen a wildly bearded, shabbily dressed specter standing in the archway. And though her intellect tried to deny it, Val had known at once who he was. Val was on her feet, running toward him before he hit the floor.

"Jonas!" Val's scream had shattered the sudden silence and the confusion in the minds of others. "My, God! Mary Beth, Jean-Paul, help me! It's Jonas!"

As she dropped to her knees beside Jonas, Val noticed another man stepping into the foyer. She was too distracted to see that he was uniformed. Before she could question his presence in her home, the man stepped forward to identify himself.

"Officer Switzer, ma'am, state police," he said respectfully. "Can you identify this man as Jonas Thorne?"

"What?" Val blinked, then nodded with distracted impatience. "Yes, yes, of course he's Jonas Thorne. I'm his wife." She moved her head to indicate the couple sinking to their knees on either side of her. "This is his daughter and son-in-law." While she spoke, Val's hands moved restlessly over Jonas, touching, searching, caressing his body, his face, his beard, his closed, sunken eyelids...*Jonas*.

The officer had proven to be of inestimable assistance. Not only did he volunteer to take care of the formalities by officially notifying the authorities about Jonas's return, he also helped Jean-Paul carry Jonas to the bedroom, undress him and get him into bed.

Val's right hand had made a more comprehensive examination of Jonas's face and body several times since then. She had rested her fingertips against his pulse, his steady beating pulse, at least a dozen times. Her left hand was enclosed within the steel-like grip of his right hand.

The first time Jonas awoke, Mary Beth broke away from Jean-Paul's supporting arm and flung herself onto the bed beside him, sobbing, "Daddy!" in a voice sounding like a young girl's.

"I'm here, honey. Don't cry. I'm all right. Everything's all right now."

Jonas's voice was calm, comforting. Only Val noticed the betraying tremor in his thin hands as he moved one restlessly over the girl's back, and the way the fingers of his other hand clenched in her hair, as if reassuring himself of his own reality by touching the flesh of his own flesh.

While holding his daughter close, Jonas's eyes, glittering with a frantic light, shifted searchingly. The frantic light only dimmed to a glow of satisfaction when his eyes settled on Val's soft violet gaze.

"Val." Jonas fell back to sleep with her whispered name on his lips.

It was late when Jonas woke again. Val was alone in the room. Promising to return in the morning, Mary Beth had gone home to report the incredible news to Marge, Lynn and the company employees. The first words out of his mouth brought a smile to Val's soft, trembling lips.

"I'm filthy. I need a bath and a shave."

"You need food," Val corrected him.

His smile was tired, but it was there. "I'll make a

deal with you," Jonas said, shoving back the bed covers. "You get the food while I get a bath and a shave."

"But Jonas!" she exclaimed anxiously. "Will you be all right on your own in there?"

His smile grew wry. "Sweetheart, I walked most of the way here from Central America," he drawled chidingly. "I think I can make it to the bathroom and back."

Val shuddered to even think of him walking that distance, then concentrated on getting together a light but nourishing meal for him, and worried about how he was doing in the bathroom.

As it turned out, Jonas did fine. He came out of the bathroom a few minutes after she returned to the bedroom. Her chest contracted at the sight of him, and she had to bite her lip to keep from crying out in concern.

His bones stood out in stark relief in his thin, hollow face and on his tall, angular frame. In fact, stark naked, he looked all bones, with skin stretched tautly over them. But his face was free of the bushy growth, and even drawn and gaunt, the face was definitely Jonas's.

He had barely wolfed down the meal before he fell asleep again, but before he did, he grasped her hand. Jonas had held on to her since then, his fingers tightly clasping hers even in slumber.

Grace had been in and out of the room countless times, bringing the baby to Val to nurse and supplying her with meals and coffee, fussing and generally checking on the condition of both of her employers. Earlier that morning, Val had asked Grace to call

Jonas's family to inform them of his progress and to suggest that they wait to visit until tomorrow, since it was becoming obvious that Jonas needed as much sleep as he could get.

Now it was dusk again, and Val sat beside him, her hand in his, her eyes adoring his terribly gaunt, terribly drawn, terribly beautiful face.

As if he felt the loving warmth of her gaze, Jonas opened his eyes and stared directly into hers. His smile was beautiful. His voice was low, sexy, an open invitation.

"Why are you sitting there when there's so much empty space in this great big bed?" His hand tugged at hers.

Val blinked against a rush of happy tears. "I didn't want to disturb your sleep," she whispered.

"I'm not asleep now." His hand tugged again. "Disturb me."

Val didn't need to be coaxed. Slipping her hand from his, she stood and began walking around the foot of the bed, leaving a trail of discarded clothes in her wake. His warm gaze followed her every move. His hand groped for the edge of the covers, lifting them for her.

"Oh, Jonas. Oh, Jonas, you're home!" Crying openly now, Val slipped into the bed and into his crushing embrace.

"Yes," Jonas groaned, gliding his lips over her face and his hands over her trembling body. "Yes, I'm home," he repeated, crushing her mouth with his own.

"Jonas, wait!" Val cried out, laughing, when he

released her mouth and moved his body over hers. "I have something exciting to tell you...show you!"

"It can wait," he growled against her mouth. "I can't. I remember, Val," he said starkly, settling into the silky cradle of her thighs. "Oh, God, I remember at last."

Val could hardly think for needing him, wanting him to be a part of her after so long. While her hands clasped his hips to draw him to her, she frowned and said, "Jonas, I don't understand. Why wouldn't you remember?"

Jonas laughed; it had the pure sound of joy. "It's a long story. I'll tell you all about it later. But right now—" his mouth brushed hers "—I need to kiss you, touch you, be absorbed by you."

Jonas and Val were one again, in unison, striving together for the ultimate perfection of ecstasy. When release sent them soaring, they joyously cried out each other's names.

"Jonas!"

"Val!"

Surprisingly, Jonas didn't go back to sleep. Exhausted, this time pleasantly so, he lay sprawled on his back and grinned at his wife.

"I want my present."

Val frowned. "What present?"

He arched a brow. "Didn't you say you had something exciting for me?"

Val's eyes flew wide. Then she laughed. She flew from the bed. Pulling on a robe, she dashed from the room, calling, "I'll be right back with your present. Don't you dare fall asleep."

When Val reentered the room a moment later, her

arms cradling a sleeping infant, Jonas was yawning. His yawn melted into a soft smile as she approached the bed.

"My grandchild?" he asked softly, sitting up to get a look at the baby.

"No, Jonas," Val murmured, handing the sleeping child to him. He shot her a confused look. "Your son," she whispered. "Jonas Thorne, junior."

"My son?" His hoarse voice held awe and wonder. For long moments Jonas gazed down at the baby. When he looked up again, his eyes were wet and tears ran unheeded and unashamedly down his face. "Our son," he corrected her, almost choking.

"Yes, darling," Val whispered, slipping onto the bed beside him. "Our son."

Baby Jonas spent the remainder of that night sleeping peacefully in the big bed, between the protective bodies of his mother, Valerie, and his father, Jonas Thorne.

* * * * *

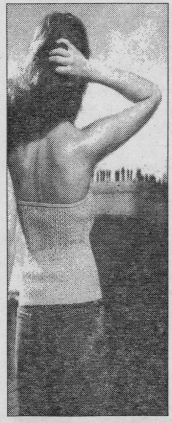

LONE STAR
LSCC
COUNTRY CLUB
EST. 1923

Where Texas society reigns supreme—and appearances are *everything.*

On sale...

June 2002
Stroke of Fortune
Christine Rimmer

July 2002
Texas Rose
Marie Ferrarella

August 2002
The Rebel's Return
Beverly Barton

September 2002
Heartbreaker
Laurie Paige

October 2002
Promised to a Sheik
Carla Cassidy

November 2002
The Quiet Seduction
Dixie Browning

December 2002
An Arranged Marriage
Peggy Moreland

January 2003
The Mercenary
Allison Leigh

February 2003
The Last Bachelor
Judy Christenberry

March 2003
Lone Wolf
Sheri WhiteFeather

April 2003
The Marriage Profile
Metsy Hingle

May 2003
Texas...Now and Forever
Merline Lovelace

Only from

Silhouette®
Where love comes alive™

***Available wherever
Silhouette books are sold.***

Visit us at www.lonestarcountryclub.com   PSLSCCLIST

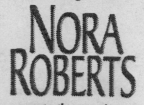

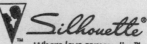